The Evolution Of Spring

The Qrie, Mad Mac and the Mer

Book 1
Second Edition Revised and Expanded

J. M. Hair

The Evolution Of Spring
Copyright © 2020 by J. M. Hair

Library of Congress Control Number: 2020909213
ISBN-13:   Paperback: 978-1-64749-123-9
           Hardback: 978-1-64749-270-0
           ePub: 978-1-64749-124-6

Printed in the United States of America

GoTo Publish

GoToPublish LLC
1-888-337-1724
www.gotopublish.com
info@gotopublish.com

CONTENTS

Acknowledgments ix

PROLOG

The Qrie Continuum and the Universe xi

PART 1 A Few Episodes of Breath's Evolution

1. AWAKENING 3
2. OAI 13
3. CONCEPTION 21
4. PHONE CALL 31
5. ARGUMENT 51
6. JOB 59
7. MERMAID 77
8. OAI 2 89
9. WHALES 93
10. CALGARY 107
11. MIAMI 125
12. USCG 141
13. OAI 3 153
14. COMMANDER 155
15. OAI 4 159
16. COMMANDER II 161
17. SCRIPPS 173

18. SUB 187
19. REGGIE 199
20. XENOPHOBES 209
21. OAI 5 225
22. FARM 227
23. TEXAS 235
24. BIG CHEESE 241
25. OAI 6 247

PART 2

1. CORAL SEA 253
2. OAI 277
3. HOME 279
4. DISCUSSION 285
5. SATURDAY 307
6. BARBECUE 313
7. PHONE CALL 341
8. JIM 351
9. MONDAY 373
10. SCHOOL 381
11. BARBECUE TWO 385
12. DEEP WATER 395
13. DISCOVERED 403
14. CAIRNS 411
15. MEETING 427
16. DECISIONS 435
17. RESTAURANT 441
18. ACCORD 449
19. OAI 2 463
20. A SCIENTIFIC LOOK 465

THE CURSE OF THE WANDTHE QRIE,
MAD MAC AND THE MER BOOK 2

The continuing saga of the Qrie, the Mer, and the
Spring family 485

ACKNOWLEDGMENTS

This book has taken a number of people to produce, and I would like to thank them all for their endurance. If I missed anyone, please fuss at me later.

Thanks to Sondra Van Havryk for helping me translate and clarify the technical portions of this tome. She took the alien language and the strange workings of my mind and put it into a more readable English.

Thanks to long-suffering Toni Greene for slaving over the many rewrites, rereads, and revisions. Without her help I would never have been able to make this book readable.

Thanks to her husband Dan Greene, who just wanted me to say a very short word, so okay, here it is: "Hi."

Thanks to the artists and editors for hammering on me until I got it somewhat right.

PROLOG
The Qrie Continuum and the Universe

Eons ago, long before the universe began, the continuum was homogenous. The Qrie forces and energies co-mingled with the physical forces and energies. Then *Prime Cause* initiated Creation. The physical matter, forces, and energies separated and formed into bubbles within the continuum. The continuum now looks somewhat like the fine uniform head of foam on a good beer. The uniform gas bubbles are the physical parts separated by the Qrie parts, which form the walls of the bubbles. Each of these physical bubbles is a universe unto itself. The universe bubbles are separated from all the other universe bubbles. The Qrie continuum permeates everything. Only Qrie forces and energies can pass into and from one bubble to the next. No physical forces or energies, can leave its bubble. Our universe is but one single bubble in an infinite froth of universal bubbles within the Qrie continuum.

PART 1
A FEW EPISODES OF BREATH'S EVOLUTION

1. AWAKENING

Breath stomped up the front porch steps and stormed through the door, slamming it hard enough to make the warm beige stucco of her home shiver.

Witnessing the young girl's distress from the vantage point of their pure energy perspective, the Solar System's Qrie Stewards Morning and Beauty were concerned about the young, powerful, telepathic, and extremely rare Qrie-human child, under their protection. They alerted her Qrie-human mother, concerned that if the child lashed out, the consequences could be dire.

Heidi Spring helped Breath remove her dirty green Fremantle Primary School surf shirt and wiped the tears from her angry daughter's eyes. "What's the matter, love? What's got you so upset?"

Breath cuddled deep into her mother's comforting arms. As they sat on their paisley patterned overstuffed velveteen sofa; the kind you can lose yourself in. All of the mismatched multicolored furniture in the house was obtained at various thrift shops around the area. The couch originally was covered with tattered, cat scratched, and torn tan Naugahyde. Heidi reupholstered it herself.

"The kids at school are so mean. They call me names. Tease me about my baggy clothes. And they say I stink. They throw mud and stuff at me. They don't want me around. Mum, why can't I be normal like the other kids?"

"Love, I know the other kids can be mean. I think they're just jealous."

"Why would they be jealous? They're all older and bigger than me. Why can't I be normal?"

Heidi hugged Breath. "I don't think age or size has anything to do with it, love. I think they're jealous because you've skipped so many grade levels, and you're so much younger than any of your classmates. I think that's what makes them jealous.

"I have some hot cocoa on the stove. I know it's your favorite. I even have some small marshmallows for it. Let's get some."

Breath clung tight to her mum. They walked hand in hand into their multicolored kitchen. The many hand-painted daisies on the walls, each a different size and color, brought peace and pleasure to Breath. There were red ones, orange, yellow, green, blue-green, blue, violet, indigo ones, and many other mixtures of colors that mankind didn't yet have names for. Breath smiled and sat down at the old kitchen thrift store table. The top was so rough and uneven that she and her mum decided to cover it with a piece of plywood, which of course got a floral scene painted on it, and a hard coat of lacquer over that. The odd assortment of kitchen chairs gave a well-used feel to the room.

"Remember Breath, no matter how mean they are to you, you must never be mean to them. And positively no hitting, because you're much stronger than they are, and you could cause serious harm to someone. That would not be good, and you want to be good. Don't you?"

"Well yeah — GP always helps me when the older kids come around. He helps me say things, like compliments. So, they won't get mad and say bad things to me. But it didn't work this time. They still threw mud at me. GP won't let me tell the other kids about him, or that I even hear and talk to him.

"Why can't I be normal, and why can't I tell, Mum? Some of my classmates have invisible playmates."

"Because Breath, we're different. Their invisible playmates will eventually go away, but we're Qrie, and our voices will be with us all of our lives. If you admit to hearing voices in your head, then regular humans will think you're insane or possibly worse — weird." Heidi tickled Breath's belly to make her giggle and lighten her mood.

Breath calmed down, of course hot cocoa and marshmallows didn't have anything to do with that. She pondered. *My voices have been with me all my life. I like them. They make me feel safe. There's nothing wrong with me; thank you very much!*

The unusually well-toned young lady, with violet-indigo eyes and Scandinavian golden-blond hair, just like her parents, is named Breath Of Spring. She lives with her mother in Fremantle, Australia. Breath is exceptional, not deranged. Her loving, devoted, and sometimes over protective mother, Heidi, has told Breath many times that all the Spring family were part human and part Qrie. Hearing voices is normal for them. Heidi told her daughter the voices started before birth, but Breath didn't remember until she began to talk.

Heidi projected into Breath's mind using telepathy. *I can hear the voices too, and Breath you must remember — never tell anyone that either of us can hear the voices.*

Breath replied in the same manner. *Mum, what are the Qrie and GP?*

They're unique and valuable friends and teachers. Now that you're old enough, you should learn to pay close attention to the voices because they'll teach you so many things. Like how GP and I taught you to read. I'm so proud, and a little jealous, because your vocabulary is almost better than mine. You're so smart, and I love you so much. Heidi gathered Breath into her arms and gave her a big hug and many kisses all over.

I love to read, Mum. What are the uh — voices? Why can't I hear them with my ears?

They're the Qrie, and they communicate mind to mind.

What are the Qrie, Mum?

Breath knew she wouldn't get an answer to that old question. She continued to ask it anyway, along with thousands of other questions that little kids just have to ask.

You'll have to ask them. They'll tell you when you're old enough and can understand.

Breath was tracing the little circles on the kitchen table as she sat next to her mum. After receiving what her mother had just projected to her, she became confused and frustrated. She closed her hands into fists and called out to the strange voices in her head. *Why can't you talk to me like GP, Mum, and Dad do? They use words. I don't understand all these fast-moving images, feelings, sounds, tastes, smells, orientations, and all those other indescribable things. How am I supposed to know what to do with them? And who're you anyway?*

Breath's Qrie-human mum and dad, Heidi and William Spring, through telepathic projection came to Breath's aid. *Breath, you must calm down. These images and things are the way the Qrie Stewards communicate, and you'll have to learn to understand them. We know it's frustrating, and it'll take patience and time to learn, but you'll get it.*

We know you can hear other people's thoughts and feelings in your mind. We know this can be upsetting and scary, but their thoughts and feelings can't hurt you without your consent. You have the full support of GP, Morning, Beauty, your father, and me. You have nothing to fear.

After a few minutes of calming thoughts and caresses, Breath calmed down enough to get up and pour herself and her mother some more hot cocoa.

After she sat the cups of hot cocoa on the table. Her mother took Breath's hands in hers. "Love, you will have to embrace your Qrie part. It's part of you and will be with you all of your life. You can't escape it. GP will help you with this. Just as he helped your father and me. I know you want to be normal, and you will be normal — a normal Qrie. GP, your father, and I will be with you every step you take. We know that you're capable and up to the challenge. You will never ever be a normal human, but you must learn to pass for one." Heidi could feel the fear and trepidation in her young daughter and gathered her into her loving arms. Mum's hugs and kisses always helped relieve Breath's fears.

***

Breath thinking back in time pondered. *Mum and dad were right — I did come to somewhat understand the two strange voices. I even learned to call them by their names, which are Morning and Beauty. Well — with a lot of help from GP, who sounds, in my head, like a man with a deep, gentle, comfortable, mild, and what GP calls a Southern U.S. drawl, that will put anyone at ease. It's soothing. Of course, I don't know what he sounds like because I've never heard his actual voice. GP, Mum, and Dad tell me all us Qrie folks talk mind to mind with a form of telepathy.*

***

When I was about two years old and learned to speak well. I asked the main voice in my head what his name was and what are the Qrie. Before that time nobody in the family knew a name to put with that main voice. So, I asked it. *I like to call people by their names. So, what's your name?*

There was a long stillness before the voice replied, *Y'all may call me GP.*

Thank you, Mister GP. I...

GP interrupted. *No, Breath. Just GP. Not Mister.*

OK, Mis...

GP chuckled and interrupted again. *Not Miss either.*

Breath laughed and thought, *A telepathic chuckle is really strange.*

OK, then, just GP. The other two voices are hard for me to understand. The ones that feel different in my head. What are their names?

Y'all may tell which one is which in time, and y'all can call them Morning and Beauty.

Is that like a beautiful morning?

No, Breath. Those're the names they call themselves.

Are they male or female?

The Qrie don't have gender, either male or female.

Oh, okay! What do they do, GP?

Well, Breath, they're like pure-energy intelligence farmers.

What's pure energy mean?

Pure energy means they don't have physical bodies.

Like a ghost?

Well, something like that, but nice friendly ghosts.

OK! What do you do?

I'm kinda like — a librarian, but I just don't look like one.

What's a librarian supposed to look like?

You know Breath, I'm not sure.

GP, why're we called Qrie?

Breath, it's what the Qrie energy names itself. The Qrie don't voice — the sound that energy makes, when it first moves. For instance, take a deep breath and hold it with the back of your tongue. Now smile and release the air by sliding your tongue forward and releasing the air. What sound did that release of air make?

I had to think about that for several seconds. *It makes the sound of Qrie, except as a whisper.*

That's right, Breath. All energy tends to make this sound upon release or change. If you'll listen, you'll hear nature saying its name. Turn on a faucet, and when the water begins to flow, that sound will be heard. A wave crashes against the rocks on the shore, and it makes that sound. And if you listen with your Qrie part, you can hear the energy say its name. Each time the Qrie energy moves or a Qrie Embrace is felt, it's accompanied by that sound and feeling.

GP, I think I like that.

I thought y'all would, Breath.

***

Heidi Spring charged out the solid front door, putting on her old blue Japanese silk kimono, chasing her exuberant daughter. "Breath, stop right there and come back in this house." Breath kept running. Heidi yelled after her daughter again. "Breath, get back in this house right now!" Breath kept running. This time Heidi projected, with force. *Breath, you ran out of the house in the nuddy again. Get back in the house and put some clothes on. You can't be out in front of the house like that. You must put on clothes.*

This got Breath's attention.

Breath stopped in her tracks and looked down at herself. Sure enough, she was naked. She whirled and ran back into the house. *I'm sorry, Mum. I forgot again. I don't understand why we need clothes on in the front yard. We don't wear any clothes inside or in the backyard.*

"Breath, I've told you many times, regular humans wear clothes all the time. Their clothes don't disintegrate when they wear them. Ours do. And clothes are expensive. We have to be careful and take care of what we have."

"I can understand not wearing clothes inside the house, but we never wear them in the backyard. What's the difference between the backyard and the front yard?"

"No one can see inside our house, so we don't have to worry about our clothes inside. And we have a solid three-meter board fence around the backyard with a vine trellis all around the top, so no one can see us in the nuddy there. You have to learn to wear clothes around normal humans, just like they do."

"I know, Mum, and I'll remember. But I still don't like clothes. They are baggy, itchy, bind up, and smell bad. The other kids make fun of me."

"I know, love. I don't like clothes either, but we have to wear them, just like normal humans do. Especially when we're around normal humans. We Qrie have problems with clothes or anything worn close to our skin."

"Is there anything we can do to help us remember — about the clothes, I mean?"

"Yes love — I think there might be. I saw a full-length mirror at the thrift shop last week. If it's still there, we can put it inside the front door. So, before we go out, we can see if we've got clothes on. How about that?"

"I think that'll work, Mum."

***

Heidi, I know you've got a question.

Yes, GP. Why do you, Morning, and Beauty treat Breath so special?

Because she 'is' so special.

I know she's special. She's Qrie just like you, her dad, and me.

Yes, Heidi, I know she's Qrie, but she's more than just Qrie. She's more than y'all can imagine. She must be trained in the proper manner, but not in a way that she might fail or reject the promise of her future. She mustn't know until the time comes what and how exceptional she is.

I say tell her. She's a smart girl and can understand. William and I were never treated like Breath is treated.

I'd love to tell her, Heidi. I told y'all and William because both of y'all were her parents and needed to know, and she needed to know that she was Qrie. The problem is, if I tell her everything, it'll change her whole perspective on life. And it'll interfere with critical decisions that she'll have to make without help from anyone else, including me.

Well, GP, you can tell me.

Heidi, y'all couldn't keep a secret from Breath if your life depended on it.

That's not true! I didn't tell her about... well. I didn't tell her about... or... well... Okay GP, maybe you're right.

You're a true gem, Heidi, and I love y'all for it.

By the way, what happens if she fails or rejects what's planned for her?

She'll lose her opportunity to reach her full potential.

Oh, GP, that sounds like a high school counselor trying to get a student to do his homework. Do you mean rejection, like what William and I did?

Yeah. Not that much different from y'all and William, but a positive outcome will be awesome, but she's got a long way to go.

2. OAI

The Office of Anomalies Investigation (OAI), based in Roanoke, Virginia. It is a tiny, obscure, classified, Federal Government organization. It is tasked with investigating possible alien artifacts, crop circle aliens (CCA), unidentified flying objects (UFOs), and any unexplainable phenomenon. The group has been passed around from agency to agency. It has been ridiculed by those agencies since its inception in the mid-1950s. It has suffered from many uncomplimentary nicknames, such as the Office of Alien Idiocy, Obscure Anomalous Insanity, Office of Absolute Insignificance, and so on. It is now under the auspices of the National Security (NS) Adviser, who has been told by the President of the United States, "Don't bother me unless the aliens are attacking. Oh, and keep the agency around just in case."

John Kingman, director of the OAI, is a hard, smallish, bald man with a broken nose no one can miss. His reward for many skirmishes with bullies, and his total unwillingness to back down. He is the perfect director for this much-maligned agency because he never stops looking for the answers.

His determined, tall, nerdish codebreaker, Tatelin 'Tate' Westworth, never quite fit into the other agencies. He ended up at the OAI because of his unabashed belief in aliens. As well as, his unquenchable drive and desire to find them. The remainder of the staff are all excellent investigators. They each have been shuffled into the OAI for one unusual reason or another. It would be an honest assessment to say that the OAI is a bit quirky. However, its work ethic is second to none. Well — it has to be.

John sat in his non-descript office. A folder entitled CCA Decoded and marked Top Secret (TS) / Sensitive Compartmented Information (SCI) stamped in bold red letters was lying on his desk.

John sat back and smiled as he opened it, scanned it, and reminisced. *I gave these crop circle aliens the acronym CCA many years ago. The other agencies will soon know — we are for real.*

Before I took over the agency fifteen years ago, the OAI had been established to see if crop circles had hidden codes within them. The running question at the time was; is there more to crop circles than meets the eye? Well, apparently so — after many years, insults, degrading remarks, and assholes! As it turns out, a few circles do have codes. After many missed starts, numerous levels of codes have been discovered.

My agency and I may not be the most popular. We've had our ups and downs, but we're gonna show them now. Tate has been with this agency almost as long as I have, and he's taken the verbal abuse and insults, with quiet grace. He deserves the promotion. I hope the higher-ups don't want to move him to a more prestigious organization. He's a good man and one extremely fine codebreaker.

Tatelin Westworth, the OAI senior analyst, and his team had worked for the last ten years trying to decode the information hidden in the crop circles. They explored many false paths. Two breakthroughs came in the last two years that allowed steady progress. The decryption of the crop circle code began to fall into place. The code was deciphered when a pre-Sumerian language was discovered. This language has not been used in over seven thousand years. Progress was made when this decoded language was combined with some advanced mathematics. The hint came from that same pre-Sumerian language.

The code is always found in a simple type of crop circle where the grain stalks were bent but not broken. All man-made circles break the stalks near ground level. All true alien crop circle stalks were bent at various heights above the ground. Years of increasing frustration became elation and vindication almost overnight.

John closed the file. He called and told his secretary to schedule a meeting with the whole team for the next day.

As soon as he hung up the phone, two of his agents George and Robert knocked on his open door.

"Come in. What can I do for you guys?"

"We just got some information on the dig in India. It's in this file, and it looks interesting." George laid the file on John's desk.

"John, here's a group of photographs and video that were taken by one of our military aircraft, while in encountering a UFO. I think you'll find the video very interesting. Because it's a clean video and close-up of one of the craft." Robert put the package in John's hand.

"What do you think it is Bob?"

"Don't know. I don't think it's anything we built. It could be Russian or Chinese."

"Thank you guys I'll look into this."

***

Tate astounded everyone, including John in the long meeting, with the overall significance of what he reported. Although becoming hoarse, Tate charged on with enthusiasm. "I think everyone can see the implications of what we've discovered here. It means we can build a communication device that can speak to the CCA that left us these messages. I'd say we should be able to build this device and have it operational within about a year.

"The only question we've got to ask ourselves now becomes, should we build it? And if so, what are the ramifications of communicating with a CCA civilization?"

Top government officials, short of the President, held secret meetings for several months over those questions.

The NS Adviser, along with the Director of National Intelligence (DNI) and several other top agency chiefs, made the decision to build the communication device. Their decision was made because the CCA had known about civilizations on Earth, and they had done nothing for the thousands of years that the crop circles had been appearing. After months of deliberation, the President signed the communications go-ahead order.

Homeland Security wasn't happy. They didn't think the aliens could be trusted, although the main reason they weren't happy was that the President, by executive order, shifted some discretionary funds from them to the OAI.

The President vetoed the idea to involve other governments.

***

The Qrie GP communicated with the other Qrie entities Morning and Beauty. *Should we allow the humans to communicate with the Anasso Consortium?*

Morning and Beauty replied. *We have been watching the OAI. We have contacted the Qrie in the Anasso Consortium. We have informed them on what the Anasso may and may not tell the humans.*

***

Meanwhile, back at the OAI, Tatelin danced with excitement. "John, the CCA beacon synchronization signals have been received. The beacon is outside the Kuiper belt, well out past the orbit of Pluto. We've spent months searching for the signal. The last alien crop circle we decoded told us where to look to find the beacon they left. The problem we had was people trampled a lot of the stalks and destroyed some of the code before we got there. We just found the beacon last week. Once we found the signal, we got the stressor to lock on."

John looked at the stressor and reminisced. *I remember watching its construction over the past year. It's a huge cylinder with a large stack of lens shaped fifteen-foot diameter, three-inch-thick, ceramic plates inside. They resemble something like a stack of hard pancakes on extreme steroids, and are all attached to a large tracking mount. The cylinder holds a vacuum to allow the plates to move without air resistance.* He turned to Tate. "Does anybody have any idea how this thing works?"

Tate looked puzzled and shrugged. "No John. The special stack of ceramic plates stresses space — we think. That's the best our physicists can come up with. As you know, the physicists call the whole apparatus a stressor. We haven't been able to detect the signal with any of our instrumentation. The signal isn't electromagnetic in any way. We think the plates themselves interact by electric fields and these electric fields change the shape of the plates — and is like an enormous and thick piezoelectric speaker, similar to the kind in some cell phones. We built several smaller stressors to test our signals. We know the signals going between the stressors are much faster than the speed of light. How much faster we can't measure yet, but we now have a communication system that can send signals faster than light. We can do this through any solid object. It doesn't make any difference what the material is; we even sent signals through the Earth. We do know that once the stressor signals lock on, the signal beam width narrows down like a laser beam and won't deviate between the two stressors. We don't know how that works either.

"Right now, the only thing we can send is ones and zeros, and not much faster than about one hundred words a minute. However, as we learn more, our speed increases."

The group spent some time trying to decide what the first message to send the CCA should be. The message sent was

"Hello from Earth. We received your message." This message was sent out once a week.

***

Almost one year passed before the team at OAI received a reply. They recorded the signal in every conceivable way. Decoding the signal took another three months.

Whenever John went down to Tate's decoding lab all he saw was confusion. There were charts and graphs and mathematical equations on the whiteboards and post it notes pasted everywhere. Besides Tate, there were people at six other desks, all with computer monitors and more post it notes on them. Those six people were surrounded by piles of books and papers from ancient manuscripts to treatises on modern mathematics. John had no idea what was going on in the minds of these people. He just knew that they were the best in the business.

When Tate entered John's office he began to talk about the communiqué. He made several quotes from a summary sheet at the beginning of the rather thin message. Tate was talking so fast John couldn't get a word in edgewise. He held up his hand, and Tate stopped talking. "I know you're excited Tate why don't you just give me a summary. Oh, and start where you stopped talking."

"Okay John, sorry, but this is such great news. From where I stopped." Tate looked down at his summary sheet. "Uh — okay. And — progress was accomplished when the translation of the pre-Sumerian language to English was made. The message is amazing John. It tells of an extensive civilization with over two hundred inhabited planets involving over three hundred billion inhabitants of many different intelligent species. All the stars and inhabited planets lie within a sphere approximately five hundred light years in diameter. The civilization is called the Anasso Consortium, and it's led by a species called the Atoom, which are a member of the Galactic Community. They are the OAI's only contact with the Consortium. We don't have a clue as to what the Galactic Community is.

"The civilization's center lies a little over a quarter of the way around the Milky Way's Galactic disc, about forty thousand light-years from Earth.

"Earth, as it turns out, is in a rather backwater area with just a single handful of intelligent species spread over several thousand light-years. The communiqué also indicated that physical travel is inconvenient due to time and distance. Communications alone will have to suffice. The message also stated that the Anasso will not enhance our technology base any more than it already has through the stressor communications device.

"The Anasso explained the probe the OAI found that was left in our solar system to monitor Earth when the Atoom first visited thousands of years ago. From time to time, the beacon would send a drone to generate crop circles in the hope that we humans would be able to decode the information in the circles and contact them. They explained that the technology of the pre-Sumerian culture wasn't up to the task.

Tate handed John the complete file. "Isn't this great John? This is the very first communiqué from an extraterrestrial intelligence ever! What do you think?"

"Well, Tate, it is remarkable, but I guess we're on our own. Of course, I didn't expect them to give us any more technology. They probably don't want backwater hick planets cluttering up their nice Galactic Community."

Tate laughed. "Can't blame them John. Who would want to be exposed to us?"

John laughed. "Too true. By the way Tate, I've seen where most of the crop circles are man-made. How many circles are CCA?"

"Not many. Only about one or two out of about two hundred and fifty circles per year. Except for the embedded code, they're plain, not elaborate at all like the man-made circles."

The communications between the Anasso and Earth began in earnest but under tight security. There'd be only hand-carried documents. No emails or other electronic communications were allowed. The only outside individual who was informed was the

NS Adviser. Informing anyone else was at the discretion of the NS Adviser himself, possibly the President, the Department of Defense (DOD), the DNI, and the security agency chiefs only.

The OAI budget was increased to a great extent.

John had a worried smile, when he realized just how big his job just became, and just how much infighting there was going to be with the other agencies.

3. CONCEPTION

The young, beautiful, blue eyed, blond, spirited, country girl, (hey she calls herself girl so...) Virginia Spring was in her kitchen. She called it her kitchen because William Spring, or Will as she called him, didn't spend a lot of time there. She considered it her domain. Will's domain was outside taking care of the farm, it's machines, and the animals. Of course, she didn't mind Will coming into the kitchen and helping her. Her problem was when Will washed and dried the dishes, he put them where he thought they ought to be, and not where she knew they should be. She knew she had to give Will some slack in the kitchen since she had moved into the farmhouse a couple of months ago. But the kitchen was taking on Virginia's touch. With her towels and curtains hanging just so, and the dishes sorted just so. Her cookbooks were stacked neatly on the shelf along with pictures hanging on the walls of the large country kitchen. She loved the antique style gas stove, but what she loved most was the huge electric side by side, stainless steel, restaurant quality, refrigerator/freezer that Will bought her when she first moved in. It replaced the old gas-fired refrigerator that had been moved out to Will's shop in the barn.

She and Will had just made love that morning. She was happy and humming while preparing breakfast, wrapped only in her house robe. She thought. *I'll pop the biscuits in the oven and take a quick shower.*

As she closed the oven door, the universe opened up, and an unbelievable, wondrous, and overpowering feeling of well-being flooded into her. Then the fillings in her teeth began to fall out. She felt wonderful and in a panic. *Oh My Gawd, what's happening to me?*

She was at home on their farm northwest of Calgary, Alberta when this happened. She grabbed a hand towel and spit the fillings into it. In her panic, she ran to the bathroom to inspect her teeth. She fumbled in a drawer and found the little plastic dental mirror. She tried to inspect her teeth in the bathroom mirror, but something was wrong.

Her husband, Will, came into the bathroom and put his arms around her. She felt another wonderful calmness flow through her.

She glanced at Will in fear. "Not now, Will. Something's happening. I can't understand why I can't see with this stupid mirror!"

Will bent over and kissed her on the forehead while reaching up to remove Virginia's glasses.

"Will, I need those glasses to see! I can't... wow... see. I... Will — I can see!" She looked at her hand and then back into the mirror. The cavities were evident. "How's this possible?"

Virginia looked at Will's reflection in the mirror. He had a strange smile. "Virginia, my beloved, there's something that we need to discuss."

***

They'd been married for two months. Virginia had met Will Spring when Sarah brought him home with her several years ago. Sarah met Will in California when she went there to visit friends on vacation. She was a pretty brunette, five foot five with smooth olive skin and large brown eyes that seemed to laugh at everything Will said.

They fell in love. It was love at first sight, and after a short whirlwind romance, and marriage in California, he came back to Calgary with her. They never had any children but they had a happy life. Will discovered he loved the farming life, and did everything he could to make the farm perfect. He knew he and Sarah could never make it perfect but they tried.

Sarah told Virginia her suspicions about Will and the many strange things she saw him do. Virginia was very curious, but never let on to Will about anything that Sarah had told her.

The devastating tragedy of Sarah's death from a massive cerebral hemorrhage a year ago brought Will and Virginia closer than ever.

Will blamed himself for not preventing her death. He was in Calgary getting some parts to repair one of the farm machines when it happened. The solar system Steward, Morning, informed him that by the time the Qrie were aware of Sarah's problem, the brain damage was already too extensive for them to repair. They assured him that there was nothing anyone could have done. He shut down and wouldn't talk to anyone for six months.

Virginia is ten years younger and always had an unexplained magnetic attraction to Will, but, for Sarah's sake, she had willed herself never to do anything about her love for him until recently. Will, an electronics engineer, was always reserved around other women. He and Sarah had made a good life for themselves. Now that the farm was his, he decided to stay. Virginia broke through Will's silence and let him know that she was there for him. They consoled one another's pain and after a few months he began to see her for her true self and fell in love with her.

***

Virginia was inspecting her teeth with single minded intensity. Will leaned over and placed a gentle kiss on the back of her neck. A feeling of tremendous warmth and love again flooded into her. He put his lips close to her ear and whispered.

"Our dreams and wishes are coming true. We've just conceived and are pregnant."

She thought in panic. *I've always wanted children, but how's this possible? No one ever knows when conception occurs; it just happens.* It was all too much. She sat down on the toilet and began to cry. She didn't know whether she was crying because she felt so wonderful, or because all her fillings had just fallen out, or her husband had just told her they were going to be parents — or perhaps all of the above.

Will was on his knees beside her with his arms around her, kissing her neck, her cheek, and her forehead. This didn't help her tears at all.

Somehow, she knew Will was right. *How could he know? Unless he 'is' magic like Sarah told me. Could it be? Could I have married a mystical being? Are we going to have an enchanted child?*

Will leaned close and kissed her again on the cheek. He placed his lips near her ear and whispered, "I love you."

This was too much. She fainted. She came to just as Will was laying her on their bed. She looked up at Will with wide-eyed panic. "I've gotta get to a doctor! I've gotta get to a dentist! I've gotta get..."

Will smiled down at her. "Everything is going to be just fine Sweetie."

She gave him an incredulous look. "That's easy for you to say! You're not the one having a baby! And you've never been to a dentist or had a cavity in your life! Your teeth are perfect! How's that possible, anyway?"

Will gave her a lopsided grin, shrugged, and held her tight. Her tears slowed, and she tried to calm herself down. A few moments later she'd calmed down enough to stop crying. She looked up at Will. He gazed down at her as his love encompassed her. "It's good that you're lying down. What I've got to explain is going to be a bit of a shock.

"My great grandmother and Heidi's great grandmother went through the same thing you're going through now; I suspected that you might go through it too. In order to bear our — children; your body must be perfect. And it will be. Any foreign object will be removed, such as fillings and crowns. Every part of your body will be healed and made perfect. Your teeth, your eyesight, your hearing, your senses of smell, taste, and touch, any scars — even former broken bones will all be made perfect. It must be so because the energies required to bring our children to term will be serious.

"Before Breath was born, Heidi, and I were told we were Qrie. They told us about Breath and what it'd take to bring her into this world. What's happening now confirms my suspicions about what our child will be. I've also been informed to handle our children, assuming we have more than one, different from how Heidi and I handled Breath. You and the children must be told early on who and what the Qrie are. That wasn't done with Breath, and it caused — uh — problems."

Virginia's eyes were still fixed on Will. "I've never met Breath, we've talked on the phone a few times, but from what I know about her, she's sweet and wonderful. How's Breath different from anyone else, and how are our — uh — kids going to be different? What kind of problems?"

Will leaned down and kissed her again, and again that wondrous feeling flowed. "I promise you; our child and I hope — children, will be a handful. They'll be wonderful, unique, special, and the closest thing to magic you can imagine.

"Breath is wonderful and quite talented. She loves the ocean and all the various animals, especially dolphins. Whales come around her, and it drives Heidi crazy because they'll let Breath ride them. When she's out walking, birds will flock around her and land on her shoulder, but only when she invites them. The kids at her school tease her unmercifully and call her a klutz, but she's not. She's regal and graceful. It's just her unusual abilities that make her look klutzy. For instance, anything that's thrown at her will veer away from her. She's extraordinary at dodgeball. And she can throw a fastball that no one can hit. She's uncanny with a bow and arrow or darts. She's the kindest and most loving person anyone knows. Of course, that's her proud father talking."

Virginia sat up, then stood up beside the bed. Will helped her up and wrapped his arms around her waist as he sat on the edge of the bed. She looked around at the clothes strewn around the room and the unmade bed. Then she noticed her panties were hanging on her copy of Starry Night on the Rhone. She looked down at Will as he was also looking where her panties were hanging. She giggled. "I don't think Vincent had that in mind."

"I don't think Vincent would have minded at all."

"Well, I still need to straighten up, make the bed, and I need to take a shower and think about this for a while. We can have some breakfast. Then we need to — talk!"

Virginia's pink, lightweight, satin, dressing robe, had come open in the front. Will placed his head on her belly. Then with a slow deliberate motion he sat up. He gazed deep into Virginia's eyes as his own eyes glazed over.

"What is it Will? You — look different!"

Will's grin was huge. He then took a long slow deep breath and let it out in a long slow happy sigh. He leaned close to Virginia and whispered. "Twins!"

Virginia again felt the wondrous flood of peace and love spread over her body. She thought that if Will hadn't had his arms around her, she would've fallen.

She grabbed Will around the neck and held him tight against her body. She didn't want this wondrous feeling to ever leave her.

Will held her like this until she released him. He smiled up at her as she pulled away. "I'll finish breakfast. I took the biscuits out of the oven. Take your time in the shower."

They each ate their breakfast with slow introspection, lost in their own thoughts. Virginia sat next to Will, in their little breakfast nook, sipping chamomile tea to calm herself down. The silence allowed her the realization that she could hear the pilot lights on the stove burning and the multitudes of various scents were now obvious, where before, she had to put her nose close to the containers to smell them. She gave Will loving but skeptical sideways glances, all the while inspecting every inch of his body.

When she was done, she gave Will a suspicious look. "You said earlier you were informed about handling our children different than the way you handled Breath. How do you know all this, and who informed you?"

Will inhaled a deep breath and let it out in a long sigh. "Now that we're pregnant, everything must be known. You're now part of my world. There are entities in this universe that're older than the universe itself. Two of these entities are associated with this solar system. These two entities created — or, in their terms — assembled this solar system and everything in it. We are known as the Qrie and command unbelievable amounts of power.

"Heidi, Breath, and I, our children, and one or two other Qrie-humans on Earth have the capability to manipulate the Qrie energies. Heidi and I decided not to be trained in the complete manipulation of these energies. We believe that no person should have unlimited power. Breath is coming to the age when she must make that decision for herself. Our children will also have to make that decision. Decision or not, the energies still flow through us. Heidi uses it to make her health potions and soaps, and she also uses it to give health readings.

"I've tried to hide it as much as possible; the government would like to have someone with this capability under their control. I don't want and will not be someone's guinea pig. We didn't want that for Breath either.

"The Qrie have informed me that they'll handle things the Qrie way with our children. They're concerned that with the technological advancements occurring now, the Qrie and another race of people will soon be discovered. When this occurs, the cat will be out of the bag so to speak. Heidi, Breath, and I have had to take extreme care to remain hidden so that no one knows our true abilities. Our children will also have to remain hidden, so no one else knows, until the proper time."

Virginia asked with concern, "Do we have any choices in this matter?"

Again, after some delay. "No! The babies will go to term unless they miscarry. The Qrie won't allow any interference whatsoever. They — the Qrie, that is — are making certain that everything is perfect with and for the babies.

"The pure-energy Qrie beings are shepherding planets with intelligent corporeal beings in order to nurture them into ascending towards True Intelligence. When this occurs, it gives us Qrie the chance to advance our understanding of ourselves and the universe. Due to the delicate and fragile nature of intelligence in the physical universe, the Qrie, with their power over universal forces, won't allow any interference in their quest whatsoever.

"You're thinking right now, what gives them the right to make these decisions for us?

"The twins and I are part Qrie. Please trust me. Life will be good. The Qrie now consider you part of the Qrie family along with me, Heidi, Breath, and the twins. The power of the Qrie is incomprehensible. They will love, protect, and help us in ways unimaginable. Everything will be explained and all your questions answered."

Will became quiet. *What is it GP?*

Will, the babies are going to require a considerable amount of Qrie energy. The babies are third-generation Qrie and will be powerful. Not as powerful as Breath but powerful just the same. Virginia must be able to handle these energies. So, I'm gonna give her what will amount to a continuous Qrie Embrace. *I'll also give her the ability to communicate with y'all, Heidi, Breath, myself, and the twins, after they're born, via our form of telepathy. Here's what y'all must do for her...*

Virginia was concerned about Will's sudden silence. "What is it Will?"

"Virginia, I think you need to lie down for this. The Qrie have analyzed your situation and have realized that you need extra Qrie support. This is what I want you to do. Take a deep breath and..."

A few moments later Will could tell Virginia was now under the influence of the Qrie energies and had been taught the ways of the Qrie. He sent her a telepathic message. *How do you feel?*

"Wow! I heard you in my mind!"

Yes, and you will feel this Qrie Embrace *for the rest of your life. You will also be able to communicate with the Qrie through your mind link. This is how you use it...*

The next morning, feeling wonderful due to her *Qrie Embrace*, Virginia looked into her dressing mirror without her glasses. Her teeth were perfect, no more cavities. She was overwhelmed. The tears began to flow again. She thought. *Everything Sarah told me was right. He 'is' a mystical being. What have I gotten myself into?*

4. PHONE CALL

The farmhouse landline phone rang three times. "Will Spring here, can I help you, Breath?"

"Hello, Daddy. I wanted to talk to you on the phone. I know we talk all the time mind to mind, but I just wanted to hear your voice."

"I like hearing your voice as well, Breath. I know mind to mind is very intimate, but I do like hearing your actual voice. I also know that you have been crying. So, take a deep breath and tell your old daddy. What have you got on — your mind, eh?"

Breath chuckled at her dad's lame joke, but it did make her feel a little better. "I'm having a little trouble with Mum. I just received a huge scholarship to the University of Melbourne, but she doesn't want me to go there. She wants me to stay here, in Fremantle and go to University here or one in Perth. But it's going to cost a fortune here because none of these local schools have offered me a scholarship of any kind."

"Don't worry about that Sweetie. I think your mother and I can pay for your schooling there if you want to stay in Fremantle. The money will be tight. But I think we can pull it off."

"I appreciate that Daddy and I want to thank you for all the support you send us. I know you and Mum probably could make it work. The thing is, Melbourne has a much better overall program and it will be free with the full advanced scholarship."

"Sweetie, the only one that can answer the question as to where you need to go, is you. I know your mom wants you to stay in Fremantle, but 'you must decide what is best for you.' I also know that the Qrie are going to put considerable pressure on you. But no matter what, the decision is still yours."

"Thank you, Daddy. I needed that. But Mum is relentless. I just wish I could get my mind off this for a while."

"I know your mom can be a bit obsessive, but this is your life, not hers. You have to do what is right for you. Listen to GP. He won't steer you wrong."

Even though they were speaking on the telephone telepaths always communicate on several levels, and Will could feel Breath's appreciation of his words.

"Breath, I think you've already made up your mind on what you need to do, you're just wanting an ally on your side. If you need to talk, why don't we change the subject for a while? How about if you tell me — some of the things that GP has taught you over the years. I know we have linked our minds while he was teaching you. But I would like to hear you say it in words, for a change."

"Uh — okay, where should I start? You know that words can't express the detail of what a mind to mind link can express."

"I know that Breath, but we are not normal people. We're Qrie and even though you're speaking, we still have the telepathic link."

"Okay well, what age would you like me to start at?"

"Whatever age you think is good. I'm all ears."

After a few moments in thought, Breath began. "Well, at about age four we — that's GP and me had a lot of fun. He encouraged me to do things. Things that'd give Mum a heart attack. Like jumping off — things."

Will gave his daughter a little chuckle. Not because of what she said, but the way she said it and the little mental twist she put on it.

"At first, I didn't want to do it — because it was scary. But when I did, GP would give me what he called a *Qrie Embrace*. It was like a warm loving hug. The kind I get when I fall asleep cuddled up close in Mum's arms."

"That's a good start, Breath, continue."

"You know, Mum and I live about three blocks from the elementary school. Next to it is a park with a playground that has swings, a merry-go-round, and monkey bars. There's a ladder attached and a whole lot of sand.

"A man from Japan is the caretaker. And he just loves to rake the sand. I never knew his name. I just called him Mr. Japan. He'd make these circles and wavy patterns in the sand with a rake. It looks nice till the kids come. They never seem to notice, but I do. The next day, the sand will be nice and neat again."

"That was good, Breath, but was that all GP taught you?"

"No, of course not. He taught me lots and lots of stuff. Do you want me to tell you everything?"

"Yes, I need to know lots and lots of stuff. Besides, I just love the sound of your voice."

Breath knew her dad was teasing her a bit, and she liked it because she could feel the telekinetic hug to go with it. "Well, okay... Uh — when I was 5 years old, the lady next door was always trying to get Mum and me to go to church with her. I always refer to Sundays as Ford day. Which means Mum and I would work on our old Ford pickup truck. We did go to church a few times. One Sunday the preacher quoted, 'Be still and know that I AM God.' I didn't know what that meant. So — I asked GP."

"Later at the park, GP told me." She lowered the pitch of her voice and tried to imitate GP's southern drawl. "'I want y'all to calm your brain. We're gonna work with the other part called your Qrie, your I AM, or as the humans might say, your God part.'"

"I didn't know what he was talking about, So I just sat real quiet-like. Now that is just plain boring for a kid that likes to run and climb the ladders and play on the monkey bars."

Breath sensed her dad chuckling.

"At the time, GP seemed to be impressed, he said. 'Y'all sit pretty still. That's a considerable accomplishment for a young person.'

"GP talked like that. He never talked down to me, like most adults. They always talked to me like I was a puppy dog or a kitty cat, but not GP or Mum.

"I also like GP's southern drawl from the US. It always makes me feel safe and comfortable."

"Well then, GP continued. 'To be still' means to still your brain or make it quiet. Y'all have thoughts running through your brain all the time. You've gotta make the thoughts go away. Think of your brain as a pond of water. Think of your thoughts as ripples on the pond. To still your brain, you must make the pond smooth with no ripples.

"'When you're able to do this, you'll notice that there're two parts of your awareness. One of those parts is your brain. We're gonna work with the part, which's much more subtle. For the time being, we'll call the I AM part, your inner mind. Your inner mind is what we're gonna use to sense the Qrie energies or the flow of the Qrie power which is the I AM.

"'When you reach this state, you'll be at peace with yourself and everything else around y'all. You'll be able to love yourself and all those around y'all. Love and rational compassion drive the creative engine of True Intelligence. With love, you'll be able to sense and begin to control the Qrie powers within. When y'all reach this state, there'll be no limit to your abilities.'

"Well, at first, it was hard for me to do that, but GP was patient and, with his help, I learned how to make my brain go 'still' and not think about anything at all."

"Wow Breath, that sounds pretty complicated. And you make it sound just like GP. Is that exactly what he said?"

"Well, no, but I think I said it pretty close."

Breath stopped for a moment to feel her dad's encouragement.

"Anyway — after I learned this, GP and I would communicate mind to mind for hours. He took me places and showed me things in my mind, many wonderful things that I'd be able to do. Like I could fly, move objects, and make things with my mind. I could jump from place to place in an instant. I could feel and experience the full Qrie power. I could also see more of the color spectrum than I ever knew existed or could imagine. Strange colors from radio waves, to regular light, to gamma rays and beyond."

"Would it be okay if I did the GP voice again?"

"Of course, Breath. I like your GP imitation."

"Oh good, here goes." She dropped the pitch of her voice to further imitate GP. "'Breath, y'all have just started and you've got a huge amount to learn. It'll take a lifetime. We'll begin by feeling what's around you. Y'all already produce a considerable Qrie field. Y'all must now use it as a sensing field within the Qrie continuum. Once this's done, y'all can sense everything around ya out to a great distance, like the ground, the dirt, the insects; and all of the objects that're on the ground, like the playground swings, slides, and monkey bars. You'll also sense people and animals.'"

She coughed and stopped trying to imitate GP.

"I still remember the first time I reached what GP liked to call the state-of-stillness. It was like I was two people. I could sense my brain, but I could also sense something else — something much bigger. It was like I could sense the whole world: the trees, the animals, the people, all the amazing new colors, and everything else and all this with my eyes closed. I couldn't tell what the people were thinking or what they were saying, but I knew they were there. I could see them. The problem is, if I looked at one thing in particular — my brain would begin to focus on it, and I'd lose everything else. I'd have to go back and make my brain still again. It was like I could think of, and be two things at once. After a while, I began to see what GP called the flows of energy and the power. This was hard because I had to still my brain so much just to sense them. But once I could see the energies, GP showed me how to move the energy flows around. It became a game with GP and me, and it was a lot of fun. GP told me to move around in the energy, and as I did, I also noticed I could move around in the world with my inner mind.

"When we started all this — it made my head hurt. But the more I tried. The more comfortable I became. I got good at sensing everything around me. When I got good, GP had me play on the monkey bars with my eyes squeezed shut. GP always wrapped me in his *Qrie Embrace* shield. It was a good thing too because sometimes I'd miss and would fall to the ground. Falling with the shield embrace was like jumping into bed. I got good at climbing, sliding, swinging, sensing, and well — falling — lots of falling." Breath giggled.

"It sounds like you like falling into this shield embrace."

"Oh, Daddy. It's so wonderful; I just love it."

"Yes, I remember GP giving me that same shield embrace and it is wonderful. Well, tell me more."

"Sometimes while climbing on the monkey bars, I'd just let go and fall into the shield embrace because it felt so good. GP had me put a blindfold on and run through the woods in the park as fast as I could, and never touch the trees, the branches, leaves, or anything.

"When I was in the woods, I could sense the animals, and they weren't afraid of me. They'd come up to me, and let me touch and pet them. The small animals and birds were fun. Even the larger insects would come around, like butterflies, dragonflies, and such. The smaller insects would never fly around my face and bother me, even though I knew they were there.

"A fun thing to do was to have the shield embrace around me and run into the trees and shrubs in the woods and bounce off them. It made me feel like the shiny ball in the pinball game at the arcade.

"GP then started teaching me how to play with the sand. He'd have me build sand castles, which was fun, but he wouldn't let me touch the sand with my hands. I had to do this, with my inner mind, while still sensing everything else around me.

"That's when the real fun started!"

Breath stopped her steady flow of words.

Will asked, "Is that all?"

"Oh, there's a lot more. I didn't know you wanted to know everything."

"Well, are you feeling better about your decision or do you need to tell me more so you can make that decision? Or is there something else you want to talk about?"

"Well, no — I just needed someone to listen and understand."

"Good enough, now are you ready to go in and argue with your mom?"

"I'm not quite there yet."

"Well then, go on?"

"Okay — When I was about seven years old, I liked my bath time. So much so that Mum would have to fuss at me to get me out of the tub. GP used this fun time to teach me to do neat stuff with my mind.

"It always started the same. He'd say, 'Breath, still your brain.' ... then something like, 'Imagine making bubbles out of the water instead of soap suds. It can be fun.'

"The problem was, I thought I was making water bubbles, but they were underwater and I couldn't see them.

"Then GP told me to make some water float in the air, like when he showed me how to move the sand.

"Then GP told me." Breath cleared her throat and tried to sound like GP again, "'Y'all do this by making a lump of water on the surface. Then pull that lump out above the water like this.'"

She cleared her throat again. "I watched as GP made a ball of water float in the air, and at the same time, he gave me detailed instructions as to how he did it.

"Soon, I made a glob of water float in the air like GP did, but it didn't look like a bubble."

"That's wonderful Breath, then what happened?"

"Well, I think I said something like, 'Wow! GP, I did it.'"

"Then GP said. 'Good now, just relax your mind, but hold the water in the air. Watch what happens.'"

"And I asked, 'What's supposed to happen?'"

"He told me, 'Don't hold the water so tight; let it be free in your mind.'"

"After a while — I got it and said. 'Look, GP, a perfect water bubble.'"

"Then GP said something like, 'That's wonderful. Now make a few more.'"

"After several baths and with GP's help, I got it, but each time when I made a little progress, Mum would fuss at me to get out of the tub. I didn't want to and would plead for just five more minutes.

"Then, after maybe a few minutes GP would say something like, 'Breath, it's time to get out. We can continue this again next time.'"

"I got good at making water bubbles. Then one day, GP told me, 'Now Breath, take that little dolphin toy you've got there, and make the water into that shape.'"

"I got good at making my own water toys. GP knew I'd do almost anything for one of his strong *Qrie Embraces* and he always rewarded me when I succeeded. Mum knew what I was doing and would let me stay in the bath longer and longer with GP there, but would fuss at me, in a fun way like calling me her water baby, when it was time to get out. I loved that time!"

"Would you like to hear more, Daddy?"

"Absolutely, Sweetie, as much as you want."

"Ok — I was still about seven and would go over to the playground. GP would tell me, 'Breath, walk on the sand, but don't disturb it.'"

"I'd argue, 'That's what it's for. And what're the Qrie?' I've asked that question a thousand times of both Mum and GP. They both ignore me, but someday I'll find out."

"One day GP said, 'Visualize walking to the monkey bars but don't touch the sand.'"

"At first, I wasn't good and messed up the sand with my footprints.

"GP was never upset and would say. 'Try again in a different spot. This time imagine the energy flowing through your body and out through your feet into the ground. That'll keep your feet from touching the ground but still able to connect to it.'"

"I asked GP what the energy looked like. He gave me an image of what could've been light coming out of my feet but it was transparent and not pretty. So, I turned the light into a rainbow.

"After about two weeks of visualizing the energy and not disturbing the sand when I walked on it, my footprints weren't nearly so deep."

"GP was always patient. He knew I was trying and would let me play, even when I failed. I would try to project myself into the sand and understand what GP was endeavoring to teach me.

"The first time I did, it was like I was on roller skates and fell — a lot. GP showed me how to make the rainbow light grab hold of the ground so my feet wouldn't slip. After that, I could walk on anything and not slip or touch the ground. He also taught me how to do this using my hands and knees as well, so I could climb right straight up the side of a smooth wall."

"That sounds super Breath, I'm glad GP was there to help you and teach you."

"Yeah, Daddy. It was neat. Do you want to hear more?"

"Of course, Breath, if you're up for it."

"Well, okay. When I was nine. I was at the playground, sitting on one of the swings but not swinging."

"GP came to me and asked. 'What's the matter Breath?'"

"I told him, 'Mum's upset with me.'"

"Then GP asked me, 'Why's she upset with you?' or actually 'y'all, which is the way, GP says, you.'"

"You know, Breath, you don't have to say it just like GP does. I don't want you to hurt your throat. If you want to use the accent, then do so, but say everything in your regular voice."

"But I thought you liked my GP imitation. It makes you smile!"

"I do, Breath, but not if it hurts your throat."

"Okay... Now, where was I? — Oh yeah. Mum says I've been playing outside too hard and wearing out my clothes."

"Then GP said. 'Well, Breath, there's a reason for that. Y'all know how your mother wears clothes lined with seaweed?'"

"Yeah, she had me wear some underclothes made out of seaweed and a dress lined with it. I won't wear the seaweed underclothes if I don't have to because they're uncomfortable, scratchy, and rub my skin raw. I don't like clothes."

"Then GP said. 'The reason your mother uses seaweed is that it'll last longer and won't disintegrate as fast, when the Qrie energies are flowin. Many things from the sea can be worn around the Qrie energies for a while.'"

"That may be true, GP, 'but they smell like seaweed.'"

"Then GP laughed. 'Breath, there's nothing I can do about seaweed smelling like seaweed.'"

"'I know, GP, but the kids make fun of me.'"

"Then GP got kinda serious. 'The reason your clothing wears out so fast is due to the Qrie fields that form around y'all when y'all use the fields; the seaweed makes the clothes last a little longer.'"

"Mum wants me to wear her baggy sack, T-shirt, and muumuu dresses, with no belt, all the time outside. But I like store-bought clothes because they're soft, fit nice, and aren't so baggy."

"GP then agreed with Mum. 'Your mom understands that baggy clothes are better and last longer.'"

"But the kids make fun of me."

"Then he made the same argument Mum makes. 'I'm sorry, Breath, but your tight-fitting clothes will fall apart.'

"Why?"

Breath sensed her dad chuckling.

"What are you laughing at Daddy?"

"You, I'm laughing at you! Do you always argue with GP?"

"Well, no, but sometimes questions have to be asked!"

"Well, I still think it's kind of funny. But I do understand what he's saying because I have had problems with my clothing as well. Just ask Virginia. But go on, tell me more."

"Well, where was I? Oh okay. Then GP said, 'Breath, hold your arm straight out and point your finger at something. Now look down your arm with your eye close to your arm. Do y'all see the watery like sheen that's surrounds your arm and hand?'"

"Yes, what's that?"

"Then GP said something like. 'That's your Qrie energy field that's around your body all the time. When it gets strong, such as when you're using the energy to not make footprints, that watery sheen energy field gets bigger and stronger. It doesn't tolerate things like tight clothes made from materials from the land. Clothes made from some materials that come from the sea can survive better. That's why your mother wants y'all to wear clothes made from seaweed.'"

"Is that why my socks, shoes, tight T-shirts, panties, and dresses with belts always seem to fall apart before the floppy clothes do?"

"'Y'all got that right, Breath.'"

"I think I understand now, GP. What am I going to do when I get older and I've gotta wear store-bought clothes all the time?"

"GP didn't give me a good answer. 'You'll either have to wear loose-fitting clothes, buy a lot of clothes or y'all can do like your mom does and line your clothes with seaweed. However, in the future, you'll learn about other types of clothing and linings that can be worn.'"

"Yuck! Now I understand why my bathers fall apart so quick. Mum hates it when I go swimming because I can only wear my bathers one time. Whenever we go to the beach we always go where there's no one around and Mum has us take off our bathers and we swim in the nuddy. If she senses someone coming, she'll get our bathers and we've gotta put them back on before anyone sees."

"GP said, 'It's the same thing.'"

"GP, are there more people like Mum and I that can't wear clothes without destroying them?"

"'Yes, Breath, there's a whole race of people that can't wear clothes and have to go naked when they're swimming. Although, they can wear store-bought clothes when they're not using the Qrie energies.'"

"That sounds great, GP. Can I meet them someday?"

"'Yes, Breath, someday I'll introduce y'all and y'all can even swim with them.'"

Breath could sense her dad pondering — then he said. "Thanks, Breath. I knew the clothing problem was — was something like that but I didn't know how it worked in reality. You just answered a question for your old dad. But then you are my genius daughter."

"Thanks, Daddy, I didn't know you had clothing problems too."

"Well, Sweetie. I do. And I now realize, so do all of us Qrie."

"Will there ever be a time when we can wear regular clothes like the humans do?"

"No Sweetie, I don't think so."

"Well, that's a bummer."

Will could sense Breath's mood. "Should we go on Sweetie?"

"Yeah, I guess so. I don't like the fact that I won't be able to wear nice clothes."

"Just because you can't wear tight clothes doesn't mean you can't wear nice clothes."

"Yeah, I guess that's right. Maybe there are some nice loose clothes out there. Well, anyway you wanna hear more?"

"Yes, if you wanna tell me more."

"Yeah, but let's change the subject from clothes. Let's see, — GP would always say, 'Breath, always sense around outside the play area to make sure no one can see you.'"

"If anyone came towards the play area where people could see me, I'd leave. Whenever I left the play area, footprints would form in the sand.

"I asked GP, why do I have to leave before someone comes near where they can see me?"

"He told me. 'Breath, you're different and special. If someone sees y'all doing things different than normal, they'll become curious. If the wrong people see y'all doing these things, they'll wanna know how y'all do them and will want to study y'all. I've seen people who're different have their lives ruined by well-meaning curious people and the government. It's why ya must be careful and not ever let anyone know what y'all can do until ya have full control of your Qrie abilities.'"

"He reminded me about this all the time. So, I asked. 'What're the Qrie?' I didn't expect an answer."

"I also asked, 'GP, why do footprints form in the sand several feet behind me when I do walk on the sand?'"

"He replied, 'I make the footprints or disturb the sand so if someone's watchin,' they don't see anything unusual.'"

"Then one day I said. I wish I could make myself invisible, so no one could see me."

"He replied, 'It's possible Breath and I'll show you.'"

"I could feel his smile. GP showed me how to put the rainbow energy around my body. When I got good at holding this energy stable. He then showed me how to change the density of the air around me. He told me that different air densities cause the light to shift directions. And if I shift the light just right; I can make the light pass around my body; and I become invisible. This took a while because I had to learn to sense the air itself, and what GP called dynamic air density. I got pretty good at this. Such that, I could move this air density as I move my arms and legs. It was a lot of fun, but it also took a lot of time standing in front of the mirror. Once I learned how to do this, I realized that I could make myself disappear. I couldn't see with my eyes because there was no light. I had to use the Qrie energies to sense my surroundings."

"So, Daddy I asked him. 'GP, why is this so?'"

"GP just laughed. 'Breath, think about it for a moment. If all of the light is bent around your body, will there be any light left for your physical eyes to see?'"

"I had to think about that for a while before I realized it was true. Then I understood that if I can't see out, no one can see me, and I am invisible. I practiced this a lot.

"GP warned me that even though no one could see me if I didn't have the fields and densities just right. People could see the shimmer as I moved. Getting rid of the shimmer was hard. I started calling my air density control field, my invisible cloak.

"The real problem with being invisible is that my clothes disintegrate very quick. Almost from the moment I start. So — I have to make sure that I take all my clothes off and do the invisible thing in the nuddy. Which is kinda fun since, I don't like clothes any way, especially those that smell like seaweed."

"I asked GP if he could show me how to do this underwater since there was no air. He told me that doing the invisible thing underwater is a thousand times harder. And that I was nowhere near ready for that challenge.

"He did tell me about something called I think he said it was a conjoogut mirror, or something like that, that will reflect light back to where it came from. And another one he called a black body that absorbs all light."

"Uh — Breath I think it's called a 'conjugate mirror.'"

"Conjugut. Okay I've got it."

"No Breath, it's conjugate not conjugut."

"Conjugate. Is that right? I think I got it right in my brain. I just couldn't get my mouth to make the right sound."

"You've got it now. Did you learn how to do it?"

"Yes, I did and its easier than being invisible. It's also good to use when the sun is too hot. He also showed me how to be selective while doing it. So, I can select which beam of light I want to reflect; like I can reflect the bright sunlight and still see everything around me. It's kinda neat but it's very complicated, and takes a lot of practice.

"GP taught me many things and introduced me to new challenges, like jumping off high stuff, that was pretty scary because I came down 'fast.' But I did get the hang of it, after a while. GP would always put the *Qrie Embrace* around me, like he was holding me, and I knew he wouldn't let me get hurt. I also put the rainbow lights around myself."

"GP would remind me that when I played with the other kids, I had to do only what they did. If they were playing in the sand, I had to mess the sand up just like they did."

"Would you like to hear something kinda scary?"

"Is this something I should keep from your mom?"

"Well, I think Mum already knows."

"In that case tell me more."

"By the time I was nine years old, I could jump off anything and not leave footprints on the ground.

"GP had me climb to the roof of the tallest building in town one late afternoon. Some workmen had been building a sidewalk around the building and they had lots of smoothed-out sand.

"Besides jumping off things, GP taught me how to climb using my hands and feet. The building was twelve stories tall and locked up. So, GP had me climb up the outside of the building, which I didn't think was all that much of a challenge."

"GP then told me. 'Breath, I want y'all to jump off this building into the sand without messing it up.'"

"That made me a bit nervous, knowing I hadn't jumped from that high before."

"But he said, 'Y'all can do this. Put your rainbow light around you. If y'all never disturb the sand, you'll never be hurt. If y'all jump from this height, y'all can jump from any height. I'll be with ya all the way.'"

"So, like a fool — I jumped, and GP was right. The *Qrie Embrace* was wonderful."

"Mum knew about what GP was doing, but I never told her about jumping off things. I didn't tell Mum that I'd jumped off the tallest building in town."

"GP told me. 'Don't worry Breath. I shield our training sessions and conversations from your mom. However, your mother and all Qrie can always tell when you're not telling everything or lying, so never lie. A temporary omission is permitted; lying isn't. You'll soon learn to detect the difference.'"

"That's very good advice, Breath, you should always listen to GP."

"I know Daddy. I always have to be careful around Mum. I slipped up a few times, and of course Mum would fuss; I found out very fast how not to lie. I told her my happiest secrets, never my deepest, darkest ones. GP would help me with those."

"You know Daddy. GP always seems to know what's going on, because one time I was sitting pondering something that Mum had said."

"GP asked me, 'Is there something on your mind, Breath?'"

"Well, yes, GP. The other day Mum said that she felt good that we're beginning to sound the same when we talk. I didn't know what she meant, that we sound like the same person speaking. I think that's crazy because I don't sound anything like Mum. Her voice is lower. What's she talking about?"

"Then he told me. 'Breath, when two Qrie entities are linked via telepathy like yourself and your mother or father, the word usage begins to sound like the same person. It's as if all y'all are using one brain for the conversation. As you get older, you'll notice the same thing with other telepaths, and perhaps even Morning and Beauty. However, that might take a while. To develop your own telepathic voice may take some time and work. Most telepaths learn to detect other telepath's personality signature, which is part of their personality structure. I'll teach y'all how to do this later.

'Telepathy emerges from a much deeper part of the brain. A concerted effort must be applied to give a different mental feeling of the telepathic communication. I do this to produce the mental feeling of a southern US gentleman, but it's not easy. When a telepath speaks aloud, they are also sending information telepathically at the same time, along with their vocal speech. This is why telepaths tend to sound alike and have similar speech patterns, as they are linked brain to brain, as well as by sound.

'Also, since telepathy comes from a deeper part of the brain than does speech. It's why when you're using telepathy to communicate you hear, what sounds like an echo. There's no real echo just a perception of one. Another thing, telepathy is not language. It's thoughts, feelings, impressions, and images, just like what Morning and Beauty do when they want to communicate. Your brain translates these telepathic thoughts and feelings into language and that is also why all telepaths sound alike.'"

"I'm gonna have to think about that GP. I'm not sure if I understand what you're saying."

"Then GP replied. 'Give it time.'"

"This is fun Daddy. Do you want to hear more?"

"Of course, how could I not want to hear what my sweet baby daughter has to say."

"Oh, Daddy, now you're just teasing me."

"Of course, I am, but it's still true and I do want to hear more."

"Well, okay. I just don't want to bore you."

"Not possible. I missed so much of your childhood by not being there that I want to hear as much as possible."

"Well then — When I was in junior high, I learned how to walk on mud. GP and I started off with the hard stuff first and worked up to the real mushy stuff. Then that real mushy mud got even mushier, and ended up just being cloudy, silty, dirty water, and then just water itself. I learned in church that there were two people who were able to walk on water. I guess now there're three. GP warned me not to ever let anybody ever see me do that, until my training was complete."

"Mum and I live about two kilometers from the ocean. My friend Alinta and I'd be in the water every chance we got. I never told Mum that we skinny dipped. But GP told me that Mum knew because my bathers were still intact.

"A lot of the time, I'd go there by myself. GP would teach me how to hold my breath for a long, long time and how to swim fast using the Qrie energies. Dolphins are a lot of fun and will always come around when I'm alone in the ocean.

"In high school, GP began teaching me how to jump. At first, we started off with small stuff and then got higher. I could jump flat-footed onto the roof of the house and then to the top of the big old eucalyptus tree growing beside the house.

"One evening GP told me, 'Ride your bike out to the town's tall radio antenna. I want y'all to learn how to jump up to the top of that antenna.'"

"I was really nervous. That antenna was a long way up and a long way down. Sometimes when I jumped down, GP would have me make my rainbow lights much stronger, and I'd stop in the air. I'd just hang there and float around; it was a lot of fun. Of course, we did this at night, so no one could see me in the nuddy or I'd use my invisible cloak. I learned that flying fast and high off the ground will destroy my clothes. I either had to do the exercise in the nuddy and bring extra clothes to have something to wear home or put my invisible cloak around myself. My invisible cloak got used a lot during the day.

"Should I go on Daddy?"

"Absolutely Breath. You haven't told me near enough, I need to know lots and lots more."

"Well then — when I was eleven and in high school, there was an old man that came around. Everybody called him crazy because he heard voices in his head. I started wondering about myself because I heard voices too. So, I went to talk to him. Maybe, just maybe, he was hearing the same voice in his head that I was hearing. But I think maybe, he was delusional because what his voices were telling him was nothing like what GP told me. The difference between me and that crazy old man is that I don't argue with my voices — well not all the time. And when I talk to the voices, I don't say anything out loud.

"I then knew the stuff I could do was quite strange!"

"GP warned me, 'Always remain quiet, never let anyone know that I'm here, and never talk out loud to me, like that unfortunate old man. If the wrong people hear y'all, they could put y'all in a mental institution.'"

"I learned to fly better than GP imagined. I could build and move some medium-sized things with my mind. I could do a lot of things that no human being could even dream of doing. I told Mum about what I could do and asked her if she could do these things too.

"She told me that she'd chosen not to. However, I've seen Mum move things without touching them and float off the floor to reach the top shelf. She could also light candles without a match just by pointing her finger at them. That made me wonder why she'd chosen not to, but Mum would never tell me. I told her that I knew she and I must be from Krypton or some other planet like Superman because we weren't human. I liked not being normal with a wonderful friend like GP. Mum vowed that I was born here on Earth like any other normal human being."

Breath stopped talking.

"Well, Breath, do you feel good enough about yourself now, that you can go in and have your argument with your mom. If not, I am still all ears and would love to hear more."

"Thanks, Daddy, I think I'm okay now. I just needed someone to talk to and clear my head."

"That's wonderful Breath sweetie, I'm glad for you. I know you'll make the right decision, and I know that GP will help you. I'll do all that I can to help you as well. Oh, and Breath, tell your mom, I'll pay for this call. I don't want your mother to have to sell the truck or the house to make a down payment on these telephone minutes."

Both Breath and her father laughed. "Thanks, Daddy, for making me feel so much better. All I have to do now is challenge and convince Mum."

5. ARGUMENT

Breath was going through a growth spurt and was now at 170cm or 5 feet 6 inches, 5 cm or about 2 inches taller than Heidi. This made Breath uneasy looking down at her mum when they were arguing. In Breath's mind, looking down at her mum was almost like arguing with herself, they shared the same shape face, fair skin, golden Scandinavian blond hair, and bright violet indigo eyes. The family resemblance was striking.

The argument about college between Breath and her overprotective mum had been going on since Breath had received a full advanced scholarship to Melbourne University, several weeks previous.

This portion of the argument started in the kitchen, then moved to the living room, to Breath's bedroom, and even to their well-organized backyard jungle of a garden. Heidi was high energy, wiry, and always relentless even when Breath was cuddled into her mum's safe, warm, and loving arms.

Breath began to remember her life growing up in this wonderful home with her mum and GP. She let her mind wander around the kaleidoscope of amazing handiwork and paintings. The house was decorated in hippie fashion which was Heidi's idea of art. It was home, but also her fetish. Even the front door had what she called happy daisies painted around the full-length mirror.

She gazed around the living room at the garden scenes that she and her mum had painted on the walls. Her mind reminisced on the large collection of what she called hippie knickknacks. They covered most of the free spaces on the desks, tables, and windowsills in the room. She liked but wondered why her mother always insisted on having string beads hanging in the doorways of every door in the house. Well except the doors leading outside.

***

The next morning the battle was rejoined and Breath was pleading, "Mum, we've been through this argument a hundred times. I graduated junior-college with top honors, and I can now go to school for free. I'm almost thirteen years old, and I've got a full scholarship. I know I've got to be careful. I know I'm special. I know I'm part human. I know the schools are a long way away, but ..."

Heidi kept cutting Breath off. "There're good universities right here in Perth. That University is all the way across the country. We can work out a way to pay for school here. I know you want to be normal and what's normal is going to school here. It's the right thing to do."

"What's right for me is to go to Melbourne. I know they've got schools of oceanography here. But none of them have given me a scholarship at all, much less an advanced scholarship. Melbourne is the best and I want to go to school there."

"That may be what you want but it's not what's best for the family."

"What do you want me to do Mum? Stay here for the rest of my life? You know good and well that someday I've gotta leave. You can't hang on to me forever." Breath knew that these words would hurt her Mum, but felt they had to be said to bolster her argument.

Stung, her Mum took a deep breath and continued. "All I'm saying is, there's nothing in Melbourne that you can't get right here at home. Besides, we can be together here. How're you going to live?" Heidi blurted, "You don't have any money. Don't think for one minute that I'm going to send you money to live that far from home. I'll close your bank account so you can't even write a check."

Breath knew this was a ploy. She knew her mum would never let her go without, even if it was her last cent. "I'll get a job. We just scrape by month to month, anyway. With me gone, you'll have more money to spend on yourself. Plus, I already closed my bank account. I needed the money to buy the plane ticket. I was surprised that going by plane is cheaper than going by train. Who would've guessed?"

Breath crunched her face in determination and projected, *Mum, you don't have to worry about me. I've got GP with me all the time.*

Heidi looked hurt. She pouted and with some rejection she projected. *I know, but I want to be with you too. I'm still a young woman and I don't want to be left alone.*

"We're as close as a thought. We always have the telephone and we can always Skype."

Heidi knew the real truth about how special Breath is. She knew Breath had to bloom, but she still felt desperate to keep her daughter safe. Her baby was leaving home. Even though she knew there was nothing she could do about it. The Qrie had other plans for Breath, but she had to try.

"Breath, please! What'll you eat? There's nothing but processed foods out there, it's not good and it's not natural."

"Cancer is natural, and not good for me either. I'll eat hamburgers, hot dogs, and ramen if I've got to. Besides, Mum, they've got farmers markets there. I'll be okay and GP will be there with me all the time."

Heidi knew she was losing this argument and began grasping at straws. "You know; we don't have any suitcases. You can't use paper bags. There's a rule or something."

"I went to that dusty old surplus store yesterday and got two duffel bags and two padlocks for them as well."

"GP and I can teach you everything you need to know here. There is no need to leave. What about all your friends here? You're just going to go off and leave them? Just like you're going off and leaving me?"

"What friends? That guilt trip won't work, Mum. Alinta Mitchel, the only real friend I ever had, moved away. Everyone else here either calls me a geek, a klutz, or a hippie freak. I don't think any of my so-called school chums are going to miss me for a nanosecond. They probably will be glad I'm gone. Well — that may be a partial truth, because when I'm gone, they won't have anybody to..."

She knew she needed reinforcements against her Mum's emotional stance, and she called upon GP for support.

GP, why's she so insistent on keeping me here? She knows I've got to go.

Truth is, Breath, to your mother, you're still her baby girl. Y'all must also remember that you're not even an adolescent yet. You're not even a teenager. It's a mother's job to protect her children. She knows what y'all can do, and she knows how special y'all are. She fears that y'all won't keep your secret. In truth, she hasn't learned to fully trust you yet.

Breath paused, *Oh, I didn't realize that. But what'd it hurt if people learned our secret?*

I've told y'all a hundred times, ever'body in your family is special. All y'all can do things that no one else can do, and there're people who, if they knew your secret, would exploit your abilities to their advantage. They'd use your family and friends to get their way. This can't be allowed. Other people would wanna know how those things are done. All y'all would become their guinea pigs. So, until your abilities are complete and under control, it's best to keep hidden and maintain your secret. Your mother's afraid that you'll spill the beans, so to speak.

Breath paused, *Oh, I didn't realize that, either.* She turned back to her Mum, who was patiently waiting. She had known that Breath was speaking to GP, and hoped that his counsel would help settle the argument to support her position. After all, GP was wise and experienced... wasn't he?

"Mum, you can trust me." She continued with a softer voice. "You know why I'm going to Melbourne? The scholarship there's the big one; everything's paid for. I get tuition, books, room and board — everything. They even have the staff to help the students in the gifted program with anything they need. Why do you think I've been working so hard all this time? All that hard work is starting to pay off. I'm going to get to live my dream. Don't you want that for me?"

"Every mum wants her daughter to live her dream. But the truth is, I'm frightened that you'll leave, and I'll never see you again. Breath, you've no idea how special you are to me."

Breath knew she had to remain strong. "We'll see each other again. It's not like I'm moving to the other side of the world, just the other side of the country. I'll be a short phone call away, and we can talk anytime you want. Well, maybe when I'm not in class or working." *Besides, we're always as close as a thought.*

"I know, Love, but it's so far, and you're so young and I've had you for such a short time. If you could just wait a little while longer." Heidi made a long sigh of dejection.

"Anyway, I don't like anything military, and those two — what'd you call them — duffel bags look pretty military to me."

Breath knew now 'everything' was going to be okay and she brightened up. "Well, they were cheap and they'll hold all my stuff. I washed them to get the musty smell out and painted them pink with flowers on them, just for you." Heidi gave Breath a halfhearted grin.

The argument abated but continued until it was time for Breath to leave.

Her mum dropped her off at the airport. She handed Breath an envelope. "These are all the permission papers you'll need. They include papers that'll allow you to work while at school."

Heidi hugged and kissed her goodbye, then turned and hurried back to her old pickup truck so Breath couldn't see her cry.

GP gave Heidi a comforting *Qrie Embrace.*

Breath watched her walk away. The porter took her bags and placed them with the others. The airport was noisy, even after she got on the plane. She sat down in her seat and started biting her lower lip. With all the brave face she put on, she was still scared and was going to miss her mum very much, and their quiet oasis called home.

GP?

GP gave Breath a strong *Qrie Embrace. Yes?*

Just checking.

I know.

***

Heidi had discussed the situation with Breath's father William, but no resolution had ever come from these continuing discussions. Both of them had been restrained by the pure-energy Qrie beings Morning and Beauty from telling Breath exactly who and what she was. William and Heidi, both being part Qrie, knew the problems that Breath was going to face, but they didn't understand why the Qrie wouldn't let Breath know what she was capable of. They'd told Heidi and William what they were, right up-front before Breath was born. Why not Breath? They thought about it and asked themselves, *Morning, Beauty, and GP hover around Breath like she's some kind of little princess. What's going on between them and her? We're all Qrie, what's so special about her?*

***

Breath called her mum when she arrived at Melbourne University. They talked for more than an hour.

Heidi told Breath. "I know you're a bit scared and uncertain of the future, love. All you have to do is get back on the airplane and come home, which I think is the best solution."

Breath bit her lip, and with tears in her eyes. "No mum, I am here and I am going to do this no matter how scary it is. I love you Mum."

Just before Heidi hung up. "Breath, never let anyone know you hear the voices. Because if you do, people will have you committed for being crazy. Listen to GP. I love you Breath."

GP projected, *Heidi, I'll take care of and teach Breath what she needs to know. I'll also make sure she has everything she needs.*

6. JOB

Breath discovered that even with her full University scholarship, living wasn't free. Heidi had sent sufficient seaweed cloth, to be used as a replaceable lining, to protect Breath's clothes and make them last longer. What she needed was toothpaste, girl stuff, snacks, bus fare, laundry stuff, and a hundred other little things. She needed money, which meant a job.

Breath looked around her dreary white room. Coming off the hall in the dorm was her white door. Behind her door were shelves, drawers, and a place to hang her clothes, also white. The end of that was a second door that led into the bathroom, also white. Behind that door was a toilet and next to that was a sink along the adjacent wall. A shower was across from the sink and the shower curtain was you, guessed it, white. One delightful thing about the restroom was that it had a high window across from the toilet that let light in.

In the main room next to the door was a single bed that had a headboard with shelves for books, a lamp, and a clock. There was also a landline telephone on the headboard shelf, and guess what — it's white. On the wall next to the bed and opposite the bathroom was a long shelf for a desk with a set of drawers at each end. There were two power plugs along that wall for plugging in computers, lights, etc. and — it was all white! Opposite the main door was a large window, to the left of the bathroom, that looked out over the courtyard and allowed light into the room. There was a set of white blinds that could be lowered and adjusted to control the light through the window. Overhead there was a single light with a frosted glass cover over it and it was — yes — white. Along the wall adjacent to the bed and also adjacent to the window are cabinets, closets, and shelves again — all white. Breath thought, *I'm glad I have a pair of sunglasses to protect my eyes from this room!*

She was disappointed in the woman counselor that the University Center for Gifted Students had provided. She didn't tell Breath about all these incidental problems. Her mum sent her what little money she could spare. Breath discovered her support system was minimal at best, and she was at times homesick. She longed for the warm, secure embrace of her mum's loving arms, the wonderful aromas from the kitchen and her mother's homemade potions. She dreamed of her mum's gentle stroking of her hair.

Breath pondered with frustration and some lonesome fear. *I just bought this used bicycle at the thrift shop with what little money I had left. At least it has a lockable basket and a cable with a combination lock, but now I'm broke. Did I do the right thing?*

She lamented that she hadn't gotten to University earlier. *All the older students got here early and had taken all of the good jobs. This is hopeless. Two weeks of job searching and rejections, and still nothing!* Discouragement rained in the form of tears soaking her lonesome white pillow.

Breath, you're Qrie, and the Qrie solve problems in unusual ways.

That may be true, GP, but the one job I've found is washing dishes in the cafeteria. No one else wants it, so I guess I'll take it. It doesn't pay much, but it's nights and weekends, and they don't mind students studying on the job when time allows.

At least it's better than nothing. The university counselor is helping me with my permits, but that's going to take time. Then the counselor made this dumb joke about me looking good enough to be a child model. It's just not fair.

Breath, life isn't always fair. Your counselor was trying to cheer y'all up, and I agree with her about y'all looking good enough to be a child model, but we ain't gonna do that. We don't want all those pictures. Hang in there kiddo. Something will turn up.

Yeah, a pile of dirty dishes.

***

Over the last week Breath was signed up for all of her classes and was back in her room lamenting, when GP projected. *Y'all need to get out of this dreary dorm room. Take a break and go for a swim. It'll do y'all good, and besides, y'all might even have some fun.*

It was early Saturday morning when Breath rode the five kilometers or so to the beach and found it almost deserted. She missed the ocean but even more she missed the beach walks with her mum.

She got some strange looks because she had a large, customized monofin that looked like a combination of an orca and a dolphin tail strapped to her back.

At home in Fremantle, she'd become frustrated swimming with normal scuba diving flippers. She tried a monofin. It wasn't to her exact liking.

When she started high school, she decided to design a monofin swimming device that suited her. She soon discovered she needed to learn a lot about physics, hydrodynamics, materials, and engineering.

Undaunted and with GP's advice and teaching, she dove into the project. She and Heidi had a small shop attached to the back of their house where they spent many hours making wooden whirligigs and decorative windmills to sell. It took a lot of study and several iterations before Breath finally discovered how to make her modified monofin work. She never stopped improving on its design. She discovered that trial and error breeds success.

A few beachcombers populated the beach with their metal detectors, looking for lost treasure, and there were a few screeching seagulls. She found a public bike rack adjacent to the beach. She put her towel, T-shirt, jeans, and thongs in her basket and locked it and her bike.

She started wading and walking aimlessly on the beach. She had walked about half a kilometer of the beach when she came upon a pod of dolphins playing in the surf. She put on her seaweed-lined monofin and swam out to join the fun.

Breath is at home in the water. She's a powerful swimmer with her monofin. With the help and training from GP, she is super-fast, and can hold her breath for an amazing amount of time.

She can hear boats and all manner of sea life underwater quite well. She noticed that ferry boats and pleasure boats, are loud and noisy to the point of being uncomfortable. Some of the bigger boats are so loud it hurt her insides.

In Fremantle, when she was troubled, GP would sometimes have her go to the ocean and swim to and around Rottnest Island and back, which was about forty kilometers altogether. Sometimes she'd just swim to Carnac Island if she wasn't up for a long swim, only fourteen kilometers. She did learn to stay away from the noisy ferry and pleasure boats and so did the dolphins.

She even learned to mimic the calls of the dolphins and whales. She learned a few of their calls and wasn't sure if she got them right, but she thought she sounded pretty convincing. She figured the dolphins and whales thought she was just babbling like a young one. She knew enough dolphin and orca calls to get her point across, although she knew she couldn't do the ultrasonic sounds.

She never told anyone at school about this; she didn't want to be more of a freak than she already was.

She often wondered how people could drown in the ocean. All you have to do is stop swimming, roll over on your back, and float forever — or wait for the dolphins, and they will take you to shore. What's the big deal? It wasn't until a year or so ago that she understood other people couldn't do that. They didn't have a relationship with sea mammals like she did.

Another thing she didn't understand was why people couldn't see as clear underwater as they could out of it.

***

Breath reminisced about how GP had taught her how to manipulate water and gather it about her body to form it into any shape she wanted, as she did with her bathtub toys. She congealed the water to give it some body. GP called this congealed manipulation a *mental gelatin encasement.* Since she had been gelatinizing and encasing the water with her mind, she'd practiced making herself a dolphin tail that started at her waist and covered her hips, legs, feet, and her custom monofin. The monofin had a pouch attached to the metal piece that came up between her calf muscles for carrying items such as her bathing togs, which she never wore with the mental gelatin encasement.

This encasement gave her much better efficiency and speed. She also made herself a pair of gelatin-encasement water gloves with webbed fingers and a paddle-like arrangement that went up to her elbows. Her webbed fingers and paddles acted like seal or dolphin flippers, which made her an even more efficient swimmer. She even made herself a gelatin top to keep the fast-moving water from irritating her nipples. She had been getting better at forming her mental gelatin encasement, but it still took her almost a minute to get everything formed. It just took a few seconds to put on her monofin. She thought, *I've gotta get better at this.*

Breath also reminisced about the many variations she'd tried with her gelatin encasement. She'd seen many pictures of mermaids with frilly streamers trailing from their arms, hair, and flukes. She practiced making these streamers and even tried to make them multicolored.

Breath also remembered the argument — or the discussion — with GP. It went something like this:

GP, we can't call this stuff I make surrounding myself a mental gelatin encasement. It just doesn't sound right.

But Breath, that's what it is. You're encasing water as a gelatin with your mind. I suppose it could be called a telekinetic gelatin encasement.

Yuck! That's even worse. We've gotta come up with something simple, like an aqueous flipper or liquid suit.

Well, how about telekinetic enclosure or translucent enclosure?

Those are just as bad. We need some kind of catchy name, like waterproof tail or maybe water tail. No, I don't like the sound of those either.

How about something like enclosure suit? At least that kind of describes it.

Well, that's better, GP. What if we combined some words? Like aqua suit? No, actually, I'm not fond of that one either. But I do like the aqua *part.*

Breath, I'm about to run out of suggestions. How about aqua fin, or aqua flipper, or even aqua costume? Do y'all like any of those?

They're not bad. What if we combined aqua and costume and made it one word? You know, like Aqume?

Breath, are you becoming 100 percent marketing on me? Aqume — you know, it does sound pretty good, and since it's just between us, we'll know what it means. It should be okay. Do you like it?

Yes, I think I do.

Then Aqume it is.

GP, do you think I'll ever get faster at producing this Aqume?

You know what they say: practice makes perfect. And here's something else Breath, you're always saying you want to be normal. Let me tell you something you're not a normal human being, but you're a normal Qrie-human being. And you're learning. How many other kids can do what you can do? Just ask yourself how many kids on the swim team at school could swim even a tenth of the distance to Rottnest Island and back. The answer to that is none of them and they are normal humans. I will praise the day and you when you truly understand what you are.

There was a long pause before Breath said anything.

GP knew that she was trying to absorb what he had just said.

Well — that was fun, GP. We'll have to do that again.

Okay, but next time, I won't be so easily swayed.

***

It wasn't long before she and the dolphins were out of sight of land. With her Aqume, arm flippers, and fluke, she felt at home with her new dolphin friends. Her mind was still on trying to get a decent job to help pay for the things she needed. She wasn't paying close attention to her dolphin friends or her surroundings.

About three hours into their play, she was surprised by a boat coming towards her. It was a boat full of tourists from Port Phillip Bay Explorers. The twenty or so tourists were having a wonderful time photographing all the dolphins and trying to get a photograph of her, but the dolphins kept getting in the way.

She panicked. *GP, why didn't you warn me about the boat? I don't have my bathers on; it's in my monofin pouch, and I don't have time to put them on.*

Y'all should learn to be more observant. You've been worrying too much about getting a job. Pay attention, I can't believe you didn't hear that boat. Y'all learned how to sense your environment through the Qrie energies. Y'all could hear the boat from some distance away. Ya just weren't paying attention. Besides, there's an opportunity with these people.

What, to see a girl swimming in the nuddy? Is this another test?

Swimming in the nude never bothered y'all before, although y'all shouldn't allow yourself to be photographed.

Oh really, GP, you think! You know, sometimes you can be so — frustrating.

Yes, Breath, but what would ya do without me?

Why do you push me so hard and with such urgency?

You'll understand soon enough.

There's my frustration again.

No comment.

I love you too, GP.

I kinda thought so.

Two diver guides in wetsuits put on flippers, masks, and snorkels and jumped in the water. When the divers swam towards her, several dolphins got between the guides and her.

Breath asked the closest diver. "What's going on?"

"We're trying to save you."

"Why? I don't need saving."

"But, miss, you're out in the middle of the bay by yourself."

"OK, so what's the big deal? Besides, I'm not alone. I've got my friends here."

"What do you mean friends? We don't see anyone else. Are there other divers or people here with you?"

"There are no other people here, only my dolphin friends."

"You'll have to come with us, Miss. We can't leave you out here alone."

"Why? I got out here, didn't I? And I'm not alone."

"How did you get out here? It's at least fifteen kilometers from shore."

Breath gave the man a wicked little smile. "I swam. How else would I get out here? Anyway, fifteen kilometers is nothing for a mermaid."

Be careful, Breath, GP warned.

"Mermaid? There's no such thing as mermaids!" He wasn't quite as sure of his conviction as he could've been, because he ducked his head underwater to see if she had a mermaid's tail. At least, that was what Breath thought he was doing.

Breath thought. *Guess what? No tail. I've got my monofin today, and my dolphin friends to protect my embarrassment, although it does kind of look like a tail. And my clear Aqume can't be seen underwater. Besides, they won't be able to see anything anyway, with all my dolphin friends around me.*

"If you won't come with us, you'll have to at least give us your name and where you live. Would you please do that?"

"Why should I give you my name? I'm not doing anything wrong."

"You may not be doing anything wrong, but if we don't bring you back to safety and this gets reported, 'we'll' be doing something wrong. We must at least get your name and address; in case something happens. Please, miss, we don't want to get into trouble."

Breath thought that was made up, but she relented. "Okay, my name is Breath Spring, and I go to University."

"That's not a real name, miss. We need your real name, and you're too young to go to University."

"My name, the only one I have, is Breath Of Spring, and I do go to Melbourne University." With that, she made a couple of dolphin calls, dove under the water, and swam off with her dolphin friends. When she dove under the water, she exposed her Aqume and tail above the water for a second or so. With the sun light glistening off the water, the tourists couldn't make out anything but the shape. But, in their minds, there was no doubt. Neither she nor the dolphins were seen again by the tour guides or the tourists on the boat that day.

Breath, I've made it such that they can't tell anyone about you. The only people on that boat who'll know about y'all are the crew, the divers, and their boss.

I wanna discuss something else with y'all. I noticed that y'all were becoming quite empathic with your dolphin friends.

So, what's wrong with my expressing empathy with my dolphin friends? When I'm in the water with them, I wanna be like them.

Breath, y'all can never be a dolphin. You're a Qrie. As a Qrie, y'all can feel sympathy and rational compassion for your dolphin friends, but you can never be a dolphin. As a telepath, y'all are also an empath and can sense another's emotions. There's nothing wrong with being an empath; it's part of what you are.

Strong empathy can cause problems for the empath. Empathy can draw y'all into the other entities' emotional worlds. Their problems become your problems. Their joys become your joys. Their enemies become your enemies. This is dangerous because as a Qrie, y'all can't have an enemy, real or imagined. Y'all must always be sympathetic with love and have rational compassion for all entities, even enemies. People can become quite violent through empathy. Those people who take on another's emotional life and their enemies, can in some cases, become more of a threat than the enemies and can even become evil themselves.

I'm not saying be selfish and immoral; on the contrary, be a good and caring person. Always use love, sympathy, rational compassion, and intelligence when dealing with any situation, but never empathize. It can isolate you from the rest of the world. Empathy will make you feel alone, and it can get you into serious trouble. The Qrie never want to take on someone else's problems. Y'all must always use love, sympathy, intelligence, and rational compassion to help others solve their own problems.

Breath was quiet and introspective. Then, after a moment. *That's interesting, GP. I never thought about it that way. Can't you have empathy for the victim as well as the perpetrator?*

No, Breath, empathy doesn't work that way. You can have sympathy and rational compassion for both, but not empathy.

I'm going to have to think about this, GP.

I thought y'all might. Make it part of your being.

Well, GP, for now, I'll just think about it.

That's all I can ask.

***

Monday afternoon, Breath was returning from class. Her head was down in concentration, since she was still worried about a job. She stopped when she saw three men standing outside her dorm room. One of the men — she recognized him as the diver she'd talked to during the incident on Saturday — pointed. "That's her, Boss."

GP, what are these people doing here?

They're curious and concerned. I warned y'all about curious people.

How did they get my dorm address and room number? All I gave them was my name and that I went to University.

She was a little intimidated and irritated by their presence. She walked up to them, "What are you doing here?"

Breath sensed and felt telepathically, from their point of view, the three men as they watched in awe as she regally walked towards them in a blue muumuu dress that her mum had made her. They'd never seen a person move so smooth and effortless in their lives. It was as if she were floating rather than walking, with her bare feet just touching the floor, if at all. The older man watched to see if her bare feet did indeed touch the floor, and he noticed they did. Well her heels didn't but the balls of her feet and toes did. He thought. *In comparison to runway fashion models or ballet dancers, her elegant grace and economy of motion was perfection.*

Breath blushed and dropped her head to hide her embarrassment and her intrusion.

The diver she'd talked to on Saturday had the name David embroidered on his shirt.

Breath's amazing beauty was offset by her awkward lack of social understanding. When she walked into a room where no one knew her, she attracted the attention of every person in the room. That attention was what made her so uncomfortable. She rejected social interaction and became businesslike to the extreme, when finding herself in social situations. She had no concept of how beautiful and striking she was.

The oldest of the three men looked at her for a long moment. Just staring into her eyes. "We... ah — wanted to see if you were okay. I didn't believe what the two divers told me. I had to see for myself. How'd you disappear, and how'd you get back?"

"I swam. How do you think I got back? As far as disappearing, I just swam underwater for a while."

"That was an extraordinary amount of time to hold your breath. Do you often go out swimming like that with the dolphins?"

"Yes, every chance I get, although sometimes I swim with the whales or seals. I'm not as fond of the seals; they stink, but they're so playful."

"Whales... seals... are you a mermaid?"

"Oh, come on! Do I look like a mermaid to you?"

"Well, Saturday you had us pretty well convinced that mermaids do exist, swimming and talking to the dolphins in their own language. Besides, no one knows what a real mermaid looks like anyway."

"I can promise you, I'm not a mermaid. I've been able to do stuff like that with marine mammals all my life. It's just something I do. I like it, and they seem to like it too. Does that make me a mermaid? I don't think so."

The older gentleman looked at the others with a sheepish grin and then back at Breath. "Would you 'like' to be a mermaid?"

"What? — Why would you ask me that, Sir?"

"I own Port Phillip Bay Explorers, and everyone just calls me Boss. I take tourists out so they can see and swim with the dolphins and fur seals. If you can repeat what you did Saturday, I can give you a good job if you're interested.

"The tourists on the boat couldn't stop talking about the mermaid and even booked more tours in the hopes of seeing you again."

"That's interesting, I need a good job. But Saturday is the only day I've got off from school. Sunday, I've gotta study and do my washing and other chores to get ready for the school week."

"That'll be perfect. Saturday is the one day we do all-day cruises. Do the dolphins come around whenever you're in the water?"

"Yes, anytime I go for a swim, they're always there unless I put out the feeling that I want to be alone."

"Always?"

"Yes, always. We're family; I'm part of the pod."

David said. "So, you are a mermaid...?"

Boss cut him off. "That's good to know. If you can always bring the dolphins, I can pay you well. Because sometimes when we go out, we don't see dolphins at all. We can always see the seals because they stay close to shore. The dolphins don't. If the tourists don't see dolphins, many times they demand part of their money back. So, if you can bring the dolphins close so the tourists can see them and even swim with them, and we don't have to refund money, that'd be great.

"I pay well, and I know you need a job. We need some way to bring the dolphins. It's a perfect match — great! Is there anything you need, like swim fins, wetsuits, anything like that?"

Breath thought for a moment. "I can use a new custom monofin. Mine is getting pretty old, and it needs constant repair. I'll also need a bunch of bathing togs; the one I had Saturday is the only one I had left, and it's no longer any good." She thought. *This guy never lets up. He must be desperate.*

"We can handle that. How about masks or snorkels?"

"Oh, I never use masks, snorkels, wetsuits, or anything like that. I don't like them. They get in the way."

"How do you stay warm without a wetsuit?"

"Oh, I never get cold, even when it's freezing. I don't know why, so don't ask me."

The older man stopped a moment and mumbled to himself with astonishment. "Wow, a girl who never gets cold. That's gotta be a first.

"Well, you'll need some kind of mask to hide what you look like. I know from experience that if you do something like this, people, especially the paparazzi, will never leave you alone.

You'll never have a free moment to yourself. You need some kind of disguise to hide your true identity."

Y'all know the man does have a point. If people find out about y'all; you'll never be free. So, a mask it is. I have an idea. I think you can use your Aqume over your head and upper body to hide your real identity. We'll have to make it look plastic and not transparent underwater. I know you're up for it. I'll make sure that the divers, crew, and Boss never reveal your true self.

Boss continued. "Okay then, I think I can arrange to get you some new equipment. Where do I find one of these monofin things?"

"I designed the one I use and built it myself. With a little money and some help, I can build another."

"What is a monofin?"

He looked at David, who rolled his eyes towards the ceiling. Boss shrugged, palms up in a pleading gesture. "What? I've never seen one."

Breath said. "Your divers use standard snorkel diving flippers, one on each foot. A monofin has one large surface, like a very large flipper, and both feet fit into the foot cups on it. To use it, you swim like a dolphin."

"Would you mind showing us your monofin so we can see what we're up against?"

"Sure. It's just in here." She being young and naïve led the men into her dorm room. Hanging in her closet was a complicated-looking device made of metal, stiff plastic, rubber, and seaweed padding, which she took down and laid on her bed.

Boss asked her. "Would you tell us how it works?"

GP, should I do this?

It's up to you, Breath. I've analyzed them, and they're honest people. I'll not allow them to divulge any of your secrets. Do you want a good job?

Yes!

Well then!

GP, did you set this up?

No comment.

Breath punched the air with her index finger. *I just knew it!*

Breath paused for a moment pondering and then looked at Boss and the others, with an expression of embarrassment. "It's much easier if I show you." She recovered from her silent punching and picked up the monofin.

"My feet go in these foot cups, like so. These clips attach to the flat bar here go between my legs and strap around my calf muscles."

Sitting on her bed, she leaned over and pointed to a hinge. "This hinge here at my foot cups has a spring and a release pin. The cable from the release pin runs up inside and to the top of the flat bar and between my legs at my knees. If I pull this ring on the cable, I can release the fluke, so it'll swing free on its hinge.

"I can slip my legs out of the clips and foot cups, stand up, and walk around... normal flippers and monofins allow thrust only on the downstroke. This bar arrangement allows me to have a powerful thrust on the upstroke as well."

She then showed them, with her legs and feet strapped to the device, how her feet could sense pressure and control the angle of the large fluke below her feet. "Swimming with the device takes a considerable amount of coordination as well as a great deal of strength in the legs, hips, and body core."

Even after she explained the device several times, the men still didn't understand how it worked. They were, however, impressed with its clean lines. There was nothing that'd interfere with water flow around her legs or the device itself.

Boss asked, "Saturday would be a good day to start. We'll do some test runs for the next three Saturdays and then see how we're doing and how much I can pay. Is that okay?"

"I can't wait a month. I need money now. I've got a job washing dishes in the cafeteria."

"OK, what if you started last Saturday? And every Saturday the dolphins come; I pay you two hundred dollars. If the dolphins don't appear, you get fifty. And we can reassess after three more Saturdays. Does that sound fair?"

Breath was excited, but she held her emotions intact. "That sounds fair for a trial period. But after three Saturdays, we renegotiate."

"I can agree to that." Boss pulled out his wallet and counted out two one-hundred-dollar bills and handed them to Breath. "This is for last Saturday. One other thing: when you're in that monofin contraption, you don't look much like a mermaid. I have a friend who can make something that'll go around your legs, along with a pair of webbed-fingered gloves, if that's okay with you. I'll see you Saturday morning at eight o'clock."

GP, what've I gotten myself into? He wants to make me look like a fish.

The only thing that Breath perceived was GP laughing.

***

"Guess what Mum? I got a job." For the next twenty minutes, Breath told her mum everything about her new job with the tour boat.

Heidi Spring loved hearing Breath's voice on the phone. She got a chance to speak after a bit. "That's wonderful Breath. I'm so proud of you. But you've got to be careful and guard your secret. I don't want you being captured by the government or some bad people who want to study you. There's still so much you don't know. Couldn't you get a job at the University itself instead of one in the open ocean?"

"I thought you were going to be happy for me Mum."

"I am, Breath. I'm ecstatic, but I'm also afraid for you. I love you so much and want you to be safe. It's my job!"

"I'll be safe Mum. I'll have GP and the entire boat crew there with me in case anything happens. GP told me that he won't let anyone talk or do anything concerning my secret, even if they find out. He'll also guide me, with keeping the secret."

"Breath baby, I'd love to talk a lot longer, but I have someone coming in right now for a reading. Please don't show anyone anything you shouldn't. I'll call you later. I'm glad for you, and I love you. Listen to GP. Bye-bye Love."

"I love you too Mum. Talk to you later."

***

For the remainder of the week, Breath and GP spent every free moment in the water practicing building a full-body Aqume. When the Aqume was out of the water, it looked plastic, but Breath hadn't perfected the underwater plastic look yet.

Saturday after getting on the tour boat, Boss handed her a package. When she opened it, Breath found a tube-like thing with painted fish scales that wraps around her legs and waist and a special hood that goes over her head and upper body, and a special pair of webbed-fingered gloves. Breath swam with her fish-scale tube, hood, and gloves until they started to fall apart. Boss came in with another package. Although this set of tubes, hoods, and gloves looked the same, they were more robust and didn't disintegrate as quick as the old ones did. Boss told Breath his friend had made the interlining out of sharkskin and silicone rubber. Breath guessed this was the reason they didn't fall apart as fast

***

Breath, you've got to learn to make your Aqume opaque and multicolored so no one can see your face and physical body. While you're doing this, you might want to make a snorkel-like arrangement that goes around to the back of your head so you don't have to lift your head out of the water to breathe.

Good point GP. I think when I can do that, I'm going to stop wearing my bather togs under my Aqume, to save on having to buy so many. Nobody will be able to see through it anyway.

Good point, Breath.

You know it's going to be difficult to get in and out of the water with this thing on. It's cumbersome and heavy on dry land and the boat.

After more experimenting they figured out a way to allow her to remove her monofin and leave her Aqume around her body and legs but still walk and climb the ladders on the boat. It was heavy and cumbersome but doable.

Well, this all just adds to the mystique. Breath, y'all know Boss and the crew will know for sure that you're a mermaid.

I know GP, but I need this job.

Well just don't let anyone take a good picture of your face.

I won't GP and thanks. I know you set all this up. And I love you for it.

No comment on the set up, and I love you too Breath.

7. MERMAID

B oss wanted Breath to visit his tour boat before she was to be the mermaid on it. When Breath got to the dock that Friday afternoon, Boss and David met her in the parking lot. As they walked down the jetty Breath asked Boss. "Why do you want me to see the boat? I have already seen it."

"Well yes but that was a dolphins eye view. I'd like for you to see all of the boat."

As Breath approached the boat, she saw the name Esmeralda in gold letters painted on the three-meter-wide stern and under that was Port Phillip Bay Explorers. "Esmeralda is an unusual name for a boat, where did it come from?"

"Esmeralda is my mother's name." Boss announced. "And it will be the name of my next boat if I ever get one. We all call her Essie for short."

Under the names was a large hinged platform with a ladder going down to it. Breath had seen these additions on other boats and knew that they were used for allowing divers easy access to the boat. As she walked along the side of the boat, she saw a blue line about thirty-centimeters-wide, painted just above the water line and above that was all white. She counted ten thirty-centimeter diameter even spaced portholes along the side just above the blue line. There again the name Esmeralda was painted on the bow of the fifteen-and-a-half-meter long boat. The name Port Phillip Bay Explorers occupied the middle of the white section also in gold lettering. She assumed it was the same on the other side.

The observation deck went all the way around the pilothouse from the bow to the stern. Two sets of stairs allowed a person to step up into the pilothouse which was about two meters above or descend to the deck below. There was a ladder on the right or starboard side of the pilothouse where one could climb up and onto the highest point on the boat, about nine meters above the waterline. Two three-meter park benches were back to back down the middle of the rear observation deck. A shorter set of park benches were on the foredeck ahead of the pilothouse.

Breath was most interested in how she was going to get into the boat from the water. She went back and inspected the diver platform and its ladder leading up the stern and into the boat. She pondered the difficulty of climbing that ladder with her full Aqume on. The steps and rails down from the top of the three-meter gunwale that surrounded the observation deck, would be no problem.

Boss took her around to the front of the pilothouse and opened the door. Inside was a room with a couple small bench seats and lockers. "This is where you and the other divers will store your diving equipment when you're on the boat. Come let me show you what's down below.

"This is what we call the lunchroom. The fixed one-meter wide table down the middle is where we serve lunch. The step over benches on either side of the table are also fixed. We don't want them bouncing around in rough water. Along the sides is a set of lift seat benches were people stow their stuff. We always tell everyone to make sure to leave with everything they brought with them. You wouldn't believe the stuff they leave behind. Behind us here are two heads or restrooms for the landlubbers. Further back is the galley. It's small but it has a large freezer and fridge. We rarely ever cook on board. We always order from the caterers before we leave port. We order in on Saturdays because it's the one day we're out all day from nine AM to about six PM. During the week we, the crew that is, bring a sack lunch. Any tours we have during the week we encourage the patrons to bring their own food." Boss opened another door. "And down these steps is the engine room. Where we have two 500 horsepower diesel engines, storage, a freshwater still, and bunks for the crew.

"We work with a crew of four. The engineman who makes sure the boat is in proper working order. The two divers who you've met and who also act as stewards during the lunch break. Then myself as the Captain, the guy who talks a lot over the sound system during the tour. You will make the fifth crewman."

Breath noticed that all of the interiors were painted sky-blue.

***

Each Saturday morning Breath would climb to the highest point on the tour boat and look out to sea. She was encased in her Aqume without her full tail or the monofin but still looking like a scale-covered mermaid in a plastic wetsuit. She did this to be alone with GP. Her purpose was to get a feel for where the dolphins might be, with GP's coaching. She'd climb down and approach Boss and point in the direction where she thought their best chances were. It became their routine, because talking through her Aqume was difficult.

Breath had asked Boss not to call her by her real name when anyone else was around. So, he and the crew started calling her Ariel, like the Little Mermaid.

***

Boss didn't tell Breath that he had an airplane flying around over the bay, trying to spot the dolphins. As it turned out, Breath was better at locating the dolphins than the airplane. After three months, Breath had never failed once; the owner rewarded her by doubling her pay, which was very much better than washing dishes.

Breath also didn't know that Boss had begun to advertise her as a special dolphin-wrangling mermaid, because whenever there were dolphins or seals nearby, Breath was in the water with them. The tourists loved her because she introduced them to her dolphin friends so they could touch and swim with them. Word got around that the tour company had a real live mermaid.

Breath pondered. *I think this boat could attract a lot more sea life if it wasn't quite so noisy. The dolphins don't like to come around because the engine and propeller noise is too loud. Maybe I can talk boss into some changes.*

A news crew came out to the tour boat one Saturday and were quite disappointed when they saw Breath wearing her custom Aqume wetsuit with fish scales painted all over it. The resulting article said, "The girl nicknamed Ariel is a good swimmer, but of course, a real mermaid she's not, with her rubber and plastic mermaid outfit. The entire thing is nothing but marketing hype."

Breath chuckled and thought, *Real mermaid indeed.*

***

On a Wednesday, the boat crew was testing the engines after some maintenance when they hit a floating log in Hobsons Bay. At the high speed they were going, the steel keel broke the rotten log in two. The two ends swung around and caused serious damage to the forward half of the fiberglass hull on both sides. The quick action of the crew allowed the boat to limp back to the repair facility.

After the inspection, Boss feared the repairs would be extensive, more than the company could afford.

After some discussion, the owner of the repair facility, who had enjoyed the tour boat trip several times, suggested an alternative. "A yacht owner ordered some clear polycarbonate sheets for some windows, but his boat sank before we could install them. No one wants to use them because they're too thick — about one point two centimeters, I think. They've been in my way for years; they're yours, and they'll make a good strong hull. Plus, you can see through them. They'll make a nice glass-bottomed boat."

Boss thought. *This sly old coot is just trying to get rid of some scrap.*

When the builder showed him what he had though, Boss agreed with a sly smile. Two weeks later and with some interior changes and seating rearrangements the Port Phillip Bay Explorers tour boat had a glass — or, rather, plastic — bottom and sides, extending forward of the head, lounge, and pilothouse. Just perfect for underwater viewing. The boat builder was also persuaded by both Breath and Boss to rebuild the engine mounts and bulkheads around the mounts to make the boat much quieter. The builder only charged for the labor.

Boss thought. *I think I just made out like a bandit.*

***

There were always a lot of people around the tour-boat dock on Saturdays. For some reason, the crews of the nearby boats and sometimes the harbormaster and his assistants would be conversing with the tour-boat crew and the tourists. Everyone was there just in time to watch Breath swim up from underneath the boat and pull herself up onto the diving platform. All conversation stopped. They all seemed to be waiting for the mermaid. The paparazzi got so bad that Breath asked Boss to pick her up about a mile out in the bay, where she left the boat when it was coming in. That way the paparazzi would have to buy a ticket if they wanted to see the mermaid come on board.

***

Breath was doing quite well. She even taught David how to swim the boat's bow wave if the boat was going slow enough. Their bow-wave riding caused quite a sensation. She also felt much safer since she'd talked Boss into changing to much quieter propellers and putting sound absorbing shrouds around those propellers to protect her, David, and the dolphins from injury. Breath felt proud of her ability to persuade Boss and was thankful that he did what she asked.

Breath, if you make the gelatin in your Aqume around your ankles a bit stiffer, you'll get better control. However, I do suggest that the continued use of your monofin around people will help deflect suspicion.

Good idea, GP. I'll give that a try, and yes, I'll continue to use my monofin, just for you.

Thank you, Breath.

Always glad to help, GP.

She conspired with Boss to put a special compartment under the boat to store her monofin. She could swim much better now, using her Aqume by itself. She did have to make the tail portion of her Aqume look like her fish-scale tube and regular monofin, metal parts and all. When she came to the boat, she'd retrieve her monofin from the compartment, swim up to the diving platform, and place it on the boat before she pulled herself up on the platform. Before she did this, she'd remove her Aqume fluke so it would look as if she were just swimming with the monofin.

There was no doubt in the minds of the crew that Breath was indeed a mermaid, since they had seen her produce her Aqume many times. Plus, Breath would always come aboard and leave the boat a mile or so from the marina. Thus, adding to the mermaid mystique and discouraged the paparazzi.

***

One Saturday after a successful day with the dolphins, the crew of the Port Phillip Bay Explorers was having a get-together at one of the local restaurants and pubs. They'd all pleaded like little kids, "Come on Breath, please? You never come with us. How do you know you won't like it if you don't try?" They were trying everything, including trying to make her feel guilty, to get her to come with them.

She felt kind of good that they were so insistent; it made her feel a part of something. But she was apprehensive of crowds.

The four guys who made up the crew of the tour boat were beginning to feel like family to her. She even accepted David as the big brother she never had.

"Well, okay, if you insist." She looked down and smiled. She thought, *I'm going to make myself go to a pub.* At that moment she felt an electric shiver run from the top of her head down to her toes.

She was excited and having a good time, even though the crowd made her apprehensive. Since she was always thirsty after spending most of the day in the water, she was drinking a lot. But she had nonalcoholic drinks, partly because she was underage but mostly because she'd not liked alcohol the few times, she'd tried her mum's homemade wine.

She couldn't wait any longer. She stood up. "If you'll excuse me, I need to go to the loo, since these wonderful libations seem to be passing through in a hurry."

As she turned to leave for the lady's room, several of the crew chuckled. One laughed. "Libations? Whoever says libations? We all know Breath is different, but libations."

Even Boss chuckled at this. One of the other crewmen refilled her glass.

As she was returning, one of the more amorous and well-lubricated patrons tried to stop her. She put her hand over her mouth and nose after smelling his very alcoholic breath. She dodged around this large young man and continued to her friends. Again, this large young man tried to stop her. Her friends, seeing this, started to her rescue. The young man grabbed her arm.

She'd taken jujitsu and judo as an athletic elective in junior college and was quite proficient, much to Heidi's chagrin. Heidi hated violence of any kind. Breath used a simple release technique, broke the man's grip, and continued on her way. Every person in the room saw this and held their breath. The man didn't get the hint. He grabbed her a second time, far stronger than he had before.

Breath looked up at the man and shouted, "Let me go! Leave me alone!"

He didn't, or at least he wasn't paying attention. Instead, he pulled her towards him. Before he could react, she'd moved into position. Just as her instructor had demonstrated and she'd practiced. She threw the man over her shoulder, crashing him onto a table. The table shattered into pieces. She then gave the man a Qrie push. The man and the table remnants went sliding across the floor and up against the wall.

Her fellow crewmen appeared beside her, ready to take on all comers. They then knew that Breath was no mere wisp of a girl. They knew she was quick, skilled, and well-muscled, like an Olympic gymnast. They now understood just how skilled. At slightly over 127 kilograms, or 280 pounds, the man weighed over twice what Breath did.

She apologized to her friends and left the bar without returning to her table.

GP gave her a strong *Qrie Embrace. Y'all went into a bar. Y'all drank some libations.* GP projected a chuckle. *Y'all kicked some ass, and y'all made it out alive. Good on ya kid!*

Thanks, GP. I don't think I like pubs.

Y'all can't blame the bar, Breath. It's the people in it. Most people are celebrating, relaxing, or trying to escape life in some way.

Well, still, I don't think the pub scene is my thing.

OK, if y'all say so Breath. Y'all still did good.

That young man is okay, isn't he?

Y'all know how to check, Breath. So — check on him.

She paused a moment. *He'll be okay, GP. The only thing that was hurt was his pride.*

You're learning, Breath. You're getting there.

***

Breath and GP had never missed finding the dolphins since she started with the tour boat. Breath liked it, the dolphins liked it and the now quieter tour boat, and the tourists liked it. Boss liked it so much, he stopped using the airplane spotter and gave part of that money to Breath.

She sent most of the money she made on the tour boat home to her mother. Heidi never took a dime of it but put it all in the bank for Breath.

With the little money Breath kept for herself, she sold her old bicycle and bought a new electric tricycle that had a special custom windshield cover that went overhead to keep the rider dry when it rained. It also had a rainproof storage container, much better than her old bicycle.

***

Karol Manor walked into the office and tossed the tour-boat flyer on his brother Rob's desk. "It says here that this tour-boat company has a real dolphin-wrangling mermaid. Think we should check this out? This mermaid could be a Star Child. If half of what they say she can do is true, we might've found ourselves a winner and solid proof. All we've got to do is fly to Melbourne and book a tour. We play tourists for a while and take all the pictures, videos, and sound recordings we can. You in?"

Rob and Karol Manor had founded a small organization called *Star Child Quest*. Their office was a clutter of earmarked magazines and newspaper clippings. The best you could say about their office was that it was in an ordered disarray. Earmarked magazines on one side and torn out newspaper clippings nearby. One would wonder how they could even see their computer screens with all the Post-it notes stuck around the edges. They were always on the lookout for strange people who could have genetic anomalies or be alien. They considered these strange people to be of possible alien origin, therefore Star Children who could be the saviors of mankind.

They published a small online and printed newsletter purporting to reveal government cover-ups and conspiracies with an occasional alien exposé, it was quite thin, with few readers. They were associated with a like-minded pair in Santa Barbara, California, run by sisters Erin and Cheryl Ziegler.

There was an organization that read the *Star Child Quest* that didn't consider Star Children as possible saviors of mankind. They used the newsletter as a means to ferret out 'evil' aliens.

***

Breath was feeling good about her success. However, on this particular day when she climbed to the top of the tour boat, she sensed something was different. The day seemed like any other — nice and sunny, a slight breeze and calm sea.

She climbed down and went to the bridge. She made sure no one was watching and pulled her Aqume covering her face aside. "Boss, there's something different. I'm not getting my usual sense of direction. However, in that direction" — she pointed — "is something I haven't felt in a while. If I'm right, no tourists will be swimming with the dolphins today."

"What do you think it is Breath?"

"I suspect... it's just a feeling... I'll tell you what." She pointed. "Continue in that direction. David and I will swim the bow wave for a while, trying to get the dolphins to come. If they don't come, we'll try Plan B."

About an hour later, the tour boat stopped at Breath's request. David and Breath came aboard, and she climbed to the top of the boat again and tried to get a feeling of what was happening.

The tour group knew there was something going on. The old salts (that's what Boss calls his tour regulars) knew that something was irregular. They knew the mermaid never needed to hunt for the dolphins more than once. There was definitely something up and the tension was high.

Breath glanced around and could feel the tension and excitement from the tour group. They knew something was up.

She came down a few minutes later and told Boss to shut down the engines and drift. She looked concerned. "Don't let anyone in the water, including the tour divers. I'll be back."

She walked to the aft of the boat, stepped down onto the diving platform, and picked up her monofin. Then she dropped into the water and disappeared.

The tension mounted on the boat. The tour group gripped the railings on the observation deck straining to see what was about to happen.

About fifteen minutes later, Breath was back, clinging to the dorsal fin of a huge orca with the entire pod following close behind. Under normal circumstances, everyone would've been taking photographs. This time, everyone just gawked at her and what was happening.

The tourists began to fumble for their cameras, not quite sure what they'd just seen. Was that her, or was it just water streaming off her body? The large orca, with Breath clinging on tight, moved farther away from the boat, making any real identification that much more difficult.

Rob looked at Karol. "Did you see that?"

Karol had a huge grin. "Yes, I did Rob. And I got it all on video. We've got our proof."

The pod of orcas stayed around the boat for about thirty minutes.

Breath just let go and came over to the boat. Two divers stepped onto the diving platform and helped her up onto the boat.

Everyone was looking at her in awe. She felt a little embarrassed. "I'm sorry, everyone. I couldn't keep them around any longer. It's hard to ride an orca that way. It took considerable persuasion just to get them to come over by the boat and stay here. I apologize. Is everyone okay?"

No one changed their expressions, including the Captain, divers, and tour guides. Excited conversations among the tour members — exploded!

What Breath hadn't controlled was that when she rode the orca, each time it came up to breathe, she was exposed and in her Aqume. She didn't look like a girl with a special diving suit around her head and body and a plastic monofin. With her

Aqume, she looked exactly like the classic mermaid, tail and all. Karol's camera showed it all in high-resolution detail.

***

There was no doubt whatsoever in everyone's minds including Rob's and Karol's, that they were looking at a real mermaid, even if now she was barefoot and wearing a custom diving suit. Breath walked over to the cooler, got a bottle of water, and plopped down on a bench.

Rob turned to Karol. "She can't be human. Did you see her eyes!"

"Yes, even through her — mask. A person could get lost in those eyes."

Boss gave her a huge bonus that week.

A short time after the orca incident, Breath confronted Boss. "Please, Boss, I'd appreciate it if I weren't advertised as a mermaid any longer. It makes me uncomfortable." This discussion went on for some time. He was reluctant but agreed to no longer advertise her in the brochures as a real mermaid. However, he didn't stop his marketing people from telling those who called in that the mermaid was still working on the tours. He also didn't tell Breath about this. People began to book tours more to see the mermaid than to see dolphins, seals, or whales. This too, made her uncomfortable.

Rob and Karol Manor knew after a few more tours and after reviewing the photos and videos that they had a winner. They'd found their Star Child. They knew no human being could do what that mermaid could do. They were exuberant when they called Erin and Cheryl. Their *Star Child Quest* newsletter had a lot larger readership.

8. OAI 2

After reading the *Star Child Quest* online newsletter, John Kingman and Tatelin Westworth agreed that the photographs were somewhat Photoshopped. However, they agreed that there could be something to the story. Director Kingman dispatched OAI agents to Melbourne, Australia, to investigate this mermaid. With close tracking, they soon discovered Heidi Spring, the mermaid's mother, in Fremantle and William Spring, the mermaid's father, in Calgary, Canada. Tight and almost invisible surveillance was placed on these people.

The OAI contacted the Australian Security Intelligence Organization (ASIO) through the National Security Adviser's office and discovered that the ASIO was already investigating the mermaid. The two agencies decided to collaborate, with the Australian government graciously allowing the OAI to pick up the bill.

The OAI agents knew, after detailed investigation, these people were born here on Earth. They were also quite certain they weren't a hundred percent human. Telephone communications intercepted between Breath, Heidi, and William confirmed that they knew they were part something called 'Qrie.'

The agents asked the Anasso if there were any species within their knowledge that could do the things the Spring family could do, and what the Qrie were.

A ten-month cycle was about the fastest the communications loop seemed to be able to go.

When the Anasso message came in, it read, "Warning. If our interpretation of your quarry is correct, extreme caution should be taken with the Spring strain of beings. If they are Qrie or are associated with the Qrie, use extreme caution.

"The Qrie are the creators or, as they prefer, 'the assemblers' of the universe. They are older than the universe itself. They use what is known as Compulsion to maintain their secrets. It is a mental block that prevents an entity, under compulsion, from informing anyone, not under compulsion, about the Qrie. There are two Qrie entities associated with a local set of star systems, until a planetary civilization achieves True Intelligence. Those two Qrie are responsible for those star systems. They do not consider any beings short of True Intelligence to be intelligent. If these Qrie or their created entities are 'interfered with' the consequences can be 'disastrous' to the extreme. It's our recommendation that any observations be made from a safe distance. The Qrie do not tolerate interference."

Tate gave John a nervous look. "What do we do with this piece of information?"

"I'll brief the National Security Adviser."

"Pass the buck, in other words."

John chuckled. "Well, that's what we do best."

"Do you think one of the agencies is going to detain and interrogate them? We should give this information to the ASIO before they do something rash."

John was slow to answer. "I wouldn't even think of interfering after reading that report from the Anasso. They know more about these entities than we do, and they make it extremely plain not to interfere with the Qrie."

Tate asked. "How do we know we can trust the Anasso? For all we know, the Qrie could be their agents. After all, their relay station is in orbit around our Sun."

"I think we should heed their warning until we learn more. No matter what, we still have an interesting situation."

Meanwhile, the ASIO contacted the OAI agents in Australia and told them they were going to detain Breath Of Spring.

Upon hearing this, John Kingman went to see the NS Adviser to discuss the situation. Part of the discussion was whether the ASIO should be told about the Anasso and whether that would violate national security. The NS Adviser and the OAI were concerned and requested that the ASIO refrain from detaining her until they got more information on the entire family. It was decided that in the interest of national security, the ASIO should be informed about the Anasso.

The ASIO agreed to wait until John could meet with them in person.

The ASIO agreed not to detain Breath after Kingman went to Australia and showed them the Anasso communiqué.

9. WHALES

The Royal Australian Navy (RAN) called. Well, they called Boss at the Port Phillip Bay Explorers office.

Boss left a voice mail on Breath's phone. When she got out of class, she called back. "What can I do for you? Is there something wrong?"

"Good morning, no, nothing is wrong Breath, except I've got the RAN people calling me, wanting to talk to the mermaid." He chuckled.

"I asked you not to call me that. What do they want?"

"They want you to help them get the blue whales out of the bay. Have you been watching the news?"

"Yes, and you know my thoughts on that. When the whales want to go, they'll go on their own. Whales come into the Bay all the time. We don't need to disturb them. They can take care of themselves. Those misguided Save the Whales people, or whatever group is harassing the Navy, would do better stopping the whaling than to worry about a few free-swimming whales. We've discussed this."

"Yes, Breath, but they've asked for your help. Please come in this afternoon and talk to them. It'd make my life easier."

"I guess I can. My afternoon class was canceled today, so I'm free. I'll be there in a little bit."

"Good. I'll call them. We'll meet them here at the office, if that's okay."

***

Breath walked into Port Philip Bay Explorers' offices, which was bright and well-lit by open windows on both sides of the long office building, and with overhead fluorescent lighting. Looking at all the people in the office cubicles she realized most of these people didn't work for Port Phillip Bay Explorers. She was amazed by the multitude of different colors for the walls of the cubicles. She stopped and tried to figure out the color scheme. After a few moments she gave up and decided that a color wheel had thrown up and there was no rhyme or reason. Boss was renting out office space to other organizations. The posted signs of the other organizations were a dead giveaway.

She walked into Boss's private office with her long golden blonde hair hanging down in her face. She always did this in case someone she didn't know was in the office. With her hair placed like this, it was impossible for anyone to make out her face.

GP, what if they want me to do something for them?

This's a good opportunity, Breath, and I'll make it so they can't tell anyone who doesn't already know.

I thought we were supposed to keep a low profile. I'm not sure I want to do this. Playing mermaid with a plastic suit is one thing. The tour company was already doing everything I do except with male snorkel divers. If I go out there and start wrangling whales for real, people will start asking questions. This is the military you know.

There's that possibility, Breath. Your recent orca incident could've been a mistake. However, with the technology that's being developed, our kind will be discovered soon enough. We've got to have good relations, with the government, the military, and in particular the Navy to build trust. This'll give us a good chance to put ourselves on the positive side of that trust.

Well, okay. If you think it's important, I'll do it.

There's that excited enthusiasm that I always love to hear.

Oh, go jump! Breath never told GP, but she just loved this little verbal sparring game she and GP played.

And GP enjoyed it too, as he chuckled. *I love you too, Breath.*

Boss introduced Breath to the two military men in his office. Commanding Officer (CO) Lieutenant Commander George Marsdurban seemed pleasant enough but had a curious expression on his face. "Miss Spring, I've heard and read some rather strange reports about you. If less than half of them are true, I might just have to start believing in mermaids. You may be the one who can help us with our whale problem." Chief Petty Officer (CPO) Goins turned away from his CO, rolled his eyes, looked skeptical, and then stifled a chuckle.

Breath saw this and smiled. "Well, Mr. Marsdurban, don't believe everything you hear. I've the been trying to get these guys to stop calling me a mermaid for a long time now. I've just about given up."

"Do you think you can help us? We're under a considerable amount of pressure and would appreciate any help you can give us."

GP, you know my feelings about this. These people seem desperate. Should I do this?

Yes. Y'all need to learn what these people can teach ya. As y'all know, the whales can take care of themselves. That's not what y'all or they are here to learn.

GP, did you set this up? What am I supposed to learn?

Many great and wonderful things.

That's not a real answer.

No comment, Sweetie.

Sometimes you can be so...

Breath paused several moments, trying to make up her mind — "It's possible that I can. I've swum with the big Blues before. They're gentle, shy, faster than most boats, loud to the point of deafening, and have bad breath to the extreme. However, I must ask you. Do you want the whales to leave the bay? Or do you just want the government and the Whale people off your back?"

Commander Marsdurban barked a laugh and was doing his best to stifle it. He nodded his head and mumbled, "Yes," between chuckles. Breath looked puzzled not understanding his mirth.

He took a deep breath and forced himself under control. "The RAN captured a Chinese whaling ship illegally harvesting blue whales. They were chasing a pod of six big blues when they were intercepted and arrested, and their ship was impounded at Bass Strait just outside the Rip into Port Phillip Bay.

"The whales were moving fast and caught the tide into the bay. They have been swimming around Port Phillip Bay for about five weeks now, and the authorities are concerned. Every time the whales get anywhere near the Rip or a ship, they turn back. The Save the Whales people or whoever, through political pressure, enlisted the RAN in an effort to herd the six whales out of the bay."

Breath fixed her eyes on him. "I can't guarantee anything. I'll help, but only if you'll do what I say."

He averted his eyes. "I'll have to check with my superiors, but I don't think there'll be a problem. Please excuse us for a moment."

GP, they're going to find out about me.

I know Breath, but they're going to find out about the Qrie anyway. We've got to make it happen on our terms. And you've got to learn a lot more about your abilities.

Maybe so, but I'm still not comfortable with this.

There's that rampant enthusiasm I was looking for.

Then you go play mermaid.

Well — not today!

The two Navy people walked out of the room. The CO pulled out his cell phone, dialed, and began talking. After he hung up the two talked and a few moments later, they returned. "We've got the authorization to go ahead with the operation. We're to follow your lead. When can we start?"

"Right now, if that's okay. I need to get my monofin off the tour boat and get into my bathers."

Boss nodded to one of the crewmembers in the room, who took off running to the tour boat.

Breath shouted to him. "Be sure to get the green suit; it's lined."

He returned a few minutes later with Breath's latest monofin and her bathing togs.

She took the items then added a distracted, "Thank you."

"OK, Commander Marsdurban, I'm ready to go."

"Please Ma'am, Commander Marsdurban sounds way too formal. CO is what everyone on the boat calls me. By the way, how old are you?"

"I'll be fourteen in two months, just before I graduate."

The CO was surprised and thought. *Thirteen! I could've sworn she was older than that! What's going on, and what the heck have I gotten myself into? I know Admiral Lynch okayed this operation. A kid running this operation? This better work, or I'm going to have egg on my face.*

She and the two apprehensive Navy personnel walked out of Boss's office, down the jetty, and got on board the RAN patrol boat HMAS *Portland*. Then they headed out into Port Phillip Bay.

Can you sense them, GP?

Yes Breath. Do the exercise to still your mind, and then feel the gentle changes the whales make. Y'all know how to do this.

Breath was silent for a few moments. *Wow, GP, I didn't think anything that big could be subtle! I've gotta remember that. Thanks.*

That was all y'all Sweetie.

Breath and GP collaborated and settled on a direction.

Then Breath pointed towards the center of the bay. "Sir, if you'll take me out in that direction fifteen kilometers or so and drop me off, I'll do my thing. Then go out three or four kilometers and begin a slow circle of my position. Make sure no boat of any kind comes within three kilometers of me in any direction. Is that understood?"

"But, miss, how will we communicate? How will we know what's happening? What if you need our help?"

"Don't try to communicate with me at all. Don't come pick me up. When I've done what I need to do, I'll swim to this boat."

"That's a rather strange request, but we agreed to do as you say. However, please take this transmitter, in case you get into trouble. Just hold it above the water and press this button." The CO lifted a protective cover on the transmitter, and exposed a bright red button underneath. After showing it to Breath he flipped the cover back down and handed the transmitter to her.

Breath slipped it into the pouch on her monofin.

Less than an hour later, the boat slowed to a stop at Breath's request.

She and the CO climbed up on the deck above the bridge and looked around. She pointed. "There are the big Blues. Drop me off here and begin your circle of the whales. But never get closer than about four kilometers from them. We don't want to scare them away. Your boat's pretty noisy."

They climbed down, and she walked to the fantail and stepped into her monofin. "Go!" she called as she dove into the water wearing her green seaweed lined bikini and her monofin.

Five hours later, the Sun was low in the sky. Breath had calculated her intercept course to the boat. Two men were standing by the aft-port (rear left) railing when Breath leaped out of the water and grabbed the aft portside upper railing and hauled herself on board. If the men hadn't been holding on to the portside railing, the crewmen would've fallen backward onto the deck. Before the men had gathered their wits, Breath was already on board removing her monofin. Then she stood up.

Breath looked at the expressions on the two men and asked, "Are you two okay? I apologize for my sudden appearance. The boat was moving a little faster than I anticipated." She turned and walked towards the bridge. The two men followed.

The CO had seen what had happened and started running towards her, grabbing an iridescent-yellow rain slicker in the process. He intercepted her, put the slicker over her shoulders, and then guided her to the ready room. Several others came into the compartment.

Breath looked down at herself and thought. *My top is gone, and my bottoms are in tatters; I've gotta thank CO for this slicker.*

Breath began the briefing. "CO George Marsdurban, this is rather a delicate situation. Don't ask me how I know what I know, because I won't tell you. Is that agreed?"

"Yes, Miss Spring. We agree."

"The whales are frightened. They've seen several members of their pod killed by a boat. They don't like boats and don't understand them. They can sense boats on both sides of the Rip and are reluctant to go through. We've got to get the boats away from the Rip on both sides and have them far enough away so the whales feel comfortable enough to go through. We'll also have to wait for the correct tide. And I'll have to do some coaxing." She paused for a response.

The CO and crew just stared at her, not knowing what to think. Then the CO broke the silence. "When can we move the whales out?"

"How soon can you get the boats and ships moved away from Bass Strait and the Rip?"

"Well let's see." CO stared at the ceiling for a moment. "We can't do it by Thursday or Friday, but by Saturday, for sure."

"Saturday is a good day. Make sure the tide is going out. I'll see you then. Would someone please pick me up about six o'clock Saturday morning? Also, I have to okay this with Boss. Right now CO, I need a lot of water and a place to rest."

CO Marsdurban agreed. "Six o'clock Saturday morning it is. See you then." He indicated to one of the crewmen to get Breath some water and a place to rest.

After Breath left the room, one of the two men that were at the rail said. "CO, I don't know if you saw her, sir, but she had to have leaped two and a half maybe even three meters out of the water to grab that rail. She's not human, I tell you. No human can come out of the water like that."

***

Lieutenant Commander Marsdurban had been in a meeting on board the HMAS *Portland* for over an hour with a nervous Vice Admiral Winston Lynch, the ASIO, and the OAI. The Lieutenant Commander was briefed about the Anasso and the Qrie — how ancient the Qrie are, how to handle himself around Breath, and how sensitive the situation could become. Admiral Lynch told the crew of the *Portland* that they'd all been put under Compulsion by the Qrie Breath Of Spring, which meant no one could communicate about this to anyone not under Compulsion.

As Marsdurban directed the patrol boat out into the bay that next Saturday, he watched Breath's every move. She stood by a railing and gazed out to sea. He noticed something clear and shimmering around her body, unlike anything he'd ever seen.

Breath, these people know about y'all. So y'all don't have to be so secretive around them. I'll not let'em disclose to anyone who doesn't already know what y'all can do.

Thanks, GP. That takes a lot of pressure off me. I was unsure of how I was going to pull this off. I didn't have my Aqume on when I came into the office.

That's not gonna be a problem. Everyone on this boat is under Compulsion.

CO Marsdurban approached Breath and started a conversation. He had already discovered that she was easy to talk to. He was quite nervous after his meeting with the Admiral, the ASIO, and the OAI, but this conversation put him at ease.

She smiled at him and then turned and climbed to the highest point she could find on the boat. After a few minutes, she climbed back down and went into the bridge.

She looked at the CO and pointed. "Go that way."

After about forty-five minutes and more pleasant conversation later, she stopped and gazed off into space, then turned back to the CO. "Stop here." She stood frozen for a moment and then nodded her head. The CO noticed the shimmer was stronger. The only thing she had on was her tiny two-piece seaweed lined swimming togs and the slicker that CO gave her from the last time.

"I'm going to get off here, and I'll bring the whales through. I'll meet you where we agreed, about forty kilometers South of the Rip, after the whales are running free. After I leave the boat, go four kilometers due east then head for the Rip."

The CO looked at her in amazement. "Forty kilometers South of the Rip and we're now about twenty kilometers North of the Rip here, in the bay. That's an enormous distance to swim. How will you even find us?"

"I found you before. I can do it again."

"Miss Spring, that's a good sixty kilometers. That's an awful lot of swimming."

She gave him a dismissive gesture. She winked at him, grabbed his sleeve and pulled him close, then whispered in his ear. "That's no distance at all for a mermaid." She paused a moment and took a quick look around. "Don't you dare tell anybody I told you that! It's our little secret. One other thing, CO. I can't wear my monofin and swim with the big Blues; they don't like the sound it makes. Please have this rain slicker ready for me when I return." She had it draped over her shoulders.

They walked together towards the fantail of the boat. She stepped close to the edge, stopped for a moment facing away from the CO, she untied her string bikini and then handed him both parts of her togs. "If you'll also hold the collar of this slicker, please."

George stifled a smile and uttered. "Sure thing." He was left holding her togs and the slicker as she dove into the water. He pondered. *How in the world is a naked teenage girl going to swim sixty kilometers in this cold water, and persuade Giant*

Blue Whales to go anywhere? I know the Admiral says she's Qrie, whatever that means, but still...

***

Breath formed her Aqume around her body and began swimming towards the whales. When she swam up to Big Mum, she gave all the whales in the pod her most powerful *Qrie Embrace* and they responded by making comforting sounds in reply. She again began mentally persuading Big Mum to move towards the Rip. It took several tries, and the huge whale began to move.

Breath didn't notice the temperature of the water, but she did notice how clear it was on that particular day. Several days ago, it was difficult to see the whole pod at once, but today she could see every whale in the pod with ease. She didn't have to worry about chasing around seeing if they were all keeping up. Knowing this she took a strong grip on Big Mum, held on tight, and continued her encouragement.

***

The patrol boat was sitting dead in the water, with the main engines idling, as Breath had requested. Almost everyone was on the aft deck, anxious to see this mermaid fly out of the water like a dolphin.

Breath didn't disappoint. She knew she'd have to propel herself farther out of the water this time, which meant she had to fly. The boat was pitching and rolling much more in the open ocean than it did in the bay. This time, she went high over the upper rail. Everyone was amazed. For five to ten seconds she was the classic mermaid floating in the air. She was exposed — tail, webbed hands, arm flippers, in all her glory. Then her aqume washed back into the ocean. George came running up to cover her with the rain slicker as she floated down to the deck.

She smiled up at him and declared, "Mission accomplished CO! Guys we did it. The whales are safe. Now, if you'll excuse me, I've got to get a lot of water and someplace to rest."

She took a shower, put on the clean blue flowered muumuu dress that she'd brought with her that morning, laid down on one of the bunks, and went to sleep. When she woke up, she went down to the galley to see if there was something to eat. She ate two sandwiches and drank two liters of cold tea. After that, she started feeling normal. The CO, the Executive Officer (or X), and several members of the crew came down to the galley when they found out she was there.

The CO stepped forward. "Everyone is bugging me. So, I've got to ask. How can you swim so fast and far? And how do you jump so high out of the water without being a real mermaid?"

"I know you've been briefed about me, but I can promise you, I'm not a mermaid. Animals come around me, and I know what they want and need. I can think about what I want, and things just happen. That's all I'll say about that. Nothing else.

"As for swimming, I've been in the water all my life, and I could always swim fast.

"I never get lost. I always know where I am and where to go. I also don't get cold or hot. As for jumping out of the water like I do, I think any good, strong swimmer who knows how to swim well with a monofin could do what I do. Once you learn how to swim with a monofin, you'll never want to swim with anything else again. I must say, though, it takes a fair amount of training, strength, and practice to get good at it."

Everyone was quiet. Then CO glanced around the room at the unbelieving crew and then back at her. "Yeah, that's a real fancy explanation Breath. It's not possible for anyone to swim sixty kilometers in that cold of water in that short period of time. I don't care how good that monofin thing is. Besides, you didn't use it this time, and when you returned, you floated in the air. Another thing: How'd you know where the whales were?"

"Well — I didn't swim far at all. I swam about maybe four kilometers before I met the blues; then I just hitched a ride with Big Mum and kind of directed her and the others through the Rip and forty kilometers south of there. I sent them on their way and then swam to the boat — about ten kilometers. All in all, it's not much more than about fourteen or fifteen kilometers, not far at all. So, you see, I'm not a mermaid after all!"

Almost everyone in the boat's galley laughed and exclaimed in unison, "Bull," and shook their heads! Then X continued. "We saw you float in the air! We saw your tail! You can't fool us! You're a mermaid!"

She knew the crew knew her secret, and she took a long look at everyone as she scanned the room and became very serious. "Everyone on this boat has a Qrie compulsion placed on them. You can't communicate to anyone, except to someone who already has the compulsion, about me or what you have seen."

Then George and everyone else raised their hands as if making an oath. "We'll all keep your secret. We promise."

Even though GP said it was okay she still wasn't comfortable with that many people knowing her secret.

That Saturday was the first Saturday since Breath had started working for the tour group that the boat didn't find any dolphins.

***

Breath and Heidi had been talking for some time about her graduation from Melbourne. "I'm so proud of you, two years of junior-college and one more year at Melbourne to graduate is exceptional! Breath you should be proud of yourself.

"I know we had our differences when you left, but that doesn't change my love for you. I know you'll do well."

"Mum, I'm going to have to run. Boss and the guys on the tour boat are throwing me a little party. I love you Mum, but I have to go. Talk to you later. Bye-bye."

Breath knew she couldn't leave until she'd also talked to her dad. "Hello, Daddy. I wanted to call to tell you that I just graduated from Melbourne University with honors, in marine biology, and oceanography. I'm going out to see Mum." There was a long pause, and then she continued with not quite as much enthusiasm she had before. "Then I'm going to come see you, Virginia, and the twins in Calgary before I start school for my master's and PhD at University of Miami in Florida." Another long pause. "Daddy, they gave me another full accelerated scholarship. I can get my master's and PhD in oceanography in less than two years. Then I've got to do a nine-month internship at Scripps Research Institute in California." Breath brightened up and continued with a solid stream of words explaining her recent adventures.

"I love you, Daddy and Virginia! Hug the twins for me. I'll see you guys soon."

"Well, just be careful. I'm so proud of you, and let us know when you get to Fremantle. We love you. Bye now."

"Bye-bye Daddy."

GP, Morning, Beauty, I want to thank all of you as well.

That's what we're here for Sweetie.

Breath felt a massive *Qrie Embrace,* and the feeling of peace and accomplishment flooded through her.

10. CALGARY

Melvin Blanchard had hated aliens since his father's abduction. He knew when it happened because his dad had told him enough times. That moment had occurred with an auto accident in which his mother was killed. His drunken father survived unharmed, without a scratch. His dad claimed that there was a bright light from a spacecraft above the car. He was transported out of the of the driver's seat, leaving it to run into the tree that killed his wife.

The police did not believe his father's abduction story. They did find an alcohol level of two point three in his blood. They also found where he had been ejected from the car due to his not wearing his seatbelt. They surmised that as the car spun out of control the driver side door opened and he was thrown out. His wife was not so lucky with her loose but buckled seatbelt. She was thrown into the dash and windshield and received fatal brain trauma due to the fact that her airbag did not function. His father received five years of probation and mandatory alcohol counseling.

His mother had shielded her son Melvin, against his father's abuse. After the incident, his father drank more and became even more abusive towards young Melvin. The beatings were sadistic and cruel. Melvin blamed the aliens for his father's brutality. Although, he knew that his father had been vicious long before the incident.

Melvin left home as soon as he was old enough to join the US Army, which he did the week after he graduated high school. He was determined and got into the Army Rangers. A short time after he joined the army, his sadistic father died. For Melvin, this was a relief. He had learned a lot from his father, which was unfortunate for anyone who got in Melvin's way.

His tycoon grandfather died when Melvin had sixteen years in the army. He left the army, took over his grandfather's businesses, and started a secretive paramilitary organization called Earth Only to find and eliminate space aliens. No one in the Earth Only organization except Melvin knew the real names of anyone else in the organization. Everyone used code names.

Melvin, who was now going by the codename TDog, subscribed to the *Star Child Quest* online publication, among others. He had just finished reading the latest issue. His ears perked up, his eyes dilated, and he became very interested in this mermaid in Australia. He knew mermaids didn't exist. If the people who wrote this newsletter had found one, she was an alien. From the firsthand report and photographs, there could be no doubt. The reporters of the *Star Child Quest* were good, and had found several other aliens. This mermaid drew his specific attention. He sent one of his team leaders, codename Dixon, and an associate to find her and get as much information as they could on this 'mermaid alien.'

Dixon found the mermaid and tracked her using drones. He followed her to the University and discovered that her name was Breath Of Spring. He subsequently found that she came from Fremantle, Australia, where her mother lives. He began keeping an eye on Heidi Spring, and his associate watched her daughter Breath in Melbourne. Dixon also looked into public records and found that Heidi was a psychic and a healer. He uncovered a number of psychics in the area and decided to call a few. They all held Heidi in the highest regard. He also noticed some were quite jealous of Heidi and her amazing protégé daughter. Dixon thought, *if these two aren't aliens, then they're damn sure witches.*

Dixon relayed all this and more to TDog in his lengthy coded email report. He relayed the fact that Breath Of Spring had just graduated from Melbourne University and was now going to attend the University of Miami in Florida. His associate also sent TDog a number of photographs of Breath that he'd taken at the University.

TDog told Dixon to follow her when she left for the United States. He had no idea that she was going to Calgary first, but he caught the next plane out. He told TDog before he left where Breath would be if TDog wanted to have someone intercept and follow her when she landed in Calgary.

TDog did just that and found out about William and Virginia Spring and the twins. William's parents were no longer living. He also began looking into Virginia Spring's background and found her family owned a huge exotic animal sanctuary in Texas called the Safari Ranch, a couple of hours northwest of Austin.

***

It was late in the evening when the plane landed. It had been delayed in Melbourne twice. She told her mum to go home from the airport and she would take a taxi when she arrived.

Breath bounded out of the taxi dragging her two pink duffel bags with her. She bounced up the front steps and into her mum's arms. They remained this way for a few minutes just hugging, kissing, and being glad that they were together again. Breath untangled herself from her mum's arms and pulled her duffel bags inside and dropped them in her room. She shed her clothes and walked back into the living room, where her mum was placing a large painted sheet of woven seaweed cloth on the overstuffed paisley couch. Breath was delighted to see the sheet; with every color of painted Daisy she could imagine.

Breath knew what the sheet was for. She knew that she and her mum were going to be passing so much Qrie energy between them that without the seaweed sheet they would destroy the unprotected couch.

The next morning, they both cooked a huge breakfast. They celebrated the day with work in the house and in the backyard jungle garden. Breath felt comforted by just being home and doing normal home things. Things she had missed for so long.

That evening they found themselves again on the seaweed covered couch tangled in one another's arms. Heidi asked while stroking Breath's hair. "Now that you've graduated from Melbourne, what are you going to do?"

Breath looked down at her knees for several moments pondering in private what to say, after their previous arguments.

"I don't know mum. I've applied for PhD scholarships at a number of universities but only one has granted me anything. I was hoping that University of Melbourne was going to extend my scholarship, for my PhD, but they didn't. Reeftown University turned me down and none of the universities here in Perth or Fremantle wanted anything to do with me. I thought I was going to get a scholarship in Brisbane or Townsville but they fell through too. The only one that granted me anything is in the US at University of Miami. I don't know whether I want to go there. It's so far to go. It's on the other side of the world. Mum, I'm afraid and I don't know what to do."

Heidi took a deep breath closed her eyes and kissed the top of Breath's head. "Well Breath the decision has to be yours. You seemed to do pretty well on the other side of the continent. So, perhaps you'll do well — on the other side of the world." She bit her lip after she said this and a lone tear started leaking down her cheek. She took another deep breath. "Only you can decide your future."

"I know Mum, but it's so far away. I won't know anyone."

"Well love, you didn't know anyone when you went to Melbourne, and you made a few friends there. I am confident that you will make friends in the US as well." Heidi took a deep breath and forced herself to calm down.

"Thanks Mum I needed that. I'll — uh call the University to tell them I'm coming.

Heidi and Breath clung to one another. Neither of them could clearly see the gaily painted room. Too many tears.

***

Breath was up early, bright eyed, and bushy tailed. With her decision made she was excited about seeing her father, stepmum, and little brother and sister. She couldn't wait to get there. She was going to celebrate Christmas in Canada this year. Maybe even a white Christmas.

Twenty-two hours flight time from Perth to Hawaii to refuel. Then she flew on to Vancouver, with a six-hour stopover there. Then a short hop to Calgary, all this will remove the bright in your eyes and take the bush out of your tail. She was just glad to be alive. Her backside was pressed flat; almost thirty hours of sitting can do that.

She brightened when she saw her dad, Virginia, and the twins. The greetings were... well... chaotic and grand. There wasn't a silent moment from the airport to the farm.

***

Breath had seen the inside of the farm house through the eyes of her telepathic father. She was comforted as they drove up to the white clap board sided two-story house. They had stopped at a pizza parlor on the way from the airport to the farmhouse. Breath was hungry and it was all she could do to stop herself from attacking the pizzas.

When they walked in Virginia said. "Breath, you're upstairs, first door on the right. The kids are across the hall from you and the bathroom is at the end of the hall. Make yourself at home. I'll get the pizzas ready."

It didn't take long for Breath to get her bundles on the bed and back down the stairs. She did notice that several of the treads on the hardwood stairs creaked, and there were a couple boards on the hardwood floor downstairs that also creaked.

When she walked into Virginia's kitchen, she took one look at the stove. "Oh! Virginia I just love your stove. It reminds me somewhat of the one we have at home. And I wish we had a refrigerator like this as well. Let's eat. I haven't eaten since I first landed in Vancouver."

That next week, Breath received a large international parcel package delivered to the farmhouse. In it were the rest of her clothes, her books, and anything else she could get in the heavy cardboard box to pack around her two latest custom-built monofins.

Breath was excited. She wanted to teach her family how to use these wonderful swimming aids. Of course, that wasn't the only reason she was there. She was desperate to meet her Canadian family.

She inspected the two monofins for damage. One had been broken and modified to fit a friend of hers in Melbourne who wanted to try it out. When Breath repaired it, she decided to make it adjustable to fit her friend and other people.

Will and the twins, Bill Junior and Samantha, came into the room while she was examining the items. Well, Will walked into the room. Bill Junior and Samantha sneaked peeks around the door frame and then tried to sneak in without being seen.

Will asked, "Breath, what are those things?"

"Oh, hi guys."

Bill Junior and Sam looked a little disappointed when they hadn't fooled their sister. "What is that awful smell? It smells like dead fish." Samantha put her fingers to her nose and pinched it closed.

"I'm sorry about the smell Samantha. It's the woven seaweed cloth that I use to protect my clothes from the Qrie energies that I produce. You will learn about this soon enough. And yes, it does smell kinda like dead fish. Mum has some stuff she makes and puts on the cloth to make it smell better, but I have run out of what I had. I need to have Mum send me some more."

"These're my monofins that I use for swimming and some stretchy zip-up tubes that my boss gave me when I first started playing mermaid in Melbourne. They fit over my hips, legs, and feet. At first, I didn't want the tube coverings at all. Boss, the tour operator, bought the coverings and wanted me to use them. He even had the divers on the boat wear them to make them look more like mermen after they'd learned how to use their monofins. We even painted the monofins to make them look like dolphin and killer whale tail flukes. I had to adjust my Aqume to match them. He got the tubes from a friend of his who had a textile research facility.

"The material is shark skin and silicone on the inside, with a spandex-like strong, stretchy material sandwiched between it and a special outside coating, which is extremely slick whenever it gets wet. Boss's friend made me five copies of the special tubes that duplicated the requirements of my old spandex tubes.

"Boss also got several pairs of web-fingered gloves made of the same material. They had skin-color silicone rubber on the palm side and the other special super slick material on the outer side.

"I asked Boss if he could get his friend to put some special finger tips on the gloves so when I grab something, I can hold on to it. The silicone rubber is usable, but it could be much better. My web-fingered Aqume gloves don't help at all, especially if I want to grab a fish.

"His friend did an amazing job of making a retractable claw on each fingertip. The claw will extend if the last joint of the finger or thumb is bent. That means I can control whether the claw will extend or not. Kinda like a cat's claw. The thumb and fingertip pads are made of special silicone material, so I can pick up small items without them slipping. I think the man is a genius.

"Oh, and he gave me this." Breath pulled out a heavy canvas bag. She reached into the bag and pulled out a rolled-up piece of lumpy canvas. She untied the cord and rolled it out on the floor. "This is something he thought I would need to fix my monofins. Look at this it has all kinds of screwdrivers of different sizes, saw blades and saw blade handles, chisels, hammers, pliers, and wrenches. I left my electric drill and grinder with my mother. They won't work over here because they run on 250 volts. I read where Canada and the United States uses 120 volts, and my mother could use them. I'll just have to get some that run on the voltage here."

"Well Breath, that looks like a good set of tools." Will ran his hand over the tools as he inspected them. "You know what, we have a good hardware store that has all manner of electric tools. I'll just bet we can find a good hand held portable grinder and drill that will work on 120 volts. Were your other electric tools battery-powered?"

"No, they were all plug-in. They were cheaper than the battery-powered ones."

"Well we'll just have to see about that. I'll just bet the hardware store has battery-powered tools. We'll have to go into town and get you some good tools that work on this continent."

Breath bounced up and threw her arms around her dad's neck and kissed him on the cheek. "Thank you, daddy. I'm looking forward to it."

Breath offered to show Virginia and Will how to swim with the monofin. She apologized to Bill Junior and Samantha because she didn't have any for them to wear.

Virginia observed. "I'm not Qrie like you two are, and I can't take the cold, but Will, if you want to try it, then I say go for it."

Her dad was eager, grinning like a little kid. They went to Ghost Lake to try it out. Once he learned the body motions, how to keep his knees straight, and how the feet controlled the tail fluke, he could swim quite well with it, and he even managed to breach clear out of the water. He wasn't as fast and couldn't jump as high as Breath, but he was no slouch, although Breath suspected that he could float off the ground like Mum. He liked the clawed web-fingered gloves and the tube a lot. She was proud of her dad; he wasn't bad for a rookie. The whole family except Virginia, had a wonderful time swimming and playing in the lake.

Breath never used the hood or tubes around her legs after she left Australia. Although she liked the feel of her latest monofin, she always opted for the total freedom of her Aqume.

Will found the tube useful since he couldn't form an Aqume like Breath. Breath experimented with her Aqume to change the fins around her webbed hands to extend all the way up her arms. She then made her arms and hands look and function more like real flippers. She also added more color to her Aqume. She now had a darker, iridescent blue tail as seen from above and skin color on the underside, with no scales. She decided she didn't like scales and using her telekinesis removed the painted scales on the tubes. They were mammals, after all. When swimming with her father or by herself, she never used the Aqume over her head or above her waist. She did use her seaweed lined top when she was around Virginia.

Breath had been bragging to Virginia how good her dad was at swimming with his monofin. Virginia mentioned to Will. "Why don't you two take a road trip to Vancouver and swim in the ocean? From what she tells me, she swims in the open ocean all the time with dolphins. Why not go see if you can find some dolphins to swim with?"

Will replied with concern. "I don't know whether that'd be such a good idea. We'd be leaving you here with no one to help."

Virginia held up her index finger to stop Will. "I've been discussing this with Betty." She looked over at Breath. "She's the woman from the next farm over. She's been bugging me to let her come over here to help with the twins. I told her that I was going to propose this to you, and she jumped at the chance to come over and help.

"Will, you've only visited and held your daughter once, when she was a baby. Sure, you talk to her all the time and have seen her on Skype, but it's time to get to know your daughter better with a little quality father-daughter time. I'm not going to take no for an answer. You're going, and that's all there is to it."

Breath and Will looked at each other and smiled. Then he grinned. "Yes dear. Whatever you say dear."

***

On the trip to Vancouver, Breath researched the best places to see dolphins and whales in the area. While Will drove, Breath studied the map. "I found a place called Telegraph Cove on Vancouver Island. Do you think that'd be a good place to go?"

Will replied. "I've never been anywhere on Vancouver Island. If it looks good to you, then it looks good to me. By the way what does it look like?"

Breath laughed. "Oh, just lots of hills, lots of trees, lots of rain, lots of clouds, and a lot of water. Did you ever see the Twilight Vampire Movies?"

"Yes, I did, both in the theater and on TV."

"Well then, you know pretty much what Vancouver Island looks like."

They caught the ferry from Vancouver to Nanaimo on Vancouver Island in the afternoon. Then they drove to Telegraph Cove and parked the pickup at the end of Ella Bay Road.

Just after sunrise the next morning, they got their gear together and walked out to a convenient place to get in the water. Will slipped in and put on his tube, monofin, and gloves. Breath got in and put on her gloves and formed her Aqume.

Some local dolphins soon discovered them. They played with the dolphins for a couple of hours, until the dolphins disappeared. Not long after that, they heard orca sounds and went to investigate. Will was a bit apprehensive about swimming with killer whales. Although, he sensed that the solar system's Qrie Stewards, Morning and Beauty, were watching and his tension subsided.

A few minutes later, the orcas found them. Breath knew orcas were a curious bunch, in particular this bunch because they'd never seen humans like these with orca-like flukes who could swim as fast as they could. They swam and played with the orcas for several hours.

Breath taught Will how to swim the bow wave. Somehow, she persuaded one of the large orcas to allow her and her dad to swim its wave. It was a real trick to learn because whales don't produce much of a wave.

Another of the large orcas would swim up between Breath and Will and present its flippers. Breath got the idea that it wanted her to hold on to the flipper. When she did, it took her down and came up fast and breached, coming almost clear of the water. It was all she could do to hang on. Then Will got the idea for each of them to hang onto a flipper while it breached.

The whales seemed to be having as much fun as Breath and her dad. Then, when Breath did a breach, all the whales seemed to take it as a challenge to show her how it was done, proper-like. Will even got into the game. They'd become members of the pod.

The game stopped. The whales began to sound and use echolocation. Breath knew they were hunting; she just didn't know what. A few minutes later, she saw the whales make for a school of huge Chinook salmon. They began to swim with the whales to round up the salmon and herd them. Breath and her dad knew this was a rare treat.

Later, a few dolphins, understanding that the whales had finished eating, reappeared. There was also a boat moving out into the bay. Breath recognized it as a tour boat for dolphin and whale watching. She saw that the boat had water jets instead of propellers, was quieter than most boats, and she thought, *Why not?* She indicated to her dad to follow her. They joined several dolphins riding the boat's bow wave. Will discovered that after riding the bow wave of a whale, riding the bow wave of a boat was much easier.

This attracted no small amount of attention from the people on the boat. One man was intense and curious. He had a stopwatch, camera, clipboard, and was taking copious notes. When the boat slowed, the dolphins left. The orcas came closer. Breath and her dad went to join them. The games began again. The whales started putting on a show for the tourists.

Breath called her dad over. "Would you like to have some real fun?"

"Breath, what kind of evil scheme are you cooking up now?"

Breath gave him a wicked little grin. "Well, Dad, when I was in Australia, everyone liked to see me swim as a mermaid. Maybe we should give these tourists a little mermaid show."

Will looked at her. "If you do, you'll be giving them a real show." He pointed to his chest.

Breath looked down and saw that her top was gone. She had no idea where it could be. Then she looked at her dad. "What the heck? Merfolk aren't supposed to wear tops, and we're Qrie anyway. Besides, I'll put my Aqume up over my chest and a thin part over my face so nobody can see anything. Let's go for it. My Aqume will look like real skin and tail, not plastic and manufactured monofin."

She stopped for a moment and looked for anyone else around. The only other person she could see was her dad. *GP are we about to do something we shouldn't? I don't want to do anything that will jeopardize the Qrie.*

I don't think it'll do any harm to play mermaid as long as y'all don't show what y'all look like for real. As I've said before, the Qrie and the Mer are gonna be discovered. The technology that the humans have developed make this inevitable. So as long as you're nice and friendly and show everyone that y'all mean them no harm, I don't see a problem. It may even help us when the discovery comes. So y'all have fun now, ya hear.

She saw the big whale that they'd been doing the breaches with and swam over to it. It obliged them by rising up between them so they could hold on to the flippers and then breached close to the boat, with both Breath and Will hanging on. This didn't go unnoticed. The passengers took photographs and videos. Breath and Will let go of the large whale and did a few breaches of their own, to the delight of the tourists.

The boat had stopped, and several of the whales had moved next to it. The boat operator told everyone they couldn't touch the whales; they could just look. The whales seemed to be as curious about the humans as the humans were about them.

Breath motioned to her dad. *Let's go over and play whale and look at the tourists like they're looking at us. Just don't say anything.*

He smiled and shook his head in disagreement. *You go have your fun; you know what you're doing around tourists. I don't. I'll just stay out here and watch. You can show me how it's done.*

Breath came up under two whales swimming near the boat. She'd put her face Aqume in place to hide her identity. She looked up at the people on the boat. There was considerable excitement. One little girl had a piece of candy still in its wrapper and leaned over the rail to give it to Breath. She rose out of the water doing a tail stand, to take the offering.

She'd learned to do this in Australia by copying dolphins. Then she relaxed back down with her head above the water, holding the candy up. The little girl had a similar piece of candy, and she put it in her mouth. Breath copied the young girl and put the piece of candy, wrapper and all, in 'her' mouth. Then Breath took it out, made a funny face, and dropped it.

She disappeared under the water. A few seconds later, she reappeared with a tiny fish dangling on one of her lethal-looking clawed fingers. She rose up and offered the little girl the fish. The little girl took it and smiled. Cameras took pictures and videos with furious intensity.

One of the whales moved a little too close for comfort, and she couldn't move down between them because the space was too small. With a subtle movement, she laid out on her back on top of the closest whale. And then, with liquid grace, she slid off the other side. It gave everyone on board a long, full frontal view of her as a mermaid.

Will projected to her. *We should start back. It's starting to get dark.*

Breath made a few whale-like sounds and then started swimming away. She hoped that her calls to the whales meant. "We must go." When Breath and her dad left, all the whales went with them. That night she and her dad laughed and swapped stories and told jokes around a small campfire. Will had stretched a canvas over the bed of his pickup truck. With their sleeping bags in the back of the truck, and roasting fresh caught salmon over their campfire everything was wonderful. They stayed there another four days, playing with their dolphin and whale friends and visiting the tour boats. It was one of the best times Breath had ever experienced, and this time it was with her daddy!

After all the camping gear was packed in the pickup, Breath went over and gave her dad a tight hug. She looked up at him with tears streaming. "This time here with you has been so very precious. I'll cherish this memory for the rest of my life."

Will looked down at his daughter, and he couldn't stop the tears either. He gave her a powerful *Qrie Embrace* and she gave him one even stronger. They held this quiet embrace for several minutes. Will finally took a deep breath and said, while trying to keep his voice steady. "Honey, we need to get on the road."

Breath stepped back, reached up, and gave her dad a kiss on the cheek.

***

On the ferry trip back to Vancouver, Breath and Will listened to the excited buzz that an actual mermaid and merman had been sighted at Telegraph Cove. There were even pictures in the local newspaper.

When they got back to Vancouver, they were getting gas as the television in the store featured a segment about them with video and several still pictures of them with the whales.

One man identified as a marine biologist was saying he'd measured the time the mermaid had remained submerged, which was an average of four to five minutes. "No human being can swim as fast as a dolphin. A human being can't breach its entire body out of the water, and hold its breath for that long. They also can't be that active, in near freezing water, without some type of protection. Hypothermia would be quick to set in. They had no thermal protection at all. We observed these creatures for more than an hour on the first day and over three hours the next day, with no apparent ill effect whatsoever.

"In addition, after close examination of the video and photographic data of the mermaid — the merman stayed well away from the boat — there's no evidence of any man-made manifestation such as swim flippers, swimming aids, wetsuit, or any other technological gear.

"The merfolk couldn't be human. Wild orcas would not allow humans to be that intimate with them."

He continued to say the merfolk seemed to be part of the orca pod. The mermaid made dolphin and whale sounds, communicating with the dolphins and whales themselves. She was the one who signaled all the whales to leave. When the merfolk left, all the whales followed. He sounded quite convincing.

***

Breath and Will were laughing when they walked into the farmhouse. They stopped laughing upon seeing Virginia's stern look and raised single eyebrow. "I know it was you two; there's no doubt. Every news crew in Western Canada and the United States is converging on that poor little village."

She still had a stern look on her face. But she couldn't hold it that way for any longer. She broke into a huge smile and laughed. "Well, did you two have a good time?"

Breath and Will exclaimed in unison. "Yes, we had a fabulous time! By the way where are the kids?"

"Ah — they're running around in the woods in their birthday suits, I just can't seem to keep clothes on them. You want me to call them in?"

Breath smiled. "Yeah why not. They'll want to hear what fun we had!"

Virginia became silent for a moment. Breath knew she was using her telepathic link to call the twins.

A few minutes later the twins returned less than clean, with snow in their hair and mud on their bare feet.

Will started telling Virginia just how good a mermaid Breath was. Virginia told them she had recorded all the newscasts about the mermaid on Vancouver Island so they could see them when they got home.

Breath and her family, including Heidi via Skype, were laughing again. For the next several hours, they recounted their adventures, played with the twins, and watched the videos of the merfolk. They even saw a video where Breath was speaking whale.

***

That summer was different for Breath. Well summer in Australia; winter in the northern hemisphere. She, Virginia, and Will spent many enjoyable hours talking, laughing, and just getting to know one another. She'd never had the opportunity to work on a farm before. Her mum had taken her to several farms, but she'd never gotten to work on any of them. She and Heidi always had a large lush garden in their backyard in Fremantle. They never bought vegetables and sold some at the markets, and they canned more than enough to see them through the winter.

The one thing that set the farm apart from anywhere else she'd lived was that Will had a well-equipped shop. In the barn, he'd set up a well-insulated and outfitted place to work during the winter. He had all manner of shop tools such as drill presses, sanders, saws, and hand tools. He even had a multipurpose lathe–milling machine combination.

Breath spent a major portion of her summer — or rather winter in that shop. Will helped her build a new monofin. She knew her old monofins were lightweight, but they were bulky and difficult to carry. She wanted to make something that would lie flat and would fold neatly into a bag or case.

She and her dad spent many hours designing and building what they called her origami flipper. After a number of trials, they achieved a beautiful mechanism that was both strong and lightweight and would fold into a small space. The entire monofin apparatus worked better than she'd anticipated.

She put a small pocket on the bar, to hold her swim togs and short T-shirt. Virginia made her several loose-fitting crop top T-shirts, out of a thin material that totally repelled water. The crop tops last much longer than the standard cotton T-shirts she was used to, and almost as long as her seaweed lined muumuu dresses.

She was reluctant to start packing for her trip to Miami. Besides her two pink duffel bags, Virginia gave her a small backpack loaded with clothes and personal items. Breath was of two minds. She was sad to leave her family but was also excited to start school.

While Breath was saying goodbye to her dad and Virginia, she pulled him aside. "Daddy, I wish you could have been around when I was growing up. I had the most wonderful sum... winter, with you, Virginia, Billy, and Sam." She looked at her dad as she put her head against his chest, and a tear presented itself.

Her dad took her in his arms and gave her a strong *Qrie Embrace.* "I, too, wish we could've been together much more than we were. But things didn't turn out that way. We've got each other now, and we've always been able to communicate with each other, so let's continue that. You've gotta come back to visit the twins, at least." He gave her another *Qrie Embrace,* this time much stronger.

***

Erin and Cheryl Ziegler contacted their friends Rob and Karol in Australia. They sent them the television footage and still pictures they'd intercepted from Vancouver.

***

TDog contacted Dixon. "Get to Miami with a crew. This mermaid can't stay away from water for long. Make arrangements to follow her and take care of the — situation. It might be best to have a good tracking device and a fast boat — maybe a fishing boat with nets. We know she's strong and capable. Just get the job done."

11. MIAMI

Breath, now that you're at the University of Miami and can live in comfort on your savings from Australia, you'll need to take time and do two things. One, y'all need to begin to mingle with other people. Learn social interaction and get yourself some social contacts. Two, y'all need to learn how to lift and manipulate large heavy objects, and make physical items that you might need, plus a few other little minor... things.

GP, lifting heavy objects is easy, but this social contact thing is difficult. Why do I have to do this social stuff, anyway?

Breath Sweetie, the only real friend you've ever had was that sweet little aboriginal girl Alinta Mitchel, in high school. Y'all never considered the tour-boat crew as your friends. They looked at y'all as a means to an end. Y'all need to learn this because someday you'll have a job that requires y'all to interact with people. The secret to this is to learn to love yourself. After you've done this, y'all can pass this love to everyone. You're still learning, but you're getting there.

First, y'all need to find someone who can be a friend who has no agenda. Try joining a club that isn't associated with your course of study.

What club would you suggest?

You're from Australia. That might be a good place to start.

GP, I'm not comfortable doing that, sooo — do I have to do this? All I want to do is do my schoolwork and explore the waters and reefs all around southern Florida.

Yes, Breath. Y'all need to learn how to be comfortable around other people. And I didn't say you couldn't explore. Just be safe.

Well — okay, if you say so.

I just love your enthusiasm.

I love you too GP.

Breath researched the organizations on campus and decided the best fit was the International Student and Scholar Services (ISSS).

***

Breath had just finished unpacking her clothes and placing them in the nice dark wood antique dresser with an attached mirror in her garage apartment. The double bed was a nice change for Breath. Most of her life she had slept on single beds. The twenty by twenty-foot multipurpose room, over the garage section, was a larger room than any other place she had ever lived. The door at the top of the outside stairs opened in the middle of the large room. To the right of the door and behind it was a full-size refrigerator and a kitchenette to the right of that. There was a two-burner electric stove along with a small sink, a microwave, and a large toaster oven, on the counter. There was no table. She guessed if she wanted a table, she'd have to get one herself. A student desk, chair, and lamp filled out the remainder of the room's decor.

A nice ten by ten-foot bathroom, with bath, shower, vanity, sink, mirror, and toilet, was built over the concrete patio below. In addition, another ten by ten-foot room was next to the bathroom also over the same patio below. Breath reasoned that this was her closet, again larger than anything she'd ever had. She rarely had lived with carpets, instead having linoleum or hardwood floors. However, some fluffy antiskid throw rugs might be nice. The sky-blue paint on the walls and ceiling along with ample windows and curtains on three sides, gave the room an open and airy feeling.

She was apprehensive about this upcoming meeting of the ISSS, and was dragging her feet as much as possible.

GP, in what seemed like a continuous coaxing exercise, shoehorned Breath into the crowded room. Without his insistent coaxing, Breath would've run screaming back to her apartment. The gifted student program had made arrangements for her to live, with a nice older couple. The apartment was built over their garage and patio.

Breath attended the first meeting of the ISSS for the January school semester. She chose a seat in the last row of the hall, as inconspicuous a seat as she could find. The feeling in the room was crisp and excited, as if something new was about to happen. Breath felt dizzy and nauseated. To her, four people were a crowd. There were more than a hundred people in this room.

She kept scanning the room, scrutinizing each person's trustworthiness. With so many people in the room, she felt closed in and pressed. She couldn't make out any of the conversations from the noisy din of all those people talking. She tried telepathic probing. There were so many people standing so close together, and she hadn't yet learned to separate them. The many and varied attitudes she was sensing confused her. There were feelings of joy and anxiety about starting the new semester. Others had fear and some were homesick and still others were anxious about a new course of study. All Breath wanted to do is get away from the confusion.

She'd never been around that many people in her life. Her sensitive nose began to pick up the smells of all the perfumes, deodorants, hairspray, laundry detergent, washed clothes, and the unbathed. All of it made her a bit nauseous. Her anxiety, nervousness, combined with her nausea, began to make her skin crawl.

Making a getaway plan, she noted to herself. *There are about two hundred chairs in the room and two double doors at the back. There's a double door up near the right front and two double doors on the left. When the lights go down, I can sneak out.*

You'll stay seated. Close your eyes and take a few deep breaths. You'll be okay. I know you're a bit panicky right now, but I'm here, and nothing's gonna harm y'all. He gave her a *Qrie Embrace*, and she relaxed a bit.

But GP, it smells like... like — too many people.

You'll live through this Breath.

But... do I have to?

GP chuckled. *Now, Breath, think about what y'all just said. Wellll!*

It seemed to Breath a never-ending amount of time elapsed before the meeting started. As they were closing the doors, two people entered and sat down beside her. She didn't know whether to move or stay where she was. She immersed herself in a nervous concentrated study of the handout literature.

When the meeting eventually did start, the speaker droned on about how wonderful it was that everyone was there. He then called for the lights to be dimmed. A video presentation began. Breath thought, *I can flee.* But then two of the largest bouncers from deepest, darkest Miami came in and closed the only doors that were still open. Escape now was out of the question. She'd just have to endure.

Breath was distracted by the crowd, and got only a small portion of the presentation. When it was over, the two bouncers opened the doors. No sooner had they done this than caterers wheeled cart after cart of food into the room. Again, escape was eliminated.

Breath felt someone tugging on the sleeve of her violet, knee length, crew T-shirt dress. She spun around then had to look down. There was a young light blond girl, with blazing blue eyes, looking up at her.

"Hi. My name is Kristin B. Iversen, and you do not have a name tag. You are supposed to have a name tag." The young girl stated, in a matter-of-fact manner, in properly enunciated English, but with an accent that Breath couldn't quite place.

Breath was flustered and glad to focus on a single person. "I didn't see any place to get one."

Breath looked at the young blue-eyed blonde girl's name tag. Upon the tag was the name, in large, neat, printed capital letters, KRISTIN B. IVERSEN.

"That's okay. I accidentally got two, and you can have one. Here is a pen to write with. You need to put your full name on the tag."

Breath's anxiety lessened. She took the tag and pen from the girl and wrote 'Breath Of Spring' on it. She peeled the back off the tag and placed it on her chest.

Kristin asked, "Is that your real name?"

The woman with her turned around. "Kristin, you should not ask questions like that."

Breath felt a little less tense. "That's all right. I've been asked that question many times, and yes, it is."

The young woman, with the same hair and eyes as the little girl, and shorter than Breath, had a tag with the name Hipsi B. Iversen. "Hi. I am Hipsi, and this is my little sister, Kristin."

Kristin interrupted. "We have the same middle name — Britt. We are from Norway. Where are you from?"

Breath replied, "I'm from Australia."

"Oh! That is farther away than Norway. What are you here for?"

Hipsi said. "Now, Kristin, that is not polite. You should be polite."

Breath had almost forgotten the crowd. "Oh, that's okay. I'm here to get my PhD in oceanography."

"Hipsi is going to be a famous movie director. But this year, she is going to learn set design and construction. I am thirsty. I am going to get something to drink." Kristin took off running.

Hipsi turned and called after her. "Kristin, stay close." Then she turned back. "I am sorry. My apologies. My little sister can be a bit precocious. She starts junior high here in a few days. She came to stay with me since our parents recently died."

Breath was silent for a moment as she sensed Hipsi's grief. "I'm sorry to hear that. Do you have other relatives here?"

Hipsi looked sad. "No, the two of us are all there is now. I was living in the dorms when the accident happened. We've just moved into an apartment, which is better for the two of us. I can continue my studies, since my parents left us a considerable endowment. Do you have any relatives in the area? And if you do not mind, how old are you?"

"My closest relatives live near Calgary, Canada. I'm alone here as well. I'm fourteen and trying to get oriented before I start class."

"Wow, that is young. You are going for your PhD in oceanography, so you must be a prodigy. Kristin is twelve, so you are only two years older than she is. And you are here by yourself."

"Yes, I'm alone. I'm in the advanced masters/PhD program."

"Well, then, we should be friends. It will be like having two sisters. Several of my friends graduated last semester and have moved to California. And you know what they say. You can never have too many friends."

Here's your chance Breath, go for it.

Breath was silent for a second after GP's interruption, then replied. "Yes, I think that'd be great."

GP gave the still nervous Breath a mild embrace. *You're doing great kiddo; keep it up.*

Breath stayed close to her new friends as they indulged in the drinks, cookies, and pastries the caterers had set out.

GP wouldn't let Breath leave until she got the names, telephone numbers, and address of her new friends.

***

TDog sent his team leader Dixon to Brandy, Texas, to find out what was going on at the sixteen square-mile exotic animal Safari Ranch, which is owned by the Moreau family, Robert,

Monique, Vincent, Desiree, and Virginia. He discovered that Greg Updike, their neighbor, had been in a long legal battle over water rights with the Moreau family and the Safari Ranch. He also discovered that the sheriff, a good friend of Greg Updike, didn't like Robert Moreau. TDog saw an opportunity here to aid Greg Updike and the sheriff in their battle against the Safari Ranch and the aliens.

TDog didn't know whether the Moreau family were aliens, but the simple fact that Virginia Moreau was married to Will Spring was enough to make them all part of the same conspiracy.

TDog directed Dixon to influence, by ingratiation, the sheriff, Greg Updike, and his two sons, Glenn and Gary. He knew that with the animosity that existed between Greg Updike, the sheriff, and the Moreau family, and with a little urging from Dixon, he could turn the existing situation to Earth Only's advantage.

Dixon was excellent at the casual meeting situation. Through intel and close observation, he just happened to bump into the sheriff and Greg Updike together in town and struck up a conversation. The three of them became fast friends. He began helping Greg Updike with his legal battles against the Safari Ranch. He began interjecting suspicion into the sheriff's mind that the Moreau family wasn't all they seemed to be. He fed the sheriff bogus documents that seemed to support those suspicions.

After a few weeks he reported back to TDog that the plan was in place.

"Thanks Dixon, sounds like things are moving along well. I've got a crew in Miami now, preparing a little surprise, for that alien bitch — Breath Of Spring.

***

The next month was busy for Breath. GP was putting her through a tough regimen of both mental and physical exercises, while she still played mermaid.

Breath, what makes y'all think lifting a small object is easier than lifting a large, heavy object? You've got all the Qrie forces and energies. They don't care if it's a grain of sand or the star of the planet that grain of sand sits upon. To these forces, they're the same. The only difference is your perception, which is an illusion.

GP, you control of all the forces in this star system. I'm just starting out!

Breath, y'all weigh about seventy kilograms, and y'all can fly. You've been able to do this for quite a while now. Y'all think flying is easy and fun. Why's it so difficult for ya to lift fifty kilograms of water?

It's not me!

That may be true, but don't forget, you're approximately sixty percent water. Think of it as yourself and go flying. Breath, let yourself go and be free in your mind, and y'all will do amazing things. Overthinking everything limits your abilities. What you've got to do is stop overthinking, and you'll find y'all can do anything. In other words, don't think about it. Just do it!

I know these exercises are difficult. I struggled with them myself, so I know what you're going through. I can tell ya that your sense of accomplishment when y'all succeed is far greater than the struggle y'all think ya went through. Here's a simple exercise for y'all to try: do a tail stand, and push the water off your body and out of your hair. In other words, dry yourself off.

Breath did the required tail stand. Her upper body was out of the water all the way to her knees. She began to push water away from her body.

Wow, that works neat! Why didn't you teach me that earlier? It beats the heck out of drying my hair with the towel or a hair dryer. I'm gonna use that from now on. Thanks, GP.

Breath, you're evading your task. 'Lift' the water!

Breath chuckled. *Yes, oh, great taskmaster. Okay, as you command.*

Breath, enough with the snide comments. Just do the exercise!

***

Breath was helping Hipsi work on the sets for the new play, with the university's art department. She was daydreaming about the arduous exercises that GP had been putting her through, over the last few months. Some of those exercises were fun, but others were quite exhausting and required tremendous concentration.

Hipsi sat down beside Breath. "What is the matter? You look distracted. Do you not like working on the sets?"

"On the contrary, Hipsi. I find the work on the sets relaxing and quite enjoyable. I know you think I'm just doing this to please you, but I like the camaraderie! I've always been afraid of crowds. Three or four people have always been a crowd to me, and I didn't know how to handle myself around them. But I'm learning to interact with the creative and flamboyant people of the theatrical company here. I'm part of the crew. They treat me like family. I still get apprehensive when I realize there are so many people around me. You know what they say: two's company; three's a crowd. But I'm learning. And it's all thanks to you and Kristin. For that, I thank you!"

Hipsi was surprised. "Breath, I did not realize that you had trouble like that. You always seem so open and friendly. I am glad that we have been able to help you. I do not know what I have done, but I am glad I am here for you."

"I've always been bullied throughout my school life for being weird or a klutz, or being the baggy-dress hippie freak, and it always came at the hands of a group of kids. I never even went to assemblies at school because of the crowd. I now understand that all crowds aren't mean."

Hipsi put her arms around Breath. "You are right; most crowds are not mean, and they cannot all be judged by the bad few."

"I guess. The people here are pretty good. I just wish all groups were this good."

With Hipsi, Kristin, and GP's help, Breath was beginning to come out of her shell. She still didn't like crowds, but she wasn't as stiff and reserved as before. As time went on, Breath began to trust her friends, and they became more comfortable with one another.

Hipsi had never seen anyone quite as reserved and socially awkward as Breath. This made her wonder, had Breath ever talked to another student the whole time she was here? It was as if she were a walking encyclopedia, because she was so intelligent. Encyclopedias do not go on dates. Intelligence can be sexy, but only to some. Hipsi decided that she and Kristin were going to have to educate Breath in the fine art of dating. The question was whether Breath was old enough to date. She was not old enough to drive yet.

Hipsi almost gave up several times, admitting that perhaps she had tackled a lost cause. But as time continued, Hipsi was encouraged as she took Kristin and Breath on outings with some of Kristin's male friends. The first few did not go well. Breath opened up a little and even began to enjoy being out. She always went with Hipsi, Kristin, and friends but never with just a boy alone. Without Hipsi or Kristin, Breath had no idea what to say to someone with a Y chromosome.

Hipsi told Breath that she was a real heartbreaker. Breath did not understand the reference. Hipsi told her it was a reference to her great beauty and then went into fine detail. After that, Breath began to pay more attention to Hipsi's makeup and wardrobe advice. Hipsi, after all, had studied theatrical wardrobe design and makeup. Hipsi told Breath that theatrical makeup had nothing to do with going out on a date. Breath enjoyed getting makeup and wardrobe tips during sessions with Hipsi and Kristin. It became a fun creative game and drew the girls closer together.

With Hipsi and Kristin's help, Breath began to learn about being a girl.

GP was pleased.

Breath also spent many hours in telepathic communication with her mum, Heidi, about... well, boys. She had a lot to learn.

***

Breath introduced Hipsi and Kristin to her world. Hipsi was the same size as Breath, but Kristin was smaller. Breath fixed her adjustable monofin to better fit Kristin. It was the oldest of the three she had, but Kristin didn't seem to mind at all. Kristin learned to use the monofin as if she were a natural. Hipsi had a little more trouble but was a good student.

Mixed in with her friends was her Qrie training with GP.

GP, have you noticed the people who've been following me around?

Yeah, Breath, I have. I don't know who they all are, but I get the feeling some of them ain't all that friendly. I'd try to steer clear of them if at all possible. I know some of them are from government organizations that seem to have taken notice of y'all. I'll keep a close watch on them.

Thank you, GP. Should I be — afraid?

I wouldn't say afraid. Let's just say cautious. Just be sure to keep your shields up like I taught ya.

Breath had been at the University of Miami going on a year. She and her friends had taken numerous trips in and around Miami and out to the Keys. This weekend, she, Hipsi, and Kristin went to Marathon Key for some fun in the sun. She'd modified one of her original spandex tubes for Kristin. She brought two of her upgraded tubes for herself and Hipsi. She thought it'd be fun to play mermaid with her friends.

When the three arrived at Sombrero Beach, Breath said, "Kristin, if you'll please get the goggles and snorkels out of the box in the back, I'll show you something special." She got a special box from the back seat that'd been taped up so Kristin couldn't see inside.

She pulled out three swimming tubes, one for each of them. The smaller tube, she handed to Kristin. "I hope this fits you,

Kristin. Hipsi and I have been working on it just for you. Let me show you how it works..."

"So that is what Hipsi has been doing with the tape measure. I thought she was making me some kind of dress. Waist size, hip size, leg length, foot size, ankle size, and every other size she could think of. With all those measurements, I thought it was going to be a dress for Morticia, like in *The Addams Family*."

Breath laughed. "Well, almost. You won't be able to walk in this, either."

Breath showed Kristin how to put it on. She then showed Hipsi. "It's obvious you can't put everything on here and walk to the beach. You'll have to put the monofin and tube on when we get in the water."

Hipsi asked, "Are they safe? These things look cumbersome."

"Yes, Hipsi, they are. I've used them for years. They make swimming much easier. Besides, I'll be right there with you."

Hipsi was skeptical. "Well, okay, but I do not want to get in too deep until I am comfortable with it."

"I agree. I know the tube prevents you from slipping out of the monofin. However, it does help you swim much faster and with less resistance."

Two hours later, the three looked and swam like real mermaids. They were quite a sensation along the beach. Breath was trying to teach her friends how to breach and get their whole body out of the water. Hipsi could get about half her body length out. However, Kristin could get almost her entire body out. The things she failed to clear were her feet and monofin.

They were swimming out from shore a good distance but not out of sight of the beach when they saw two young boys in a canoe.

Kristin took off her goggles and snorkel and handed them to her sister. She then swam underwater and came up next to the canoe. "Hi, boys. Having fun?"

The two boys almost jumped out of the canoe.

"I was just swimming by and thought you two would like to join me in the briny deep."

The older boy exclaimed, "Holy crap, you're a mermaid!"

"Yes! And I was just wondering if you would like to join me for a swim? I promise we will not go far. Maybe twenty or thirty miles." She smiled sweetly and batted her eyelashes at them.

"This isn't possible. There's no such thing as mermaids. You look like one of those girls at the large aquariums dressed up like a mermaid."

Breath and Hipsi were laughing. "Here, Hipsi, take my goggles and snorkel. I think the boys need a lesson in mermaid." Breath disappeared, and a few moments later, she breached, leaping over the canoe, Kristin, and the boys.

The older boy again exclaimed, "Holy crap, a real mermaid!"

Kristin was laughing and still batting her eyelashes. "Why yes, we are real mermaids."

About that time, both Breath and Hipsi came up beside the canoe. All three mermaids were laughing.

The older boy asked. "How did you do that? I've never seen anybody able to do anything like that."

"Years and years of practice."

The older boy looked close at the three girls. "You're not real mermaids. I can see your waistbands. And I see your monofins. I have a monofin myself, but I can't breach that high out of the water. Although, now that I think about it, I did see something like that on YouTube."

Kristin laughed. "Well, it was fun while it lasted. I hope you do not mind me holding on to your canoe. I am getting a little tired."

"You can hang on as long as you want. We're heading home now, anyway."

The younger boy was still looking at Kristin. "But she looks like a mermaid."

"No, Chuck. She's just playing."

"Well, she's pretty, anyway."

"Thank you, Chuck." Kristin looked at the older boy. "What is your name?"

"I'm Rob Walka. This is my little brother, Chuck Walka."

"Well, Rob and Chuck, can my sister hold on to the canoe as well?"

"Yeah, but we can't paddle if you're hanging on."

Breath interrupted. "Don't worry. Give me my mask and snorkel, and I can push everyone to the beach."

The remainder of the afternoon involved a rather animated conversation about all thing's mermaid. Breath and Hipsi noticed Rob was quite taken with Kristin.

Rob's cell phone rang. It was his mother, telling the boys to come home. She invited the girls to dinner. Breath at first refused, but Mrs. Walka, being quite persuasive, talked Hipsi and Kristin into coming. They then convinced Breath.

Rob leaned close to Kristin. "Kristin, if you'll help me take the canoe home, Chuck can show Breath how to get to our house."

Chuck confided to Breath that he preferred to be called Charlie.

Hipsi smiled and confided to Breath that she thought it was Rob's idea for him and Kristin to be alone.

It worked.

The meal was wonderful, and the conversation was better.

There was however, one minor problem: Charlie was still convinced that Breath was a real mermaid. He even began to convince his brother. As time went on, even their parents, Jack and Wilma, began to suspect.

For the remainder of their time at the University, Breath, Hipsi, and Kristin spent many good times with the Walkas. Jack was a large-animal veterinarian, and Wilma was a nurse practitioner. They'd retired young and moved there from North Carolina.

The Walkas had many family discussions about Breath being a mermaid. After they discovered Breath was from Western Canada, they were sure. They had seen the Vancouver videos proving that there were indeed mermaids and her hair was the right length and color and so was the color of her eyes.

***

GP was proud of his protégé. *Breath, you've succeeded at two major milestones in your training.*

First, Hipsi and Kristin have done a wonderful job getting y'all over your fear of crowds. I know you're still apprehensive, but y'all know that a crowd isn't gonna attack ya. Y'all owe Hipsi and Kristin a debt of gratitude.

Breath, y'all now realize that the energy controlled and directed by y'all can move a raindrop or a cubic kilometer of water.

I'm very proud of ya. You've learned how to make things y'all need and to move large objects as well as water. But y'all know what they say: Practice makes perfect. Just don't let your concentration waver. Y'all might get wet.

Well GP, I must admit these exercises have been rewarding and in many ways' fun, but why do I need to know all this stuff?

To be able to accept a challenge that's more satisfying and wonderful than anything y'all can imagine.

Just what would that be?

You'll see, Breath. You'll see.

When?

When you're ready Breath, and not before.

GP, you can be so infuriating. Sometimes you're worse than Mum.

I know, Breath. But I don't want to spoil the surprise. I think you're gonna love it.

It better be as good as you say.

I love you too Breath.

Breath felt pretty good about herself, and the *Qrie Embrace* that GP gave her made her feel even better.

***

Dixon texted TDog from Texas. 'Things are going well here. Have some more work to do. Might be a while.'

TDog texted back. 'Got a crew here in Miami. Going to give that alien bitch Breath Of Spring a little surprise.'

12. USCG

Friday afternoons and Sundays were light for Breath. She liked to take a swim at these times. The forecast called for cloudy, a light breeze, and misting rain. Breath liked these days because for some reason people didn't like to swim in the rain. She couldn't understand that. What's the difference between being wet with rain and wet while swimming? She didn't mind because on rainy days there weren't so many people. She could play with the dolphins, without being observed.

She was walking towards the bridge over the waterway a couple blocks from her garage apartment when a young man came running up behind her. "Miss — Miss, you dropped this." He placed in her hand a small plastic ornament pin, about the size of a quarter, of a small dolphin. It had an open clasp on the back.

Breath looked at it for a second. "This isn't mine."

The young man turned and pointed a short distance behind them. "I saw it drop from your clothes. It must be yours. Perhaps it's one of your friends,' and it got mixed up in your clothes."

Breath sensed the young man's nervousness, but she didn't probe his mind. "I've never seen anything like that on any of my friends. However, it may belong to my landlady. I'll check later."

"Have a nice day Miss, and I hope you find its owner."

"I hope so too. You have a nice day as well." She looked at the dolphin for a moment and thought it looked rather pretty. She pinned it to her T-shirt, one that Virginia had made for her.

***

Divya Khatri and Ramesh Ramananda of the OAI were concentrating on the remote tracking drone aircraft video screen. Divya and Ramesh came from another government agency where they had gotten into a little bit of well — difficulty. Not enough to get them fired but questionable enough to get them transferred to someplace where they couldn't cause any more — difficulties. Their primary problem was they asked too many — uncomfortable questions. Both John and Tate had reviewed their history and realized these two were quite good at what they did and they both knew that these two would be a perfect fit for the OAI.

"Ramesh, do you see that? We've got two signals. I've got the tracker chip that we put on Breath coming in fine, but there's a second one. Would you see if you can tune that one in better?"

"I'm on it... and — I got it, and it's on Breath for sure."

"How did it get there? Is somebody else tracking her?"

"Maybe it was that guy earlier."

"Could be." Divya looked closer at the drone monitor. "Could you widen the view a little bit?"

"OK. What are you looking for?"

"That fishing boat looks like it might be following her."

"Are you sure? They're still in the waterway, and they might not even see her."

"You may be right. Maybe it's just my imagination. Let's watch for a while. How about something to drink?" She left and walked forward to the small refrigerator in their large 20-foot observation and surveillance van. A few moments later, Divya yelled, "Let's see... we've got 7UP, Dr Pepper, and Coke."

"Yeah, I'll take anything diet. Thanks."

Divya returned, her arms loaded. "Here's your soda, and I got some chips as well. What's happening?"

Ramesh studied the screen. "Well, would you look at that? It 'is' following her all right. I don't think there's any doubt now."

At that time, the drone must've caught an air current. Ramesh watched the screen jump and then settle back down. "Wait. What was that?"

Divya and Ramesh focused on the monitor. Divya pointed to the screen. "Zoom in on that."

Ramesh adjusted some controls on the monitor. "I think we should call the Coast Guard."

Divya started dialing the phone. "I agree." She waited on the phone until a male voice answered. "Hello, can you get me the Coast Guard dispatcher, please?"

"This is the dispatcher. How can I help you?"

"There's someone swimming out into the bay with a boat following close behind, and they're heading towards some orca whales. You need to get someone out there to get whoever is swimming out of the water. They've just entered the bay from Coral Gables Waterway and are headed southeast."

"Thank you; we'll look into it. Please give..."

"Thank you." Click. Divya thought. *We don't need any bureaucratic entanglements.*

"Ramesh, let's tune into the Coast Guard channels and listen."

"Already there."

Breath sent a greeting call to the orca pod she knew was close by. She knew by the return soundings that they could be friends and wanted to interact. The afternoon held the promise of fun. These Orcas communicated with a different accent than the ones she had encountered off Vancouver Island. Regardless, they still sent friendly soundings, and she looked forward to meeting them.

If it weren't for this noisy boat, I could hear the fish as well. But that's how boats are. I'll just use its bow wave to get me further out to the clean clear water of the reefs. Where the orcas and I can have fun.

***

"This is Coast Guard helicopter number H-26 to the cutter *Vigilant*. Over."

"This is Captain Russell of the *Vigilant*. Is this the boat we've been dispatched to check on? Over."

"Yes, Captain. It is. We can see the boat, and there's something in the water swimming the bow wave, most probably a dolphin. We don't see any human swimmers, and up ahead, there looks to be the pod of orca whales reported. Over."

"This is *Vigilant*. You say there are no swimmers in the water? Over."

"This is H-26. That's right, Captain. We don't see any swimmers at this time. Only dolphins. Over."

"This is *Vigilant*. We'll hang back to see if the boat steers clear of the whales. Over."

"This is H-26. Captain, that boat just dropped its net and accelerated. There're men on the deck with guns. They look like they're trying to catch or kill whatever is swimming the bow wave. I think we need to intervene. Over."

"This is *Vigilant*. I agree; move ahead to intercept. We're accelerating to catch up. Over."

"*Vigilant*, this is H-26. The men on that boat are shooting at something in the water. It looks like maybe one of the dolphins or something. I can't make it out here; maybe we can see better with the telescopic HD video camera. Over."

Breath felt a searing pain rip into her body. Her swimming became erratic and she could no longer maintain her position on the bow wave. She began to struggle to get away from the boat and the deadly propellers. Then she was in a net.

There was a pause, and the helicopter copilot began talking. "Captain, you're not going to believe this, but I think what the guys on that boat are shooting at... What looks an awful lot like, ah... well, it looks like, um..." The copilot trailed off. "Oh! Over."

The Captain came on the line. "This is Captain Russell. What is it man? What are they shooting at? Over."

"It looks like a... um... err... a frilly, multicolored mermaid, Captain. I know it sounds crazy, but that's what it looks like in the video. It's right at the surface, with long, flowing blond hair; a long, deep-blue-colored tail and a tail fluke shaped like it should belong to an orca; and lots of multicolored streamers. We've got a good picture of it. It was swimming the boat's bow wave. Those men hit it, and it's bleeding bad. There's blood in the water. Over."

"H-26, we'll be there as quick as we can. Over." He turned to the helmsman. "All ahead full."

"This is H-26. *Vigilant*, you're not going to believe what's happening now. All those orcas are attacking that boat, and it looks like the boat is losing. We're getting it all on video. Over."

"This is *Vigilant*. Keep us informed. Give us a running description of what's going on. I'll have two rescue crews in the water as soon as we get there. Over."

"Understood, Captain." The H-26 copilot began a running commentary. "The men on that boat caught her in the net and pulled her up on board. We got a good video of it as a mermaid with flippers, tail, and all, but now it doesn't look like a mermaid at all — just a naked, well-muscled human female. They're shooting at the woman, but they're getting themselves tangled up in their own nets. One man, not in the net, has what looks like a sniper rifle and fired it at her from point-blank range. The nets and cables are all moving. The man who fired dropped his rifle, and it looks damaged. He just picked up a spear gun and fired it. She now has the spear all the way through her.

"The orcas are ramming the boat, and it's taking a beating. They've already cracked the hull in several places. Over."

Divya told Ramesh. "Don't miss a second of this."

"H-26, we're launching two rescue boats now. They'll be there in about a minute. Keep video going. I want everything. Over."

"*Vigilant*, this is H-26. All those men are now tangled up in their own nets and cables. Orca whales are swimming around the boat. I hope our rescue crews are going to be okay.

"The woman has freed herself from the net and just flew or actually floated in the air, over the side of the boat, and is now in the water. One of the orcas has come up and lifted her out of the water on its back. Over."

"H-26, keep a close eye on our crews, but keep the video on that mermaid woman. Be ready to extract our rescue crew members. Over."

Breath was in severe pain from the bullets and the spear through her. *Thank you for being here for me my ocean friends. At that moment several orcas shifted their attention from her to two fast moving small boats coming in their direction.* Breath, even though she was in extreme pain, projected her consciousness at the two boats and realized what they were. Just as the orcas were about to attack the small boats she projected. *Those boats are our friends do not attack them. They're here to help.*

"*Vigilant*, the orcas have made a clear path for both rescue boats.

"The corpsman is with the orca and the mermaid now and is checking her condition. He just cut the spear gun line. We're dropping a basket as we speak. Over."

"H-26, is she still alive? Over."

"*Vigilant*, the corpsman says she's lost a lot of blood and is barely conscious but still alive. He's trying to stop the bleeding. And we're headed to the hospital. We've already radioed ahead. Over."

"Good. H-26, keep us informed. We'll take care of the boat. *Vigilant* out."

***

William Spring was aware of the situation and was already on his way to the Calgary airport. Virginia booked him a round trip ticket to Miami.

Several hours later, after Breath came out of the ER and the operating room, two military people walked into the ICU. They were intimidating and quite insistent. The hospital staff told them to leave, but they wouldn't.

About twenty minutes later, Will hurried into the room without saying a word, and with one stern look from him, the two military people left.

A sudden commotion on the other side of the ICU had everyone's attention riveted there. Will raised his hands over Breath. He moved his hands from the top of her head to her feet. There was a strong light between his hands and her body.

***

Will stayed with Breath until she left the hospital. "Breath, I love you and wish I could stay longer, but I've got to be back home Monday morning."

Breath gave him a powerful *Qrie Embrace* and thought, *I love you too, Daddy, and I'll always have the telepathic link with you, mum, Virginia, and GP. Hipsi and Kristin are always there in spirit.*

Will projected before he left. *Breath, there are two people following us — more likely you — since we left the hospital. They were also in the hospital room when I came in. I suspect they're military and now know about you. I want you to know this and for you to be careful. I love you Breath, and I so wish I could stay.* He kissed her goodbye and left.

Breath, all your blood and tissue samples that were taken while at the hospital and on the Coast Guard helicopter, as well as the CT brain and body scans, have been destroyed. All the blood that was in the water and the lift basket have also been destroyed. Y'all need to be more careful. That little escapade was irresponsible. Y'all know better.

I know GP. I'll be wary of boats in the future. Unless I know the boat, I won't swim its bow wave, okay?

Good. Breath, you'll have to be careful from now on. The U.S. Coast Guard is now going to be investigating y'all. Up to now, you've been considered a sideshow or a curiosity; however, now you're a person of interest. Y'all will also be investigated by other American agencies like the OAI. From this time on, you'll have to be looking over your shoulder, as they'll be following.

Is there anything you can do about it, GP?

No. I can keep them from harming ya, but I can't control their actions. One other thing: the five crew members of that boat that fired on y'all and captured ya have disappeared from the Coast Guard cutter and are now sequestered. I'll tell y'all more about that later.

Your shield stopped the bullet from that very high-powered rifle. That was no easy task. I'm sorry y'all got hurt. But y'all kicked ass. Let me worry about the names.

Oh! So! My getting shot with bullets and skewered with a spear gun and almost killed, isn't being harmed? Is it possible for me to just be a normal human? I have always longed for and wanted to be normal. I just don't know what that means.

It's impossible, Breath. You'll never ever be a normal human being. You're destined for greatness — such greatness you can't imagine now. And as for being harmed and a little weak, are y'all okay now — or not? Ya look fine to me.

Greatness? What are you talking about, GP? What do you mean, greatness?

You'll soon understand, but y'all have a lot to learn yet. Like being Qrie and keeping yourself safe.

GP, sometimes you're — so — so... exasperating.

I know Breath. For now, it can't be helped. It hurts me down deep that y'all had to go through this. However, I think you've learned a powerful lesson.

Did you set this up, GP?

I didn't set anything up. However, I didn't choose to interfere with the progress of the situation.

What if I had gotten killed?

I wouldn't have allowed that to happen, or allowed y'all to be seriously injured.

So, you just let me blunder on like an idiot.
Yes, but like I said, I'd never allow you to be seriously injured.
You know, GP, sometimes I don't like you very much.
Yes, I know Breath. I love y'all too.

***

When Hipsi and Kristin found out about Breath's ordeal, they were both afraid for her and upset with her at the same time. After they found out how swift she had recovered, Kristin, with some help from Hipsi, started an all-out search for mermaids and mermaid lore.

Kristin asked Hipsi. "Do you think that Breath could be an actual mermaid?"

Hipsi replied. "I do not know, but she did push that canoe very fast with the boys inside and both of us hanging on. It does make you wonder!"

***

Breath didn't miss any classes, and no one asked anything about what had happened to her, which was just fine as far as she was concerned. She figured that the government must have hushed up the incident. Her first order of business was to go to the US Coast Guard station and thank the people who had helped her. They were gracious, but she got some curious looks from the people there. Her next stop was to the hospital to pay her bill.

She did notice that everywhere she went, there were always one or two people following her. If she went anywhere by car or on her bicycle, there was always another car following. She suspected it was someone from the Coast Guard.

She projected to her dad in Calgary and told him about being followed. He informed her there was nothing she could do about it but to trust GP. *If it's military or government and they haven't done anything up to now, there's a good chance they aren't going to do anything. They just want to see what you're up to. We see them here watching the farm also. Just keep an eye on them. Think of it this way, Breath: If it's military and they're that interested in you, then if someone tries to do something to you, they might be able to help.*

***

Every Friday afternoon, Breath put on her swimsuit bottoms, strung her clawed gloves around her neck, and wore one of Virginia's T-shirts over that. She did it that way so no one could see her gloves. She walked from the garage apartment to the little bridge across the waterway on Granada Boulevard. She walked down by the side of the bridge, where there was a little path to the underside, jumped in the water, formed her Aqume, and began swimming towards the yacht basin. She thought she'd swim down to Elliott Key and check out the reef.

Hipsi and Kristin knew Breath disappeared on Fridays and wanted to surprise her. They'd just pulled into the driveway at Breath's apartment. They saw Breath walking towards the little bridge and jumped out of the car to catch her attention. They planned to surprise her with a pizza. She disappeared under the bridge, and the girls ran onto the bridge to see if they could find her. They did — she was swimming as a full-blown mermaid: with iridescent bright-blue tail; clawed, webbed fingers; skin-colored flippers; and all.

"Oh My Gawd! Hipsi — did you see what I just saw? OMG! Was that our Breath?"

"Yes — it was — and I am speechless!"

When Breath didn't return after about an hour, Hipsi turned to Kristin. "Well — now we know what she does on Fridays. We have got to find out a lot more about mermaids!" Hipsi cranked the car and as they drove away Kristin asked with an excited and nervous giggle. "Do you suppose — she could be a real mermaid — do you?"

Hipsi glanced at Kristin and said with a nervous giggle. "I guess we will find out in time. Kristin you 'cannot' say a word about this to anyone, swear to me. She is our friend and we must protect her."

"I swear Sis, with all my heart. But still..."

***

The OAI and the military people who were following Breath had realized early on that a twenty-mile swim was nothing. She'd do that at least once a week. On the weekends, she'd take on larger challenges. They also noticed that she stayed well clear of boats since being shot. She played with the dolphins, but when they started swimming the boats bow wave, she didn't go with them.

***

The Coast Guard investigation supervisor was talking to his Commander. "There's considerable speculation between the agents as to how she can be walking barefoot with a T-shirt and a swimsuit bottom one moment and seconds later be swimming as a mermaid with a tail, flippers, and clawed webbed fingers."

The Commander nodded. "Well, we won't have to tail her much longer." He chuckled. "We've got one more week of observation. Then we bring her in and just see what makes her tick."

13. OAI 3

John Kingman was allowed into the National Security Adviser's office. The man looked up as John laid a file on his desk. "What's this?"

"It seems our little Miss Breath Of Spring got herself shot and injured in Florida. It's a miracle that she healed from those injuries in just twenty-four hours. She seemed a little weak but the hospital did release her. The Coast Guard rescued her, and now they're investigating her as well. I think we need to intervene. The more we find out about this family, the more we're convinced they indeed 'are' the Qrie. If the Coast Guard Investigation Service (CGIS) or any other agency detains and interrogates the Qrie Breath Of Spring or any other member of her family, this could be interpreted by the Qrie as interference. If the warnings of the Anasso are serious, that action could result in dire consequences.

"You should also know that the five men on that boat that shot her have now disappeared. We think the Qrie have considered those five as 'interfering' with her."

The Adviser looked at John. "This whole alien thing scares the shit out of me. If the Anasso are as apprehensive of the Qrie as they seem to be, then I think we should heed the warning.

"I'm going to issue an advisory under tight security to the CGIS group in Miami to observe but don't approach. John, continue the noninterference surveillance. I want to know everything we can find out about this family. I also want you to find out who set up that ambush on that boat."

"Yes, sir. One more interesting tidbit: she tried to pay her hospital bill with 300-year-old Spanish gold coins!" He chuckled.

14. COMMANDER

The next Friday, Breath rode down to the kiteboarding school at Matheson Hammock Park. It was pretty quiet, just before the weekend. She parked and locked her bike to a convenient palm tree and walked with her usual grace to the water and dove in. A few minutes later, she was heading south again to the Biscayne National Underwater Park at Elliott Key.

As she started out, she observed a personal watercraft. The pilot didn't look too stable. She thought she'd watch awhile, just to make sure he was okay. It turned out he was not. He made a sharp turn. The watercraft went one direction. He went the other.

GP, this man needs help.

Breath, I'll be here if y'all need me. Y'all know what to do.

Divya and Ramesh were watching her every move.

She swam to the unconscious man, while dodging his watercraft.

"This idiot doesn't have a life vest on." She grumbled. She looked around to see if there was somewhere safe, she could tow him to. *I've gotta get some air into his lungs.* When she did, he coughed and then was out cold again.

At least he had enough sense to wear the kill strap.

Breath began swimming with him towards his watercraft. She labored him onto the craft. He was draped over the seat. She gave him a few more breaths. She then pushed him and his watercraft to a small sandy beach. She pushed and floated the watercraft as far up on the beach as she dared. She glanced around to see if anyone was near enough to help.

When she found no one nearby, she floated onto the beach, not touching the ground. She grabbed the man's arm. She pulled and floated him off the watercraft onto his back. She checked and found his heartbeat. She began giving him mouth-to-mouth. He began to breathe but coughed up some blood. He woke up in a daze.

"Don't move. I'm going to get a car. I'll be right back."

Pondering her next move. *Should I run or swim? Let's see — it's over a mile if I run its less than three quarters of a mile if I swim. I can swim faster than I can run. So, swim it is!*

She turned and again floated until she was in the water.

She ran through the parking lot looking for someone with a car when she saw a man driving a van. She ran over waving her arms to get him to stop which he did. "Please sir. I need your help! There's a man on the other side of the park that needs to go to the hospital. Can you please help?"

"Sure thing, just tell me where to go." She directed the man East and then South to Matheson Park Road and then to its end where the little beach was.

The van that she'd flagged down pulled up beside the injured man. She jumped out and grabbed him up. She placed him in the back with gentle care. She then climbed in beside him. She slammed the door, and the van driver sped off.

The van pulled up to the emergency entrance of Doctors Hospital in Coral Gables. The driver honked his horn. Breath opened the door, picked the man up out of the back, and ran with him to place him on a gurney. This surprised the two EMTs who were pushing the gurney.

A short time later, she was telling the ER admitting nurse what had happened, although she left out a few minor points such as — well — her tail. She wrote the man a note telling him where to find his watercraft and signed it. The nurse stapled it to his paperwork.

Breath thanked the van driver for his help and for returning her to her bicycle.

Twenty-four hours and a multitude of tests later, Commander Wesley Montague walked out of the hospital. He had had an allergic reaction to certain local shellfish. The beers hadn't helped matters either. He called his buddy to give him a ride back to the park where his car was. They found his buddy's watercraft where Breath's note indicated.

GP, did you put that guy on the watercraft under compulsion?

No Breath I didn't. I'm keeping a close watch on him though.

Do we have anything to fear?

I don't think so. Like I say, I'm keeping a close watch on him.

15. OAI 4

The National Security Adviser walked out of his office and saw John Kingman coming towards him. He turned and waved John into his office. "What is it this time John?"

"The Qrie Breath Of Spring has done it again. This time, she rescued a Navy Commander, so now the Navy is investigating as well. I'd suggest you have the Navy and the Coast Guard work together on this."

The adviser perused the small file that John handed him, not wanting to place the file on his not-so-neat desk. "This little gal better start watching her backside because she's becoming a not very well-kept secret.

"Could the Qrie be up to something?"

"According to the Anasso, they never know what the Qrie are up to, since they cannot read the Qrie telepathically."

The adviser looked concerned, and then he brightened. "Oh, I wanted to ask how that Piper M350 was working out for you. It should cut down on the travel time between Roanoke and DC. I know it's not much, but we're working on something faster."

"Oh, it's working great. I used it on these last two trips to DC. Beats the heck out of driving. As you know we can't use electronic communications in these situations. We still have to take commercial airlines to the crop circles. That's not a bad problem because most of the circles are made by man, not by the crop circle aliens. However, the CCA ones get trampled pretty bad before we can get there."

"Yes, you've mentioned that before, and we're trying to set the OAI up with something much faster — a 2X plus supersonic, as a matter of fact. It has some kind of sonic-boom deflector to allow it to fly over land. I just don't know when we'll get it."

"I guess we'll just have to wait and see. Thanks a lot for the effort. We appreciate it."

"The OAI is a hot commodity right now. Several of the agency chiefs want to get in on the action."

"A hot commodity is okay as long as it doesn't turn into a hot seat."

Both men laughed.

16. COMMANDER II

Breath had just gotten to campus and, with her usual graceful stroll, was going to class in a fluffy pink, short sleeve, seaweed lined, muumuu, when she heard a voice behind her. She turned and saw a tall, well-built, powerful man in a Navy officers uniform walking towards her. She recognized him as being the man on the watercraft.

"Hello — Miss Breath Of Spring. I'm Commander Wesley Montague. I called your apartment, and when I didn't get an answer, I did a little internet search and found your address. I went to your apartment with these." He pulled a bouquet of red roses from behind his back. As he did, he noticed Breath was carrying a pair of flip-flops and was barefoot, and standing tiptoed with her heels maybe a half inch clear of the ground. "Your landlady said you had already left for the University and told me what you were wearing. So, I took a chance. I want to thank you for saving my life. I owe you big time."

Breath was suspicious. Her shields flew up strong as she challenged him. "How did you get my address and telephone number? I didn't leave that information on the note. The University said they wouldn't give my phone number or address to anyone. So how did you get it?"

"I'm sorry; I can't give you that information. Let's just say the military has its ways. I'm sorry if I startled you; that was not my intention. You saved my life. I wanted and needed to thank you. If there's ever anything I can do for you, just name it." He offered her the flowers along with a thank-you card with his name and contact information attached.

Breath took the flowers and cradled them in her left arm. She put her hand out and shook Wesley's large hand, giving him a healing *Qrie Embrace*. He looked startled but held his ground, and then she put her hand around his neck, pulled him down to her, and kissed him on the cheek. This time she gave him a powerful *Qrie Embrace*. She had to surround him with a Qrie shield just to hold him up. "I'm so glad you're okay. I was so afraid something terrible had happened to you." While she supported him, she realized she had never seen Commander Montague standing. She was tall but he towered over her. He was well over six feet and well-muscled like most of the military people she'd encountered. His sandy blond hair, receding hairline, and glasses gave him an intelligent studious look.

His face had an expression of pure ecstasy. "Oh my goodness, what was that?" After a long pause, he smiled. "Something bad did happen, but something wonderful also happened — you. It's not every day you get saved by a beautiful angelic mermaid."

She pulled her hand from around his neck and stepped back. "Please, keep your voice down. I am not a mermaid! I keep trying to tell everyone that! Why won't anyone believe me?"

Wesley, still recovering from the embrace, chuckled. "Maybe it's like the duck."

Breath gave Wesley a quizzical look. "What's a duck got to do with it?"

"Well, if it looks like a duck, quacks like a duck, walks like a duck, and swims like a duck, it must be a duck. Even in my bad nearly drowned condition, I saw you as a mermaid. There was no doubt."

Several expressions of confusion crossed Breath's face. Her head tilted slightly to the left. "But I..."

At this moment, two other Navy men approached, one a huge muscular, fair skinned man, six and a half feet tall or more, with blond hair and blue eyes. His companion was almost a foot shorter, had to build like an Olympic weightlifter, with walnut colored skin, light brown eyes, and a shaved head. Both men walked up to Wesley and Breath. The shorter man interrupted. "Excuse us Ma'am." He then looked at the Commander. "Sir, if you'll come with us." The Commander turned and looked at the two men. He recognized Navy Security the moment he saw them.

Wesley looked back at her still recovering from her kiss. "Thank you again, Breath. Remember, I mean 'anything.'" As he started to walk away, he stopped and turned back towards Breath. He cupped his right hand over his mouth and whispered. "I promise I'll keep your secret." He left with the two men.

***

The next CGIS meeting between the agents and the supervisor had a different tone altogether. Tate and John from the OAI sat in silence at the back of the briefing room.

The supervisor began. "Gentlemen, these briefings are top secret." He didn't mention the OAI people.

"In light of new evidence — that being — that our 'mermaid' suspect saved a Navy Commander — the Navy has requested all our information on the young — uh lady and the two incidents. We'll not be apprehending her anytime soon. The Navy and Coast Guard brass don't want her interfered with in any way — just watched, at least for the time being. If there's an opportunity to talk to the young — lady during our investigation, we're authorized to do so, but it's not to be an interrogation.

"They've also requested we do a joint investigation. I don't think I need to mention that this could involve a considerable amount of time. But since the Navy is providing for everything, all we've got to do is provide some additional personnel. Are there any questions?"

There were several Navy personnel in the meeting. One of the young officers stood up. "We've all seen the video of Miss

Spring lifting Commander Montague onto the seat of that watercraft. The seat of that large watercraft is over two feet above the water. The Commander weighs almost twice as much as Miss Spring. We tried to put a dummy the size and weight of the Commander onto the seat of the same type of watercraft, while it was in the water. It took four men to do it. Two men were required on each side. It looked like she just tossed him onto the seat. She pushed that same watercraft, with the Commander on it, up on the beach farther than those four divers could push it. It's obvious, no single man could do it. She also pulled him off the seat once the ski was on the beach with one hand and rolled him over. She did leave what looked like claw marks on his arm. We also have to question the obvious — tail, webbed hands, and what looks like flippers instead of arms. And the way she moved when she was on the beach.

"When the van came to get him on the beach, she just picked him up like he was a baby and put him in the van. Also, when they got to the hospital, she picked him up again and — 'ran' with him to put him on the gurney.

"Does anyone have any idea how she did that? Another obvious question is where did her tail, webbed hands, and flippers go?"

The room was quiet. No one had an answer.

Then one of the CGIS people stood. "We've analyzed photographs of her claws taken during the Vancouver incident. Our analysis shows those claws can easily rip a great white shark open. The Commander is quite lucky that all he got was marks.

"We analyzed the bullet taken from her shoulder after the shooting incident. It was from a high-powered .50-caliber sniper rifle. We haven't figured out how she stopped that bullet."

Again, the room was quiet.

***

Tate called John into his OAI lab. "This is a full-spectrum video of the fishing boat incident. Look at the shimmering... My best guess is, it's heat or a plasma of some kind around Breath

Of Spring's body, and tendrils of that plasma go from her to the net and cables that are wrapping around those five people. This can't be seen with a standard monitor. She's doing something unusual."

***

About two weeks later, Breath went to a little diner coffee shop a short distance from the University. She had just set down and was sipping her hot chocolate with whipped cream when a man, whom she had never seen before, approached her and sat down. She knew he wasn't one of the military people.

He showed her a number of photographs of her as a mermaid in Australia and in Vancouver. At the bottom of each photograph was a label marked *Star Child Quest*. She had seen these same photographs before and realized they must be from that publishing group in Perth, Australia. He began to badger her. He wanted her to tell him about being a mermaid. She told him several times that she wasn't a mermaid and that she had been wearing a costume. She started sipping her hot chocolate much faster. Her burning tongue made her realize that drinking fast wasn't a good idea. He was insistent and started making a scene in the diner. She got up and started for the door. He ran over and blocked it. Everyone in the diner was staring.

"You're not going anywhere little missy, until you tell me what I want to know."

She tried to duck under his arm to get through the door. It almost worked, except he stuck his leg out and tripped her. She did a judo roll on the sidewalk outside, and came up on her feet. She started to run, but he grabbed her. Before she could stop herself, she slapped him across the face. He went down like a sack of potatoes. Then she turned to run again and almost ran into a huge man coming to a stop in front of her.

She turned and ran back into the diner. She ran through the diner, looking for another way out. She saw her purse and snatched it up. She stopped for a microsecond thinking about chocolate. There was no other way out, and again she ran for the door.

When she got to the door, the same man was there again. He was bleeding from his mouth. She decided not to stop. She put her arms out in front of her to push him out of the way. She hit the man in his shoulders on both sides of his neck. She heard a crunching sound. The man yelled and fell to the ground.

She ran to the end of the block and around the corner. She stopped and looked back around the corner. She wanted to see if the man was following. The two military-looking men who had been following her that day were bending over the intrusive man. He was lying still on the pavement. The smaller of the two military men looked up and faced her. He smiled, and nodded. Then he pulled out his phone and dialed. The military men were preventing the intrusive man from moving.

***

Three days later, Breath saw the same two military men she had seen with the Commander and the intrusive man. They were following her again, this time on campus. She walked around the corner of the nearest building ahead of them, and stopped out of sight. When the men came around the corner, she stepped out. They froze.

"Thanks, gentlemen, for helping me the other day. Can I please buy you each a cup of coffee? It'd be my pleasure."

They looked at each other and just shrugged and then nodded. "Uh... well, yes, Ma'am. We'd like that."

The smaller gentlemen asked, "How long have you known about us following you?"

"Well, the shooting incident happened on a Friday, and I noticed you Monday morning as I was going to class."

The large gentleman chuckled. "We didn't fool you for a second — did we?"

"Well, not really. I do have to ask, though, why're you following me, and who are you?"

The small man explained. "We're from the Coast Guard Investigation Service, or CGIS for short. We're supposed to follow and see if you do anything — unusual. That's about all we can say for right now. We're not even supposed to give you our names if asked. I don't know how it'd hurt anything, but that seems to be the procedure."

Breath snickered. "Well, I guess the other day was a little unusual."

"Yes ma'am, it was."

Breath looked concerned. "I hope that man is okay. He's okay, right?"

The large gentleman chuckled. "Well, if you consider three missing teeth, a fractured jaw, and two broken collarbones okay, then that man is just fine! Otherwise, he still has three missing teeth, a fractured jaw, and two broken collarbones. I might add that the man was a reporter from one of those sleazy tabloid journals. He has been in trouble with his strong-arm tactics in the past. The police are investigating the incident and with all the witnesses' statements, he's in trouble. We gave the police our statement, but they want to speak with you. We informed him that he should keep well away from you in the future."

Breath, with a shy smile, stammered a bit as she looked up. "I... I didn't mean to hurt him. But when he grabbed my arm, that was kind of it. I just slapped him to get him off me. Then I turned and almost ran into some huge guy. Then I made a mistake by running back into the diner. I was looking for another way out but couldn't find one. I saw my purse and grabbed it and was going to run out the door again, and he blocked it again — déjà vu. This time, I wasn't going to let him stop me, so I just put my arms out in front of me and ran into him. I didn't want to hurt him so I thought I would just push him at his shoulders. He went down, and I kept running. I feel bad about hurting him."

"That was one serious slap, and that huge guy you almost ran into was me. We were running over to see what was going on. We were worried you might've been injured, although you seemed to have the situation pretty well under control."

He chuckled and then began again. "By the way, we're looking for some good people to protect us when we go down dark alleys. Do you think you'd like to have the job? We could sure use your help. We're in great need of someone who can slap that hard."

Both of the gentlemen laughed.

Breath blushed. "Now you're just having me on. The next time it's your duty to follow me, why don't you just walk up and say hi? We can walk together and enjoy one another's company. That seems a lot more civilized than skulking about. Don't you think?"

The smaller, dark gentleman smiled. "That wouldn't be proper procedure, Ma'am."

"Do you always follow proper procedure? What's the real reason you're following me anyway? What are you trying to find out?"

The larger gentleman looked uneasy, started shifting his weight, and rubbing his hands together. "We — uh were told about and shown videos of you swimming with the whales and dolphins. You were also swimming in front of that boat with the dolphins. No human can swim that fast and stay underwater for that long. We were just supposed to follow you and see if you changed or something. We're not sure of what we're looking for."

Breath spoke with irritation in her voice. "Look, I'm not a mermaid or anything like that. I can hold my breath for a long time, and I can swim as fast as most boats. I've been in and around water all my life. Swimming is second nature to me. And I have help. I have no more classes this afternoon. So, take me home, and I'll show you what I use. My swimming isn't a mystery."

***

A few minutes later, they pulled into the driveway in front of Breath's upstairs garage apartment. They all went up the stairs and she invited them in. Breath went to her closet, and pulled out her latest monofin. It didn't have the tube with it. She looked at the two men. "This is a monofin and it's what I use to help me swim, such as swimming the bow wave on that boat. That boat wasn't moving fast, and with one of these, anyone can swim that wave if you know how to use it. If you'll wait just one moment, I'll show you how it works."

She walked into the bathroom. She changed out of her muumuu dress into a skimpy, two-piece, pink bikini bathing suit. She came out, took the monofin, and unfolded it. She began to explain. "These cups fit my feet like so. These clips here clamp onto my calves after I've slipped my feet into the cups." She continued to explain how everything worked. "Once you've learned how to swim with a monofin like this, you'll never swim with anything else. It allows you to swim much faster than you can swim with standard flippers."

The men were amazed at the device's simple and efficient design. They still couldn't believe that she could do the things they'd seen her do in the video.

The smaller man asked, "Is this the one you had when you were shot?"

"No, but I had another like this one. It must've taken a hit with a bullet about here." She pointed.

The men weren't convinced.

She continued. "I suspect that seen from above, I'd look like a mermaid, and the fluke was a blue-colored material." She laid the monofin out flat on the floor and then sat down on the floor with her feet in the foot cups. "I think you can see that if you were in a helicopter with binoculars, looking into the water at me with this thing on. And if you can imagine the tail fluke being blue, it would be easy to see how you could mistake me for a mermaid. Now do you understand?"

Both men stood there staring, almost drooling, at her gorgeous body lying on the floor in her skimpy pink bikini, with her feet attached to that — whatever thing. They both were unconvinced and with a distracted, almost hypnotic, simultaneous reply said. "Yes!"

Breath smiled ever so sweetly. "Well, then, all you've got to do is take a picture, because that'll be better than a thousand words."

The smaller man left the apartment on a dead run to get the camera out of the SUV. Breath continued lying there until he came back and started taking pictures. She said to the big man, "Mobile phones have cameras, you know."

Breath teased. "Now, wasn't that better than skulking about waiting for me to grow scales and a tail?"

The large man chuckled. "Well, no! I liked the skulking about, watching a beautiful, regal, graceful, and gorgeous young woman glide all over the place."

Breath turned red all over. It became difficult to discern the line between Breath and her bikini.

Breath, y'all must be careful. The Qrie know that lies are not just evil, but they corrupt your being into evil as well. Lies are insidious and have a way of sneaking up and compromising your integrity. So, don't lie. I thought I taught y'all better.

What should I do? I didn't know what to say.

Y'all can evade, delay, or refuse to answer.

I understand, GP. I'll try.

Do more than try.

The big guy chuckled. "Like Ricky Ricardo says — 'Loocee, yoo got some splainin too doo.' Breath this explains just one tiny part of the mystery. Even if we do believe you about your monofin tail, it doesn't explain anything as to why all those whales were out there with you. Or why, after you got shot, they went ballistic on that boat. Or why they circled the boat until we got there. It also doesn't explain why, when the Coast Guard crews came rushing up there in their rescue boats, the whales made a path for them.

"It also doesn't explain the excellent photographs of you and your father on Vancouver Island, swimming and breaching all the way out of the water. You were also photographed in detail swimming with both dolphins and orca whales. It doesn't explain how you were able to talk, in their language, to both the dolphins and the whales in those videos. And how was it in those videos that when you communicated to them and left, they all followed you?

"And that doesn't even come close to the reason that you've got the strength of several men. And there are more — little minor inconveniences, you might say. How do you explain all that?"

Breath looked at the two men with the expression of a guilty little girl caught. "Well, I..."

The big guy held out his hand. "Yeah, that's what I thought." He looked over at his companion. "Yep, she's a mermaid! She can't even deny it."

The other man opened his wallet, took out a dollar bill, placed it in the big guy's hand, and grinned. "This is great! We get to watch her graceful gorgeousness a whole lot longer."

Breath's blush returned. She mused. *I just love these guys.*

***

GP, is there anything I can do to help the man I hurt?

I've been waiting for y'all to ask that question. Yes, y'all can go to the hospital. Stand outside his room and send him healing and loving energies.

But GP, I don't love him.

It's all part of loving yourself and learning the ways of the Qrie. Breath, y'all asked me what ya could do, and this is it.

I understand. Okay, I'll do it.

That's my girl.

***

Erin and Cheryl sent emails, pictures, and videos to Rob and Karol about Breath Of Spring acting and looking like the mermaid in Vancouver. She was the right size; her hair color and eyes were correct. She was in the same area when all the photographs and videos were taken. It must be her.

***

Breath's swimming activities came to a screeching halt when her work on her PhD doctoral thesis and dissertation reached its final stage. That time was just plain work. When she received her PhD, she felt a tremendous weight lifted from her. But it wasn't over yet. She still had a postdoc internship ahead of her at Scripps in La Jolla, California.

17. SCRIPPS

Breath, Hipsi, and Kristin spent the whole weekend just having fun. It was a bittersweet time because they knew they wouldn't see one another until Hipsi and Kristin moved to California.

Breath also called the Walka family to wish them well and say her goodbyes. She realized that she had become quite attached to the Iversen sisters and the Walka family, and didn't want to leave them.

The three girls packed Breath's two pink duffel bags to the brim. She was ready for the long bus trip from Miami to Scripps Research Institute near San Diego, California.

Breath carried the bag with the monofin strapped to it while Kristin struggled with the second pink duffel bag. The bus driver grabbed them up and put them in the luggage compartment of the bus. The three girls hugged one another while tears rained down. Breath could feel a hollow spot forming in her soul and she didn't want to leave, but she knew she had no choice. Hipsi lightened her mood when she said that she and Kristin would be moving to the Los Angeles area soon. Breath got on the bus and was blowing kisses to Hipsi and Kristin until the bus pulled away. The tears didn't stop just because the bus left.

She noticed that the seats on the bus were no softer or more comfortable than the seats on the plane ride from Perth to Vancouver. She pondered. *It's a good thing that I have a couple stops on the way.* She wanted to go for a swim in Pensacola, Florida, and Galveston, Texas, but was anxious to get to California and take a swim in the Pacific Ocean.

***

When she arrived at Scripps Research Institute, she was introduced to a woman everyone called Mother Hen. Mother Hen's job was to make sure all the new interns and students ended up in proper care. People under Mother Hen's protection were called her chicks.

Breath chuckled. *Okay, so now I'm an 'official' chick! Would that be Dr. chick?*

Mother Hen gave Breath the address of a nice couple who lived about four blocks from the ocean. Breath was excited and thought. *OMG! It's absolutely wonderful to be within walking distance of the institute, and the ocean. I just wish Hipsi and Kristin were here with me.*

When her taxi pulled up in front of the house, a navy-blue SUV pulled up behind her. Two uniformed Navy officers got out and walked towards her. One of them approached Breath. "Hello. Are you Miss Breath Of Spring?"

Oh, come on! I haven't been here five minutes and I'm not even settled in yet, and here they are already following me around again.

Breath gave the man a guarded look as the taxi driver opened the trunk of the cab and took out her two duffel bags. "Yes. What can I do for you?"

"I'm Commander Barnes, and this is Captain Stein, and it's not what you can do for us. It's what we can do for you Ma'am."

Breath was a little confused. "I don't understand. What can you do for me? Why do you want to do something for me, anyway?"

"Well, Ma'am, it seems you saved the life of a rather important naval person a while back. The U.S. Navy would like to thank you. If you'll come with us, please. We think you'll like your new accommodations better; it's much closer to the beach."

Breath was apprehensive, guarded, and uncertain. Her shields went up.

GP, is it safe? Should I go with these men?

Yes Breath. I know where they're taking y'all. You'll be all right.

"Well, okay. I guess I can delay moving in for a little while longer."

The two men picked up her duffel bags and put them in the back of the SUV. One of them held the door open for her.

She climbed in, and they went back towards the beach. They turned onto a street called El Paseo Grande. A few houses down on the ocean side, an elderly man walked out and waved at the two officers. He looked as if he'd just walked off the beach in flip-flops, bathing suit, and an outrageously gaudy Hawaiian shirt. He greeted the two officers and opened Breath's door.

"Miss Breath Of Spring, I'm so glad to meet you. I'm retired Rear Admiral Clifford Yokum. Please, just call me Cliff. I assume you've already met Captain Stein and Commander Barnes. Welcome to my home. May I please show you around?"

She thought. *What's this all about? I suppose it won't do any harm to look.*

She followed the Admiral into the house. Her pupils dilated when she saw the beach through the open glass doors in the living room.

Cliff made a sweeping gesture and gave her a huge smile. "Welcome to your new home!"

"But I already have a residence a few blocks from here."

"Yes, we know. We thought you might like to be a little closer to the ocean. And you can't get much closer than this, unless you're aboard ship. Plus, the U.S. Navy is picking up the bill."

Breath's red flags flew up. "I'm sorry, Sir. I can't take any kind of gift like this, especially from the United States Navy. It wouldn't be appropriate. I'm not, nor will I ever be, a part of the U.S. Navy. I can't accept this. I'm sorry, Sir."

"Commander Wesley Montague, the gentleman you saved in Florida, is a valuable member of an elite organization within the Navy. Without his contribution, we would not be able to fight terrorism, as well as we can with him. We also contacted a Commander George Marsdurban of the Royal Australian Navy, who told us how you helped them with a whale problem. So, you see Miss, you've already aided us, and we're now trying to pay you back. There are no strings attached to this offer."

She gazed at the Admiral for a second. "George told me he'd never tell anyone. I'll have to fuss at him for that."

"It's not his fault. He had to make a full report to his supervisors. Besides, they knew about you before he did."

Breath turned away. *GP, is this a good idea?*

Breath, these people already know about y'all. Y'all can't hide from them any longer. I also don't sense any animosity in their motives or their offer. There's also a great opportunity to learn.

OK, if you think it's all right.

Breath paused, contemplating what GP had just relayed. She turned with some apprehension back towards the man with the gaudy shirt. "Can I get that in writing?"

The Admiral laughed. "I can tell we're going to get along famously." He looked at the two officers. "I like her already. She won't take any guff from anybody, no matter whom she's talking to or what kind of outrageous shirt he's wearing." He looked back at Breath. "Yes, you can have it in writing."

Breath looked at him and cocked an eyebrow. "Okay, but you've got one week."

No sooner had she agreed than Cliff waved an arm and a couple sailors swarmed the SUV. It was empty in seconds. *Where did those sailors come from?* She pondered.

She looked at the house and realized it was painted the same color as her home in Perth.

They went upstairs, and she got her first good look at her new accommodations. The thing she liked about it most is it has direct access to the beach. In less than thirty minutes, she was moved in, clothes hung up, dresser filled. Even her toothpaste and toothbrush were in her new huge bathroom. All of which was upstairs.

She has a kitchenette with a sink, counter, two burner electric hot plate, and tiny refrigerator. Her full bathroom is along the upstairs walkway next to her kitchenette.

She also has full access to the large main kitchen, dining, and living area which is all one big room, except for the kitchen bar counter area. The main kitchen and dining area were to the left as you walk in the main entrance. On the right of the main big room was Cliff's master bedroom. Straight through from the main entrance is a wall of glass and a set of double glass doors leading to a large outdoor patio. Beyond that is the beach.

Upstairs above Cliff's master bedroom are two guestrooms and another bathroom. A second-floor walkway balcony surrounds the large room below. Upstairs, on the ocean side is a set of double sliding glass doors leading to an outdoor balcony.

All the interior walls are painted an off-white with no pictures or art hanging. It reminded her a bit of her dorm room in Melbourne. However, the beach more than made up for any shortcomings.

She perused her new home and compared it to her garage apartment in Florida. This was much better; it felt homey. She knew she'd be happy living here; she already loved it.

The sailors left; their job was done. The two escorting officers remained.

She was anxious and excited as she went up to her room. She put on her swimsuit bottoms and one of Virginia's T-shirts.

GP, since they already know about me, do I need my monofin?

Cliff and the other Admirals know about y'all, but those officers don't. So yes, y'all need your monofin.

She tossed her monofin over her shoulder and went downstairs. She walked into the room with the three men. "Would it be all right if I went for a swim?"

Cliff made another grand sweeping gesture. "It's now your home, too, so yes, you can go to the beach anytime. Also, we've contacted Mother Hen and the Institute about your new living arrangement."

The three men watched her run into the ocean and disappear. All three went out to the beach to see where she'd gone, but she was nowhere to be seen. Commander Barnes asked Admiral Yokum if they should go look for her. "She doesn't have a mask or snorkel. She might be in trouble."

"From the briefings I've had on this young lady, she could swim to Hawaii and back and never be in trouble. I don't think she's in trouble now. If you want to wait awhile, you're more than welcome. We can go up to the balcony and watch for her.

"Two other things from the reports: While she was in Florida, she was approached by a young man from a tabloid journal. When he tried to manhandle her, she slapped him. That slap resulted in three teeth being knocked out and a broken jaw. She also broke both of the young man's collarbones.

"The other happened while she was still in Australia. Some large inebriated fellow in a bar in Melbourne grabbed our little Miss Breath. The next thing that man knew; he was waking up on the other side of the room. So, I'd say you'd better treat her with respect. She's much faster and stronger than she looks."

***

GP projected, *Breath, I want y'all to start doing a new series of exercises.*

Oh, GP, do I have to? I just got here. I just got wet.

This won't be that kind of exercise. Y'all can do this while you're in the water, swimming. You've been able to swim with your Aqume for quite some time now without even having to think about it. I want y'all to learn how to manipulate the minerals in the water to make things y'all might need. I'd like for y'all to start making talons for your fingertips similar to the claws on your gloves, only these talons will be made of silicon carbide extracted from ocean water. Y'all can get silicon from sand and carbon from plants, plankton, and dead animals, or all of it from the water, like the Mer get the gold for their bodies from the ocean water.

This sounds very complicated, GP.

It's not nearly as complicated as it sounds. However, rather than working with large items, you're gonna be working with microscopic things and molecules.

I know we do a lot of fun things, but we also do a lot of training. What's this all about? You're always so evasive, it's always push, push, push, train, train, train!

I want y'all to be ready when the great opportunity comes along.

What opportunity would that be?

A glorious wonderful one. Now, this is what I want y'all to do... GP gave Breath a detailed explanation of what he wanted her to learn and how to go about it.

***

The three men watched and waited for Breath for about three hours. Then Captain Stein pointed. "There she is! She just walked up out of the water. How in the world did she do that? I've been watching with the binoculars. And I haven't seen a head pop up, anyone swimming — nothing. She wasn't there one moment; the next she was. And she's dry, hair and all! What's going on here, Admiral? I don't think you're telling us everything, Cliff. Like why'd Admiral Winscott assign us this job when a seaman could do it?"

"Yeah, that drying-off thing was also in the briefing. As to why you were assigned this job — well one you're my friends, and two you'll find that this young lady is different. You'll find out in time. Part of your job will be to see that she's... well, not messed with. Pay close attention and observe. That's all I can say."

Both officers glanced at each other and then back to Admiral Yokum. They both replied in unison, "We understand, Admiral."

Breath walked into the living room and picked up a bottle of water she'd left on the small table by the door. She downed about half of it. The three men came down and joined her.

Cliff asked her. "Did you enjoy your swim?"

"Yes, it's great out there. The ocean floor goes out in some places a mile or so, and then it drops off kind of sudden. I'm going to have to explore that. This is going to be fun. There are dolphins, humpbacks, and seals out there, all friendly. There are more great whites than I'm accustomed to, and you know how grumpy they can get, but I'll get used to it." She continued for some time describing in detail the ocean floor and its flora and fauna. "And there are some beautiful kelp gardens and seaweed. I could gather some and make a wonderful salad."

The three men listened to her excited, animated, and sometimes matter-of-fact description of the ocean bottom and wildlife that only local divers, with expert training could talk about. The three men were watching her during her vigorous passionate description, and were grinning as they tried to stifle their amazement. They'd never encountered anyone quite like Breath!

***

The next morning, a little before 6:00 a.m., Breath was sneaking into the kitchen so as not to awaken the Admiral. She was surprised to see he was already up, had coffee brewing, and was bent over looking in the large freezer/refrigerator. Breath wondered why he needed such a large refrigerator for just him. She had looked into the refrigerator yesterday afternoon and noticed how vacant it was.

The refrigerator was next to a set of floor-to-ceiling cabinets, on its left side. The refrigerator and cabinets were on the outside wall and against the wall between the kitchen and the garage and underneath her bedroom. On the other side of the refrigerator was a counter with a large sink centered in it with cabinets underneath. Next to that was the stove and oven combo. Above the counter, sink, and stove were overhead cabinets. Opposite that was another long counter with underneath cabinets at the same height as the first one and behind that and into the other room was a high bar counter and barstools. Then there was the breakfast and dining nook beyond the bar, which was part of the downstairs great room.

"Morning, gorgeous. The coffee is on and will be ready in a few minutes. I was just looking for something to make for breakfast. It looks like I'm almost out of everything. Guess I'm going to have to go to the grocery store and pick up a few things. Right now, we've got three eggs, a couple slices of bologna, and a couple sodas. There's some bean dip in here, but we're out of chips. I've got some butter but no bread to put it on. On top of that, I'm almost out of pancake mix. Not near enough to make ourselves a stack. I'm embarrassed for not planning better.

"There's a little hole-in-the-wall restaurant not too far from here that serves a great breakfast. How about it? My treat." He closed the refrigerator door and looked at Breath over the top of his glasses.

Breath was standing there in her bathing suit bottoms and T-shirt. She had two medium-size spiny lobsters wriggling in her hand. "Good morning, Admiral. I was going to surprise you with breakfast. I just caught these two trying to sneak into the kitchen. Perhaps we should invite them in? Do you have a big pot and plenty of water?" She was trying her best to put on a relaxed and congenial manner. She wasn't sure if she was pulling it off.

Cliff looked at the lobsters and noticed that Breath's fingernails were claws and black or dark blue. "Wow, lobster for breakfast. I could get used to that. Of course, in about six months, I'd weigh five hundred pounds. You say these two were trying to break 'into' the kitchen? Now I know what all that scratching has been in the mornings over the last week or so." He was saying all this, while he was digging under the counter for a large pot. He filled the pot and set it on the stove. He also got a small saucepan and put a stick of butter in it.

She put the lobsters in the sink. "I just love your house, Admiral. It's too bad though, that you can't be closer to the beach." She smiled and made a little nervous giggle.

"Breath, please call me Cliff. We're going to be living here together for a while, and I don't want things to be so formal. It'll take us a while to work out our routines around each other. So, let's be as comfortable and as casual as we can."

"Thank you, Cliff. I'll admit, I'm nervous. I've never lived with a man in my life. My parents split up when I was just a baby. I had a boyfriend for about two months that Hipsi set me up with, but we didn't live together, and he broke my heart. Too young, I guess. This is a first for me, and I'm not well versed in the etiquette. I want us to be friends; I've hardly ever had any. People always seem to think I'm some kind of freak. I know that I'm different, and I hope that doesn't come between us.

"The only real friends I've ever had was an aboriginal girl named Alinta Mitchel in high school, the Walka family in the Florida Keys, and two friends I met at the University of Miami, Hipsi and Kristin Iversen. I went on some blind dates that Hipsi set me up with, but I wouldn't call them friends." A tear started down Breath's cheek. It was gone with a quick swipe. "I lost track of Alinta after she moved to Karratha, and I would like to see her again one day. I hope you can meet Hipsi and Kristin sometime, and I'm rambling. I'm sorry!"

"Breath, we'll work it out. I know sometimes I can be a grumpy old man. But if I do, you call me on it. My late wife would never let me get away with anything. She made me toe the line, and I expect you to do the same. She'd have loved you. I just wish she could've met you."

Breath excused herself; ran upstairs looking forward to going grocery shopping. She took a quick shower and put on some nice loose jeans and a floppy polo shirt, all lined with seaweed and sprayed with her mum's new concoction to eliminate the smell. When she came down, the water was boiling. She reached into the sink and picked up the two lobsters. She became still for a moment and a light formed around her hands and the lobsters.

The two lobsters became limp and stopped moving. Then she placed them in the boiling water.

Cliff was shocked and tried to look as if nothing had happened. She began helping Cliff set the table for breakfast. He noticed that her fingernails were no longer claws and were normal in color and shape and had a jewellike sheen.

Breakfast was wonderful. Grocery shopping later was even better. Breath was pleased that Cliff had a manner about him that put people, especially her, at ease. Life was good.

***

Breath fell into a routine at Scripps with her studies, her internship, and her postdoc work. She was in the water every free second. She'd become a 'California Beach Babe.'

One afternoon when Breath was walking back from the institute, she noticed a familiar car parked out front. She dashed inside. It was her friends Hipsi and Kristin. There were hugs all around, and squeals of delight. Kristin danced around the room when she wasn't hugging Breath.

Breath introduced her friends to the Admiral. He then excused himself and left.

Hipsi said. "We moved here to California a short time ago, and I've got this new job. We have been so busy with this new movie that we have had no time to do anything. The director got sick and gave us all a few days off. I called a couple times, but you never answered, so we thought we would surprise you."

"I'm so glad you did. I've been missing and thinking about you two as well, but I've been so busy that I haven't had a chance to get back with you. So, tell me what's been happening."

Kristin threw her head back and tossed her hair over her left shoulder. "'I' am in the movie. It is not a big part, but I get to say a few lines." She raised her chin to the right and flipped her hair over her other shoulder. "It will be my springboard to fame and fortune."

All three laughed and started talking at once. Breath talked about her work and studies at the institute, and Kristin and Hipsi talked about their work on the movie.

Hipsi and Kristin gathered Breath up, and they went shopping. It was rare for Breath to go shopping, and then just for essentials. Hipsi and Kristin knew this and knew that Breath needed a wardrobe and makeup upgrade.

Kristin picked up Breath's hand and started looking at her fingernails. "Why do your fingernails come to such a sharp point?" She dug in her purse for a nail file and started trying to dull the sharp points. Nothing happened; the nail file wasn't up to the job. "What's going on here, Breath? I've never seen any nail polish this hard. I can't even touch it with this file."

Breath pulled her hand back. "Oh, that's just a little experiment a friend of mine wants me to try."

The three friends tried on Breath's new acquisitions in various combinations and had about as much fun as three young women can have. They even inflicted their wardrobe and makeup acquisitions upon Cliff, who turned out to be a good sport.

Cliff had been preparing flounder with all the trimmings for himself and the girls. A little bit before he called them down, Hipsi and Kristin nodded to each other and became quite serious.

Hipsi began. "We know that there is more about you than you have told us. We followed you one time, trying to catch you in Coral Gables, when you walked under a bridge and became a mermaid. We both saw you."

"Oh — you saw that?"

"We also have these videos of you and your father in Vancouver on two separate occasions. You talked to the wild dolphins and whales. We know it was you because of your hair, body shape, and the tail. Also, while we were in Florida, we noticed people and some kind of little flying thing following you everywhere you went. Would you care to explain?"

GP gave Breath a cautionary warning. Breath was ready to spill the beans but thought better of it.

"Hipsi, Kristin, I'd love to tell you, but I can't right now. I promise when I can, I'll tell you everything. I'll tell you this, there's more to the story, but for now, you can't tell anyone. Please, keep this to yourselves. It's much safer this way. Right now, the U.S. Navy and I are on friendly terms, and I'd like to keep it that way. I'll say that I'm different, and my life is... well — complicated. I also don't want anyone else to learn any more about the situation than they already do. I hope you understand."

Hipsi hugged her friend. "We do, Breath, and they will not learn anything from us."

Breath felt relieved. "I can always trust you. I miss you so much. We have to stay in touch better than we have. We've gotta get together more often. I'm so glad we're all in California now. But just remember..." Breath put her right index finger to her lips.

***

Cliff was in the living room, watching television and putting together a jigsaw puzzle. When Breath came in from the beach. "Oh, I like jigsaw puzzles. Do you mind if I help?"

"Sure. The more the merrier."

As they were assembling the puzzle, Cliff began to notice that each time Breath picked up a puzzle piece, her fingernails, which hadn't yet returned to normal, scratched the glass top on the coffee table.

18. SUB

Once a month, Admiral Yokum has several of his friends over for poker night. On these nights, Breath would excuse herself and take in a movie. This was her sixth movie, and she found herself becoming somewhat bored with them. At first, they'd sparked her imagination. But with GP's guidance, and her ability to project her consciousness, she far exceeded anything she could see in a dark room filled with hundreds of people. She did find romance movies interesting and even educational. They gave her ideas for the future — just in case.

When Breath returned that evening, the boys' night in was still in full swing. They were all setting around the dining table in the kitchen nook. The breakfast bar between the dining table in the kitchen proper, was the depository for a number of cell phones, several sets of keys, a bottle of scotch, and some shot glasses.

It was also a celebration because Captain Victor Russell had been promoted to Rear Admiral. The other flag-rank officer in the room was Vice Admiral Archie Winscott. As Breath glided into the room, both Admirals stopped what they were doing and paid close attention to her. The new Rear Admiral had just been briefed about Admiral Yokum's houseguest. Navy Captain Stein and Commander Barnes remained quiet and just watched.

Breath set her purse on the bar counter, and was going into the kitchen when the room shook. Dishes rattled, the sliding glass doors going out to the patio also rattled. She could feel the shaking in her feet, but it wasn't near enough to make her lose her balance. She did however, grab the kitchen counter. She exclaimed. "Oh, my goodness! What was that?"

Winscott leaned back in a nonchalant manner. "Oh — I'd say maybe a four point five. Could be a four point eight on the Richter scale. What would you guess Cliff?"

"Yeah, I'd say you're pretty close; nothing over that, though." He continued to deal the cards.

Breath exclaimed. "You mean that was an earthquake!"

Cliff looked at her over the top of his glasses. "Yeah, we get them all the time; nothing to worry about. It's when things start falling off the shelves and kitchen drawers start flying open that we get concerned. That was just a little tweaker."

Breath wasn't convinced. She looked around the room, checking to see if everything was okay. "Sooo — nothing to worry about — rrriiight?"

Cliff was still looking at her over the top of his glasses. "That's right, Breath. It's nothing to worry about, at least not something of that magnitude."

Breath was still glancing around the room. "Ooookaay!"

Breath was in the kitchen when a cell phone vibrated, lying on the breakfast counter. Breath answered it. The person on the other end asked for Commander Barnes. She looked out into the dining area where the men were playing. "Commander Barnes, it's for you."

Barnes got up to take the phone.

When he returned from the kitchen, his face was ashen. "Gentlemen, we've had an incident. That drug-running submarine we were doing a practice raise has just shifted and trapped two of my divers. This was supposed to be a safe training dive. We've used that submarine for training exercises for the last two years. It just turned serious. Please excuse me Gentlemen and Ma'am."

Admiral Winscott asked, "Commander, is there anything we could do to help?"

"I don't know what you can do, but you're more than welcome to observe."

Breath asked, "Is there anything I can do to help?"

The five men looked at one another for a moment. Then Cliff motioned to the other two Admirals to join him in the kitchen.

Archie asked. "Cliff, what's this all about? She's a civilian, not even American. What can she do?"

"We've all been briefed about her, and we'll never seen a better diver on this planet. Some of the things that I've seen her do right here are beyond belief, so I'd say let her come. She may be able to help. She certainly can't hurt anything!"

Cliff and the new Admiral returned from the kitchen. Cliff looked at Breath and nodded. The Vice Admiral remained in the kitchen and made a quick phone call.

"Great! I'll just grab my purse."

They left in two cars, traveling as fast as traffic would allow to the base, where a hard-bottom inflatable transfer skiff was waiting. When they got aboard the dive ship, Commander Barnes and his party were briefed on the situation.

Barnes asked Admiral Winscott. "Why are they putting up all the hi-res cameras?"

"Just go with it. Consider it more training."

Barnes nodded to the briefing officer to continue. "This was supposed to be a training mission. A drug runner's submarine had sunk several years ago in about three hundred feet of water. This training mission was to get inside, retrieve the log if it had one, or take pictures if they couldn't find the log. The second part of that mission was to attach lines to the submarine and lift it. Then everything was to be put back like it was, so we can do it all over again.

"Two hardhat divers, Chief Petty Officer Farnsworth and Diver Second Class Hastings, had gone down to get the log.

While they were inside the submarine, it shifted and rolled over, trapping the two men inside."

Barnes looked at the dive master. "Earthquake?" The dive master nodded his head.

The tension on deck was thick. A second team of divers was on its way down to render aid.

Farnsworth's report was grim. "Our lines are crushed. They are trapped under the submarine. We're not getting enough air. Hastings's communication line has been severed. There's no air coming through Hastings's line. He's passed out. I'm sharing my air line with him, but he's not coming around."

There was indecision as to how to get the men out of the submarine. The earthquake shift had allowed the submarine to roll over and block any way out for the divers. The sub didn't have a conning tower. The decision was to send divers to tunnel under the submarine to the access port. Or they could take cutting torches and cut an access hole through the hull. This was all they could do at present. Since, the crane barge to lift the submarine hadn't arrived yet. At that moment, two divers were descending to make an inspection and a decision. Whatever they did was going to take a long time.

GP, those two men down there are in serious trouble, perhaps dying. Can't you do something, please?

Breath, I know Hastings's air is running out. He doesn't have enough time to be rescued by the other divers. And Farnsworth isn't much better off. If the submarine shifts even a little bit more, he'll die as well.

I'll not let those men die.

Then, Breath, y'all know what to do. So just do it!

Breath went to the head. She changed into a two-piece bathing suit she always carried in her purse. When she returned on deck, she received some strange and serious looks.

Captain Stein stopped her. "Miss, I don't think you quite understand the gravity of the situation here. This isn't a pleasure cruise. Please, step aside. We've got people to handle this."

Breath ignored the Captain. She walked over to Cliff. She handed him her purse and clothes. "Sir, if I don't do something now, Hastings is going to die for sure. I know the situation down there. There's nothing those two other divers can do." Before anyone else could stop her, she walked over to the side of the ship and jumped into the inky, cold, dark sea.

A cartoonish-sounding voice came over the dive intercom. "Commander, you're not going to believe this, but there's a mermaid down here with us. She just waved at us."

Barnes leaned over and said into the dive intercom. "You guys must be getting the bends. There aren't any such things as mermaids. You men are seeing things! Get your mind on your jobs, and let's save these men!" He turned from the intercom to another petty officer. "Check those divers' triox mixture. There may be an imbalance in their lines."

"Commander, she just picked up the entire submarine and rolled it over, exposing the hatch. One of the lines is cut and bleeding air. It looks like the other line is crushed as well, and the heavy steel hatch is bent and stuck. She's having some trouble with it. As she tries to force it open the whole submarine moves. As soon as we get down, we'll help her with that hatch.

"She just squeezed through the partially open hatch and went inside."

Commander Barnes turned to the dive master. "Get another two lines ready to send down for Farnsworth and Hastings."

"Commander, she's just squeezed out through the hatch and went over to where we think Farnsworth and Hastings are inside the sub. She ripped a hole in the hull and peeled it open like it was a can of soda."

The cartoonish voice came back on the intercom. "Commander, she's got Hastings, and she's coming up. She's got a bubble of air around him."

Breath, y'all cut your back coming through that hole y'all made. Are ya okay? Can ya make it?

Yes, GP. It hurts bad, but I'm not stopping. I can check it on the surface.

About a minute later, everyone was hanging over the side of the ship to see the mermaid bring Hastings up. Breath and Hastings burst out of the water and landed on the fantail of the ship a good fifteen feet above the water line.

Breath called out in an irresistible, commanding voice, "Get the suit off him. He's not breathing. He hasn't had air for several minutes. Revive him and get him into the decompression chamber." Everyone just stared. She raised her voice. "Now, Gentlemen!"

People started scrambling.

Several corpsmen and Rear Admiral Russell were compelled to remove the suit and give Hastings respiration and oxygen. Captain Stein watched, frozen with his mouth agape.

Breath hadn't had time to get rid of her Aqume. She was covered with glistening red-tinted blue water in the shape of a mermaid. Everyone else aboard just stared. She then remembered to release her Aqume. A few seconds later, water flowed all over the deck from her. She was dazed.

Cliff ran over to her. "Are you okay? That was over three hundred feet, and you were down for a long time."

Breath stood up and looked at him. "I'm okay, Cliff. I'm dizzy. That took a lot out of me. I just to need sit down a minute." Breath thought. *I can make it through this. I've been through worse.*

Cliff stared at her for several seconds.

"Is there something wrong, Cliff?"

"You were a mermaid — or at least you looked like a mermaid. What was that tail thing just a moment ago? And what are those?" He was pointing at her hands.

Breath gave him a pained look, and in a coy, strained, and offhanded manner, she replied. "Oh, that was my Aqume. And I open cans with these."

"Your what... cans?"

She started to stand up. "I'll tell you later, but I've got to get back to Farnsworth."

A corpsman was looking at her back and touched her with something cold. She didn't mind the cold, but the stinging sensation hurt. She turned so quickly, she knocked whatever the corpsman was holding out of his hand as she tried to remain standing.

"What are you doing? That stings."

"But, ma'am, you're cut. And pretty bad too. You're bleeding."

Breath looked down at herself and felt blood running down the back of her leg. Her top was gone, and her swimsuit bottoms were in threads.

Vice Admiral Winscott was standing close by and helped Breath remain on her feet. "Miss your injured and losing a lot of blood."

She grabbed Cliff's arm to steady herself as she rocked back and forth and almost fell. "I don't have time for this. Farnsworth is still down there and in serious trouble."

She released Cliff's arm and walked, struggling, and unsteady over to the dive master, who she thought might be in charge of the dive training. Cliff was trying to stop her since she was bleeding badly. She grabbed the man's arm to help balance herself. He started to pull away from the sharp pain but couldn't. He looked down and saw the claws and blood beginning to darken his sleeve.

Breath's voice was strained. "Do you have another line? Farnsworth needs it. His line is trapped, and he's not getting sufficient air. I'll take it down to him, and you can bring all the divers up, so they can decompress."

The man gave immediate orders for another line. Breath took it and dove back into the water under the protests of Cliff, Admiral Winscott, and the corpsman, who then went to the dive master to attend to the wounds Breath had left on his arm.

The cartoonish voice came back over the intercom. "Did she get Hastings to safety? We're at the sub but we're having trouble getting in. Farnsworth is having trouble."

The Commander replied again into the dive intercom. "Yes, Hastings is going to be okay. She's on her way back down now with another line."

The strange intercom voice came back. "Here she is with the line. She's going into the sub now." There was a pause of several minutes. "She's coming out now with Farnsworth. She's motioning us to help Farnsworth to the lift cage. We've got him, and his lines look good and he's coming around. Commander, she doesn't look good. She's going up, and she's in trouble."

GP, help me. Breath returned to the surface. This time, she didn't burst out of the water. She floated to the surface face down.

Four divers were immediately in the water. She was put in a lift basket and lifted to the ship's deck. She was still bleeding. Two corpsmen started working on her. They were having trouble getting through her gelatin encasement. Breath still dazed, realized what she needed to do. All semblance of her bloody mermaid tail and arm flippers washed away.

She was disoriented and dizzy, but she thought she'd be okay.

Breath, I'm giving y'all a strong embrace, and I'm flowing healing energies into ya. It may take a while, 'cause y'all lost a lot of blood. More than you lost in the Miami incident. But you're gonna be just fine. Let the Navy Corpsmen do their thing.

Tell my father he doesn't need to come to San Diego.

Only if y'all don't go into a coma. Breath, I don't like seeing y'all get hurt. You've got to remember to hold your protection shield about yourself. Your Aqume isn't a shield.

The ship's doctor and the corpsmen finally stanched the bleeding.

She smiled but protested. "Please — I don't need all this attention. I — can heal just fine on my own."

Much to her chagrin, her protests landed on deaf ears. The Admirals insisted that she be taken to the base hospital and examined to make sure she was in perfect health.

"I don't nee..." as she fainted.

***

The doctor was talking to the Admirals. "Sirs, she's lost a lot of blood, but..."

Cliff interrupted. "Then give her blood!"

"But sir, there's a problem. We can't figure out what her blood type is. We've done every test we can think of, but she doesn't have a normal blood type. We don't dare give her whole blood if we don't know what her type is. We're giving her plasma and saline to bring her volume up. If she makes it through the night, she'll probably be okay."

That night Cliff, Barnes, and the Admirals and later Hastings, and Farnsworth, after their decompression, stood watch over Breath. She was delirious and began talking. Some of the words were in English, but then she started making dolphin and orca sounds. She seemed to be carrying on a conversation with someone, some dolphins, and an orca.

The two divers looked at Cliff and the Commander. They all looked back at Breath in amazement. Cliff made sure the door was closed so no one else could hear.

The Commander and the two divers looked at Cliff. The Commander leaned close to Cliff. "Admiral, you know her better than anyone. Did she just do and say what I think she did?"

Cliff looked just as amazed as the others. "You saw her on the ship, tail and all. Look at those — talons. Those aren't ordinary fingernails. She ripped the steel hull of that submarine open with those things. Who knows what's possible with her?"

Two days later, her talons were gone. After the doctors had taken just about every test they could think of, they were amazed that she had healed so quick. Breath was allowed to go home. Cliff was there with three other Admirals, along with Commander Barnes and Captain Stein from the poker game. She went home with a full Navy escort.

Breath, you're healing just fine, but it's gonna take a while for your physical body to fully recover.

Thanks, GP.

Should I fuss now or later?

Later please, oh and thanks GP.

For what?

For being there. I just wanted to let you know.

I love y'all too Breath.

From that moment on, Breath could do no wrong, according to the U.S. Navy. They didn't care who or what she was. And what she was — was hungry. Anyone standing close could hear the grumbling.

***

The word got out to the fleet Admirals that Breath Of Spring and her immediate family existed, were off limits, and were protected by the U.S. Navy.

It took the Navy less than a day to put tight ground, air, and personal around-the-clock surveillance and security on Breath Of Spring. It took another week to work out all the kinks with the OAI.

Using the Qrie fields, Breath could sense the surveillance the Navy had put on her. She noticed that they were discreet, and most of the agents tried to stay well out of sight. Even the vehicles were close to invisible and as unobtrusive as possible. But there were always one or two that were easily spotted. She assumed that these people were there as a reminder for her assurance. She was comforted by the Navy's presence, but was weak and a little worried, since she had never lost so much blood before.

***

At home in the beach house, Breath had plenty of time to spend with Cliff. They spent many hours talking and just getting to know one another better. Breath, a couple days after the submarine incident, brought up in quiet conversation, what she thought might be a touchy subject.

"Cliff, I can detect people who have errant mental characteristics, such as psychopaths, sociopaths, narcissists, egomaniacs, power mongers, to name just a few, but since I have been around your military, primarily the Navy and the

Coast Guard, I have not sensed any of these types of individuals. Is it possible that you could enlighten me?"

"Well Breath, a few years ago the government of the United States started a similar program that is used in Switzerland and Israel, where all young people out of high school must do government duty either in the military or some other government service. The instability of some governments and the constant threat of terrorism brought this on. Over the years we have seen people with the aforementioned mental deficiencies that have caused considerable problems for the military. All personnel entering boot camp or officers training school, after college graduation, are given an extensive psychological evaluation, with a thorough in-depth training in reality and critical thinking. The military then weeds out all those individuals with the various mental aberrations and deficiencies. We have found that by doing this the overall capability of the military is improved. Everyone on active military duty has been thoroughly, psychologically, and critically vetted.

"I might also add, that all government positions and appointments must now come from former active duty military personnel, or go through the full vetting process. As it turns out, the former psychological vetted military personnel are also used by most states in their hiring. Large corporations are also hiring from these vetted persons.

"We knew when we did this vetting process that about ten percent of the population would not be fit for the military or the government agencies, and it was overall an excellent decision."

"What happens to the people who fail the vetting process?"

"They are watched and given as much psychological support and help as possible. Many do quite well, however, most can still have considerable problems."

19. REGGIE

A couple weeks out of the hospital, and after convalescing at Cliff's beach house. Breath was feeling much better and was walking home from the institute, late in the afternoon. She sensed a young Navy Ensign following her again.

Those blazing green eyes and light brown hair set off by that strong jaw makes me quiver. His muscular well-toned body doesn't hurt the combination at all. Oh my! He can put me at ease anytime with that marvelous relaxing smile. He's a few inches taller than me which is just great because I can cuddle my head on his neck and shoulder. She immediately recoiled at these errant thoughts. *What the heck am I thinking.*

Oh, what the heck, why not? She slowed a bit and placed a more concentrated telepathic sensing field on the young Ensign. She slowed and turned her head, he stopped and turned away from her, darting behind a convenient concrete-and-glass wall. She extended her senses towards him still stronger.

Pleased by the results of her scan. *He is nervous but harmless, which is quite endearing. I haven't sensed an inviting, comfortable individual like this since being with Mum. He is human not Qrie, but he is still more compassionate, caring, and loving than normal humans.* She chuckled; *he is trying quite hard to stay inconspicuous.*

A warm comfortable loving feeling passed through her body all the way to her toes. *Maybe, just maybe? Why not? GP, what do you think? Should I go for it?*

She sensed GP's elation. *By all means, Breath. This is a big step for y'all. I've been waiting for this moment for a long time. I have a good feeling about this young man.*

Me too, GP. But I'm still a little uncertain.

Well, Breath, it's just like swimming. Take a deep breath and dive in.

She stopped, turned around, and glided back towards the Ensign so fast that he didn't have time to react, all the while maintaining her telepathic link with him. He just as fast started trying to find a doorway into which he could dart. There was none; he was surrounded by glass walls and concrete. Trapped!

She listened to his thoughts. *I'm going to blow this duty assignment. This is my first job out of officers training. She's going to see me. What the hell am I going to do? There's simply no place to hide. Should I make a run for it? Oh My God, she's here!*

Breath hooked her right hand around his left elbow. She smiled sweetly and batted her eyelashes at him. "Guess what? You sir, are going to escort me home, since we're going to the same place. I'm Breath Of Spring. What's your name?"

With her telepathic link she could hear his thoughts, his elation, his discomfort, sense his elevated heartbeat, and his history. *I'll let him tell me his history when we know one another better.* She thought.

The Ensign's mind raced. *I've been briefed about her being a person of interest by the security supervisor. I know she is someone unusual because the U.S. Navy doesn't follow just anyone. Okay, okay calm down — I've got to keep my wits and find a way out of this.* He could find none. He was still trapped!

She projected a strong *Qrie Embrace* into him to calm his nerves.

He staggered. *Oh man, what the heck was that? Am I going to pass out? Maybe it's because she surprised me. They didn't tell me about that, and why not? She's here with her hand around my elbow. I guess there's nothing for me to do except play along. That is, if I can stay upright.*

"My — my name is Regi... uh... Reginald, um... Kotak, but everyone just calls me Reg or Reggie."

Gesturing to his Navy uniform. "Well Reggie, I hope I'm not breaking any rules by having you walk with me. Please calm down. I'm not going to bite."

"Uh... no, Ma'am... don't bite uh — Or rather I — uh don't think walking with you — will break uh— any rules." He took a deep breath and calmed himself. "Besides, I would rather walk with you than follow you."

"Well, Reggie let me say something about that. If you want to remain inconspicuous, I suggest you shouldn't wear your uniform. You kinda stick out like a sore thumb. Even here in this Navy town."

"Well, Miss, I guess I should take your advice next time."

They both laughed. His laugh was a bit shaky.

As they walked and talked, Reggie began to relax and become more congenial. However, when they reached the beach house, he stopped at the sidewalk and was reluctant to enter.

"What's the matter, Reggie? Don't you want to come in?"

"Well, Ma'am, I'm just supposed to follow you till you get home and then follow you if you come back out."

"Reggie, I told you my name is Breath, not Ma'am, Miss, or Miss Spring, and I'm asking you to come in with me, please."

An apprehensive Reggie followed her into the house.

When they came in, Cliff was in his recliner reading the newspaper. "Hi, Cliff. This is Mister Reginald Kotak, and he and I are going to take a walk on the beach. Could you please lend him some proper beach-walking togs — um clothes? We wouldn't want to get his nice Navy uniform all sandy. We might want to sit and watch the waves a while or take a swim."

Cliff turned and smiled at Breath. Then he looked at the Ensign, still smiling, but cocked an eyebrow. Reggie became stiff with a look of apprehension when he realized who Cliff was. He had seen Cliff's picture on Admiral Winscott's office wall. "Yes, Breath, I think we can find something for... 'Mister' Kotak."

"Super. Thanks Cliff. I'll run upstairs and get changed."

When she reached the bottom of the stairs, she turned and looked back at Reggie. He had the look and a mental plead. *Please don't leave me here alone with Admiral Yokum.*

When she came back downstairs, in one of Virginia's T-shirts and a seaweed-lined bathing suit bottom, she saw Reggie in one of Cliff's swimsuits. Reggie was standing stiff and formal while listening to what Cliff was saying. He relaxed a bit when he saw Breath.

"Nice choice, Cliff. Are you ready to go Reggie? The ocean is waiting."

She grabbed Reggie's hand and bounced towards the door with excitement. Reggie became wobbly and weak in the knees.

Cliff chuckled and mumbled. "I know precisely what happened when Breath grabbed his hand." *That same feeling passes through me whenever she touches me. I'm not worried about her at all. The one I'm worried about is Ensign Kotak. I hope he can make it through this.* He watched as the pair disappeared towards the ocean. He chuckled, turned, picked up the phone, and called his good friend Vice Admiral Archie Winscott.

Breath and Reggie came back to the beach house hand in hand a little before dark. Cliff met them at the door. "I figured you kids would be back about now. I have dinner cooked and ready. The plates are on the counter, so help yourself!"

Everyone sat down at the dining table. Reggie was still stiff and uncomfortable. Cliff smiled and winked at Breath then he opened the conversation. "Dig in, everyone. How'd your walk on the beach go?"

"Oh Cliff, we had a wonderful time. We ran and played in the surf, and I hit Reggie with a sand ball, but he never hit me." She looked at Reggie and could see that he was a bit embarrassed. She took a deep breath and calmed herself down. She never felt this way before, about a young man and was still a bit unsure. "Then we just laid on the beach and talked."

"That's great. I'm glad you two had fun. Are you going to do it again?"

"Yes." Breath looked down at her plate. Then looked up at Reggie. "If you want to do it again."

Reggie glanced at Cliff, who smiled and nodded approval. He looked back at Breath and grinned. "Yes, I would like that."

After they got seconds and had finished eating, Breath offered to do the dishes. Cliff complained that she should entertain her guest. Breath didn't take the hint as she cleared the table.

Cliff and Reggie went into the living room and sat down. When Breath finished the dishes, she came out and noticed Reggie was much more relaxed around Cliff. Upon seeing that Reggie had changed back into his uniform, Breath excused herself to go change. She came down dressed in one of her nicest muumuu dresses and sat down in Cliff's easy chair across from the couch where Reggie and Cliff were seated.

Cliff watched Breath as she started what seemed to be an innocent conversation. He surmised, from his OAI briefings, that she was probing Reggie's mind for information. Reggie, while oblivious to what Breath was doing, began to relax and enjoy the conversation.

"I grew up in Kansas, and I loved to swim. Still do. I loved to go snorkel diving, and later scuba diving, in the lakes around where I lived. I helped the sheriff one time retrieve a car that had run into and gone down in a nearby lake. I'm doing Navy dive training here on assignment with Commander Barnes..."

Breath through her telepathic probe saw Reggie's memory of him standing before Commander Barnes desk. Reggie saw a photograph of Breath lying there and asked the Commander, who she was. The Commander then said, "She is someone we have been tasked to follow and I am looking for volunteers."

Reggie blurted. "I'll follow her anywhere." The Commander replied, "Good, you just got an assignment over and above your diving training." Reggie was surprised but grinned as big as a Cheshire cat.

Cliff chuckled at Breath's silent reaction and he reminded himself to ask Breath what she had discovered that made her blush and glance at Reggie.

Cliff excused himself and stood up, saying he had things to do in his office. The conversation between Reggie and Breath turned a bit more... private.

Reggie, a little later, looked at his watch. "Excuse me, Breath. I'm sorry, but I've got to get back and report in. It's been an excellent day, and I hope we can do it again."

"Yes, Reggie, it has been an 'excellent' day. I enjoyed it a lot, and we will do it again. When are you going to be on duty? Watching me again, that is."

"I am scheduled to this duty — or your duty — or this duty rotation all this week."

A line of red was rising up Reggie's collar. She smiled. She took his hand and escorted him to the door. They walked outside towards the street. "Would you like for me to walk with you to your car?"

"No, Breath. It's parked at the institute. I'll see you tomorrow."

"That's great Reggie. I'm looking forward to it." Breath stepped much closer to him than he found comfortable and stood quietly while opening a telepathic link between them and looked up at him with a sweet smile. His expression of indecision was more like someone being led to his own execution. She put a mild field of love and compassion around them both then stepped even closer, almost touching, and remained standing quietly. He got the hint and put his arms around her. When they kissed, she gave him a powerful *Qrie Embrace*. She had to hold him up to keep him from falling. They stood together like this for — well, a while.

His only thought was, *Oh My goodness, this is wonderful!*

Breath, I AM so proud of ya. Y'all have finally learned to truly love yourself, and in so doing you're now capable of allowing and being loved by someone else. This is a great step. This very act of loving yourself will multiply your Qrie power and your capabilities many times.

Thanks GP, I do feel something different. It's almost as if the universe were lifting me up, like I AM ascending to some higher level.

That's true Breath. Y'all now have the power to ascend higher than you could ever imagine.

***

Early the next morning, Commander Barnes and Ensign Kotak were standing in Admiral Winscott's office. "Ensign Kotak, would you care to explain to me and Commander Barnes here exactly what was going on yesterday?"

"Well, Sir... you see... uh, I was following Miss Spring — when she suddenly turned around and walked straight back to me. I had no place to go. She hooked her hand around my elbow — and told me I was going to escort her home. After I escorted her home, she wanted me to go inside. Inside, I met Rear Admiral Clifford Yokum. I didn't realize she lived — with him. The Admiral was surprised to see me. She insisted that we take a walk on the beach in bathing suits. Admiral Yokum loaned me a bathing suit, and Miss Spring and I took a walk on the beach. We — walked — um — played in the surf, and sat on the sand — and talked. Then we came back to Admiral Yokum's beach house. He'd cooked dinner, and we ate; then we sat and talked some more. I then left and came back to make the day's report."

"All the time that you were with her, did she do anything unusual, like swimming fast, and such?"

"Well, sir, she's a very fast swimmer. Faster than I am, and I'm as fast or faster than anyone else I know."

"And you're sure this is all that happened? Nothing else unusual?"

"Well, sir — there were incidents that I can't explain. When she touched me with her hand, I got some kind of energy flow throughout my body. It made me feel light and really good. The other was when I kissed her goodbye..."

"You what? You kissed this woman? What were you thinking?"

"Sir, yes, Sir. I didn't know what else to do. I was leaving the beach house. We walked outside. She asked if I wanted her to walk me to my car. I said no, that it was parked at the institute. Then she stepped close, almost touching me, and just stood there, perfectly still, just looking up at me. I didn't know what to do. So, I put my arms around her and kissed her good night. At that moment, the Earth simply opened up, and I fell into it. My legs went limp. If she hadn't been holding me up, I'd have fallen. I've never experienced anything like that in my life. How I made it back to my car I'll never know. I sat there in my car for at least an hour before I was able to drive. I hadn't been around a woman for a while, and I thought I was having a breakdown from the kiss."

"Did you have these feelings any other time while you were around her?"

"No, sir. Only when we physically touched."

"Ensign, do you think you can be objective and continue with your observation duties with a clear head?"

"Oh Yes Sir! I can carry on my duties. She did request that if I'm on duty to follow her, that I should walk with her. Will that be a problem, Sir?"

"I think that would be okay, Ensign, as long as you don't take it any further than you already have. Just be careful. There's no telling what might happen. Do you understand?"

"Yes Sir, Admiral, I understand."

"Thank you, Ensign. You're dismissed."

Reggie turned and left the two men in the Admiral's office.

"Admiral, I know, from the OAI, that she hasn't put Ensign Kotak under Compulsion, like she did everyone at the submarine incident. Do you think she's going to do something that would require Kotak to be under Compulsion?"

"From my briefings, Commander, we'll never know what the Qrie are up to. You know as much as I do. But I don't think she's gonna do anything that'll cause any harm to Ensign Kotak. I think she likes him. And from what I've heard about the Qrie, God help anyone who tries to harm him.

"I suspect that she wanted that kiss more than Ensign Kotak wanted it. After all, she was the one who gave him the signal." The Admiral chuckled. "At least he was smart enough to take the hint."

Over the next week and a half, Breath and Reggie spent every afternoon that she was free, and the weekends, walking the beach, swimming, going to movies, going to restaurants, and just hanging out.

Reggie had other military duties on the dive boat from time to time, which took away from his Breath observation time. Once his other military duties were done, he was eager and volunteered for — observation duty. Commander Barnes smiled at this but okayed his request each time.

Cliff told Admiral Winscott that Breath was always in a great mood when Ensign Kotak was around.

Cliff was laughing as Breath floated into the beach house from the ocean. He had just hung up the phone after talking to Admiral Winscott.

"What's so funny Cliff?"

"I was talking to Archie Winscott and he told me what you call Chief Farnsworth, Petty Officer Hastings, and Ensign Kotak. Commander Barnes says you have visited the dive boat several times, and went out with them while training. He doesn't mind you keeping an eye on your friends. But he also requested that you not call them and the boat crew your — 'Sweeties.'"

"But they are my Sweeties. That's the way I think of them. They're sweet, kind, helpful, and doing a needed job. What else should I call them besides 'My Sweeties'?"

"Well the divers are getting a lot of teasing from the crew. They would like for you to call them something other than 'Sweeties.' Chief Farnsworth suggested that he had the nickname 'Galoot' when he started his dive training. Because he looked so clumsy walking around in his diving suit."

"Well, okay Cliff. I suppose I can call them my 'Galoots' instead of my 'Sweeties,' and turn the word into a term of endearment for my dear friends. If that's what they want." Breath tilted her head to the right, gave Cliff a pleading look, stuck her bottom lip out, and pouted. The look would've had a much stronger effect, if she had held it a little longer, instead of breaking into a huge twinkling smile.

20. XENOPHOBES

Reggie had two large bags of freshly popped hot buttered popcorn from the convenience store and was waiting for Breath. She walked up, took the offered bag from Reggie, and put her nose close to the top of the bag as she inhaled the warm popcorn aroma. She reached up to give Reggie a peck on the cheek. "Thank you, Reggie. You remembered how much I love hot buttered popcorn and the aroma. They began walking back towards the beach house.

Reggie told Breath a corny joke that he'd heard from his diver buddies, and they were both laughing.

"Oh, Reggie, that joke is so lame it's..."

A black van pulled up beside them. A man shot Breath with at least eight fast acting tranquilizer darts. The man used a dart gun modified to be automatic. He shot from the vans open side doors. One dart got past her shield while she was trying to protect Reggie. Popcorn exploded everywhere! Three men jumped out. They knocked Reggie out when he tried to protect Breath. They put a black bag over her head. They crammed them both into the van and sped off. Breath was weakened from the tranquilizer. She almost passed out.

The black van lost the Navy SUV in the busy traffic. It couldn't lose the airborne drone. The drone followed the van to a small concrete warehouse. The surveillance people called for backup. The Navy security team began surrounding the warehouse. Vice Admiral Winscott put his command on alert. Then he called his boss, Admiral Harland, Commander in Chief of the Pacific Fleet (CinCPacFlt). He was on a command tour at the North Island Naval Air Station. Admiral Harland put the entire Pacific Fleet on alert. Both Admirals called for their cars. They wanted to go to the incident site. They knew this was not their wisest decision.

GP was concerned. He could sense Breath's location. He also sensed her confusion. Morning and Beauty were concerned as well. GP began to probe the minds of the abductors. He wasn't happy with the results. He analyzed both Breath and the Ensign for injuries.

He discovered that Breath had been injected with a fast-acting tranquilizer. She'd already begun to isolate and remove the compound from her body. He analyzed the Ensign and discovered a mild concussion, which he healed. He did leave the nasty cut for the corpsman. He allowed the Ensign to remain unconscious. He noticed Breath still had her shield up. However, it wasn't as strong as it should've been.

***

The people who abducted Breath and Reggie were from the group Earth Only. The alien-hating xenophobes were determined to cleanse the world of space aliens. They'd track down suspected space aliens and interrogate them through torture. After they'd gotten all the information they could extract from the victim, they'd kill that person. Then they'd go after the people that that person had implicated and torture and kill them. It was a vile modern-day witch-hunt.

She was the latest in a long series of aliens they'd been tracking. They knew she was responsible for killing the Earth

Only crew in Miami. There was no doubt in their minds that she was a space alien. They were determined to eliminate her.

***

About the same time as the abduction, a gunshot rang out in Fremantle, Australia. Heidi, as was her habit, had risen early and was picking some vegetables in her lush garden. The high-powered sniper bullet, fired from a hovering helicopter, grazed her head and exploded in her hair. She was slammed to the ground. GP and Morning were already on their way to her and caught her before she touched ground.

GP told Morning, *Get those shooters! Beauty, stay with Breath! I'll check on William, Virginia, and the kids!*

GP left a part of his being with Heidi. *I'm sorry, Heidi. I should've held the shield stronger. The bullet was deflected, but not completely. You're healed just fine, but you'll have some missing hair for a while. We weren't expecting an attack like this.*

Don't worry about it, GP. Everything's okay. I'm fine. Check on the rest of the family. Just in case.

The OAI agents in the monitoring van near the Spring farm in Calgary noticed three human infrared signatures. They sent two agents to check. The OAI agents, with their video camera, observed the three men in silence. They reported back to their supervisor who was in the van. She was watching the video, and told the agents to bring the men in.

There were two snipers and a spotter preparing to fire, but the OAI agents interrupted that activity. The spotter and one sniper turned when the OAI agents made themselves known. However, the other sniper continued to draw down on Will and the two children, who had just exited the farmhouse. One OAI agent realized what was happening. He fired a warning shot near the head of that sniper, with his silenced pistol. The sniper lost his concentration. Then the OAI agents disarmed the three assailants, handcuffed them, and started them moving towards the surveillance van.

A bright light formed around the five men. The two OAI agents found themselves walking towards the surveillance van in a state of confusion. The three culprits were no longer present.

***

Breath's mind began to clear a bit. She was still disoriented. Her breath was rapid and her heart was racing. The bag over her head stank. She felt nauseated.

We lost hard contact with y'all for a while, but you're gonna be okay.

Her head began to clear, and then she became panicky. *Where is Reggie? He was with me. Is he okay? I can't sense him. I've got to...*

Yes Breath, he's okay, but I haven't allowed him to become conscious yet. He had a nasty cut on his head and a concussion. I've already healed the concussion and slowed the bleeding, but I left the cut.

Y'all were abducted. The abductors shot y'all with a tranquilizer dart, and you're still groggy.

Who is here? I can sense Beauty, but that is all.

Beauty is with y'all. Morning and I are busy at the moment. Can y'all sense the Navy security people who've just arrived?

Yes, GP, I can sense all of them, as well as the man walking towards me.

Morning, Beauty, and I are all concerned.

Breath felt GP and Beauty. Then after a moment, the presence of Morning. It gave her comfort and... The black cloth bag was ripped from her head. The light was bright and in her eyes. She squinted. She was handcuffed. Her legs were tied to the chair. Her eyes were slow to adapt to the light. She looked around.

Her abductors were stunned to see that she was awake. They recovered and began pummeling her with questions. They knew she was a space alien. They demanded to know where she was from.

Breath was groggy. "I'm from Australia. I was born in Reeftown, Queensland. I've lived most of my life in Fremantle."

They'd have none of it. They kept asking what planet she was from. Each time they'd ask. She'd say, "Earth."

Breath, you've removed most of the chemicals that they injected into y'all. But the effects on your brain are gonna be with y'all for quite a while. Y'all should use your Qrie part because it's not affected by the chemicals.

Breath's head began to clear, but much slower than she would've liked.

Morning and Beauty are becoming more and more agitated. They're about ready to take this place apart and make a huge hole in the ground. I'm gonna get y'all out of here.

That's just fine with me, GP. These handcuffs and ropes are beginning to irritate. I'm getting rid of them.

OK Breath, but can I ask what you're doing to the building?

I'm going to turn this place into a ball of rubble, okay? I thought that'd be better than Morning and Beauty making a big hole in the ground. Either way, GP, I've had enough of these people. I'll get Reggie. She was still unsteady.

***

Admiral Clifford Yokum arrived and was being briefed by the Situation Commander in the warehouse parking lot where Breath and the Ensign were being held.

About that time, Admirals Harland and Winscott arrived and were briefed on the situation. Both men knew there wasn't much they could do to help. They just wanted to be present to see what a Qrie might do.

While they were talking, a powerful bright light formed around the building, and another dome of light formed over the entire operation.

Clifford raised his voice. "Attention, everyone. Stay between the light of the outer dome and the light dome around the building. Under no circumstances allow that light to touch you."

Then he paused. "I apologize, Commander, for that outburst. This is your command. Please continue."

"No harm done, Admiral. You know more about the situation and her than anyone else here. We've been briefed on this Breath Of Spring person, but we don't know what to expect. Can you give us some insight?"

"I'm sorry Commander. I don't know what to expect from her either. We do know she's powerful and is able to do things no other human being can do. We've never heard of, or encountered anything like this before. She also has her — observer Ensign Reginald Kotak in there with her. Your guess is as good as mine. All I can say is, expect the unexpected. God help us all if they have harmed Ensign Kotak." He lowered his voice and leaned closer to the Commander. "Who she now considers her boyfriend."

"Well, Admiral, do you know anything about the people who took her and the Ensign captive?"

"No, Commander. I only know what you know."

A petty officer came running up to the Commander and handed him a piece of paper. The Commander looked at it. "Admiral, it looks like it could be a group of nasty alien hunters. The FBI has been hunting them for some time. They're suspected and wanted for a number of murders.

"We're also isolated. We've lost all communications from outside the dome."

***

Breath, using her telekinesis, unlocked her handcuffs. She watched as they fell off her wrists. She also used the same technique to untie the ropes from around her legs. She heard crunching and growling noises and knew what they were. The two men who were in the room with her turned as the door slammed open. Three men came charging into the room.

One of the men looked at the two already there. "Guys, something strange is going on at the corners of the building.

They're beginning to fall apart and crumble. I checked the closed-circuit cameras. We've got company and a lot of it."

Breath gazed around the room. "Gentlemen surrender now and you'll only be charged with kidnapping. If not, you'll be charged with additional crimes."

The man who had been asking all the questions growled, "Get this alien 'thing' into the van. We're getting out of here. Leave the Navy guy."

As the group moved Breath, at gunpoint, out of the small office into the empty warehouse. They saw their van turn into a compact ball of steel.

Breath saw Reggie sitting against the wall near the van. He was just coming around. His hands were tied in front of him. He was sitting up and holding his bleeding head in pain. He looked up and was glad to see Breath. She sent him a strong healing *Qrie Embrace*. They were still surrounded by their abductors.

"You should rethink the getting-out-of-here part. I don't think that van is gonna take us anywhere. I hope you've got good insurance. I suggest you surrender." Breath was irritated because she was still unsteady and not thinking as clearly as she would've liked.

The building continued to crumble.

The man in charge whirled on Breath. "It won't make any difference to you." He pulled the trigger on his shotgun.

Breath had her shield up. The shotgun pellets made it as far as the edge of a glowing field tight about her body. She didn't feel them, and the pellets fell onto the floor. She smiled and looked down at them.

Wow, GP! That's such a neat trick. It works well. Thanks for teaching me that.

Count on it! Congratulations. Now protect Reggie!

She put the same protective field around Reggie.

The gunman who fired at Breath vanished after she glared at him. The shotgun fell to the floor. The other men began firing at both her and Reggie, with the same results.

Breath, in a flash of light, found herself standing outside the building near Cliff and the Situation Commander. She was carrying Reggie in her arms. The five kidnappers appeared and were suspended in the air behind her and Reggie.

Wow GP, teleportation. You've gotta teach me how to do that.

I'll do that later. Right now, we've got to get the rest of that tranquilizer out of your body so it won't do any more harm to your brain. I also want to congratulate ya. That shield that y'all put around yourself and Reggie came directly from your Qrie part. Later when ya get outta this mess, I want y'all to do that little stillness and I AM expansion exercise that I taught ya. So, your Qrie part can be a 'full' part of your being. And your shield will remain up and strong all the time. You're Qrie and I AM. So, use the Qrie inner mind power and let it protect ya.

Breath put Reggie down and turned around to watch as she continued to collapse the building. She moved a corpsman away who had come up to examine Reggie. She knelt down to put her hand on Reggie's head. A bright glow of energy formed around the two of them. "Oh, no, no, no Reggie! I'm so sorry all this happened. It's all my fault." His nasty cut was healed, but she gave him such a powerful healing *Qrie Embrace* that he passed out. *Oh no, I gave him too much. Can't I do anything right today?*

His uniform was covered in his blood as was her dress and hands. The corpsman was standing close by watching in amazement. She looked up at him. "Reggie was struck on the head. Would you please check him out? I tried to heal it as best I could."

The corpsman began by examining Reggie for injuries.

One kidnapper complained. "Damn, I just finished that building. I don't even have insurance on it yet."

Breath looked at him. "You should've surrendered when I offered."

The building was now a compact sphere of concrete, rubble, and rebar. It was floating about six feet clear of the ground. It continued to shrink until it was a polished sphere of steel and stone, a few feet in diameter.

Breath, in Florida y'all learned to lift and move a cubic kilometer of water, so move that sphere of a building into the Pacific Ocean. Y'all also might want to get rid of the outer protective dome.

Breath was silent for a moment. She made a large sweeping motion with her left hand, and the outside dome disappeared. Then made a motion with her right hand, as if she were tossing a Frisbee. The stone-and-steel sphere flew into the air and made a loud sonic boom as it left.

Breath floated up level with the five abductors. "Gentlemen, I wish you had surrendered and not shot at me and my friend. As it is now, I don't think you're going to appreciate your new accommodations." She made another Frisbee-tossing motion. The five abductors disappeared. She was surprised, but at GP's coaching, she didn't show it.

Breath pondered. *That took a lot of power. Am I ready for that kind of responsibility? I'm thankful that I could help the whales, the commander, Farnsworth, and Hastings. I was shot on that boat then injured on the submarine, and now this. Why can't I ever be normal?*

Breath calmed herself, gathered her thoughts, turned around, floated down, and put a hand on Cliff's shoulder to steady herself. He put his arm around her back to support her. He took a closer look at her. She had no clothes on except a shimmering translucent leotard like thing and he wondered what it was. A corpsman, seeing this, and her, grabbed a blanket and with Cliff's help draped it over Breath's shoulders. She looked dazed and upset, "Cliff, just for future reference, I don't like my friends or myself being shot, not with tranquilizers, guns, bullets, or anything. I also don't like interference, because now I'm going to have to put Reggie under Compulsion."

Cliff felt a tremendous irritation in his mind and body. He felt his skin crawl. When he looked at Breath, what he saw was the immensity of the universe and the infinity of time. He was shaken to the foundations of his being. All he could say was a weak, "Aye, aye, Ma'am."

"Oh, Cliff, I see you brought a lot of people with you. You didn't have to go to all that trouble, but thank you anyway. Reggie and I do appreciate it.

"I need to rest; those men shot me with some kind of tranquilizer. Since then, I've been somewhat impaired, but I'm improving. Is everyone else okay? By the way, Cliff, do you think I can hitch a ride home, please?"

Cliff, his mouth still agape, couldn't utter a sound. He just nodded. The Admirals, Situation Commander, and all the security people involved were wearing the same expression as Cliff. *Did they see and feel what I just experienced?*

GP, who was telepathically linked to everyone there just smiled.

GP, how far did that sphere go, and where'd those five people go?

The Qrie — Morning and Beauty that is — don't appreciate people interfering with a Qrie — right now, that would be y'all. The building that y'all compacted and tossed is on its way to somewhere between here and Hawaii. The abductors are in suspended animation, but their brains are still active. Just so ya know, those five are now with the five who were responsible for shooting y'all in Florida. They'll all be taught how not to interfere with the Qrie. Y'all did good, and no one was hurt in the end.

I need to know Breath. What was your intention by collapsing that building? Were y'all gonna leave the culprits inside? Ya know Breath, the Qrie almost never kill humans but don't stand in the way of humans killing other humans. The Qrie will not allow humans to wipe themselves out via all-out nuclear war or other weapons of mass destruction. We don't wanna start over again if we don't have to.

I'm sorry GP. I started collapsing the building before I made a plan to get out. I suppose next time I should plan ahead.

I agree Breath. I need to teach y'all a little exercise to ramp up your Compulsion so y'all don't become irritated and dangerous like y'all were. I interfered with y'all when y'all turned that building into a sphere. I had to make sure no one would be hurt. Y'all need to be careful because y'all scared Cliff, the Admirals, the Situation Commander, and everyone else pretty bad. We'll get to that later.

Breath noticed that GP was silent for a moment and sensed considerable irritation from him. She also sensed that he wasn't telling her everything.

Breath, y'all weren't holding your protection shield around y'all strong enough again, like y'all should've been. Y'all know better than that. If y'all had had a strong shield up, that tranquilizer dart could never have gotten to ya, and you'd not have gotten cut coming out of that submarine. Reggie also would have been safe. I know the shield used to be an unconscious thing because I did it for y'all, as I do for Heidi, William, Virginia, and the twins. I don't do it for y'all anymore. You've gotta maintain your shield yourself and remain diligent.

Breath did the mental equivalent of hanging her head. *I know, GP. I did have the shield up, but it wasn't as strong as it could've been, and there were so many darts. I just have to get better, but it's so much to think about all the time.*

I know it is, Breath, but y'all can do this. It was hard for me to learn as well. I was lucky; many times, I could've been killed were it not for Morning and Beauty. Use your Qrie part to help y'all maintain your diligence. It's part of y'all now, so learn to use it.

From now on, I will GP.

Well it's about time. Please, maintain your diligence. I love y'all too much to see y'all get hurt. I've got another little question. What was the big dome for?

I didn't know if there were any more bad guys out there. So, I put the big dome around everyone to protect them and keep them safe.

Good on ya kid! Y'all are learning how unconditional love works, and I love y'all for it.

I love you too, GP — I don't feel so good.

I know Breath and that will take a while.

***

A security detail took Breath home. Heavily armed Naval security then surrounded the beach house.

Cliff and all of the officers including the senior NCOs present at the incident went back to the base. They were going to have a serious debriefing about Breath Of Spring. All of the Admirals in charge of the surrounding Navy bases were called into the briefing as well.

Ensign Kotak was given some clean dungarees to replace his bloody uniform. He was finishing his report to the group. "... It had to be a twelve-gauge shotgun at point-blank range. Then the rest of the group must've fired fifty rounds into her. I saw them hitting her. Then they turned on me. She put some kind of energy cocoon around both of us. I could feel bullets pelting me, but that was all they did. She saved my life. The next thing I remember, we were all outside by the Situation Command Van. When she put her hand on my head, I again felt the universe open up, and again I felt the unconditional, indescribable love emanating from her."

One of the Admirals spoke up. "Yes, and just how'd she do all that? How could she be cut as bad as she was pulling that diver out of that submarine after she'd ripped it open and be able to stop all those bullets? We raised the submarine and examined the hole she ripped in it. We found a small piece of one of her fingernails or talons. It turns out that talon is made of silicon carbide. That stuff can cut steel like its butter.

"Another thing: One of the security people tossed a rock at the big outer dome. All it did was spark and bounce off, and those people who came after the dome was in place couldn't get through."

Cliff spoke up. "One, I have never seen her lift huge weights like that or transport herself like she did. Nor have I ever seen her make a dome. I had no idea she could do any of that. It's obvious, she can. One thing for sure: she wasn't happy when she came out of that building, and we all saw and felt the result of that. I think we've just seen what happens when the Qrie encounters interference.

"Two, perhaps it was because she was expecting the bullets. She may not have been expecting to get cut. After all, her mind was concentrating on getting Petty Officer Hastings out of that submarine and saving his life. She then put her life on the line to also save Chief Farnsworth.

"Three, I've seen her talons. She can make them come and go at will, although it takes her a small amount of time. When the talons aren't dark, they're clear as diamond and look like regular fingernail polish. However, those fingernails can cut glass. I've seen her do it.

"Four, she conveyed to me, through telepathy, that she put the outer dome in place to make sure everyone was safe. That message came when she looked into my eyes.

"Something you may not have noticed was when she floated down to me after making those men disappear. I had to hold her, and she had to hold on to me because she was unstable. I don't think she would've revealed as much about herself had she not been compromised by the tranquilizer."

The situation Commander and Admirals began receiving communiqués about radars tracking a mysterious object that had splashed down in the ocean approximately 1,500 miles away on a path towards Hawaii. They were wondering if it was a missile.

Vice Admiral Winscott looked at Cliff. "She just flicked her wrist, and that building-sphere thing went fifteen hundred miles at several times the speed of sound! Where'd those abductors go? Gentlemen, the bottom line is we've got a situation here. According to our calculations, that building weighed some four hundred tons. She crushed it like a piece of paper and tossed it fifteen hundred miles — 'and' she can fly. If she can do that, what could she do to one of our capital ships? We need to find out. I just don't know how to go about that. We also must tread lightly here and keep her collaborating with us. It is certain that we don't want anyone that powerful to be upset with us."

Cliff made a low whistle. "I couldn't agree more. We must keep her trust. I suspect we'll not see those abductors anytime soon."

The meeting continued till late into the night.

***

Breath was frightened, angry, and concerned about her mum and absolutely furious with GP. *How could you not tell me what was going on with Mum? She could've been killed. She almost was, and I'm just now finding out about it! You — you — sometimes you make me so — crazy. Thank God, Dad, Virginia, and the kids are okay! Didn't you tell me you put shields around Mum and Dad?*

Breath, there were too many things going on with y'all, at that time. If I'd told y'all what was going on, what could y'all have done? The answer to that is nothing. Y'all were just able to function as it was. We got the two snipers who were after your mom. We let the helicopter pilot go. He was flying with a gun to his head. We also got three snipers who were after your dad and family in Calgary. They'll never bother any of y'all again, as they're now with the men on the boat in Miami and the xenophobes here. The government people who were watching your family were a great help.

I also must apologize to y'all and Heidi because I wasn't holding the shield around your mother as strong as I should've. The rifle the sniper used was a large caliber like the one used on you in Miami, and much more powerful than I'd expected. The bullet was deflected, but not quite enough.

That evening Breath, Heidi, Will, Virginia, Billy, and Sam all talked together on Skype so they could see and physically hear each other. Everyone was relieved that the family was okay, and that Heidi had been healed. Qrie family security was a hot topic, and everyone decided to maintain strong shields around each member, including Virginia.

At their next meeting at Scripps Institute, Reggie walked up to and planted a huge kiss on Breath's lips. She responded with an eager kiss of her own. She had been apprehensive of how Reggie had taken the incident. Their kisses and tight hugs were long and heartfelt. They both chuckled when a passerby said, "Get a room!"

***

Erin and Cheryl Ziegler started following Breath around California wherever they could. They also photographed the people who were following her.

***

Two months later, Breath completed her internship at Scripps Institution of Oceanography. Upon that completion, she received several offers around Australia and the U.S. She was interested in an offer from Geoscience Australia to join the organization as a postdoc research fellow on the survey ship *Morning Discovery*. She was interested in this one because it operated out of Reeftown, Queensland.

Breath went to visit Hipsi and Kristin on Monday after she received confirmation of her job on *Morning Discovery*. It was a bittersweet reunion, but Hipsi decided to make the occasion happier by going shopping. They spent the day fixing Breath up for the next several years. Of course, shopping for clothes also requires accessories and matching makeup.

Breath thought. *I'm not sure about the makeup. If I have it on and I use the Qrie energies, it all goes flying off, and then I have to reapply. Even a little bit of Qrie energy will destroy it. It can be such a bother, but I like it. It's fun, and it makes me feel good. So...*

Breath insisted on having appropriate attire for her new position and life aboard ship. Among the three of them, Breath was set up for quite some period of time.

The next day Breath took Hipsi and Kristin to the beach. They got to play mermaid again. While they were coming out of the water, a young man came by, and Hipsi asked him if he'd take their picture as mermaids. She ran and got her camera out of the car, put her mermaid outfit back on, and all three posed on some nearby rocks. The young man took several good pictures. On the way home, they stopped and bought two nice picture frames, and they had the best picture of the group printed on high-quality paper at Walmart. Hipsi framed them, kept one for her and Kristin, and gave the other to Breath.

The goodbye hugs were long, and heartfelt tears flowed.

21. OAI 5

Tate saw John coming out of his office. He waved a handful of papers at him. "John, the Anasso have intense interest in the Qrie entities that we've discovered here. They want as much information on them as possible."

"Well, Tate, I guess we should send them as much information as we've got, considering the recent happenings. Anyone who can do that is a force to be respected. I suppose we should also tell them about the surveillance and her close contacts with the Navy. Why don't we ask them if they have any idea what these Qrie entities are doing here?

"I also think we should inform the ASIO to exercise extreme caution around the Qrie Heidi Spring.

"We've got to come up with some diversion to prevent people from thinking anything alien is going on. I think we should also come up with some kind of cover story for the events surrounding Breath Of Spring and her family. This *Star Child Quest* situation has caused us problems. We should make it sound like government experimental testing of some kind."

Tate chuckled. "You take care of the ASIO, and I'll get on the government-testing conspiracy. I'm thinking something like a stern public denial of government testing might do the trick."

Later that day, all of the email addresses to which the *Star Child Quest* was connected received an email that categorically denied that the U.S. government was doing any new technology tests of any kind with any person or persons and denied any involvement with any such alleged persons.

This spurred a furious flurry of questioning emails.

Tate again chuckled.

22. FARM

Breath had several weeks before she had to report to her new job at Geoscience Australia. It had taken her several weeks to recover from the chemicals in the tranquilizer dart and her episode with the submarine. *Why is it taking me so long to heal? I can heal anyone else in an instant with the Qrie energies.*

Well Breath, I haven't said anything about this. I was hoping you'd figure it out. You know what happens when you heal someone with the Qrie energies. Y'all have to do the same thing for yourself. Let the Qrie energies flow into and through your body to heal yourself. Just as y'all do when ya heal others. You're part human, but your more powerful part is Qrie. Y'all need to learn to use your Qrie part as a natural part of your consciousness along with your human part. Y'all need to let your Qrie part and your human part work and be free together.

I thought I was doing that GP.

Well guess what Breath, ya weren't.

Y'all were feeling sorry for yourself. I've got a little exercise I want y'all to do. It'll help y'all link up both parts of your being. Now this is what you need to do...

She felt much better after the exercise. But she found it a little tiresome that the Navy divers, Farnsworth, Hastings, and Reggie had been placed on Temporary Duty Assignment (TDA) to her, and were always armed. She didn't understand why, but Cliff made it plain for her not to interfere. The three guys were wonderful and she relished their attention, but with them around, she never got to do anything for herself. She would've liked to spend more alone time with Reggie. However, the other two guys were always there. She and Reggie had to sneak in hugs and kisses whenever they could.

She showed them how her adjustable monofin worked. She tried her best to teach them how to swim with it. Although they did well, they never got what she considered proficient. They did have a huge amount of fun trying. She also introduced them all to her dolphin friends, which they loved.

Before she left for Australia, she was going to visit her dad, Virginia, and the twins at their farm. She told Cliff she wasn't looking forward to a long bus trip. She kept trying to talk GP into teleporting her to Calgary and then on to Reeftown, Queensland. GP was teaching her how to teleport, but she was afraid to do it herself over that distance, because she might not get all of her parts back in their right places. Besides, GP told her she was not ready for that distance yet.

Cliff made arrangements with the Navy to fly her, Reggie, Farnsworth, Hastings, and himself to Calgary for her visit. They would then fly to Hawaii for refueling and on to Sydney on a US Navy Gulfstream G550 VIP aircraft. She was to report there for her new job on the ship *Morning Discovery*. She suspected GP had put Cliff up to the aircraft arrangement.

On the flight up to Calgary, Cliff told Breath that her three Navy buddies were being reassigned and would be shipping out after they'd secured her at Fleet Base East in Sydney. She would've liked to have had more time to spend with Reggie, but he had several more years obligation with the U.S. Navy.

Reggie secured a large SUV to take them to the farm. Both of Breath's pink duffel bags were left on the aircraft. She took an overnight bag, for her stay. As they were approaching the farm, Breath telepathically called Virginia to tell her they'd landed and were almost there.

She was still for a moment. *Okay, I'll take care of it. Bye.*

Cliff looked at her and asked, "You look concerned. Is there anything wrong?"

She looked at him and smiled. "No, everything is okay. It's just that Bill Junior and Samantha are having a little — play party. And you guys can't attend."

Cliff touched Breath's arm. "We won't interfere. We'll stay well back from your guests if that's what's required, but we'd still like to meet and thank your parents and your brother and sister. By the way, how old are the twins?"

They could see the farmhouse from the road. It was a short distance away. "They're eleven. We've got to stop here."

They pulled over to the side of the road, and got out of the SUV. She told them all that she could make it to the farm on her own from here. She told everyone that this was as far as they could go and explained the situation. They protested a bit, but they did as she requested. Cliff and the guys were all trying to persuade Breath to allow them to meet the family.

"Oh Cliff, I didn't say you couldn't meet the family. I just said you couldn't go to the party."

"Why not?"

"Well — guys — you know how I swim with dolphins and killer whales. Do you see any dolphins or killer whales anywhere around? My family does the same thing with other animals. So you'll have to wait here. The family doesn't want you to frighten the animals. I'll call to let you know when the coast is clear. Do you understand?"

"Not really, Breath. What kind of animals are you talking about?"

Breath smiled sweetly. "Grizzly bears."

Everyone watched, with envy, as Breath did a thorough check to see if any strange person was around and watching. Then she just floated off the ground and towards the farmhouse.

Farnsworth got a pair of binoculars out of the back of the SUV, and started scanning the area. "Whoa, guys you've got to see this. There's got to be five adult bears down there. I also count seven cubs. She wasn't kidding. Here Admiral take a look."

The kids and the bear cubs were chasing one another, like any bunch of kids on a playground "You've got to be kidding." Cliff watched for a moment and slowly lowered the binoculars. "Well I'll be. You never know what the Qrie are going to do next." He handed the binoculars to Reggie.

"Those kids are playing with bear cubs. And Breath is hand feeding adult bears what looks like strawberries. Does anyone have a camera that can record this?"

Cliff raised an eyebrow and gave Reggie a serious look. "I don't think — that's a good idea?"

"Yeah but, no one's going to believe this if we don't have a picture."

Farnsworth and Hastings were both laughing, and Cliff continued giving Reggie his serious look. "Reggie, no one's going to believe this anyway — picture or not. And remember the Compulsion."

"Well I guess you guys have a point."

***

Morning Discovery was given permission to dock at HMAS Kuttabul. Skipper, its captain was waiting dockside for his new crew member Breath Of Spring. Cliff, Reggie, Farnsworth, Hastings, and Breath enjoyed the RAN transport helicopter ride from Holsworthy Military Airport to Fleet Base East. She made the mistake of calling him Captain Skipper. He informed her that he was to be called Skipper, not Captain. Reggie and the two divers helped her load all of her belongings onto her new ship. They wouldn't let her touch a thing.

She asked Cliff. "Why did You, Reggie, and the two divers need to come with me on this long trip?"

"Because Vice Admiral Archie Winscott said so! He wanted to make sure you had a US Navy escort and would arrive safe."

"Um — okay!"

Cliff, Reggie, and the divers had to return to the United States. Breath was sad to see them go. She'd spent so much time with what she called her 'Big, Sweet, Lovable Galoots,' ungainly they were not, but she teased them because they couldn't seem to learn how to use her monofins very well. Like breaching completely out of the water, which they never mastered. Cliff said, "Well — they are the best divers and swimmers in the world with the possible exception of yourself." 'Galoots' became a term of endearment. It was okay when Breath said it, but her 'Sweetie' crew on the dive boat will never let them live that nickname down.

"Reggie, I wish you didn't have to go back and could stay here with me. You know I like you — a lot."

"I know Breath and I like you — a lot. You're very special to me too. But I think the Navy would frown on my staying here with you, which I would like to do. But I've got over four more years on my six-year Navy hitch. And I want to become the best Navy diver I can."

"I know Reggie, but when you get out. I'll still be here. You know we use divers here on *Morning Discovery*. We could use a superior Navy diver. Maybe in four years..."

"You know — I always planned a career in the Navy. There is also another problem Breath. I am becoming — addicted to you and your touch. I can't be around you without touching you. I have tried. When I am touching you nothing else in the world exists. It's caused some problems for me with the Navy and my diving. All I think about is your touch. I hate to say this but being around you is like an overdose of drugs. Of course, I've never tried drugs, but people tell me that's what it's like. And that's what's happening to me now. I hate to say this, because I do love you, but on a steady diet of your touch I am useless. Already it takes me hours to overcome what you do to me, so I can even do my job."

Breath's heart ached. Her stomach cramped. Her tears were a steady stream. Because she knew what he was saying was true.

She knew he had to leave. It was logical and reasonable but it didn't ease the pain.

"Breath, I think you know what I mean. I have seen you become distracted when I'm around. Especially after we've touched and kissed. I don't want to go, but I have no choice. I would like for you to come with me, but you have no choice either."

GP, how do I relieve Reggie of this addiction burden? I don't want him to go but we have no choice.

Well Breath, when y'all healed him after ya brought him out of the building, y'all gave him too much Qrie energy and his body and mind have been severely affected by that overload. Like he said it's an addiction. What y'all have to do to give the poor boy relief, is you must...

"I know you're right." She blubbered to Reggie knowing what she must do now. Then she grabbed him hard and he responded in kind. They kissed with equal intensity, and she gave him the most powerful *Qrie Embrace* she had ever given anyone. She followed GP's instructions. He passed out, but she held him until he came around. They kissed several more times, until Cliff called to him saying it was time for them to leave. She waved goodbye to Reggie and all her Navy friends.

As she watched the helicopter take off for Holsworthy Military Airport, she knew that was the last time she would ever see Reggie again. She took a deep breath, and let it out slowly, to calm herself. She knew he was going to be okay now.

She then sent him a strong telepathic message. *Bless you Reggie. I hope you find someone to love and that will love you. Goodbye!*

She took another long, slow, deep, breath. *If I don't stop crying, I'm going to raise the tidal level of Sydney Harbor.*

Breath recovered from Reggie, which took several hours. Later she spent quite a number of happy and tearful minutes on her phone talking with her friends Hipsi and Kristin Iversen. She let them know that she was now on *Morning Discovery* and told them how much she missed them. And plotted schemes as to when they could come to Australia for a visit.

Breath pondered. *At least now I can start living a normal life.*

Breath, I think y'all know that y'all have a lot more training ahead of ya.

Oh GP, do I have to?

What do y'all think? I know that down deep y'all want to know what your 'Destiny' has in store for ya. After all I do love y'all very much and so want to see ya succeed.

I know, but is there anyone out there who is compatible with me?

Yes, there's someone out there for ya, and y'all will know when y'all see him.

When will that be?

I love y'all Breath.

Oh GP, your exasperating, you know that don't you, and I love you too!

23. TEXAS

Monique Moreau was hysterical. She was talking so fast that Virginia could hardly understand a word. A few minutes into the one-sided conversation, Monique began to slow down, and Virginia began to understand why her mother was so upset. Virginia motioned to Will to get on the other land line phone so he could listen in.

Monique was hysterical and crying. Both Will and Virginia Spring had to listen intently to understand what she was saying. Will deciphered that someone had been murdered, someone was missing, and three others were also killed. The more he listened, the more he deciphered. He thanked the stars that Monique tended to repeat herself.

Virginia looked frantically at Will. "What are we going to do Will? We've got to go to the ranch; we don't have a choice. With Poppa Robert having been murdered, and Vincent and Desiree missing, we've got to go. Mama is in danger, and it looks like someone's trying to kill off the animals as well. Our family and three young male lions... How can anyone do something like this?"

Will took Virginia in his arms and held her tight. "I don't know why anyone would do anything like this. I know they've had a long-standing feud with the sheriff and the Updike family. But surely, they'd never resort to this!

"I'll start repairing the truck and get it ready so we can leave as soon as possible."

Two days later, Will, Virginia, and the twins started south to Central Texas, where Virginia's family's Safari Ranch was located. They'd loaded their four-wheel-drive extended cab pickup with all the personal items they needed for a long stay.

They had no idea how long they'd be there or even when they'd be back to their home in Calgary. They made arrangements with their neighbors to work the property. They asked their neighbor Betty to find a renter, if possible.

***

They didn't need to bring much with them other than clothes and personal items because the private ranch house was huge, with seven bedrooms, five bathrooms, a kitchen, a dining room, a living room, and a den. At one time it was a bed-and-breakfast.

There is now a separate lodge with twenty-five double-bed, family-oriented rooms for visitors and its own upscale restaurant. It also has a communal room, check-in, and registration area. A large swimming pool separates the lodge from the bunkhouse. The bunkhouse has a cafeteria. It also has two large dormitories with fifty bunks each. One side for girls and the other side for boys, each with its own huge restroom and shower facilities, to accommodate large school outings. They knew they could also stay in the more-than-ample staff quarters, which housed the full-time staff and ranch hands.

The Safari Ranch is quite large — sixteen sections, or 10,240 acres. It was and still is an animal rescue facility. Over the years and with so many rescue animals coming in it has turned into a humongous zoo and wildlife park. Everything is separated into compounds representing the six continents of the Earth. Each compound is divided into carnivore, herbivore, primate sections, and enclosed aviary buildings. There is just about every kind of animal represented on the ranch.

Each compound has a fully appointed multiroom bungalow with supplies for the ranch hands if they need to stay in that section longer.

There is also a large separate reptile building. No poisonous snakes, because Monique doesn't like them.

Of course, the carnivores don't mingle with the herbivores, since they don't play nice together.

People will buy a baby exotic animal thinking that they can handle it but when the baby grows up, they realize they can't handle it. The ranch, being an animal sanctuary, will take those animals. The ranch also takes in wounded and abandoned animals, as well as endangered species of all types.

Robert Moreau was an exotic animal veterinarian. He and his wife Monique started the ranch many years ago after they were married.

***

Everyone was on edge. Will consulted with the sheriff several times about the progress of the investigation. About the only thing he could find out was that the lions and Robert Moreau had been killed with two different guns. The one used on Robert seemed to be a large-caliber pistol. The one used on the lions was a high-powered hunting rifle. There was no word at all on the disappearances of Virginia's brother and sister, Vincent and Desiree.

This lack of information dragged on for months with no progress at all. Will couldn't even get information as to what the guns' calibers were. He knew that the sheriff was the son of the district attorney, and he was incompetent, greedy, jealous, mean, and lazy. The people of Brandy had been trying to get rid of him for years, but for some strange reason, he just kept getting reelected.

***

Erin and Cheryl discovered the Moreau family on the Safari Ranch in Texas were related to Breath Of Spring. They sent emails to Rob and Karol in Australia, telling them what they'd found. They also made several trips to Texas and the Safari Ranch to get a better perspective. They began tracking the Spring family and the many agents and ranch hands. To them this was huge. They'd found the mother lode. They didn't know how to correlate what they had found since this was Virginia Moreau's family and not the Spring family. Virginia and the Moreau family and the Spring family were in-laws.

They had a computer-whiz friend who had facial-recognition software. He took the photos that Erin and Cheryl had given him, and tracked some of the agents and whom they worked for. He never told Erin and Cheryl how he did it.

Emails went flying back and forth across the Pacific speculating on what the various government agents and the Star Children were doing on that ranch.

***

The OAI, the U.S. Navy, along with the Royal Canadian Mounted Police, who were charged with keeping track of Will, Virginia, and the twins, opened an unmarked office in the nearby town of Brandy. Cynthia Schultz, of the OAI, was selected as lead agent. She worked and coordinated with the other agencies.

The building she found for the headquarters was an old brick two-story furniture store with a smaller wooden storeroom as a third floor. The offices were on the second floor. The first floor was used as the parking garage. From this vantage point they could set up surveillance in town and on the Qrie at the Safari Ranch. This made it much easier for the agents. Divya and Ramesh set up their drone, video, and surveillance equipment in the converted large third floor storeroom to hide the many antennas.

GP, Breath, Will, and Virginia knew what was going on and, in most ways, encouraged it. They all knew that Monique would have to be informed about the Qrie soon. The family didn't want to upset her any more than she already was. They all decided to wait until the dust settled, to inform her.

***

Dixon, TDog's number-one hit man, strode with confidence into TDog's office. "Well, we got some of them, and it's about time! Those damnable aliens took down fifteen good men. I call that a little payback."

"Yeah Dixon, but I understand the alien bitch is back in Australia now. Unfortunately, we're going to have to recruit more people because we've lost all the good ones to those damnable, useless aliens.

"At least, there's one positive thing about this whole situation. We've got that idiot Sheriff and the three Updikes on our side now. Plus, we've got audio and video of them, so they can't back out of anything we want to do in the future. And we're definitely going to do something in the future."

TDog opened a drawer and pulled out a bottle of whiskey and two glasses. He poured a drink in each one, and handed one to Dixon. "Here's to fifteen great men, the Updikes, that stupid Sheriff, and at least three dead aliens."

Dixon continued the toast. "Hear! Hear! Now all we've got to do is get Breath Of Spring and the rest of that accursed alien family."

"Amen to that." They touched glasses and downed the shots. "You know Dixon the only thing I regret is that we didn't get a chance to interrogate any of those things. We need more info like who, what, when, and where from those alien assholes."

24. BIG CHEESE

It had been almost a year since Dr. Breath Of Spring first stepped on board *Morning Discovery*. The crew was slow to accept Breath because she was so young. However, the ship's Captain — everyone just called him Skipper — took Breath under his wing and made sure she was accepted. Geoscience Australia sent her to a short-term highly intense Ocean Seafaring School in the Australian Maritime College at University of Tasmania. She had to start her Seafaring and Shipmate's license training. Skipper continued her intense training to get her Shipmate's license as soon as possible, when she returned aboard *Morning Discovery*. As a result, he treated her like a daughter. Everyone knew that to mess with Breath was to mess with Skipper, and no one wanted to cross that bridge.

"Skipper, why does Geoscience want me to get a Shipmate's license?"

"Well, it's a lot easier to get a postdoc than a good ship's mate. Breath, the ship's science director is also *Morning Discovery's* first mate, and is getting ready to retire soon. I guess the company is just hedging their bets. Hey, somebody's got to do it, so why not you?"

About a month later, the director of *Morning Discovery* told his bosses at Geoscience Australia how they could stick their unreasonable request up their collective backsides.

What's going on, GP?

Something nefarious Breath. The authorities and the bureaucracy within Geoscience Australia are working on it. I suggest y'all wait it out. Y'all should be okay.

Oh, that's comforting. You're a lot of help.

That's what I'm here for. I just love to help.

What is it, GP? You don't sound like your normal self.

Well, Breath, I'm kinda excited. It seems that our old friends Morning and Beauty are beginning to understand and communicate in 'human language.' I've been teaching them how to use language, and I'm excited that my efforts are paying off. I'm hoping that they'll soon be able to converse with human beings without having to resort to the complex images.

That's super, GP. Can I talk to them?

Not at this time, Breath. I think they're — shy.

Shy? All the things they can do, like building star systems, and they're shy? Well, they can have their shyness. Thanks for telling me, GP. I can't wait to talk with them.

I know that once a person has learned how to understand the images, feelings, emotions, and orientations, they can get a lot more information transferred in a short conversation.

I know, Breath. The problem is humans can't understand the images, feelings, et cetera. They've got to have language. I know it's inadequate, but that's all they've got.

Well, I'm glad for Morning and Beauty anyway.

Breath had no idea what the altercation was all about. However, after that incident, the old director was gone. He had accrued a lot of vacation time. Then several auditors came aboard. They grilled everyone about even the most minute details. When they left, they indicated that they'd file a report, and Geoscience Australia would get back to them with the results.

***

Breath was leaning on the ship's railing as *Morning Discovery* was approaching Reeftown. Skipper came up to her and put his arm around her shoulder. "What's the matter Breath you look kind of down?"

"Hey Skipper, I'm okay." She glanced over at his hand on her shoulder and smiled. "You better be careful your wife may get jealous!"

"What wife would that be Breath?"

"*Morning Discovery* of course, everybody on this ship knows your married to her."

He laughed, which made Breath more comfortable. "Well I'm not the only one, everybody on board says your *Morning Discovery's* little baby girl. Tell you what, after we dock, I'll make a couple telephone calls to some of my young friends and see if we can't set you up with a date."

She pulled away from him to look him square in the face. "Don't you dare. You know how I feel about random men."

He stepped back with his hands up in a surrender position and laughingly said. "Okay, okay I won't make the call. By the way, I've got to do some shopping in town want to come with me?"

"Sure, as long as you don't try to point out 'every guy' that you think looks like my type. Last time we shopped together; you took great delight in teasing me. Pointing out the endless romantic possibilities for me as we walked around town."

"Well, if not me who else are you going to get to do the job?"

Breath's grin was huge as she punched Skipper on his shoulder. Then she put her arms around him and gave him a big hug.

Three months had passed. Still, there was no word from Geoscience Australia. Rumors ran rampant. Skipper told Breath that he'd seen situations like this several times. They always ended bad. Sometimes everyone would be laid off. The tension didn't make shipboard operations any easier. Breath wondered what had caused the old director to storm off so disgruntled. Skipper told her that the old guy was mild mannered and good at what he did. He didn't understand the situation either.

The lead scientist's leaving, left Skipper in charge. He'd get their marching orders and pass them on to the crew. They hadn't done a bathymetric sounding in three months. The work they'd been assigned since the old director left seemed like busy work. They were doing coral-density surveys, fish and crustacean counts, and taking water samples.

Breath elected to remain aboard *Morning Discovery* because it felt like home. She liked the people, the job, and being aboard ship. Breath was now the senior scientist on board as well as the third mate. She started at postdoc and had risen rapidly through the ranks. She realized that her meteoric rise through the ranks was primarily due to attrition. Attracting qualified scientific people to Geoscience Australia was not easy. The agency liked her work, and she got good offers from both inside and outside Geoscience. She always decided to stay, much to management's delight. All the other jobs were in labs onshore. The scientists above her had all gone to better onshore jobs, either within Geoscience or with other agencies.

When *Morning Discovery* pulled into its slip next to the Geoscience Australia laboratories in Reeftown, they noticed several cars with the Geoscience emblem. Everyone became nervous.

Breath saw the Human Resources woman, who was always present when someone got fired, waiting on the dock. She came on board and told Skipper to have everyone gather in the large meeting room. Skipper whispered to Breath. "This isn't a good sign."

She told everyone gathered. "A Geoscience Australia internal error caused the dustup with the old director. A minor reorganization resolved the problem, exonerating the previous director, who is now happy and retired with a full pension."

She turned to Skipper. "Captain, can you work with a new director scientist aboard this ship?"

Skipper put on a huge smile. "Yes Ma'am, I think I can do that."

The woman looked at Breath. "Breath Of Spring, please come up here. The Captain has something for you."

Skipper turned around and opened a case. When he turned forward again, he had a huge yellow ribbon with a monstrous bow on it. Written on the ribbon in large bold letters was, **Breath Of Spring, Queen of the Sea**, and in smaller bold letters, **Well, at least *Morning Discovery*.** Everyone applauded. The cooks brought out a cake from the galley as everyone chanted. "Hip, hip, hooray!"

Breath projected. *Wow, GP! All my work has paid off. I know they had no one else and didn't want someone so young, but I still got the job. You were right. Everything did work out.*

Breath, they wouldn't have given y'all that job if they didn't think y'all could do it.

You know, GP, I'm going to have to get Skipper, because he knew about this the whole time.

Well, Skipper wasn't the only one who was keeping things from y'all. If y'all fuss at him, you'll have to fuss at me as well because I helped him keep the secret. He just didn't know it.

OK, then shame on both of you! Thanks, GP.

She had a huge smile and started doing a ridiculous happy dance. Everyone was congratulating her. *Morning Discovery* had truly become home.

GP projected. *See!*

Breath stopped her happy dance. *GP, what did they mean when they said reorganization?*

Someone higher up got caught spreading negative rumors, trying to manipulate the system and the old director for their own gain. That person is gone now.

I see. Thanks for telling me. Another thing GP, do I have to let anyone on board Morning Discovery *know what I am?*

Not if you don't want them to know. You wanted to be normal and this could be your chance while it lasts.

What is that supposed to mean?

Well...

What are you up to GP?

Nothing Breath, nothing at all! You wanted to be normal this is your chance.

How long will this normal last?

I'd have to say, as long as it lasts.

That's not a real answer.

I love you too Breath.

Breath called Hipsi and Kristin Iversen. They talked for over an hour. Breath told them everything that had happened. Well, almost everything.

Breath then projected the news to her mother. They communicated in this manner for another hour.

Later, Skipper and Breath were leaning against the railing on *Morning Discovery*. "Congratulations, Breath. You deserve this promotion and your third mate's license. I guess that makes you now an officially official, official!"

Breath couldn't help but laugh and Skipper joined her.

***

Rob and Karol reported, that their primary Star Child was back in Australia, to Erin and Cheryl in California.

25. OAI 6

Tate looked up as John came into the lab. "Hey, John, the Anasso are still interested in the Qrie entities. They believe the Qrie are preparing to be discovered on Earth. However, the Anasso say the Qrie will reveal themselves only to the governments they consider friends, as they did with the Atoom. Earth's technology has reached a point where they can't hide any longer.

"They say the Qrie can take on a physical form under very restricted circumstances. The use of physical forms by the Qrie is unprecedented in Anasso history.

"They sent us a huge file on the Qrie. I won't go into it here."

Tate handed John the thick folder.

"OK, so these Qrie entities are about to come out of the closet. Do the Anasso have any idea what we can expect?"

"Not a whole lot Tate, except those incidents in Miami and California could be the first steps towards discovery. The Qrie will control everything up to the point of discovery unless a unique opportunity arises. According to the Anasso, the Qrie won't interfere with free will unless the Qrie are interfered with.

"One thing they did say was that we should inform, in secret, the agencies investigating the Qrie about the situation and how they should conduct themselves."

Tate hesitated for a moment and then continued. "I know – the Anasso sound like a broken record. Yes, and they did emphasize that last part — about being secret and safe. I get the feeling that when the Qrie showed themselves to the Atoom, the Atoom didn't do everything quite right and got their tails stepped on, so to speak.

"One other thing you'll find in the report is that the pure Qrie are more alien then we imagine; they're pure energy and don't communicate in any form of verbal language. They communicate to the Anasso through their created entities on the various planets. They have found out that 'their' Qrie do know about the physical Qrie here on Earth but won't elaborate further."

"Interesting Tate. Who do they recommend we inform?"

"If I interpret the Anasso correctly, the people we inform should be high level. The Qrie seem to be centering their activities in eastern Australia. This is where our primary subject, Breath Of Spring, happens to be. And she's associated with the Royal Australian Navy in that area.

"There's Vice Admiral Winston Lynch, who has worked with us. I think he should be the one we contact. On the American side, Admiral John Grant also knows about us. From our feelers at the Department of the Navy, Admiral Grant is supposed to soon become Commander in Chief of the Pacific. He'd be well placed to handle any adverse situation."

"Thanks, Tate. Give me all the pertinent information, and I'll take a trip to inform them."

***

Breath, I've got some information for ya.

What is it, GP?

Morning and Beauty have analyzed the fifteen culprits — the ones from the boat, the ones from the warehouse, and the ones involved in the incident with your family. They all work for the same group. It's called Earth Only. It's run by a man named Melvin Blanchard through several shell corporations. Our problem right now is locating him, since he never stays in one place long and operates under the pseudonym TDog. The FBI is also looking for him, for the murders of a number of other so-called aliens. Morning and Beauty feel that they're the ones responsible for the deaths of your stepmother's family, Robert, Vincent, and Desiree Moreau.

I have the memories of the murdered family members. Robert Moreau was shot in the back of the head with a large caliber hollow point bullet. After I analyzed Robert, Vincent, and Desiree, I realized that Vincent and Desiree were probably shot from behind with the same type of high-powered pistol. None of them have any memory of even being shot, and none of them have any memory of the others having been shot. So, there had to be three murderers.

That's at least some news, GP. We're making some progress.

Well Breath, it's something. The FBI is also looking for someone called Dixon. They don't know what his last name is or even if that is his name. He works for Melvin Blanchard and is his number-one instigator and hit man. These people won't hide from us for long.

PART 2

1. CORAL SEA

Captain Oscar Blankenship sat looking at his fingernails, there was nothing more to chew. He thought — *We only have four bilge pumps, and two of them need repair, and the last two are barely keeping up. I think my old* Sweet Lady *here's on her last rusted legs.* He glanced at a monitor screen that showed his dangerous cargo on the aft container mount of his small cargo ship. He then took a quick side glance at a bearded man armed with an AK-47 standing off to one side of the bridge. *If I could figure out a way to get rid of those terrorist SOBs, I'd dump that accursed box along with them into the sea and take my* Sweet Lady *here to a nice tropical island where we could both retire. I know this is your last trip* Sweet Lady, *and I hope we can finish everything before we sink.*

Oscar paced, and the fresh deck paint was becoming thin on the bridge.

"Oh, holy... Captain! You're gonna wanna look at this."

Blankenship turned, straightened to his full height, shoulders back, head erect, and moved with a slow deliberate stroll over to the radar screen, while trying to exude the confidence he didn't possess. He mumbled under his breath to the radar operator so no one else could hear. "What now, don't we have enough trouble?"

The radar operator looked up at his Captain and whispered. "Maybe not."

There were two blips on the screen, one circling the other, and he knew he was probably looking at a Royal Australian Navy (RAN) ship with a helicopter circling it.

They couldn't tell that it was a helicopter from the blip. Oscar surmised the truth from the relative speeds of the two blips. If he got anywhere near them, he was going to be boarded and not make port. They knew him, and, more important, they knew his *Sweet Lady.*

He thought with discouraged contemplation. *Damn, both of those blips have turned towards my ship; I can't have those guys coming on board. Maybe if I turn and make like I'm going north real confident-like, they won't decide to follow me. We just can't look like we're in a huge panic right now.*

Blankenship turned to his helmsman. "Set your heading to 340°. Do it slow like we intended to do that the whole time. Maybe they won't follow us." He watched the two blips on the radar screen for about fifteen minutes and noticed that the slower one had changed course. It was now on an exact intercept course to where they'd be in a short time.

Shit, he thought with an angry frown. *I'm gonna have to run for it, but I do get to dump that damn container. This isn't going to make the owners of that cargo happy. We'll be lucky to come out of this with our skins. Maybe they won't harm the crew and we can come out of this alive. I hope.*

He told the helmsman, "Make for international waters as fast as we can go!" He called down to the engine room. "Give me as much speed as we can get outta this tub; we gotta get outta here. We got the RAN on our asses!" The man with an AK-47 lowered his gun and pointed it at Oscar. Oscar turned towards him. "I'm open to any suggestions. You can always go back, get another container, and hijack another ship. Otherwise, we all get thrown in prison for a long time. We've gotta dump that container."

The man just stood there in total indecision, mouth open, and eyes blank. He then whirled and left the bridge.

Oscar watched the radar screen with intensity. The RAN ship was going to intercept them before they reached international waters. The helicopter was going to get there a lot sooner than that.

Man, the crap just piles deeper. He turned to the first mate and yelled, "Get as many people down on the deck as possible!" He pointed at the twelve-meter (forty-foot) intermodal container, with multiple rusted holes in it, locked down on the deck. "Get that accursed thing off my ship. As rusty as it is it'll sink like a rock. The rest will be okay."

Oscar watched pandemonium take place on the aft deck of his ship. The men were like ants climbing the overhead crane and crawling with levers, ropes, block and tackle, winches, and anything that they thought would help move the accursed box off his deck as soon as possible. He and the men knew it weighed about sixty-five metric tons. All the crewmen sprang forward with a desperate will.

The terrorists had told the crew what was in the box, and they'd all signed up anyway. But Oscar wasn't quite sure whether they'd signed on willingly, because he knew he wasn't given a choice. If the RAN found out what was in that box — well, he didn't want to think about those consequences. He could always say his ship and crew were hijacked. Which was true, but with his less than stellar reputation, no one would believe him.

Just before the box was splashed overboard, Oscar watched two of the terrorists open and go into the box and then come out a few minutes later, closing and locking the container. He pondered in a bit of a panic. *What are those idiots doing I hope they didn't set some kind of explosive charge? If they did and that thing blows up; the RAN is gonna get here and they're gonna be pissed.* A frantic few minutes later, the mysterious cargo box was dumped with vicious abruptness into the sea.

Sweet Lady felt relieved and invigorated, as she added a knot to her speed. The chase continued towards international waters.

***

Breath watched while standing on the bridge of *Morning Discovery*, barefoot and in one of her blue loose-fitting, short-sleeved, muumuu dresses, that she now considered her standard uniform. Her ship was a luxury catamaran yacht that had sunk, was salvaged, and then converted into a survey vessel. Geoscience Australia used the ship for bathymetric measurements of the ocean floor and general oceanographic studies along the reef.

Breath, now nineteen almost twenty, had been on *Morning Discovery* for about three and a half years. She loved her job as its new science director, and she loved her ship. Except for the continuous training sessions that GP had her doing, which she has had to hide from the crew of *Morning Discovery*. She now considered her life on board ship as normal. She thought. *Every one of the crew is under a partial Qrie Compulsion. Perfectly normal all over — and in every way, well — except for...*

The ship is a thirty-three-meter long steel-hull catamaran with an eleven-meter width. It can make twenty-eight knots. It has a folding drop deck at the aft of the ship for skin- and scuba-diver access. It has a fourteen-foot hard-bottom inflatable boat on drop arms on the foredeck. It also has two ten-foot inflatable lifeboats in emergency storage on the foredeck.

Breath watched with interest. The large fishing trawler or small cargo ship, a mile or two ahead of them, changed heading by one hundred and eighty degrees and picked up speed. She watched through her binoculars at the frantic movement on the ship. Something fell or was pushed off the aft end into the ocean with an impressive splash of clear blue-green water.

She scowled a bit, and thought. *That entire thing is rather strange. I think we should go and check it out. That ship threw something large and heavy into the ocean. That was their intent, since they didn't slow down or change course in any way afterwards. They seem to be trying to get as far away from that mystery object as possible.*

Breath considered her options when the crewman at the radar station yelled out to no one in particular, "That's a RAN patrol boat, and it's after that ship; the ship might be running contraband. There are two other blips on the screen. One moving fast, could be a helicopter, and the other one slower, which could be the RAN patrol boat. Because both are moving in that ship's direction on intercept vectors."

Breath called down the stairs to the deck directly below to Dr. Kavanaugh, her thin but well-built postdoc assistant. "Hey, Ben, have we picked up the last of the sonar sensors? There's something going on up here, and I'd like to go check it out."

Ben called back, "We're about done here. We've got one more sensor to pick up. Be about two minutes, and then we can head out. What's up?"

"I don't know, but there are strange things going on out here."

"I know what you mean," Ben shouted back. "I've been watching them too. There are several of them out there — four, it looks like — and they move fast. I didn't think that dolphins could swim that fast, and they seem to be able to stay down a lot longer than any dolphins I've ever seen. As a matter of fact, I haven't seen any of them come to the surface since I've been watching."

Breath took a moment to try to reconcile what she was seeing and what Ben was saying. It didn't work. "What are you talking about, Ben? I haven't been watching dolphins. I've been watching a ship out here doing strange things and dropping containers off its aft end."

"Oh, that. Yeah, that ship just dropped something off and it's big, but I thought you were talking about the blips we had on the sonar array. There are several of them; they all move fast, and they don't seem to be coming up for air. I thought they might be dolphins, but they don't act like dolphins. They're way too fast."

Breath chewed her lower lip, a habit she'd never been able to break anytime she was deep in thought or had to make a decision without adequate information. She made up her mind and quit chewing. "Have you got the recorder on so we can keep track of them?"

"Yeah."

"Good. Keep it running! We're heading towards where we saw that ship lose whatever it was off its stern. They definitely didn't seem to want it on board, and it could be bad news for the environment — maybe something toxic."

Ben appeared at the bottom of the passageway and gave her a thumbs-up. "OK, go! We've got the last sensor. We're pulling it in now."

Breath turned to the Captain, who was standing a few paces away and scanning the same spot on the ocean. "Skipper, please make for where we saw that ship lose that piece of its cargo. We might be able to pick it up if it floats, or drop a remote down and see where and what it is if it doesn't. If it's dangerous, we need to get it picked up and moved. We think a RAN patrol boat will be here in a short while, and maybe they can give us a hand."

Skipper nodded to the helmsman, who turned the helm a few points to starboard and eased the dual throttle controls forward. The powerful, idling twin diesel engines took on a deeper, vibrant growl as the ship began a graceful acceleration.

The helmsman never took his eyes off the target spot, and replied. "We're on our way."

Not bothering with the ship's intercom, Breath turned her head and called down the stairs again. "Ben, you've been watching some weird blips on the sonar. What are they doing now?"

She could tell by Ben's muted voice that he was still staring at the display of the sonar unit and not bothering to turn his head towards the door. "They're moving in the same direction we're going right now, only they're way ahead of us and increasing their distance. It looks like they might be heading for that thing that ship dropped into the ocean. They're a curious bunch, whatever they are. It almost looks like they're racing. There are two individuals out ahead of the others. They've gotta be going for whatever we're looking for as well."

There was a short pause, and Breath could've sworn she heard a long, low whistle. "Dr. Spring, these things are amazing. They've got to be going sixty kilometers per hour or better. I've watched them for about twenty minutes on the sonar, and they keep darting in and out of view; they seem like they're playing some kind of game. It's almost like a game of tag you'd see children playing in a schoolyard. I know dolphins do play games, but I've never seen anything like this. Well, guess what? We have a winner. The two that were..."

Just then, a tremendous explosion in front of their ship made the bulkheads vibrate and knocked out the sonar system.

Several simultaneous thoughts raced through Ben's mind. *Damn, I just fixed that array system last week. Man, that was one whale of an explosion. Thank God for these sound-limiting headphones! I hope those blips are okay... nice ship, nice ship, don't sink.*

Ben turned to the hatchway, which was still open to the bridge. "What the hell was that? I heard it and felt it down here. Is everybody okay? Did we hit something?"

Breath, things are gonna get a little — exciting. Stay calm and be professional. Don't do anything rash. I'd suggest y'all be just as surprised as everyone else.

What's that supposed to mean, GP? What are you telling me?

Things are gonna start happening rather fast. Just go with the flow.

GP, you sound like something serious has happened.

It has, and it's not good. Morning, Beauty, and I are on our way.

What is it?

There was no response.

GP answer me! What's happened?

You'll find out soon enough.

Uh — does this mean my time of being normal is over?
Yep — pretty much!

Breath's voice strained, and after a pause to absorb what GP had just said, she called down to the sonar lab, "Ben, get up here, 'now.' There's been a huge explosion where that thing fell off the other ship."

Ben came bounding up the stairs, two steps at a time.

Breath looked at him for a moment and had an inappropriate thought, *He is in great shape for a geek — not even breathing hard. He's taller and thinner than Reggie. Not as muscular but that's...* She applied the brakes to that thought and brought herself back to the situation at hand, albeit a bit chagrined. *What would Skipper say, or Hipsi, for that matter?*

Ben grabbed an available pair of binoculars and started looking in the direction of the explosion, trying to spot any debris.

Skipper put *Morning Discovery* into a slow and guarded circle around the explosion site. They all continued searching the area as their ship drew closer to the expanding circle of froth on the sea's surface, which marked the origin of the blast.

Both of them saw it at the same time. A head popped up out of the water, looking glaringly out of place. Not only that, but it was a human head attached to a human body, with a massive crown of golden hair spreading out in every direction. Even from a distance, the observers could sense that the being seemed to look dazed and disoriented.

As they watched amazed, another similar head appeared near the first, displaying the same long flowing golden hair. The second seemed to be struggling to pull the first and two others to the surface.

Breath and Ben both saw that they had to be people, and they were injured. They shared a split-second gaze of horror between themselves. Breath spun back into the interior of the bridge.

She started to give directions to Skipper. She found that he was already maneuvering the ship into position to get a launch off. Several crew members were running for the inflatable boat.

You never have to tell real professionals how to do their jobs. She was chewing on her lip again.

The crew moved three injured, very unusual looking golden skinned people, off the dripping rescue boat. They laid them, with care, on the aft diver access deck of the ship. The rescue team made sure the stricken survivors were safe onboard. They turned to shove off into the waves again for the fourth victim. That one had the same golden skin and hair as the others.

Breath had a fleeting thought as she ran towards the aft railings. *What's this? Some kind of nudist cruise or an ocean-going orgy? Maybe it's gold body paint!*

***

Doc, the ship's paramedic, sprinted towards the aft access deck as fast as he could go with his bag. Breath and Ben pounded in his wake. They got to the access deck, and Doc was already busy. He looked grim. He checked two of the three golden people lying on the deck. They were a bloody mess of pulped flesh and hemorrhaging orifices.

Breath had taken a course in first aid and EMT training at the University of Miami. She knew that two of these people didn't have a chance. She looked at the one who was still moving. The young, slender, well-muscled, golden-haired female was the one that doc was now working on, with frantic determination.

Still in the water was the fourth victim also bleeding, but active.

Breath was about to ask the rescue team about the fourth victim. She noticed that person had begun swimming in a circle. As she watched, the golden form began a slow rise out of the water. It was unmistakable. Other crewmen and the rescue crew saw this as well. They joined Breath in frozen wide-mouthed amazement. Here was a golden, nude young woman, with massive golden hair floating above the water. She had a bright and glowing white light all around her and what looked like huge wings of light, coming from her back. Breath realized she was also glowing. She did an exercise that GP had taught her about hiding her light from humans, but still letting the Qrie energies flow.

On closer examination, they weren't wings. They looked like huge gossamer trees with lightning-like plasma tendrils as the limbs and twigs coming out from the person's back and wrapping around towards the front, but also reaching far above and below her. When Breath took a closer look at these treelike things, they reminded her of glittering streamers of glowing plasma. The structure was always the same, just in finer detail the further out from her body it extended. As she inspected the structure through her binoculars, the detail got finer and finer until it just disappeared. The other thing that was obvious was the magnificent colors of light streaming through the structure. She could see wave after wave of beautiful colored light moving through the tendrils towards the person's back. It seemed as if the light was life-giving blood moving through veins towards the heart.

Standing next to Breath, Ben blinked and whispered, "Wow!"

Breath shot him a quick incredulous glance on this titanic understatement and then collected herself. She leaned over the railing and shouted. "Can we help you?"

The young golden woman made no comment and indeed seemed not to have heard her at all. She continued to float a few feet clear of the ocean surface. Her emanating light became brighter. Tendrils of this plasma light began to stream towards the three golden figures on *Morning Discovery's* deck.

Seeming oblivious of the spectacle occurring only meters away above the ocean surface, Doc looked up at Breath after finishing his examination of the three on the deck. "These two are dead. I can't do anything for them. This one is still alive but not for long, unless we can get her on that helo and get her to a hospital." He pointed at a RAN helicopter flying in their direction.

Someone on the helicopter called out and asked if anybody had been injured. At the same moment, two bright lights flashed around the golden person floating above the water. The helo pilot was startled. He almost crashed into *Morning Discovery.*

He caught the helo just in time. He jerked the controls so hard that one of the personnel in the helicopter was thrown out. He struck the deck of the ship with his head and fell into the sea. The pilot moved the helicopter a reasonable distance from *Morning Discovery.* He put the helicopter down in the water on its floats on the windless, calm sea.

One of the two bright lights moved over to *Morning Discovery* and began floating above the people on the access deck. The golden angelic female flew to the RAN crewman who fell out of the helicopter. She lifted him up out of the water and floated him to the access deck. She gently laid him there, with the three other golden people.

Doc was startled by this, but not for long. He started examining the RAN crewman who had a broken neck, several other bad cuts, contusions, and broken bones. He concluded that there was no hope for this man. Doc now had three dead people and one in very serious trouble, on the aft deck of the ship. The light that floated over the access deck brightened and then faded somewhat. Everyone froze. They just stared, unable to move, everyone except Doc and Breath.

Breath turned and looked at the light above them.

The light brightened. Everyone on board *Morning Discovery,* the helicopter, and the rescue crew in the water heard not a voice but a mental projection from the light. *I am the Qrie Morning. This is the Qrie Beauty. The golden one above the water and the three on your ship are called Mer. Do not touch them, and do not move them in any way.* Galactic Prime *comes.*

Breath was stunned. She'd heard the names Qrie, Morning, and Beauty all her life, but now she was face to face with the Qrie. She thought, *Is this what they're really like?*

Are you 'the' Morning and Beauty that I've known and communicated with all my life?

Morning and Beauty together replied. *Yes.*

Breath grinned a confident little smile. *Yes, of course...*

About this time, the RAN patrol boat *Queen's Shield* came up alongside *Morning Discovery*. Commanding Officer (CO) Lieutenant Commander Lawrence Tibbett called out to the Captain, "Ahoy, *Morning Discovery*! May we board your ship?"

Skipper yelled back, "By all means. We need your help. We've got several injured — on board, including one of your own helo crewmen. Please have your doctor come aboard as well."

CO Tibbett, of the refitted and modified Armidale-class patrol boat, deftly maneuvered alongside *Morning Discovery*. A Sub Lieutenant, a couple of crewmen, and the doctor of the RAN boat made their way to the aft access deck. When they arrived, their jaws dropped. They stood frozen for several seconds before they started to move again.

Breath turned and saw the Sub Lieutenant standing before her. He was tall, over six feet, with light sandy-blond hair cut in a military style. Breath noticed he had a straight nose, strong chin, broad shoulders, and nice strong hands.

As Tom stared at her, he sensed a strange form of energy pass between them. Each had unusual thoughts about the other, and both 'knew' it. There was mental and emotional linkage in some bizarre manner between them.

Breath sighed and realized this energy was similar to the energy that passed between her and her mum and dad.

They both felt a surge of energy that stopped them in their tracks. They also felt an expansion of mind that only Breath had experienced before. Both knew there was a powerful attraction that neither of them had ever felt before. Neither of them understood why this was happening. Their minds had linked, and Sub Lieutenant Tom Haynes was stunned.

Breath knew she had to get back to the emergency at hand and forced herself to break this wonderful knowing link.

She shook herself and asked. *GP, what was that? We were in each other's minds, just like the Qrie, for God's sake. Is he Qrie?*

There was no reply.

GP?

She then turned to the RAN crew. "Things are a bit strange here right now. This…" Breath paused for a moment and pointed at one of the lights. "This is the Qrie Morning. The other light there is the Qrie Beauty. That golden person floating above the water and three of those on the deck here are called Mer. The Qrie Morning has just informed us that someone or something called *Galactic Prime* is coming."

Sub Lieutenant Haynes, in a formal military style, said, "Thank you, Ma'am. Doctor, what can you tell me about the condition of these people?"

The RAN doctor turned to Haynes and pointed at the people on the deck. "Three of these people are dead. We can't do anything for them, including one of our own crewmen. One is barely alive and needs to get to a hospital ASAP."

Haynes took charge again. "OK, then, let's get that — person loaded into the helicopter and get her to a hospital ASAP."

The Qrie Morning projected to Tom and the crew. *You will do nothing. You will not move these people. We will take care of them — all of them.* Galactic Prime *comes.*

Haynes objected. "I don't care if it's the Second Coming of God. We need to get this person to a hospital now. So, get out of our way and let us do our job!"

A powerful light formed around the RAN crewman and the three strange golden people lying on the aft deck, preventing anyone from moving them. As hard as Haynes tried to break through the light, he couldn't do it. Breath had no problem with the light and was trying to help. She was secretly channeling healing Qrie energies to the injured. She didn't want anyone else to see.

"Just who do you think you are?" Tom Haynes yelled at the light. "We have people injured and dying! We must get them to hospital. And just who is this *Galactic Prime*?"

The Qrie Morning projected a brief explanation. Galactic Prime *and the Qrie are the assemblers of the Milky Way*

Galaxy and many surrounding galaxies. The Qrie Morning and Beauty are the assemblers of this solar system.

A strong *Qrie Embrace* was then felt by all present. Breath instantly recognized this embrace. She froze in her tracks. She received information on many different levels infusing her with far more understanding than anyone else there.

Oh, My God! '*I AM Qrie!*' She exclaimed to herself, as if this was the first time, she had comprehended what she was.

GP projected with a chuckle. *Well duh — Breath! And your new life starts right now.*

***

Everyone except Breath was stunned. The power, the expansion of the mind, and the feeling of peace and well-being were amazing. Breath had been through it all many times before and knew it intimately.

Everyone else had the same thought simultaneously, as if all their brains were linked, which in a way they were. *Have we just heard what we thought we heard? Can this be true? Who are these beings? We might be able to understand the Mer; they at least look human. The Qrie don't even have bodies. They're just pure energy, as far as we know, and God knows what kind of energy that is. Did we just encounter God? Anything that can assemble a galaxy or even a solar system has to be God.*

Breath let her being absorb the *Qrie Embrace*. This time, the mind link between she and Tom was much stronger.

The thought came: Galactic Prime *is here.*

A tremendous light formed at the aft end of *Morning Discovery*. *Galactic Prime* covered all the injured people on the deck of the ship with a powerful light.

Breath had no problem walking through the light. She stood over one of the injured but was inhibited from moving anyone. Haynes was still trying to get through the light but couldn't do it. When the bright light came, she was in it, along with the four on the deck and the one floating over the water.

They were lifted up and floated out over the water away from *Morning Discovery*. Breath was gently placed back on the deck in a brilliant shield of light.

The four injured were floated out over the water, along with the other golden Mer floating just off the ship. The light floated above them and became unbearable to look at. Even with their eyes shut, it was still too bright. The light came right through their skin into their bodies.

Breath basked in its glory.

This continued for several minutes. Then, as the light decreased in intensity, three of the four golden Mer and the RAN crewman were now living, breathing, healthy, active beings, and each was surrounded by a shield of multicolored light. They were again placed upon the deck of the ship. One of the Mer, the one with the horrible head injury, remained floating off the ship over the water.

Breath watched as all this happened and sensed that she had a similar shield of light around her. She'd felt this wondrous marvelous expansion of light and mind many times in her life. It began to dissipate. Within a few seconds, her light shield was completely gone, as if nothing had happened. The wondrous feeling dissipated much slower.

Several exclamations came from the helicopter. People who'd been injured in the helicopter, by its sudden motion, were also healed.

The Mer with the terrible head injuries was lifted into the center of the extreme but indistinct light and disappeared. Breath knew this Mer died and couldn't be resurrected.

Galactic Prime expanded the light to cover all the crews assembled in both ships and the helicopter. Everyone was flooded with a massive *Qrie Embrace*. *Galactic Prime* projected to everyone assembled, *I am* Galactic Prime *of the Qrie. I do not consider myself God. You now know of our existence. We will make an accord with you.*

Breath thought. *Something here feels really familiar. The only difference is the lack of the Southern drawl...*

Galactic Prime continued. *The Mer will work with both Dr. Breath Of Spring and her crew and Commander Lawrence Tibbett and his crew. You will not find better-qualified people than the Mer to help you with your oceanographic studies and the protection of the shores of this nation. In addition, the Qrie and the Mer will keep a conscious presence on the crews of* Morning Discovery *and* Queen's Shield *to make sure that they are in good health and safety.*

The Mer can handle themselves against considerable odds, whether human or natural, but the Mer cannot kill anyone human or Mer.

In exchange for this help and aid, you will maintain our secret. You will not disclose to any person or agency whatsoever who we are or that we even exist.

You can study the Mer, but you shall not take fluid or tissue samples or perform any other invasive procedures or restrain them in any way. This accord will be agreed upon this day. You will not be allowed to discuss this with your superiors except those already under Compulsion. This accord applies to all people assembled here today and will be binding until the Qrie Stewards or I release you from this accord.

By this time, Commander Tibbett had climbed aboard *Morning Discovery.* Tibbett challenged the telepathic — voice. "This all sounds ominous and commanding. I don't like it. I'm also not comfortable with this conscious presence that you talk about. What happens when I get new crew members? What if someone slips and lets the secret out?"

Galactic Prime projected. *I would like for this to be voluntary. However, I can already sense several members of the crew are considering a financial reward for this information. I am not sure anyone will believe them, but we will not take that chance.*

As for new crew members, you will inform them as to the situation with us. Before they meet the Mer, they will be subject to the Compulsion, as I will impress it upon each of them.

Dr. Spring, Commander Tibbett, we will do all that we said to help you with your studies and your duties. However, considering the sensitivity of this accord, I will place a mandatory Compulsion on all of you that you will not divulge our existence to anyone not under the Compulsion.

The only decision that you, Dr. Spring, and Commander Tibbett have is, do you want our help or not?

Breath shook herself out of her reverie. "I, for one, certainly want the help. I welcome it with open arms. I want to know everything I can find out about the Mer and you, *Galactic Prime.*"

Tibbett — still shaken by the events. "The way you put it; I really don't have a choice. The Compulsion will be applied regardless. So yes, I'll accept the help."

Breath and Tom asked simultaneously, again with one mind, "When will the Compulsion be removed?" They glanced at each other.

Galactic Prime replied, *The Compulsion will remain in force until we reveal ourselves to the world at large, which will be a long time — probably never. We know the technology of this modern world is good, and we cannot avoid being discovered again.*

We want to be discovered on our own terms and under our own conditions. We do not want a hostile government discovering us and forcing us to defend ourselves. This would not be good for us or the government and would be counterproductive.

Sub Lieutenant Haynes, the crew of Morning Discovery *is good. As they have long-range pictures of what was happening on that ship just prior to them dumping their cargo. Perhaps they will be of use to you.*

Skipper replied with confusion. "I didn't take any pictures."

At that moment, a crewman came running down from the bridge, saying, "Skipper, photographs of that ship we were looking at just showed up. I don't know where they came from, but you're not going to believe these pictures."

One of the crewmen pointed at something coming their way. "Would you look at that?" A small freighter ship with a flat aft deck was moving towards them. As it drew closer, they saw three golden people with huge wings of light flying in formation. Everyone watched in amazement as the Mer brought the old ship and left it some distance from the RAN ship. The ship had hardly stopped when Commander Tibbett ordered a hard-bottomed inflatable boat towards it.

Haynes thought. *When did the Mer leave? I never saw them go. And how are they doing that?*

The light around *Galactic Prime* increased for a moment. Everyone felt the *Qrie Embrace,* and then it was gone. The Qrie Morning projected to Breath and Tom. *Is there anything else we can do for you? If not, we would like for you to introduce yourselves to the Mer.*

Please do not touch the Mer or the human. This can discharge their Qrie field that you see about them and cause you and them considerable pain. They can, however, touch you with their hands; let them do the touching. I will take my leave of you.

Breath and Haynes looked at each other and commented together. "We've a million questions." They gazed at one another. Their minds were linked.

With that, the Qrie left, leaving a sense of well-being, love, and oneness in their wake. They also took the contraband ship and its crew. The ship just disappeared in a tremendous blaze of light and thunderous sound.

Breath and Haynes looked at each other again and asked in perfect unison, "What the..."

***

GP, it's nice to see that Morning and Beauty can use language now.

Yes Breath, it is. It makes things a lot easier.

***

Doc had his stethoscope out, preparing to listen to the chest of the crewman. The RAN doctor was about to do the exact same thing. They were asking all manner of questions when Breath and Tom ran up together and shouted. "Don't touch him, whatever you do."

Doc asked, "Why not? We need to find out what's going on here and if he's back to health."

Haynes stepped forward and placed a cautionary hand on the Doctor. "The Qrie told us not to let anyone touch them. They were emphatic about it, so we're going to take them at their word. It has something to do with that glow of light around them. Just don't touch them. I assume the light will dissipate over time. We'll just have to watch and see."

The other Mer floated down and joined the humans around them on the aft upper deck of *Morning Discovery*. Breath invited them into what was a large combination break room, conference room, and dining area with a big table and chairs. Commander Tibbett, Tom, Breath, and Ben formed a receiving line there for their visitors.

As they started filing into the room, Breath introduced herself to each of the Mer. She was startled when she saw the Mer in the light. Their skin looked like pure gold, and they were so young. Two of the Mer helped the RAN crewman maneuver into the room. Breath was startled again when the first Mer came up to her. This was the female who had been injured but hadn't died.

"How do you do, Dr. Breath Of Spring? *Galactic Prime* asked me to tell you that it knows the complete origin of your name and likes it."

Breath didn't know what to say. A small, gentle but powerful voice came into her mind. *Own your name.* And with that simple statement, she had an overwhelming feeling of *Qrie Embrace*, and she knew that it had come from *Galactic Prime*.

"I'm Kandy Bernard." She turned and pointed to the other two Mer. "This is Neil and Sophianna. The one who died and was taken by *Galactic Prime* was our friend, Cheyenne."

Breath could sense the deep sorrow and pain that Neil, Kandy, and Sophianna were experiencing as they mourned their friend.

The second Mer approached her. "Hello, I'm Neil Talmage."

For a second, Breath's mind swirled. "I know that name. I know a Dr. Taylor Talmage. Could you be related?"

Neil whispered. "He's my father."

Again, Breath's mind swirled, as if it was getting too much information all at once. She couldn't sort it out. Bewildered, she asked Neil. "Does your father know what happened here today?" Then she thought. *Wait — maybe there's a way they can communicate like I do with Mum, Dad, and GP.*

"He knows. The Qrie and the Mer are connected by a telepathic link using the Qrie energies. All the Mer and their families on Earth know what happened here today, and how you, your crew, and your ship helped save our lives."

She thought. *They're like me, Mum, Dad, and GP.*

"Yes." Neil said. "And he was relieved when *Galactic Prime* showed up, as he knew then everything would be okay. All except for Cheyenne."

"Do you go to school in Reeftown?"

"Yes, I'm in the tenth grade. I take classes just like everyone else. I go to dances, football games, field trips, all kinds of school functions. I eat lunch, and I complain about homework. I even have a girlfriend." He looked over at Kandy. "She's also Mer like me, but I can swim faster than she can."

"Do you play any sports?"

"The Mer are stronger and faster than humans. It'd be an unfair advantage, and we do have to keep a low profile. I'd like a chance to swim against some of those super swim jocks at school who think they can beat anybody in the world. Cheyenne and I used to race all the time. We could beat anybody. I'm going to miss her so much. I know Kandy and Sophianna are too."

Breath again felt the grief, pain, heartache, and extreme loss that poured out from him. "Please accept my condolences. I'm so sorry for your loss."

She'd completely missed the third Mer, the one who was floating over the water, and had absolutely no clue as to anything about her. "Neil, I must introduce myself to Sophianna." She stopped and turned around. "She was the one who was floating out over the water, right?"

Neil gave a halfhearted smile and nodded.

Breath asked, "Oh, and what's her full name?"

"Sophianna Heilsvien."

***

Breath was preoccupied with the idea that the Mer existed, and she didn't hear much of the conversation that was going on around the table. A whole new species, and no one knew! She looked at the Mer closely — the golden hair, eyebrows, eyelashes, amazing deep-blue eyes, with brilliant gold rings around the irises. She wondered. *Is the shimmer of energy around their bodies the same Qrie energy that I put around my own body? If so, how does it make their skin look as if it could be made of pure gold?*

How could anyone see this and not suspect that they even existed? And what about those exceptional physical bodies, with the hair, the skin, and the ring in the eyes? Why don't they have nipples, navels, or external genitalia? They look like Ken and Barbie dolls, not anatomical at all. For that matter, except for the females' amazing hourglass figures, astounding beauty, tiny breasts, and the larger size of the male, male and female Mer look alike.

What about these Qrie entities or beings, balls of nonmaterial energy? I'm Qrie myself. She paused a moment finally having to accept that she was Qrie. *Am I like them? What did GP mean by my new life starts now? There's so much to learn. I've gotta know. I'd better get started because it's all going to take another lifetime.*

Breath's mind came back to the conversation. Tom Haynes had asked the Mer if it was possible to safely bring up the debris of the box or container or whatever it was that had held the explosive. Neil informed Sub Lieutenant Haynes that it would be no problem, and all the Mer rose to accomplish the task.

After the Mer had exited the room, Tom said. "Those Mer people are compliant, almost as if they were slaves."

A soft voice came into the minds of all those in the room. *The Mer are not slaves; they have free will like any other human being. They do have a strong desire to help move Mer and humans towards True Intelligence.*

"Wow!" everyone in the room said in unison.

Then Tom continued. "Those beings knew what we were saying, and they're not even here."

The same soft voice came into the minds of those in the room. *We're now always with you.*

Breath thought. *That's a scary concept.* Then, aloud. "What do you mean by True Intelligence?"

No answer came. She again became lost in thought.

"Are you okay, Dr. Spring?"

Breath awoke from a concentrated daze. Someone was shaking her and was asking her a question. Her mind snapped back from a place of extreme concentration, peace, and love, where she was at one with the entire universe. It was a familiar place to her, where she was comfortable and could think. For a moment, she was dazed. Then she asked. "What?"

Ben shook Breath. "Dr. Spring, you were way out in la-la land. Do you want to go see the debris that the Mer will bring back from the explosion site?"

"Uh, yes — I'd like to see that."

Tom asked. "Are we sure the Mer will be okay handling this stuff? I don't want anyone getting hurt."

No reply came from anyone. They were already gone.

CO Tibbett said in his commanding voice. "I want to make certain there's no more unexploded ordnance in that debris. If there is, isolate it and make sure it's safe. We don't want anyone else getting hurt. Have the Mer put everything in the hard-bottom inflatable boat so we can sort through it. I don't want it on the ship until we're sure it's okay."

After this was done, Neil asked Haynes if there was anything else, they could do for him.

"No, thank you, Neil. Not at this time. Thank you for what you 'have' done."

Kandy saw Breath on the upper deck of *Morning Discovery*. She floated in the air over to her and asked. "Dr. Spring, is there anything else you need or that we can do for you?"

Breath told the Mer that there was nothing more that she needed. She was saying her goodbyes to each of them when she came to Neil. She asked him if it would be possible for her to visit him, Dr. Talmage, and his family to ask some questions.

"Sure. I don't see why not. You know who we are now. So, we've got nothing to hide from you. You can't tell anyone else, anyway."

"Thank you." She said as they shook hands. His skin was as soft and smooth as a baby's, and not unlike her own, which belied the fact of his strength. When their hands touched, Breath felt the loss that Neil was radiating for his friend, Cheyenne. She reached up quickly, touched him on the shoulder, and gave him a powerful *Qrie Embrace*.

The astonishment on his face was profound. He looked at Breath in wide-eyed amazement and disbelief. She had just reached through his powerful Qrie field to touch him, and she had not discharged his field. "You're Qrie!"

Breath quickly put her index finger to her lips. He remained quiet and quickly turned to leave with his friends Kandy and Sophianna. Neil turned as they left and gave Breath a strange inquisitive look and nodded.

***

CO Tibbitt was talking to Sub Lieutenant Haynes, the helo pilot, and the crewman who'd been thrown out of the helicopter, killed, and resurrected by *Galactic Prime*. "In light of the situation that we just went through, the fact that no one was harmed and no equipment has been damaged in this entire situation on this ship, I can't possibly see how we could make any statement as to what happened out here today. We chased the contraband ship, they threw something overboard, it exploded, but the ship got away. I know it'll be difficult to explain, but with the Compulsions, that is all we can say — and it is what happened."

Haynes stepped outside the bridge and yelled across to *Morning Discovery*. "Skipper, if there's nothing else, we'll make for port."

"Nothing more here. Thanks a lot, and smooth sailing, Sub Lieutenant."

Haynes turned to the boatswain and gave the order to unlash and pull the duffel-bag-sized boat fenders. He then turned back towards *Morning Discovery* and saw the three remaining Mer and Breath. Their eyes locked on each other, and again, it was as if they were of one mind.

Haynes waved to those on-board *Morning Discovery* and thought, *I'd like to have a long, nautical conversation with Dr. Spring. She's gotta be the most beautiful woman I've ever seen in my life.*

Breath's thoughts turned to Tom Haynes. *Wow! I'd like to have more than just a nautical conversation.* She immediately became embarrassed, and her cheeks flushed. *OMG, I know what he was thinking. Did he get what I was thinking as well?*

As Breath and Sub Lieutenant Haynes looked at each other, they again felt this strange energy pass between them, and each knew exactly what the other was thinking.

2. OAI

John Kingman walked into the OAI communications and code lab as soon as he heard a new message had been decoded. He saw Tate in his office at the back of the long lab working feverishly at his computer and walked over. "Well, Tate, I see you got the two new large monitor screens that makes four now. How do you keep up with all of that information? You know this makes me feel inadequate with my one little computer screen. Anything new?"

"Hey John, yeah these extra screens make it easier to track the decoding. I talked to some of the guys and we're going to send the Atoom of the Anasso a complete English dictionary and a pre-Sumerian to English translation file. That way we don't have so many translations and translation errors to deal with.

"I haven't had a chance to read the message over yet. From what I've been able to see so far, the Atoom have sent us a rather detailed piece on how to treat the Qrie, their created entities, who they call the Kawreak, and how to avoid conflict. They say we'll have a different name than Kawreak for these entities. Basically, the same old stuff, beating the dead horse.

"When the Atoom first discovered the Qrie and the Kawreak, the Atoom were a bit... well... anal retentive. The Qrie didn't appreciate it. They didn't go into detail about what happened, but I suspect it wasn't comfortable for the Atoom."

John laughed. "Basically, beating the same old dead horse, as you say. Well, let's hope we do better. Did they say anything more about when this great unveiling might happen?"

"I haven't gone through the entire report, but from what I understand, it should happen soon, if it hasn't already happened. I suspect we should inform Vice Admiral Lynch in Australia. He should follow the events around Reeftown, since that's where all the activity seems to be taking place. He should pay close attention to the Qrie Breath Of Spring."

***

Soon, Tate visited John with more details. "Hey, John, I've been going over the report. One thing I found was a rather glowing account of how the Kawreak can be excellent allies. They say it is rare for the Qrie to enter into situations, but the Kawreak do and can perform feats no one else is capable of.

"Here's the rest of the report and some of my comments. I know you're going to need them for your upcoming trip to Australia and your meeting with Admiral Lynch."

"Thanks Tate, and on my trip back I'll bring you a koala bear."

"Oh, gee thanks John, just what I need."

3. HOME

Mums and dads worry about their kids the world over. They've done this for as long as there have been mums, dads, and kids. The Mer are no different.

Cheyenne's Mer father, John Weber; along with Kandy Bernard's human dad, Jefferson, and Mer mum, Connie; as well as Hilga Heilsvien, Sophianna's mum, were all gathered at Taylor and Crystal Talmage's huge stone fortress home and compound. They were all assembled to mourn for Cheyenne and to find out what had happened to the other young Mer. All these people considered themselves to be one Mer family. They went to great lengths to protect one another and their secret from the outside world.

The three Mer teenagers knew exactly what was going to happen when they got home. They knew Dr. Talmage was going to examine them with a fine-tooth comb that the RAN doctor and Doc from *Morning Discovery* could only read about in science-fiction novels.

The fathers would back Dr. Talmage and agree with any findings that he might make. They also knew that their mums would ask a million questions, few of which were answerable in a lifetime. The two Mer girls and Neil lamented this on their slow float to Neil's fortress home onto the beach and up the cliff to the seaside compound entrance. Neil, Sophianna, and Kandy looked at one another; there was a massive vacancy in their hearts.

When Neil opened the door, Dr. Talmage took one look at their gold skin. His eyebrows shot up and he pointed. "You three — my examining room. Now!"

As the three turned towards the room, the mums started asking questions. No one could understand exactly what was being asked because there were too many questions by too many people, and it all sounded like confusing noise.

Dr. Talmage was businesslike. He raised his voice. "Who goes first?"

Kandy was floating closest to Dr. Talmage. Everyone in the crowded room was being quite careful not to touch her or any of the other teenage Mer.

"Kandy, you're up." He began pulling scopes, lights, electrical leads, and other medical items from several drawers, and began plugging the leads into an array of electronic instruments.

Kandy looked askance at the instruments and other medical items Dr. Talmage was digging for. She looked at her parents and Doctor Talmage several times, with nervous glances. Some of the instruments looked to her like torture devices.

Dr. Talmage told everyone in the room to remain quiet while he did his examination. He had to concentrate. He held out his left hand and asked Kandy to take it. He then began to move his right hand, using slow caution, towards her chest. When he finally did touch her chest, he moved his hand back and dropped her hand.

He began with her hair. Examining what she thought might be each strand. He then continued down all the way to her toes. He continued slowly poking and prodding and sticking things where she didn't think things could be stuck. He was careful and gentle, trying his best not to cause her any discomfort. He pasted electrodes on various parts of her body and took a multitude of readings.

She didn't know what they were for, and she certainly didn't protest. He took every vital sign that he could imagine, and some she thought he just made up. He carefully took blood samples. He even took small skin scrapings, which did hurt a little. He took hair, fingernail, and toenail clippings. He did all this while everyone else watched with intensity.

The Mer are not bothered by nudity. They don't even think about it. There's usually a sign and a mirror on the inside of their front doors that looks like the sign on a unisex bathroom with a stick figure of a man and a stick figure of a woman in a dress. This's to remind any Mer walking outside to check and see if they do indeed have clothes on.

To Kandy the exam seemed to take an hour. Dr. Talmage helped her down from the examination table. "Next."

He then went through the same extensive examination of Neil and Sophianna.

After the three young Mer had been poked and prodded in every conceivable manner by Dr. Talmage, he picked up the tray of samples he'd been working with and put it in his office fridge. "I'll take these tissue and blood samples to my office and lab in town and analyze them on Monday. We'll know more when the data comes back. Until then, we'll just have to wait. I don't know about all of you, but I'm hungry." His voice cracked, and he paused for a moment. Then, with a tear in his eye, he muttered, "Let's eat."

Everyone moved through the huge rambling Talmage home, and out into the large dining room. Crystal Talmage had set out the good plates, glasses, and silverware on the long dining table. This wasn't unusual for them, except for the good China, as they had frequent meals together and on all weekends. The mums had made a huge meal for the group during the examinations. An empty chair was placed next to John for Cheyenne. Her picture and her favorite Fulton Cowrie shell were placed on her empty plate.

On matters of Mer, the group always deferred to John Weber, as he was the elder merman of the group.

"OK, Cheye... or, rather, Kandy." His voice cracked as he corrected himself, and then he continued with a hoarse whisper. "Tell us what happened. You might also want to include why you four were where you were when all this happened. And why weren't you paying more attention to those boats? Don't you know they've got sonar?"

He didn't have to tell her to use language instead of Mer or Qrie energy, for the benefit of the humans in the room. All Mer speak human languages when out of the water. Speaking requires less concentration and energy than using Qrie energies. The Mer speak with their physical voices, unless the information isn't easily communicated, or while underwater, or over a long distance. They even use cell phones just like humans do.

Humans, in the past, have noticed Mer laughing and gesturing with one another with no words being exchanged. This isn't a good thing and is frowned upon, since it makes humans curious.

Kandy's voice quivered as she began speaking. "The four of us went out for a swim. Everything was okay until we started playing tag. Things got a little fast after that, and before long, we were pretty far out, still playing tag." She took a deep breath to calm herself down. "That was when we saw the ships, and one of them lost something. We decided to race over to see what it was." She seemed to have forgotten about answering the question about keeping away from the boats.

Kandy began again, but with slow sad intensity. "Oh — My — Gawd. You wouldn't believe it. Neil got there first and won — I guess. Like, I didn't remember anything until I woke up floating upright on the back of that ship. Even after that, things were hazy. Oh — My — Gawd," she repeated. "The power of the Qrie energy was way immense. I wasn't aware of what had happened until we all entered the conference room.

"Before we went in, we all received an immense energy surge; it explained in detail what had happened to us, and allowed us to remember a lot of stuff. I believed this monstrous energy surge was from *Galactic Prime*. I didn't say anything to anyone except to introduce myself.

"I did talk to Dr. Spring for a second. Besides, Dr. Spring was way more interested in Neil than any of us."

Dr. Talmage asked. "Why was that Neil?"

"Uh well — Dr. Spring apparently knows you. I think she was surprised that the Mer could live on land with no one knowing about us. She seemed preoccupied with this idea. Before we left to come home, she asked if she could come by and talk to you and the family. She's extremely curious, and I suspect tenacious." He paused a second, debating with himself, as to whether he should say something else or not. "Uh — when we were leaving, I shook hands with Doctor Spring. She looked at me with compassion. Then she very quickly touched me on the shoulder. Right through the Qrie field. I felt 'by far' the strongest *Qrie Embrace* I have ever experienced. Except for the one I received from *Galactic Prime*. How's that possible anyway?" Neil's voice cracked, as tears were again flowing.

Everyone in the room just stared at Neil, not knowing what to say.

Dr. Talmage finally broke the silence. "Crystal told me about the Compulsion that *Galactic Prime* placed on all the humans there. I do know Dr. Spring, and I'd like for us to talk with her. This sounds like her — all business, all the time. Perhaps she will be an ally for the Mer. Considering what you have told us about her, Neil."

Each of the young Mer got a chance to give his or her version of the events of the day. They were grilled about the explosion and their impressions of what the Qrie Stewards and *Galactic Prime* were like.

Everyone was curious. Few Mer have ever actually encountered the Qrie Stewards. Even though, the Mer are in near continuous contact with them. The Mer never had any knowledge of *Galactic Prime*. The Qrie Stewards have never mentioned an entity by that name.

Each of the Mer teenagers told the same story. That of incomprehensible vastness and inconceivable power. The magnitudes of intensity were greater than the normal Qrie emotions associated with the Qrie energy and the *Qrie Embrace*. They also talked about Cheyenne, her loss, and how they missed her.

After many retellings, the adults decided it was time for bed. The energized young Mer knew they couldn't go to bed because they might discharge their fields. They all decided to give sleeping vertically a try. To anyone other than the Mer, this would've looked strange. The three golden nude teenagers were floating vertically several feet off the ground, in the corner of the backyard compound near the house. They had huge multicolored plasma wings, called flares. These flares came from their backs. Their bodies were surrounded by an even more glorious beautiful light from the Qrie energies. Sure enough, in a few minutes, they were all sound asleep.

All the Mer families have apartments at the Talmage's gigantic home and compound. Which is over twenty-four kilometers from their homes and apartments in Reeftown. The roads in town are paved, but more than half of the roads to the compound are dirt and gravel. Sometimes travel on those dirt roads can be a challenge. All the Mer families have four-wheel-drive vehicles.

4. DISCUSSION

Breath paced back and forth in her cabin mulling over the events of the day. Sleep was out of the question. She got up and put on a pair of loose, ripped, and holey blue jeans, and an old floppy sweatshirt. She took her pacing up on deck. As she was walking towards the bow of the ship, she found Skipper gazing blankly at the other boats in the harbor, deep in thought.

"How's it goin, Skipper? At least we got back to port in one piece. Can't sleep either?"

Skipper looked at her and just shrugged and looked into his coffee cup.

Breath took a deep breath and let it out as a long sigh. "Unusual day we had today. I'm really kind of looking forward to tomorrow. At least I'll have the weekend to mull all this over."

"It's tomorrow, Breath. And I don't know whether I'm up for understatements right now. I've lived all my life thinking I knew pretty much what was happening in the world, and especially the ocean. But after the events of today, it's got me wondering what's the truth that's going on out there.

"Woke up this morning thinking I had things pretty well in hand. Then all hell broke loose. I found out that there 'are' mermaids out there, although they damn sure don't look like any mermaids I've ever heard about.

"Those Qrie things and that *Galactic Prime* thing gave me a real..." His voice just trailed off and he paused for a long moment. "When those things showed up, I told myself that the world was coming to an end. I don't know about you, Breath, but my world just got turned upside down."

"Yeah, I know exactly what you mean. There was so much going on... I was trying to make sense of it all. You probably noticed that I was a bit out of it a few times. That Sub Lieutenant Tom Haynes, seemed to take everything in stride. Nothing seemed to faze him."

"Then I don't think you noticed the looks of absolute amazement on his face — or mine. I think there could've been a few moments of outright terror, if we're going to be honest with ourselves."

Breath paused. "Do you think he was 'afraid,' or something else? He just doesn't look the type. I know I was, and still am... apprehensive."

"Everyone gets scared, Breath, and I think everyone on both ships was scared. Some were scared out of their minds. That helicopter pilot, for example, looked like he needed a whole bottle of Valium when he transferred over to the RAN ship. He was in bad shape, with the accident and all. I could've taken a couple Valium myself."

"Don't berate yourself for an instant, for feeling that you were the only one apprehensive in that situation. How could you not be at least anxious, or at most scared half out of your mind?

"I'm not sure that anyone on Earth has ever encountered anything quite like what we went through today. I really don't think I'm going to get much sleep in the next week or so. I've got a lot of mental sorting out to do."

Skipper shifted his weight and continued while rubbing his chin. "Breath, you know, I think you need to get ahold of Sub Lieutenant Tom Haynes. I noticed that he took great notice of you. I think he'd also like to speak with you about what we went through. I'm not sure that he has anyone that he can talk to."

"Do you think so, Skipper?" she bashfully muttered with a shy, hopeful twinkle in her eye. "I was so caught up in what was going on that I never noticed."

"Breath, we've been together for about three and a half years now. You can't bullshit me like that. I saw you looking at him, and I saw him looking at you. There was no doubt there were super sparks flying between you two, whether you want to admit it or not. Don't try to pull the wool over my eyes; I'm way too old for that. I say give him a call. He's at the RAN base staying in the Bachelor Officer Quarters (BOQ). I already checked him out; he's single. And I also know that you checked him out as well. Here's the number where you can reach him.

"You know, he moves like you and those Mer folk do. He has the same regal, graceful elegance that you do. I know I've told you this before. I never thought I'd see it in a man, but he certainly has it. I think you need to know this guy."

With that, Skipper handed Breath a slip of paper. Her cheeks flushed. She took the note and gave him a shy smile. His smile was encouraging and approving.

"Skipper, you don't think he'll think I'm being too forward?"

"Not possible. He's probably awake right now, sorting through the events of the day. Just like we are, he's most likely thinking about you and wondering if he should call. I say beat him to the punch. Don't argue or try to analyze it to death; just do it. Get a life Breath. Go for it."

GP, should I do this? It's after midnight.

Yes, Breath. What Skipper said. He's up and needs someone to talk to about what happened today.

She nodded to Skipper and pulled her phone from a pocket as she walked away, dialing. The phone didn't have a chance to ring before it was answered.

"Hello!" A male voice answered.

"Hello, Sub Lieutenant Haynes? I hope I'm not disturbing you. This is Breath Spring. We met today and... Well anyway, I'd like to talk to you about what went on today, if you don't mind. I don't really know how to sort this all out. I was hoping you might have some perspective."

"Hello, Dr. Spring. I was just thinking about... I was just thinking about the, uh — events of the day, too. If you're like me, neither one of us can sleep. I'm so keyed up right now, there's no way I could sleep for a week. Do you think we could get together, have a cup of coffee, and talk this over? I really need to talk to someone about this."

"Do you know where Rebecca's Diner is? Oh — and you're going to have to come by *Morning Discovery* and pick me up. I don't have my car. I couldn't get it started last time I tried. Do you know where my ship is?"

"Yes, I know where Rebecca's is, and I know where your ship is. I'll be there in about ten minutes."

"Great. I'll meet you on the dock."

Breath couldn't go out wearing what she'd thrown on for a midnight walk around deck. That just wouldn't do. For a frantic five minutes, she went through her closet, and the only clean things she had were a pair of loose blue jeans and a pink blouse. *This'll have to do,* she thought.

I really do need to do some washing, and maybe even bring a couple of things in from the apartment. She put them on and went into her cabin's bathroom and started putting on makeup. She hoped she was getting it all on straight because the light was dim, and it was hard to make out exactly how good a job she did. *This will have to do and it'll stay if I don't use any Qrie energy.*

She grabbed her purse and ran down the gangway just as Tom pulled up. *Oh, my,* she thought. *I'm thinking of him as Tom now!*

He parked his ancient gray Toyota Land Cruiser a short distance away and got out. He walked over to her. "You look — nice."

When they looked at each other, they again felt that unusual energy between them. It wasn't as strong as earlier, but it was certainly there.

"How on earth can you tell? It's dark, after midnight." Then she thought. *Breath, you idiot! He just gave you a compliment. Accept it for what it is. Don't mess it all up with a bunch of facts. What would Hipsi say?*

As Tom opened her door, she looked over the bonnet of the car towards the ship. Sure enough, there was Skipper, looking down, surveying the world, making sure she was okay. A warm feeling went through her when she saw him. She mused. *And he'll probably be there when we come back.*

***

Rebecca's wasn't fancy, it was just a place where you can get a pretty good cup of coffee and a quick meal, and it was open twenty-four hours. The coffee was okay, but the hot chocolate was excellent! She thought. *I wonder just how many sleepless nights I've spent in this café, soaking up hot cocoa. More than I'd like to remember. I've really gotta get a life.*

Breath and Tom went in and looked around. Breath went to her usual booth in the back, where no one could overhear them. She was pleasantly surprised when Tom sat down beside her. She noticed a tingling. Her heart began to beat a little faster. They didn't say anything to each other until the waiter came over and asked what he could bring them.

Breath ordered a double hot cocoa and a glass of water. Tom asked if the cocoa was made fresh or just out of a package. Breath launched into a detailed explanation of how excellent the hot cocoa there was. The waiter smiled and rolled his eyes. Breath pointed to a sign over the bar that read:

The Chocolate Used in Our Extremely Superior Hot Cocoa
Comes All the Way from California and
Is Second to None.

Tom, being a bit of a cocoa fan himself, decided to go for the double hot cocoa with marshmallows.

Someone came into the café. Breath and Tom were quick to glance, with a nervous look, towards the door. However, the man just handed the waiter something. It looked like a five-dollar bill. The man was facing away from them, and they couldn't hear what he was saying. The waiter was facing them. "You really didn't have to do that, Mate. You could've brought this in the next time. I can trust you for a piece of pie Bob."

Breath and Tom looked at each other with an expression of relief. Both felt the subtle tingling again. They didn't know what to expect. They both stopped and looked deep into each other's eyes. They thought together, with their minds linked. *We've got the same color eyes.* That telepathic communication startled them, and they both looked down at the table.

As they waited for their order, they began to make small talk about the weather and whether Sydney or Melbourne was going to win the game next week and who'd go on to the playoffs. Neither of them cared anything about football. They just didn't know what to say and didn't want to acknowledge what had just happened. They also didn't want to start the conversation until they got their order. Besides, Breath was trying to calm herself down, since her heart was racing like a wildfire. *Reggie never affected me this way.*

When the waiter brought their drinks, he asked. "Is there anything else I can get you?"

Tom looked up at the waiter. "No, thank you. Everything is fine."

"In that case, just ring this bell. I'll come out and see what you need. I'll be in the back. Be warned: the bell is pretty loud." He set the bell on their table.

"Thank you."

The waiter left. Both voiced at the same time. "God, what a day!"

Breath was surprised. "Oh, I'm sorry. Please go ahead."

"No, no, you go first, please."

GP, what should I tell him? What should I talk about? Why do I feel so strange? Is he the one?

Breath could feel GP's smile, but he didn't give her any clue about — the one.

Breath, he's like y'all. But I wouldn't bring that up right now. Y'all might just freak him out. Put yourself in his position and talk. Y'all know y'all want to — talk, that is.

OK, GP, here goes.

"Sub Lieutenant Haynes, do you think the Compulsions will restrict us from talking about what happened today?"

"Please, Dr. Spring, just call me Tom. All my friends do.

"I don't know what this Compulsion is or how it works. I don't know what we're — restricted in discussing. I think the only way we'll find out is to start talking and see where it leads."

"Please, Tom, just call me Breath. I don't really like the name, but it's the only one I've got."

"Why don't you like your name?"

"Breath Of Spring — have you ever heard such a crazy name? My mum, Heidi Spring, is a modern-day hippie, free spirit, and psychic who missed the sixties by several decades or so. I was born here in Australia. My father, William Spring, was in the U.S. Navy, doing some kind of joint exercise with the Australian and New Zealand Navies.

"My mum, was here and pregnant with me. Somehow a newsgroup got the info that Mum had just gone into hospital and that my dad Will was with another news crew on his U.S. Ship.

"The two news crews decided to hook up communications between them so that my father could see my birth. As it turned out, the connection wasn't as good as it possibly could've been. By the time the news crews got everything working reasonably well, I'd already been born. Just couldn't wait for all that news-crew folderol. The news crew with my dad told him he had a new baby girl.

"Mum asked my dad what she should name me. Apparently, Dad didn't get that question, noise in the communications or something. And he told her, 'Hold up my little breath of spring so that I can see her.' Mum didn't hear the first part of that sentence; all she heard was *Breath Of Spring*. Sooo — guess what? I became Breath Of Spring.

"To anyone on this planet other than a new-age hippie, that would've been unthinkable. To her, it was perfect and normal. I've had to live with it ever since. Don't get me wrong. I love Mum dearly, but she could've named me Barbara, Esmeralda, or Sue. Anything but Breath Of Spring. The kids at school were really rough on me because of my name. They teased me and made jokes about me, my name, and worse, they were quite cruel. There's one thing, though. I'm probably the only Breath Of Spring on this Earth."

Breath questioned herself in silence. *What's happening to me? I never tell anyone anything about myself. And here I'm prattling on like a teenage girl to a man I don't even know.* She paused a moment and then realized. *OMG, I am a teenager.*

She perceived GP laughing. *Well duh, Breath.*

She paused for a moment and then continued to ramble. "At least it makes me unique. Have you ever heard of another person with the middle name *Of*? I know I never have. Oh, sure, there's the Queen of England and Prince of Wales, but those're just titles. It's not their name, and the word *of* isn't capitalized. The doctor at the hospital wrote *Breath Of Spring* with all three names capitalized. So, you're looking at the only person on this Earth with the middle name, *Of*. I'm somewhat like the Queen — my name is a title! At least her name is Elizabeth.

"Actually, it's not the worst thing I've ever been called. When I was growing up, no one wanted me around because I was such a klutz. Every time I tried to do something, things got knocked over, spilled, or worse; it was terrible. Most of my schoolmates and the children I grew up with just called me 'hippie freak.' It's like I've got this weird force field or something. Mum says the universe put a protective shield around me."

She thought. *There I go again, spewing words. To a man, no less, and he's listening. What the...*

She spewed on. "I was never a good athlete. I did like to run and was good at it. I think it was actually because I was never good at team sports. And, of course, no one wanted an uncoordinated fumbler on their team, although I was a good baseball pitcher. I had a really screaming fastball no one could hit. The problem was, I could never seem to catch the ball; it always seemed to veer off about the time I was about to catch it. I was a killer at dodgeball; no one could ever get me out. It was the only team sport I ever excelled at. I was also quite good at darts and archery, but they're not really team sports.

"The other thing that I'm really good at is swimming. I absolutely love it! Every time I go in the ocean..." Breath awkwardly stopped midsentence. *I can't tell him about the dolphins and whales and how they come around, and they tow me anywhere I want to go and how it's like we've got an intimate connection of some type. Mum and GP would have my head.*

She faked a cough and started again to cover up the obvious pause. "The swimming coach at my high school saw me swimming and tried his best to get me to join the swim team. But it was in vain."

What is it about this guy? I want to tell him everything. She thought as she continued speaking.

"I had a job while I was in college in Melbourne, on a tour boat. I swam with the dolphins and sometimes with the seals so the tourists could see and photograph them. Before I started working on the tour boat and dressing up like a mermaid, the tour boat's divers just used wetsuits, flippers, snorkels, and masks. The mermaid and merman things were much more successful with the tourists."

She continued with the story of her life, trying to keep the strange stuff out of the conversation. She couldn't seem to stop talking; only long enough to catch her breath.

"My family has always been really — different..."

She thought. *I haven't said this many words to anyone, much less a man — a good-looking man at that. I didn't even tell Reggie all this, and he knew what the Navy knew. Well, I'm on a roll.*

She rolled on. "Mum and Dad weren't well treated, being modern-day hippies and all. It was a different time, and things have changed..."

Tom was enraptured with her voice. He knew he was hearing every word, but he was consciously absorbing only a small portion of what she was actually saying. It was as if he were in a dream state. He was absorbing the way she smiled, the sparkle of her eyes, and the gentle lilt of her voice. He was entranced.

"The U.S. Navy and Coast Guard had long-range photos of me and thought that I was a mermaid... I promise you, Tom, I'm not a mermaid, not like the ones we saw today. What the Coast Guard saw in the photographs was me 'playing' mermaid..."

I've gotta shut up. What's the matter with me? She forced herself to stop talking.

Tom's eyes brightened. He was absolutely enthralled by this woman. He didn't want her to stop talking. Her voice was like music to him; her lips were magnetic. Her eyes were hypnotic, brilliant, violet, and indigo like his own; her hair seemed somehow magical; and her scent held him immobile. But at that particular moment, there was silence. He had to say something.

"You... uh — know," he stammered. "A — similar thing has happened to me. Well, the swimming thing, anyway, not the mermaid stuff. I probably shouldn't tell you this because you'll think I'm weird, but I used to go snorkel diving, and the dolphins would come 'round. It was like I was one of them. I've never told that to anyone else."

Breath's eyes brightened, but she didn't say anything.

Tom thought. *I love her voice and everything else. I want to hear more.* He paused a moment and took a sip of his chocolate. *Wow, she's right. This is excellent, although it could be a little hotter.* He then asked aloud, "How was it that your modern-day hippie mum here and your sailor father from the United States got together and had you here in Australia? Actually, I thought that the hippie movement was in the sixties and was all over by the mid-seventies. If your mum was born after that, how could she be a hippie?"

Breath sighed and thought. *He makes me so... comfortable.* Then she continued. "She couldn't. She's a new-age or modern-day hippie, or a wannabe hippie. She just fell in love with the hippie idea. There's no doubt about my mum being different. She makes her living as a psychic and by selling healing herbal potions and vegetables out of her huge lush garden at the local farmer's market.

"Well, actually, a couple of years before I was born, my father came to Australia and met Mum. She was living outside of Perth in what she called a commune. It really wasn't; it was a bunch of separate families living in small cottages on a large farm and sharing the proceeds of the farm. My parents met, fell in love, got married — new age, I guess, hippie style — and decided to move to California.

"Mum told me they had great times trying to live the hippie lifestyle, including going to protest rallies. She even proudly stated that they made a general nuisance of themselves during those times.

"They found another commune in California, similar to the commune where Mum had been living in Perth. Everything was going great until they discovered a commune member had somehow absconded with everyone's money and just disappeared. No one ever found out how he did it and where he, or the money went. The commune people found out when the bank came out and foreclosed on the farm.

"After that, my dad was doing all manner of odd jobs to keep the two of them together. He was a good mechanic and good with electronics. He got a degree in electronics engineering.

"Mum makes natural soaps, teas, and holistic medicines. They both also excel at psychic healing and readings.

"Things weren't actually going well for them financially. Apparently, some people took exception to Mum's herbal medicines, psychic readings, and, primarily her political outlook.

"My dad was arrested for designing and building electronic eavesdropping devices for some nefarious people. He had to go to court and was told he could either join the military or go to jail. He chose the military, the U.S. Navy. It turned out that those eavesdropping devices were actually seismic sensors for a local oil company. But by the time it was all sorted out, my dad was in the Navy and couldn't get out."

Why am I doing this? She thought. *It's almost as if I'm compelled to tell him everything.*

"The same good old boys and local authorities found other minor discrepancies. Apparently, the wedding was questionable, something about a Queensland registered marriage celebrant, was used against my parents. The hippie ceremony was not completely legal. What a Perth marriage has to do with Queensland I don't know, but the good old boys got rid of my parents any way they could, legally or otherwise. They basically destroyed my family. Mum had to return to Australia, pregnant with me.

"A year or so later, after Dad got out of the Navy, he returned to Australia to again marry Mum, this time legally. It didn't work out. Actually, I think she was afraid to move back to the United States, and she'd become accustomed to living alone with a child and was afraid a man would upset her routines and her lifestyle.

"Dad was heartbroken and returned to the United States. He married a woman named Sarah. Unfortunately, a year or so later, she died. After Sarah, he married my present stepmum, Virginia. They had twins: a boy, Bill Junior, and a girl, Samantha, my little brother and sister. I finally met them when I was going to school in the United States."

Breath stopped talking, perhaps just to take a breath, and thought. *I've been ear bashing, and I can't shut up.*

Tom was jolted out of his enraptured reverie and felt he had to say something. "So, you were born in Perth?"

"No, actually, I was born right here in Reeftown. When I finished my PhD, I had several job opportunities; none of which were in Western Australia. The job here didn't pay as much, but for some reason, it felt like home..."

Breath interrupted herself. *I've gotta stop rambling. Maybe if I ask a question.* "How about you? Where're you from?"

Tom was still mesmerized by Breath's voice. He equated her voice to the soft touch of his toddler cousin's gentle and careful exploration of his face with her eyes and hands. Breath's voice moved over several octaves but was gentle, melodic, and caring, and the mysterious energy flow was soothing.

Several seconds passed before it dawned on Tom that he'd been asked a question.

"Oh... uh — I was born here in Reeftown as well. My family has lived here for generations. My dad and mum moved away a short time ago and want to move back. My last assignment was in Darwin. When this assignment opened up, I jumped at it. Like you, it felt right, and it was home."

Breath looked down at her hand. "We were born here, and I guess we've both come home." To prevent herself from continuing, she took a drink of her cocoa, which was now cold.

"It's home." Tom continued after a second. "Growing up here was great. I had lots of friends and was good at sports. Girls... not so much. I was awkward. Don't get me wrong; the girls came around. The ones who came around were always several grades behind me because I skipped several grades in school. It's just... I didn't know what to say to them. I was kind of a nerdy geek.

"Athletics came easy to me. It was almost as if I could predict what my opponents were going to do. However, I gravitated more towards the sciences and mathematics instead of sports because I was too small and young. My ambition when I was in high school was to become an oceanographer. I took a lot of classes in oceanography at the Royal Australian Naval College. I graduated college just before I was eighteen.

"At the time, I thought the RAN was looking for oceanographers, so I became a midshipman. It turned out they were actually looking for contractors. I never got to do much oceanography. I'm advancing through the RAN pretty quick, though. I should be promoted to Lieutenant soon. I suppose that life for me has been easy. I seem to be able to do anything well."

Breath said. "Maybe you can teach me how to make my life a little easier. I've always had to struggle, athletics wise. However, I was good academics wise. That part came easy. Actually, thinking about it, my life has been fairly easy, too, not counting sports."

"Why don't you change your name if you don't like it?"

"You know, I've thought about that a lot. Cavendish is my mum's maiden name, and I suppose her legal name. However, she still goes by Heidi Spring; she never changed her name back to Cavendish. Makes you kind of wonder...

"I even went down to the courthouse one time and got the paperwork to fill out. But, under the line that asked for a new name, I simply couldn't think of what I really wanted to be called. Isn't that pathetic?"

"What? You, pathetic? I think you're..." He trailed off. "I... I don't think you're..."

Tom thought. *I better shut up before I'm up a gumtree.* He flushed a bit; he could feel the red rising up his collar. *Why does this woman make me do this? I can't think straight around her.*

Breath chuckled under her breath and looked down at the table. "Well, that's the way I feel, anyway."

An awkward silence passed between them. Tom, in a desperate attempt to get out of the hole he'd dug for himself, changed the subject. "That's a beautiful necklace you have there. Where'd you get it?"

"Well, it's been in my family for generations. My great-grand mum had it, and then it passed to my grand mum, and then she gave it to Mum on her sixteenth birthday. The clasp broke on it, and Mum sent it to Dad to fix. She let my stepmum wear it until my sixteenth birthday, but actually Virginia gave it to me when I went to visit them before I went to University of Miami. I don't know where great-grand mum got it, maybe my great-great-grand mum. It must've been meant for my family because Mum told me she lost it at the beach one time. And someone found it and gave it back to her. All that happened before I was born. It's actually been in and out of the family several times, but it always comes back."

"So, you're going to give it to your daughter when she's sixteen?"

"Yes. Well, that's when I have a daughter. First, I've gotta find a man with whom to have a daughter." Breath turned red and suddenly became absorbed in the pattern on the tablecloth.

Tom thought. *I better change the subject.*

"There's no denying it, the events today happened! I've gone over and over it in my mind. I've got no real explanation for it, but I saw what everyone else saw!

"Those four Mer beings on your ship were there, and two of them were dead, as was our crewman, and the other two Mer had life-threatening injuries. The doctor told me so — confirmed it! I can't really understand or conceive of how or what that one was doing when it was floating above the water. From what everyone else was telling me, it was there — no doubt, and it certainly floated above the water! How did she do that anyway?

"Doc — my doc — told me that his examination showed that they were human inside. They might've looked strange on the outside, but their insides were human. And those light beings — I know they were intelligent beings because they spoke to us, or, more proper, they thought to us. I didn't think that was possible. I don't mind saying I was a little scared. I've seen some strange things and have been in some tough situations, but that scared me." He glanced around to make sure no one was nearby. "And what's with us? We were in each other's heads. We both knew what the other was thinking."

Tom continued with apprehension. "*Galactic Prime* of the Qrie — whatever that means — the Qrie Beauty, and the Qrie Morning all did impossible things. And where'd that contraband ship and its crew disappear to? One moment it was there. The next, it was gone. I'm so confused; my mind has been running around in circles.

"If I didn't know better, I'd swear I was going crazy. It's a good thing these Compulsions are on us, so we can't tell anyone else. That'd absolutely prove to everyone we told that we're crazy. You'd lose your job, and there's no doubt I'd lose mine.

"When *Galactic Prime* brought that Mer person and the helo crewman back to life, that really got to me. That's not possible — when you're dead, you're dead! No one is gonna bring you back. But it did! We've all heard of people coming back from the dead, but that's usually on the operating table and not with injuries as bad as that crewman or that merman kid or whatever it was had.

"I talked to my crewman on the way back to port. He told us that there was no way I could understand what he experienced when he woke up. It was so far beyond any way of comprehending that there was no possible way that he could explain it. One thing he did say was that time ceased to exist. I can't fathom that.

"I'm sorry, Breath. I've been running off at the mouth, and I haven't given you a chance to get a word in edgewise. Please, forgive me."

***

Breath thought. *Skipper was right. He was scared and just trying to make sense of everything, just like everyone else there.*

"Well, Tom, I guess the Compulsions don't prevent us from talking about it to each other. We've been thinking about the same exact thing ever since it happened. I can't think of anything else." She thought. *Well, other than you.* "You're right. If anyone else ever heard about what we saw today, they'd lock us up in the loony bin. I do think I have a way to get some answers. I was talking with one of the Mer today — well, actually, yesterday — the young merman, Neil Talmage. I know his father, Dr. Taylor Talmage. Have you heard of him?"

"I've heard of him. I think he did some work for one of my crewmen a year or so ago. Other than that, I don't know anything about him. Do you think he'd be willing to talk to us and give us some answers?"

"Yes! Neil thought that his father would be willing to talk to us. We've got the Compulsions on us, so we can't tell anyone else. Perhaps we should give Dr. Talmage a call and have a conference with him and Neil. I can set it up with him. I think talking to the good doctor and a real Mer is the only way we're going to get any real answers. I don't know about you, but I must find out as much as I can about all these entities."

"I agree Breath. I wonder if he would mind if I came along as well."

"I can't imagine why he'd mind. Both of us were there, and we helped his son, Neil."

"You know Breath, our hot cocoa isn't so hot anymore."

They sat, sipping their chocolate in quiet contemplation thinking about the conversation and the marvelous energies that were passing between them. Both of their minds were spinning. They both were absorbed in their cocoa and other things at the moment.

Tom said after a long moment. "Breath, we're not going to solve anything more here tonight as far as the Qrie, the Mer, and *Galactic Prime* are concerned."

Breath looked at him and thought. *He looks so good in those blue jeans and that polo shirt. I wonder how good he'd look out of them. OMG! I haven't even known him for twenty-four hours, and I'm thinking thoughts like that.* She blushed. *Has it been that long?* Her cheeks became as pink as the blouse she was wearing, and she felt that strange tingling sensation again.

Tom definitely felt the energy and noticed the blush. He leaned over to her. "Breath, is there something wrong?" When he leaned over, he was close enough to actually smell her hair. He didn't know whether it was some kind of strange perfume that she was wearing, but he found it quite alluring. Maybe it was that strange tingling. He thought. *My God, I've definitely gotta know this woman much better.* He began to blush himself.

Breath smiled, looking up at him. "Nothing is wrong. I've been at sea for a while myself!" Her color deepened, and she thought her heart would jump out of her chest. Breath turned in the booth towards Tom. She pulled her right knee up on the seat and hooked her right foot behind her left knee. She did this to keep her knees from shaking. She didn't have any place to put her right arm, so she placed it on the back of the booth. Tom made himself more comfortable, crossing his legs at the ankles and turning to face her. Their knees touched, and she felt a strong tingling throughout her body. Her heart raced. She felt a jolt. Tom didn't move his knee.

They continued talking, about their ships, their crews, and Skipper. Tom seemed to be having trouble. He'd start a sentence and then somehow lose his train of thought. His mind wasn't on the conversation at all.

Breath noticed that each time Tom glanced away and then looked back at her, his eyes would dilate. She knew from a bio-physiology class she'd taken in college that when someone's eyes dilate, he's interested or emotionally involved in what he's seeing. She wondered if it was just the darkness of the corner or if he was interested in her, too.

He put his arm on the back of the booth seat, on top of hers. She knew he was interested, when he started drawing little circles with his finger on top of her arm. She didn't understand it, but it felt like soothing electric sparks jumping from his finger to her arm.

"Breath, we've been talking for hours here about Lord knows what: ships, marine biology, contraband, and stuff. Have you got a clue as to what we've talked about over the past hour? I... I don't. All I can think about is that unbelievable perfume you're wearing, your beautiful blond hair, your gorgeous violet-indigo eyes, and a face that puts me in a trance. Every time I touch you, it's electric. If your eyes had that little gold ring around the iris, I'd know for a fact that you were a mermaid. You can't deny that those young women are some of the most beautiful creatures you, I, or anyone else has ever seen, and you're at the top of that category."

Breath's heart stopped. *No one, especially not a man — a good-looking man at that — has ever said anything like that to me!* Tears began to flow.

Contraband, oceans, ships, sails, and other useless things were forgotten. Much more important things were exchanged with soft, intimate, quiet.

***

The Sun was rising, and they were still at Rebecca's. They were hearing the door open and close more often, and cold cocoa was still in their cups. Apparently, the chocolate wasn't nearly as good as advertised. Or perhaps the conversation between them was more intimate and much better.

Tom noticed that Breath's eyes were red and a bit droopy. He suggested they should pay the bill, leave a monster tip, and get some rest. As he got up, he noticed that his legs were just a little bit stiff. He probably should've moved his legs around a little bit more, but he enjoyed the pleasure of the electric feeling of touching Breath's knee.

He stood up and walked around the table and offered his hand to Breath. She looked up at him, gave him her hand, and started to get up. The intense stinging in her legs let her know that they had gone to sleep. She, too, didn't want to move for fear of losing the touch of Tom's knee and the warmth it gave.

Breath was surprised. "Oh, my goodness, my leg is asleep. Well — both of them are. Would you please help me up and steady me while the blood flows back into my legs?"

"I'll hold you as long as you want." He reached down with his right arm, lifted her, swung her around towards him, and put his left arm around her.

He noticed she was amazingly light in his arms, and the electric surge was tremendous. He was holding her so her toes just touched the floor. Her head was touching his. He could smell her hair again; he thought it was wonderful. He just couldn't recognize that scent. He could detect a little bit of an ocean smell and surmised that she hadn't had a chance to take a shower before he'd picked her up last night.

Breath looked at him and thought. *My heart can't take much more of this. Is he a figment of my imagination, or is he for real?* Then Breath noticed the blood had returned to her legs. As the tingling pins-and-needles stinging started, she gave a startled sound, and Tom pressed her tighter to his chest. Electricity again surged through her body. Normally, this would've been wonderful, except for the tingling in her legs. She noticed heat rising up from her legs to her abdomen, to the hardening of her breasts, and, finally, to her cheeks. She felt warm all over.

Tom held Breath until the circulation came back into her legs and they stopped stinging. He looked into her eyes, which were wide open and intense. He was delighted that she was so light in his arms, with that strange electric heat. He noticed that he was excited and strangely warm himself. He knew he wanted to hold her tight and take care of her. He looked down at her. She looked up at him, and both knew they had come home.

They walked over to the cash register arms around each other, just for safety's sake, of course. Tom pulled out his credit card and noticed a new waiter. Tom asked about the other waiter.

The new waiter took Tom's card. "I came on at four a.m. You lovebirds haven't moved since I've been here. The other guy informed me you'd been here all night."

Tom left a huge tip and told the waiter to split it with the other guy. He thought. *Hmm, so he thinks we're lovebirds, does he?* He looked down at Breath and noticed she was blushing.

Breath let Tom help her out to his car. He opened her door, helped her into the car, and handed her the seat belt. She thought. *I can do this myself, but I enjoy him helping me.*

Tom drove her back to her ship. She took one look at the rather steep gangway and asked Tom if he'd take her to her apartment.

When they pulled up to her apartment, Tom stopped the car, jumped out, and ran around the car to open her door.

She thought. *I could get used to this.*

She fumbled for a moment in her purse, looking for her keys. As her hand came up with them, Tom took them and softly touched her hand. She smiled as he found the correct key and opened her door. She held out her hand, and he dropped them into it. He then put his arm around her back, pulled her close to him, and kissed her. She melted and kissed him back with all the pent-up feelings the night had brought about. Both felt a tremendous electric surge of pleasure pass between them. He slowly released her, smiled, and had a confused look on his face. He then turned to leave and walk to his car. He didn't quite make it. She grabbed his wrist and pulled him into her apartment and closed the door.

5. SATURDAY

Breath woke up and felt a massive sense of loss when she realized and understood that Tom was gone. She felt bereft of his warmth and disappointed that he had better things to do and would leave like that without even saying goodbye. *Men...* She harrumphed — *who needs them!* She tried to put him out of her mind because she needed to take a shower and brush her teeth.

GP, is he really gone?

No comment.

GP, sometimes you're no help at all.

I love y'all too Breath. Always glad to help.

She was still groggy and disappointed when she got out of the shower and dried herself off. Even though she could dry herself with the Qrie energies, she still liked the feel of the towel on her skin. She wrapped the towel around her hair and took a quick glance in the bathroom mirror.

She walked into the kitchen, thinking she'd make herself a cup of coffee. She felt different without him. Her skin didn't feel the same. She thought. *You don't suppose...*

She had just prepared the coffee maker and turned it on when Tom walked through the door bearing bagels, coffee, and orange juice. He announced in a loud voice. "You know, there's absolutely nothing to eat in this apartment." And then he saw Breath with nothing on except the towel wrapped around her hair.

It was a good thing that Breath had just turned on the coffeemaker and was moving away from it; otherwise, it would've been all over her and the floor. When she heard the door and saw Tom, she jumped with a startled gasp. All those overwhelming feelings she had earlier came flooding back. She immediately looked for an escape route, but there was none.

She thought. *Oh, my, he got up, didn't want to wake me, and went to get breakfast.* A multitude of feelings surged through her, and tears formed. Her eyes were electric and as big as saucers. Her face was redder than it had ever been. She looked this way and that, but there was no way out except through Tom. He stood there looking at her for what she thought was an eternity.

Then he took his sweet time as he placed the breakfast on the kitchen counter. To Breath his slowness was painstaking as he appreciated her complete body in all her glory. Her panic subsided when she realized that Tom was very deliberate and teasing as he took his sweet time at her expense. She felt that same wonderful tingling throughout her body, and that excitement and arousal was hers again. She looked at Tom with a coy come-hither smile, then put her hand on the counter and struck a provocative pose and waited.

He was deliberate with his slowness as he walked over to her. He put his arms around her, and pressed her against him. He was ever so gentle as he kissed her. She dissolved. After several long wonderful kisses, he reached down, picked her up, and carried her into the bedroom. If it had been up to her, she would've grabbed him by the hair, and dragged him to the bedroom. His way was much better.

It was midafternoon when they drug themselves out of bed. They went in and took a shower together. Tom confessed to her he'd never taken a shower with a woman before. She told him that this was her first time, too.

She looked up at him. "You are also my first time to — you know — have sex. I know too, through our energy link, that I was your first time as well."

"Yes, it's just that none of the other women seemed right to me."

Several firsts for both of them. They were making history together. Showers together were nice, and they could take a long time touching and exploring. Much longer than her usual jump in, scrub down, rinse, and out — and much more sensual.

She hadn't thought of her job, the ship, the Mer, the Qrie, *Galactic Prime*, or anything else since she brought Tom into her apartment. She was exhausted. She still had that strange, warm, wonderful, expansive, tingling sensation, and it hadn't diminished. She felt euphoric, better than she could ever remember. She wondered. *Do I have a real live boyfriend, a lover, a true relationship? Is he someone I can talk to and confide in and share secrets with? Is he someone who'll be there for me? I know I want to be there for him. We share a secret between us that few humans have ever shared. Will he still be interested in me after a month or two, or will he run away like the others when he finds out how different I am? Whenever I start talking about my work for some reason, men run screaming into the night — Hipsi is trying to break me of that habit. Could he be 'the one'?*

A scar on Breath's psyche has caused her to shy away from men in the past. At one time, she'd firmly resolved in her mind to be a spinster (Hipsi was working to break her of that, too).

She put those negative thoughts out of her head. Tom had his arms around her and hers around him. The gentle, sensual caress of the water was all she wanted to think about. She was in a world alone with Tom, and that was all she wanted.

However, all good things, as well as hot water, must come to an end.

Tom grumbled. "This is a terrible time to run out of hot water." He turned off the now-cold shower.

Breath bounced out of the shower. "I've gotta call Dr. Talmage and set up an appointment. I hope he can see us this afternoon or tomorrow. Do you think he'd mind if we came over this afternoon?"

"Well, there's only one way to find out. Call and ask him."

Breath had jumped out of the shower, not even bothering to dry off. She ran over to her phone, looked up the number, and called. The phone started ringing. Then she looked at herself, still wet, in her bedroom's full-length mirror and thought. *Well, my, my, look at me. I'm standing here totally naked, soaking wet, and there's a man in my shower. What in the world is happening to me?* She did a little giggle, did a little wiggle dance, and thought. *I 'like' it.*

Crystal Talmage answered the phone on the third ring. "Hello."

"Hi, this is Dr. Breath Spring. I met your son Neil yesterday. I asked him if it'd be all right if I could talk to Dr. Talmage and the family about what happened yesterday. And could I ask questions about the Mer and the entities we encountered?"

"Well, that was a mouthful, and yes, Neil told us that you'd like to speak with us. We're anxious to speak with you too. We've got some friends that we'd like to have in on this conversation as well. They've got questions about the incident. We're going to make up a large meal, and you're more than welcome to join us. Please, can you make it over this evening?"

"I'd love to do that. I must ask you, though: May I bring Sub Lieutenant Tom Haynes of the RAN ship *Queen's Shield*, which helped out yesterday?"

"Yes, no need to even ask. We'll all be eating around six o'clock. We're eager to meet you and Sub Lieutenant Haynes.

"I'll text you the directions. We live about twenty-four kilometers north of Reeftown in the hills overlooking the sea. I've got to warn you: some of the road is rough dirt and gravel."

"We'll be there. Thank you. Bye."

Breath took a long, slow look at Tom, paying close attention to his broad shoulders. "Tom, has your body always been hairless, or do you shave? I know I don't. I've got no hair whatsoever below my neckline all the way down to my toes except for my eyebrows and eyelashes. I was wondering about you. We look like the Mer."

Tom continued drying himself off. "I've never had any body hair, not even in my armpits, on my arms, legs, or pubic hair. I don't even have facial hair. Head hair, brows, and lashes is all I've got. It's always been a bit of an embarrassment for me."

Breath continued. "I also noticed you wear two undershirts, two pairs of boxer shorts, and two pairs of socks. Why's that? I never wear underclothes. I don't like the smell."

There was a long quiet moment. Then Tom made a slow turn and saw that Breath was as red as a beet and had no idea what to do with her hands.

Tom replied after another long moment. "I'm not quite sure how to respond to that. I have noticed that you don't wear underwear. So — I've never..." Then he started turning red.

"Uh... to answer your question, Breath, I never have quite figured that out. Mum started that when I was quite young. I go through about a complete set of underwear and socks a week. If I don't double or triple up on the underwear and socks, I go through outer clothes, shoes, and uniforms quickly, and that's expensive."

Breath thought after she recovered from her embarrassing outburst. *I wonder. Could he be like me? I've the same problem with my clothing. If it weren't for Mum's stinky seaweed liners, I probably wouldn't have anything to wear.*

6. BARBECUE

Breath and Tom arrived at the Talmage house about five forty-five that afternoon. The house was set off by itself on ten hectares. It has a three-meter-high thick stone wall around the entire property with stone turrets at the corners. It has a seven-meter-high stone wall enclosure in the monstrous backyard. There are many large eucalyptus trees and smaller shrubs around the outside of the high wall and in the front of the gigantic house. If you pass by on the road and look through the huge steel gate; you can't see the house or the cars in the driveway for the trees and tall shrubs.

Tom drove up to the automatic gate, which opened. He drove through, and parked in front of the house. Breath didn't wait for Tom to open her door this time.

When Breath and Tom got to the door, they were surprised. There were six people standing just outside the door, watching them closely with strange looks. They all had small loose bathers on, making Breath feel overwhelmed and overdressed in her loose-fitting muumuu dress.

Crystal Talmage walked up to Breath and extended her hand. "You must be Dr. Spring and Sub Lieutenant Haynes. Please, come in! We've been waiting for you."

Tom noticed Breath's discomfort. He reached out and took Crystal's hand. "Hi, I'm Tom Haynes. I was at the incident yesterday. I'm on the RAN ship *Queen's Shield*, which rendered aid. Please, just call me Tom. And this is Dr. Breath Of Spring, Director Scientist of the Geoscience Australia survey ship *Morning Discovery*."

"I'm Crystal Talmage, Dr. Talmage's wife. I'm so glad you could make it this evening. We're all preparing to go out in the backyard for a swim and barbecue. You're on time. We've just finished a memorial for Cheyenne.

"We've been looking forward to meeting and thanking you for your help. Please join us; I hope you're hungry Tom, Doctor Spring."

Breath pulled herself together. "Please call me Breath, and yes, we brought our appetites." Breath couldn't help noticing how everyone was watching her and Tom with intensity.

As they all meandered through the maze of the huge house and out into the backyard, Breath noticed the same three young Mer with their golden hair and skin. They were in the same condition they were in when they'd left her ship yesterday. Still in the nuddy, they did have a diminished glow. They still floated off the ground, and their wings were in full form. They were floating in a tight circle, talking to one another. Breath could feel the loss of their fellow Mer and loved one, Cheyenne.

Breath paused and looked at the young Mer and pondered a moment. *That's interesting. Their skin seems to be as solid gold as it was earlier, at the incident.*

Two older men, one with golden hair, eyebrows, and eyelashes came over to Breath and Tom. The other man, with golden-blond hair, just not as golden, Breath knew was Dr. Talmage. "Hello, I'm Taylor Talmage, Neil's dad. And this is John Weber, Cheyenne's father."

Taylor leaned close to Breath and Tom then whispered. "Our young Mer over there are not allowed to call you Breath or Tom, only Dr. Spring and Sub Lieutenant Haynes. They'll have to earn that privilege, and I suspect it might take a while. We're glad you came today; we just wish it could've been under better circumstances. I hope that together, we can all figure out what happened yesterday."

Breath took John Weber's hand. "I'm so sorry for your loss. If there's ever anything I can do for you, please don't hesitate to call."

Tom also took John's hand. "I, too, am so sorry for your loss. And if there's anything I can do, please, let me know."

John replied, subdued and with sadness. "Thank you both. If you had not been there, things could've been much worse. From what Morning and Beauty told us, Neil and Kandy would've died too."

While Tom was talking to John, Breath began to watch the people gathered there. They all moved with an elegant grace like Tom. Skipper told her that she moved with the same regal grace that he did. She'd never paid much attention to it because it was the way her mum and dad moved. Now she became interested in the gracefulness of the Mer.

In an effort to lighten the mood, Tom looked at the huge backyard and then at Dr. Talmage. "Impressive home and backyard you have. I like the huge swimming pool and hot tub. How was it that you've got this seven-meter-high stone wall all around your backyard? I've never seen eucalyptus trees grow that close together. They must be forty to fifty meters tall. And what's with all the birds?"

Dr. Talmage brightened. "We bought this place sixteen years ago. It was run down and a total mess. The original fort was nicknamed Dunleavy's Delirium. Back in about 1880, there was a Lieutenant Colonel Dudley Dunleavy, who wanted to become a General. He was quite wealthy and decided to help the Australian government by building a fort to protect this area from the Russians. The government was in the process of building Fort Scratchley in Newcastle, New South Wales, for the same purpose. Dunleavy decided to help the government by building a fort here in Reeftown. Of course, at that time there wasn't much here to protect. He built the walls of native sandstone twenty feet tall, with a three-foot parapet wall at the top and gun emplacements along the ocean side. There were never any guns mounted. He also built a ten-foot tall six-foot-wide deterrent wall with a continuous parapet all the way around with corner gun turrets, for soldiers to shoot from. At that time Australia used the imperial inch, foot, and mile measurements. When the military came to inspect his constructions, they found several woeful inadequacies, since the rammed earth and mortared sandstone battery walls were not thick enough, being six feet at the top and ten feet at the bottom. Not adequate for gun emplacements. The Australian government wanted nothing to do with the monstrosity.

"The whole project broke him, and his health failed. Just before he died, he gave it to the Australian prison system, and it was used as a stockade back in the early 1890s. The prison was later found to be inadequate and went unused for over a hundred years. About the only thing left of the prison are the high walls. As you'll notice, those walls are thicker at the bottom than they are at the top and are sunk deep into the ground. The huge house outside the high walls was built to provide housing for the guards and personnel along with offices for the prison and other government administration. We widened a passageway between the house and our high walled-in backyard compound." Taylor pointed. "As you can see, there's also a large wagon entry, heavy double gate, on the south side high wall. The Australian government didn't think that was adequate either. We replaced the wood and painted the double gate to make it match the wall.

"The stockade walls were still strong. The administration and the quarters building were gutted and the roof had collapsed, due to rotten wood, but the stone walls were still in good shape. We cleaned the place up, put up new rafters and a roof, added interior walls, doors inside and out, electricity, running water, wastewater treatment system, and sewer lines for the kitchens and bathrooms. The old cells and other wooden buildings inside the high-walled stockade were in such bad shape that we had to demolish them.

"The swimming pool was once the basement storeroom walls and floor of the old common room and dining facility. When we bought the place, the basement was full of water. Amazing enough it didn't leak. We drained it, made a shallow portion and a large hot tub at one end, sealed it all up with a good plaster seal and tile, put in some circulation pumps, painted it, and voilà we've got a swimming pool. We considered filling the pool with seawater, since the land ends down the cliff at the ocean's edge. We decided against that when we discovered it would've turned into a bureaucratic nightmare.

"Most of the trees were here when we moved in. We trimmed them up a bit, and they improve our privacy. We want them as tall and dense as possible so no one can see our flares from outside the compound. As for the birds, they're drawn, like many other animals, to the Qrie energies that the Mer emit. They don't interfere, and we enjoy them, but they are a bit noisy and nosy.

"Our very few neighbors still call it the old prison. It came with a lot of grounds between the three-meter outside perimeter walls and the main prison stockade high walls, which also helps us keep our privacy. A couple times each year, we have a pool party and invite our human friends. Which are the neighbors who live in the area, and my patients who live in town." Dr. Talmage seemed quite proud of the private edifice.

***

Breath had no sooner sat down when someone called out, "It's done! Everybody, gather round and get your plates."

Dr. Talmage floated up to the young Mer and told them something and then returned to the barbie. Breath and Tom were amazed that a human like him could fly. Breath thought. *He must be Mer but hides it well. And he does have a shimmer of energy around his body. Is that a Qrie field? It looks just like the one that forms around me when I use the Qrie energy.*

Breath and Tom noticed that the young Mer held their position away from the table and the barbie. Breath didn't know whether they were holding back out of respect, or perhaps, from the expression on their faces, had been told to hold back by Dr. Talmage.

As Breath and Tom moved towards the serving line, Hilga handed each of them a plate and some utensils. "De drinking cups are over by de salads. Oh, und be careful, because Taylor's barbecue ist addicting. It's almost as goot as any drug. It's not quite as goot as Crystal's gazpacho, but it's vay better dan anyting you can get in de restaurant."

After all of the adults had gotten their food, only then did the young Mer float over to fill their plates. They took their food and floated over to a high shelf built along the wall. Breath and Tom watched and understood that the young Mer couldn't sit down; they had to remain vertical.

When Breath and Tom finished their plates of food, Doctor Talmage stood up. "Listen up, everybody. I'd like to introduce everyone." He formally introduced Breath and Tom to the rest of the group. And the rest of the group stood up one at a time to introduce themselves. Breath and Tom were amazed there were so many Mer living right there in Reeftown, and they couldn't distinguish them from any other human in town. Well, except for the gold hair, eyebrows, and the gold ring around the irises of their radiant blue eyes, although, she thought. *The gold ring around their irises is much thinner and harder to see than when they're in their full golden Mer form.*

Tom thought. *I wonder if all the golden blondes in town are Mer. This being Australia, if that's true, there's one whale of a lot of Mer here.*

Breath, as was her habit, began to categorize in her mind everyone she met. *Let's see. There's Dr. Taylor and Crystal Talmage, his wife. Then there's Jefferson and Connie Bernard, Kandy Bernard's parents; Hilga Heilsvien, who's Sophianna Heilsvien's mum; and John Weber, Cheyenne's father, who all seem to be able to fly! Crystal, Connie, and John Weber are the only adults who have the golden hair, eyebrows, eyelashes, and the gold rings in their eyes; all the others are golden blondes but not the same gold as the Mer. What's with that?*

***

After everyone had eaten, Dr. Talmage suggested they get in the hot tub. Breath half raised her hand. "I'm sorry, but I didn't bring bathing togs."

Crystal jumped up. "The Mer never wear clothes if we can help it. However, no worries love. There are several for just such occasions as this. I'll get you and Tom each a suit. Besides, I want to see that mermaid tail of yours."

Breath was astounded. "How do you know about that? I haven't told anyone about my tail. I haven't even told Tom yet! How could you know?"

Connie laughed. "Morning or Beauty told us; I don't know which. We've known about it for some time. We didn't know it was you until just now. You've gotta show us."

Breath in a panic thought. *Oh no, he's going to think I'm some kind of freak and run screaming into the night.* She looked at Tom and stammered. "But I... well, I... I'm sorry. I guess — I should've told you. But I was afraid of how you might take it."

Tom leaned close. "Don't worry about it, Breath. After what's happened to us this last day or so, nothing could surprise me. When our minds linked, I knew at that moment you were something special. Go ahead Breath. I'd like to see your tail — although it can't be any nicer than the one — I've already seen. Besides, who're we going to tell?"

Breath blushed, and they followed Crystal into the huge maze of a house. They wound around the monstrous house and ended up in a large sewing room. Crystal picked up one of the two-piece bathers and handed it to Breath.

Breath said. "I've never seen bathers like these and the ones you're wearing. Where'd you get them, and what are they made of? The cloth feels wonderful, like silk."

Crystal said. "The cloth is silk. You see, the Mer can't wear regular clothes. The Qrie energies will destroy them. These are made from hagfish silk, so when we produce the energy fields about our bodies, they're not destroyed as quick as regular clothes. Let me show you."

Crystal opened a door into another room where there were spinning and knitting machines and automatic looms for making cloth. She took a regular cotton handkerchief and held it close around her abdomen. A strong energy shield formed around her body, and she floated off the floor.

"As you can see, with the energy field tight around my body, the handkerchief is beginning to disintegrate. This is what happens to normal clothing. It's also why the Mer never wear clothes unless we go out among normal humans."

"Why doesn't the hagfish silk clothing disintegrate?"

"We can wear many things that come from the sea that won't disintegrate as quick. We line all our store-bought clothes with this silk material to make them last longer, and we make it right here. Hilga makes it best."

Breath started to say "You're just like me" but stopped herself before she did. Instead, she said, "Where can I get some of that material?"

She was apprehensive. *GP, these people are just like me! Do you think this is okay?*

Yes, Breath. These people will become some of your best friends. They're, somewhat like y'all.

"Next time you come over, we'll give you a bolt and some dye to color it with. You can't use regular dye; it must come from the sea."

Everyone followed Breath to the large pool. When she dove in, everyone followed. Even the young ones were in the pool.

Breath thought. *I guess water doesn't discharge the field. Well, here goes nothing.* And she began to form her Aqume in full color with frills and streamers. Everyone in the group was amazed.

John was as amazed as everyone else. "No one has ever seen a real mermaid. We didn't think mermaids like that existed."

"As far as I know, I'm the only one. I like to play mermaid, and this seems to be the result." She didn't think it would be a good idea to tell them about GP and her voices, although they did know about Morning and Beauty.

Everyone continued asking questions. The young ones were quite curious about how she could transform into a real mermaid. Breath showed them how fast she could swim and how she could breach and get her entire body and tail high out of the water like a dolphin.

After about an hour, Breath started laughing. "You know, it's funny. I always thought I was a fake mermaid, just pretending. And then I met all of you, and I knew, without a doubt, I was a fake. You're the real mermen and mermaids. Not me."

Neil floated closer. "But Dr. Spring, we don't have a beautiful tail like you do. All the pictures we've ever seen of mermaids all have tails like you. We can't be real mermen and mermaids because we don't have tails. I thought mermaids had scales, but you don't have any; your tail looks like bright colorful dolphin or whale skin."

"Neil, I did this because the pictures and drawings I saw of mermaids were with tails. I must have a tail because it's the only way I can swim. I don't have any scales because I don't like them. I prefer the smooth skin surface."

Breath, you can swim almost as fast as the Mer without your tail. Don't forget you can form a Qrie energy field around your body, just like they do. You may not be able to swim as fast as they can. It may take a bit of practice, but you 'can' swim like they do.

I never realized that GP. Thanks, I'll try that next time.

Always here to help.

After spending about half an hour laughing, joking, and discussing who were the real mermaids the final agreement was that they were all merfolk.

Tom couldn't get into the conversation all that much. He was amazed at the situation and the combination and interaction of his new friends. He noticed that Breath had become quite comfortable around them.

When the questions about Breath being a mermaid slowed down, she asked, "What do the Mer do?"

John chuckled. "I wondered how long it was going to take you to ask that question. The Mer maintain the anchor points for the aggression suppression rings that the Qrie have placed around the Earth. There are twenty-seven — or rather now twenty-six Mer living here in Reeftown." John paused for a moment. Then he continued. "Most live and stay around the anchor point at Koala Island. Human beings are warlike and aggressive. The Qrie placed these rings around the Earth to suppress that aggression. It's our job to make sure those rings don't float off into space."

Breath looked surprised. "Will the rings float off into space?"

John laughed. "No. They've been here for over two million years. I think they're here to stay! It's our job to make sure they do, by making sure they're properly anchored."

Breath looked stunned at that statement, but all of the Mer thought it was funny.

***

When the conversation and laughter slowed down, Dr. Talmage asked Breath and Tom for their interpretation of the recent events at sea.

Tom went first and gave a detailed — military-style report of what the RAN was trying to do to catch the ship hauling contraband. He also gave a detailed report on the events after he reached *Morning Discovery*.

"I admit that I was intimidated by the Mer, the Qrie, *Galactic Prime,* and the Compulsions that were placed upon everyone there. I'm quite concerned about not being able to report to my superiors about the existence of the Mer, Qrie, and *Galactic Prime,* although Commander Tibbett does know.

One other thing that I question is how all this connects because Breath and I have had close mental linking throughout this entire episode. I now know Breath is different, and I know that I'm different as well. Are we Mer or something else?"

Breath remained quiet and became quite interested in one of her fingernails.

When Tom had finished, John Weber, noticing Breath's unease, asked, "Dr. Spring, could you please tell us how you were able to track our fine, errant young Mer? They've all been taught how to avoid sonar."

"My postdoc assistant, Dr. Benjamin Kavanaugh, has built an advanced passive acoustic array. It uses an acoustic lens with a large number of small acoustic sensors. It works much like a lens and sensor on your cell phone or a camera. It doesn't need a sonar-sounding pulse at all. The ocean is quite noisy. The output is like a grainy video signal."

John asked, "Do you know of any way to block the signal?"

"I don't know of any," Breath said. "You'll have to talk with Ben about that; he's the one who knows how it works. Ben says the RAN also has these units on some of their ships. I'm not that technical, but I'm quite sure he'd be glad to explain it to you. As you know, he's under the same Compulsions everyone else is."

"I'd like to do that. This new sonar, or passive acoustic array, as you call it, could be a serious threat to us. I, for one, am quite worried about it."

Tom said. "If you'll give us your contact information, we'll make sure that Dr. Kavanaugh gets it. We'll have him talk to you."

Breath then continued with her report just as Tom had, in as much detail as she could remember.

Dr. Talmage looked concerned and raised his index finger as soon as Breath completed her report. "Your reports agree with what our young Mer have reported, at least those who were alive and conscious at the time. I want to thank you for helping and giving assistance to our young ones. If you hadn't been there to render aid... well, I just don't even want to think about the consequences. Again, we all thank you. If there's anything we can ever do to help you, please, let us know.

"Thank you for telling us about this passive sonar system. I suppose our young Mer weren't at fault for not being able to avoid it. It doesn't, however, absolve them of the fact that they were playing tag and not paying proper attention and observing the boats in the area. We do need to learn more about this passive sonar system.

"Please Tom, can you tell me how the crewman of the RAN ship is doing?"

"He was doing just fine until we got him halfway back to port, and the doctor just couldn't stand it anymore. He just had to take some readings.

"This wasn't a good thing for either the doctor or the crewman. The crewman was floating next to and holding on to a vertical stanchion. The doctor came up to place his stethoscope on the crewman's chest. A loud bang was heard. Both the crewman and the doctor ended up on the deck. They were both unconscious for about two hours in what looked like a coma. The doctor came to first and started to go over to the crewman, but the X stopped him. A short time later, the crewman came to, and the field about him had diminished. He could then stand on his own two feet. The field was still there, but before we got back to port, the field had dissipated. You know, Taylor, I'd like to get you two doctors together to compare notes, if you don't mind."

"I'd love to, Tom. I don't have another doctor to speak to about the Mer. And I'd love to have another to consult with about the incident."

"I'll set it up."

Then Dr. Talmage, with a mischievous twinkle in his eye, said. "Well, if that's all the questions, I guess we can call it a night."

Breath looked disappointed. "But I haven't asked any questions..."

Everyone except Breath and Tom started laughing.

Breath and Tom looked at each other and knew they'd been had. They also knew that this group had a strange but good sense of humor.

Breath was still in her mermaid form. "Taylor, Tom didn't tell me about the doctor and the crewman being knocked unconscious. Can you shed any light as to why this happened?"

"Yes, I don't know if the Qrie told you not to touch the Mer while they had the fields about them. If someone touches the body with something foreign to the field and does it rather fast, the field will discharge. If the field is rather weak and the one doing the touching is human, the result is what Tom saw around the doctor and the crewman. However, if the field is strong, the human touching this field can be in for a rather long coma.

"The human just gets hit by the discharging field once. The Mer, on the other hand, gets hit twice once by the discharging field and once when the field is regenerated. Both of these situations are uncomfortable for the Mer. Discharging a field isn't recommended."

Neil asked. "Doctor Spring, how was it that you could touch me so fast without discharging my field?"

Doctor Talmage saw the uncomfortable look on Breath's face. Then he looked at Neil and cleared his throat.

Neil glanced at his father then looked down at his feet.

"Well, I think my doctor found that out the hard way," Tom said, and then he just as fast asked, "What can the Mer do, and how is it that they can fly?"

John Weber, realizing Breath was uncomfortable, started explaining. "The Mer have the ability to use the Qrie energy and the Qrie continuum to communicate among ourselves and with the Qrie Stewards anywhere we are.

"We have a special type of skin through which we can breathe underwater when we energize. Our head hair has special coatings that allow the Qrie energy to form a protective field around the head and shoulders. The eyebrows are also of that same type of hair, allowing for a field to flow down over the eyes. The Mer also have long, thick eyelashes that serve to further protect the eyes from water and other things in it. We have no hair below our eyes and normal hairline.

"Since we can flow the Qrie energy about us, we can control what a person sees by the manipulation of this energy. We can bend light with this energy and almost make ourselves invisible until we move. Even then, it's difficult to make out what we are or that we are even there. I noticed you watching Taylor when he floated up to Kandy and Sophianna. That energy field you saw tight around his body is the same thing, somewhat diminished, that is around the Mer when we use the Qrie energy. It's like wearing a tight but comfortable translucent wetsuit.

"The Mer have certain limitations when using this energy; we cannot have objects close to our skin, such as clothing. As a result, we can't wear clothing at any time while in the ocean or using the Qrie energies."

Dr. Talmage said. "We noticed that neither of you has any hair below your eyes and normal hairline. Either you have a strange case of alopecia, or you're much like us."

Breath thought. *I know I'm different. GP, Mum, and Dad all say I'm Qrie. I've got to know more.* Then she asked. "What would happen if you were wearing clothing and use the energy on land?"

John Weber said. "The land clothes would tend to disintegrate when the energies reached high enough to do any useful work, such as floating off the ground or building a sufficient protective field. However, under certain conditions, some items such as pearls, coral, and clothing made from seaweed, hagfish silk, and fish skins can survive for a while. Gold can be worn anytime and is not affected by the Qrie fields."

Tom asked. "How fast can you swim?"

John replied. "That depends on the individual Mer and its ability to manipulate its field. Young Mer can swim many times faster than any human. As the individual gets older and more experienced using these fields, their ability and swimming speeds increase. Some experienced Mer can swim over two hundred forty kilometers an hour, using these fields. I might say though, if that Mer loses its concentration, at that speed, the result can be quite uh — uncomfortable."

Tom laughed. "Wow, that's fast! If they don't have anything on and are swimming that fast, how do they prevent protruding parts of the body from being injured?"

"Yes. Tom, it is fast. Since the Mer have and can increase Qrie energy about our bodies, it prevents damage to the skin and other exposed parts. The arms and fingers are surrounded with this Qrie energy, as are the legs and feet. The ears are flattened tight against the skull and are protected by the Qrie energy and head hair. On females, the Qrie energy closes over the vaginal opening. The navel and anal openings also are covered by this field on both sexes. For males, the genitalia are pulled up into the body and covered by this field. You saw this field around Taylor.

"This field forms around any living thing we decide to lift using the Qrie energies. If we lift a human being that isn't Mer or Mer-human, the exact same field forms.

"The kids used to tease the neighbor's cat by lifting it with the Qrie energies tight around his body. That made the cat look strange. Of course, now the cat stays over here most all the time, begging to be picked up with the Qrie energies.

"When Taylor's field is strong enough to do something useful, the energy field makes it difficult to make out his white swimming suit from the rest of his skin. He looks like a skin-colored department store mannequin. Just like you, except without the mermaid tail and flippers.

"The Mer also generate a temporary skin covering. We can generate this fast-growing protection over our more delicate parts, as we just mentioned. Humans and Mer-humans cannot do this and cannot swim anywhere near as fast as the Mer. This occurs when we energize and the field is under our complete control.

"In addition, the Mer can form skin pockets on the abdomen and on the back, not unlike a kangaroo's pouch. We can use these pouches to carry objects that would be damaged by the

Qrie energies. These pouches are sealed in the same manner as our protective skin.

"You should know the Mer never wear clothes except in public. If they do the clothes will disintegrate, while using the Qrie energies. Even clothing made from hagfish silk. With few exceptions, like gold, pearls, and other items from the sea, the fields don't tolerate anything next to the skin and the outside field."

"What's 'with' all the gold?" Breath asked.

John continued. "Our hair and skin have a protein coating on it, with a gold particle attached to the molecule. These gold particles are what you see. This coating allows the Qrie field to be directed around the hair and around the body. It helps protect our eyes and our faces. When we are not energized, these molecules cannot be seen because they lie just under the skin. However, when we energize, these molecules come to the surface. This 'gold coating' is also in our lungs. It attracts oxygen and water but repels carbon dioxide, carbon monoxide, nitrogen, and nitrogen oxide compounds as well. Allowing us to breathe underwater through our skin, like I said before. It also allows us to dive very deep without getting the bends.

"Also, our skin, bones, muscles, and internal organs all have a fibrous material somewhat like silk, but much stronger. These fibers make us quite tough."

John's voice cracked, and he was silent for a moment. "But it's obvious that it's not tough enough. This fibrous silk material is transparent and makes up the top surface of our skin. This is why when you see an energized Mer, you see gold. Although it looks like an awful lot of gold there's just a tiny amount there."

Breath asked. "Our doctors confirmed that three were dead. How is it that two were healed and resurrected?"

John was silent for a long moment and then continued the explanation. "The Qrie and the Mer have the capability of healing. The Qrie can heal much more severe injuries than the Mer. However, even the Qrie don't know how to manipulate the energies to resurrect the dead. We have no concept of how

Galactic Prime can do this. Cheyenne is with *Galactic Prime* now." His voice cracked as he made this last statement.

Breath had to know and looked at Dr. Talmage. "I saw you float up to the young Mer earlier. Are you also Mer, and how'd you do that?"

He replied. "All of us here are either Mer or part Mer. If a person has enough Mer genes, then they can do some of the things that a true Mer can do, such as fly, move objects with the energies and form the Qrie field around their bodies."

Sophianna was floating in the water next to Breath. "Dr. Spring, can you fly like us?"

"I... ah... well, uh — yes. Maybe not as well as you, but I can" — she looked at Tom with apprehension — "fly."

Kandy jumped up out of the pool and floated. "Show us." The other two young Mer leapt from the pool and all three began flying, coaxing Breath to follow them.

Breath looked around the group. Everyone there had an expectant expression, including Tom. She glanced at Tom with a pleading look. Then she flew up, joined the group of young Mer, and began flying with them.

Now that was a rather strange sight. Here were three golden teenage Mer in full flare and what looked to be a real mermaid with a tail, all flying together.

Neil exclaimed when they came back into the pool. "Mum, did you see her? She can fly every bit as good as we can — maybe even better!"

"Yes, Neil, I saw her." Crystal turned to Breath. "I couldn't help but notice while you were flying that you look about the same age as my teenagers. If I didn't know better, I'd swear that you were a teenager. I know that you're the Directing Scientist on *Morning Discovery*. I also know the Mer grow at the same rate but age slower than normal humans. You've gotta be at least in your twenties. How do you command respect, and how do you stay so young?"

Breath blushed. "Oh, well — I'm nineteen years old. Skipper helps me a lot with the respect part. I've been told — by a friend that I'll have a very slow aging process."

Crystal looked amazed. "Oh, really?"

Sophianna turned to Breath and gave her a long, hard look. "We know you're not Mer. Are you Qrie?"

Breath decided to change the subject and asked, "What are the Qrie and *Galactic Prime* like? What are they trying to do?"

Crystal noticed Breath's unease, and answered before Sophianna could ask another question. "We know what the Qrie are trying to do on this Earth and what the Mers' job is in accomplishing that task. We have no concept of what *Galactic Prime* is doing here, what it is, what it wants, or how it does what it does.

"The Qrie Stewards tell us that *Galactic Prime* is a very ancient entity. As far as they know, *Galactic Prime* is the oldest entity in this universe."

Breath was amazed. "Wow! It spoke — or, rather, communicated — to my mind. It also spoke or communicated to Kandy, because she gave me a message from *Galactic Prime*."

Connie Bernard looked stunned at her daughter. "What did it say to you? And why did it give you the message for Breath?"

Kandy, surprised and uneasy about this sudden attention, blushed. "It didn't say anything! It was more like communicating with the Qrie, but with much more astounding power. It told me to tell Breath that it knew the background of her name and that it liked it. I've got no idea why it gave me the message."

Sophianna asked Breath. "We can read humans and Mer but not the Qrie unless they allow it, and we can't read you. Are you Qrie?"

The adults, seeing Breath's discomfort, looked a little concerned. Hilga interrupted, "Sophianna!"

Crystal continued the interruption. "I almost forgot we have homemade bonbons. Hilga, why don't you help me bring them out for everyone?"

Breath thought. *There seems to be more Mer here than there are humans.* Then she asked, "How is it that the Mer and humans can mate and have children?"

Connie Bernard, with a sly grin, replied. "Oh, that's easy. Boy meets mermaid; boy asks mermaid to mate. Ta-da! Kids."

Dr. Talmage, said amid the laughter. "Breath, it's not that simple. The Mer just keep their population on Earth at about five hundred. We think that the Qrie maintain this population level for their own purposes. The Mer are part human, and they can mate with humans and have children, but not all the children are realized Mer. Another factor in our population is the fact that Mer live longer than humans. Our birth rate is rather small. Mer children are a rarity and are treasured. Neil was born here. The families of Kandy, Cheyenne, and Sophianna all came here when they chose to enter human school. Their parents being both Mer and Mer-human allowed them that choice. Prior to that, they lived in the ocean and were — homeschooled, so to speak."

Everyone began getting out of the pool in anticipation of the bonbons. Breath floated up in the air and released her Aqume. The water splashed back into the pool. She then floated over to a circle of chairs. Everyone else was moving towards and started to pick up their towels.

Breath looked at her towel and then looked at Tom with a sly smile. She backed up a bit and held out her hand. She expelled all of the water from her body and her hair and formed it into a small ball of water.

Tom watched in amazement. "You've gotta teach me how you do that!"

Breath tossed the water into the pool, and, with a come-hither smile, said, "You'll have to coax it out of me later."

Crystal came through the kitchen door bearing bonbons. The young Mer started to converge on her. "Now, kids, you have to wait until our guests get some first." There was a collective sigh and grumble, but they backed up to let Crystal through.

Sophianna noticed a croquet ball on the ground. She'd been practicing refining her telekinesis for some time and decided to pick it up. She tossed the ball to Neil, who caught it with his telekinesis and tossed it back, and a game of toss started.

John jumped up and got a folding table and set it in the center of the circle for Crystal to set the bonbons on. Hilga followed close behind her with a tray of hot tea, coffee, cups, and saucers. Breath and Tom each took a couple of bonbons, put them on a saucer, and noticed the young Mer had already started a game of keep-away.

Breath was distracted as she reached for some more bonbons. As she did, she felt an electric spark jump from her hand and knock over several cups. John was surprised at this. He caught the cups before they dropped to the ground and set them back on the table. Then he gave Breath a rather amazed, intense look. She knew her klutziness had again presented itself but was amazed by John's speed and dexterity.

Tom asked. "Aren't you afraid that the ball or one of them is going to discharge one of the three?"

Hilga observed. "Yah, it vill happen. One of dem vill mess up unt vill get knocked to de ground. But a goot lesson it vill be. For certain, all right dey vill be."

Sure enough, a few moments later, a loud bang was heard, and Kandy hit the ground. Neil went over, offered his hand, and helped her up. She looked in pain but none the worse for the wear. Sophianna was saying she was sorry and flew over to Kandy to see if she was okay.

None of the parents around the circle seemed to be concerned at all. And the game continued.

Breath and Tom watched in amazement. There were three golden naked teenagers with huge wings flying around in the backyard. They were throwing a wooden ball at one another at speeds neither Breath nor Tom could even track. They were catching and dodging the ball as if it were as slow as a balloon.

***

Later that evening, Breath felt a little overwhelmed by the events of the day. She looked over at Tom with an inquiring look. Tom looked back at her and smiled. He felt the electric tingle and knew she was ready to go.

Tom stood up and shook Taylor's hand and thanked him for a most wonderful and different kind of evening. He then shook John Weber's hand and thanked him for all the information he'd given him and Breath. He then turned and shook hands with Jefferson Bernard.

He asked Jefferson, "How is it living with two mermaids?"

Jefferson laughed and nodded. "Taylor and I commiserate a lot. Life is interesting. Without Connie, I don't think it'd be possible. Kandy is a real handful. I've got no idea how Hilga does it with Sophianna alone."

Tom looked over at the Mer ball game. "I don't know how it'd be possible, either."

Connie was standing next to Jefferson. "Hilga isn't alone because she has Crystal here and me." With that, she threw her arms around Tom. Crystal threw her arms around Breath. Both of them said in unison. "Welcome to the family, you two." Jefferson and Taylor both confirmed this welcome by placing their hands on Tom's and Breath's shoulders.

John and Hilga saw this and came over, and they all joined in a large group hug. Connie's and Crystal's eyes teared up. Both women started talking at once. Then Crystal nodded to Connie. "Without you and your help, we'd not have our young ones today." John tried to remain stoic, but Hilga's eyes were streaming. All she could get out was a weak "Dank you."

Breath and Tom looked at each other and smiled. Breath had never been welcomed like that in her life, and she was a bit overwhelmed.

Tom chuckled and licked his lips. "Does being part of the family mean we can drop in anytime for some of that fabulous barbecue?"

Connie laughed. "Of course! You two can come over here any time you want. This is, after all, the local Mer family home, and you're now part of the family. Just open the door and walk in. By the way, the gate and door won't open except for family members; everyone else has to ring the bell."

Breath asked, "How does the door know?"

Dr. Talmage and John laughed, and the doctor said. "Oh, the house, backyard, and the land around them are protected by a Mer protection field. If you're compatible with that Mer field, you can come in; otherwise, you can't! Come over anytime, since we now know you're compatible.

"You must know that if you come over unannounced, sometimes the kids cook, and that can be a real challenge."

Everyone laughed as Connie and Crystal disappeared into the kitchen.

A few moments later, Connie, Crystal, and Hilga came out of the kitchen with several large glass containers with plastic covers filled with food. Crystal, laughing, handed Breath several containers. "Being part of the family also means you have to help us get rid of leftovers. It's part of the job description."

Tom then walked over to Breath. Their arms were now loaded down with leftovers. Both smiled and thanked the women for preparing such a wonderful meal and for making them feel so welcome and comfortable.

As Breath and Tom started to leave, John called. "Kids, come here and say goodbye to our guests." With that, the young Mer flew over and formed a line to say goodbye.

Breath and Tom walked over to the line to shake hands with each of the young Mer. Each of the young Mer took a glass bowl from Breath or Tom in one hand and shook hands with the other. Each time their hands touched; the *Qrie Embrace* was felt. They each thanked Breath and Tom for being there in the sea and helping them. Then they followed Breath and Tom out to his car. Tom opened the boot of the car and placed the leftover containers inside.

Before Breath got in the car, Neil leaned close to her ear and whispered. "How did you touch me, give me that powerful

Qrie Embrace, and not have both of us go unconscious or even be affected by the field surrounding me?"

Neil was standing close to Breath. She turned and with one quick motion touched him on the chest out of sight of the others. She then projected to him alone. *Please say no more about this to anyone. You'll find out soon enough.* Then she gave him another, even more powerful, *Qrie Embrace.* This one staggered him and she had to hold him up with her Qrie energies until he recovered. His eyes were the size of saucers.

She then stepped aside to let Tom open her door. She turned away from a stunned Neil and towards her new Mer friends. "I want to thank all of you for such a warm welcome and a wonderful time." Then, to hide the tear that was forming, she got into the car, and Tom handed her the seat belt.

"You know, Tom, I can reach around and get the seat belt myself. Not that I mind you giving it to me." She said with a shy smile.

"Breath, I know, you are important to me, and I want to make certain you're safe."

"In that case let's go back to my apartment? We can 'talk' about the day."

Tom said. "I don't know, Breath. I've a lot of socks to sort, towels to count, important things like that back at the Station."

Breath said, with a serious expression. "Oh, that's great. Take me back to the ship. I need to talk to Skipper, anyway."

Tom played along. "That'd be great. I'd like to speak with Dr. Kavanaugh about this sonar array of his. Will he be there?"

"Oh, really?"

Tom smiled and looked at Breath. "Well — not really."

"Well, that's just great. All ahead full to the apartment, Lieutenant."

"Aye, aye, Ma'am. Whatever you say, Ma'am."

"Don't you Ma'am me; I'll demote you to swabby."

"That just might be fun, Ma'am."

"I'll show you when I get you back to my apartment."

"That's what I'm counting on," Tom teased with a quick wicked grin.

He parked the car, jumped out, and ran to open Breath's door. Tom then opened her apartment door. He handed Breath her keys. Then they went back to the boot to get the leftovers.

Breath said. "They gave us so much. It'll take us a week to eat all this."

They went into the apartment. They filled the refrigerator with the leftover bowls. Tom went back and locked the door behind them. He followed Breath into the bedroom. They both disrobed and went towards the bathroom to brush their teeth. Tom waited outside and told Breath he didn't have a toothbrush.

"I've got an old one around that I use to brush off my shoes. Maybe that one will work." She pulled open a drawer and tossed Tom a new toothbrush still in the package.

Tom was still standing outside the bathroom.

"What are you doing out there? Come in here, and we can share the bathroom. Or are you just shy?"

"I'm not shy, but we sure are becoming familiar with each other. I just never have been with a woman like this. I 'like' it, and I also like the view and this wonderful electric tingling sensation when I look at you."

Breath almost dropped her toothbrush but caught herself and agreed. "I 'like' it, too."

She and this situation are almost overwhelming. "I'm going to get a glass of orange juice while you finish up here, and I'll get you one, too. Then I'll come in and brush my teeth."

Breath came out to the kitchen and took the glass of orange juice that Tom handed her. Then he went into the bathroom. She downed the orange juice and started to crawl into bed. As she did, she noticed the top fitted sheet of the two fitted sheets she had on the bed had developed holes. She was going to have put a new sheet on. Tom soon came out and helped her.

They lay there, arm in arm, talking about the events of the day and the barbecue that evening. Neither one of them had slept more than about two hours in the last two days. They were beyond exhausted.

They started talking about their personal preferences in musical groups and movies. Their eyes locked onto each other. That strange, wonderful, powerful energy flowed between them. It was similar to the energy they first felt when they met on *Morning Discovery*. This time it was much more powerful. They remained locked in this embrace for what seemed like hours. They didn't remember falling asleep.

***

Breath was awakened late Sunday morning by Tom carefully getting out of bed so as not to wake her. She feigned sleep and clandestinely watched him get dressed. He somehow found an old pair of blue jeans and a T-shirt. Where he got them, she didn't know. Then he crept out of the bedroom and closed the door so as not to wake her.

Breath wondered. *What's he up to?* She got up when she heard the front door open. She opened her bedroom door and sneaked over to the front window.

She watched as Tom opened her car door, leaned down, and did something near the floorboard. Then he went to the front of the car and lifted the bonnet. He bent over and looked in the engine compartment and jiggled a couple of wires. He then got back in the car and tried to start it. It didn't start, not even a click. He went over to his old Land Cruiser, and opened the rear door. He got a rag and an instrument with wires. He then went back over to her car and looked at and checked the battery. He wiped the battery and looked closely. He then stood up, shut the bonnet, and closed the door to her car. He closed the rear door of his vehicle, got in it, and drove away.

Breath mused. *I like my car, but it's given me trouble. Although I suppose the car is actually more practical than a bicycle, the bicycle is more reliable!*

I'll get some breakfast started. We have a couple of bagels. I'll heat them up, and we can have them and some orange juice for breakfast. Tom should be back in a few minutes, but I don't know where he's gone. She put the bagels in the toaster, ready to be toasted when Tom got back, and went back into the bedroom to get dressed.

She picked up the phone and called Hipsi to tell her about Tom. She left out a few minor points, such as the Qrie and the Mer. They were still talking when Tom pulled up about half an hour later.

She went over to the window and watched as he got a battery out of the back his Land Cruiser and took it over to her car. He went back over to his vehicle and got a toolbox. He unlocked her car, opened the bonnet, and went to work with the tools. Just a few moments later, she had a new battery. He got in her car and turned on the ignition. The car started immediately. She watched with tears in her eyes at his thoughtfulness.

She watched as he put the old battery and the tools back in his vehicle, wiped his hands with the rag, closed the boot, and walked towards the apartment.

"Hipsi, I've gotta go. I've gotta kiss Tom!"

"Okay! Breath — go get that man!"

When he opened the door, she jumped into his arms and started kissing him.

A few heartfelt moments later, Tom was able to take a breath. "I'm going to have to do that more often."

Breath looked up at Tom with tears streaming down her face. "Thank you, thank you. No one has ever done anything like that for me." Then she asked more quietly. "Are you for real?"

Tom stepped back and patted himself down. He looked at her with a twinkle in his eye. "Yep." He took her in his arms and kissed her soundly. When they finally came up for air, they again locked their gazes and sensed that the energy passing between them now and last night was real.

Several silent minutes elapsed while ever more powerful energies passed between them. Finally, Tom took a deep breath and reluctantly pushed Breath away. "I hate to break this up. But we need to take that old battery back to the parts place. I need to wash up. And while we're out, I think we need to get lunch or brunch or whatever. How do you feel about going back to Rebecca's?"

Breath, still reeling from the powerful energies and kisses, could only squeak out a weak, "Ok." The bagels were forgotten.

7. PHONE CALL

The waiter greeted them when they walked into Rebecca's. "How are you lovebird's doing? Thanks for that nice tip. How about some hot cocoa on me?"

"That'd be wonderful. Thank you!" Tom thought. *There's that lovebird's thing again. Are we carrying a sign on us or something?*

Tom looked down at Breath. She gave him a shy look, blushed, smiled, and leaned in close to touch him. They went back to their half booth and sat down side-by-side.

The waiter brought their double cocoas and asked them if there was anything else, he could get them.

Breath, still reeling from the energies earlier, was confused. "I always know what I want before I ever sit down, but today, I'm having trouble deciding."

Tom sighed gazing glassy eyed at the menu. "Yeah, I'm always a burger-and-fries kind of guy. I'm having a difficult time trying to make up my mind as to what I want as well."

The waiter came too soon. Breath, out of desperation, ordered the crispy chicken salad with honey mustard, and she didn't even like honey mustard! Tom, with the same uncertainty, ordered the steak with a side salad.

As they sat waiting for their meal, Tom let out a long sigh. "This has been one whale of an eventful couple days. I've met mermaids and mermen and the gods that made them, the Sun, the Earth, and everything else. I know they don't consider themselves to be gods, but I don't know what else to call them. And, best of all, I met you. Someone I can talk to and confide in, and someone I think I can love... I've waited so long for this... for you."

Breath's heart was pounding so hard, she thought it could be heard across the room. Her breath was catchy, and again, her eyes were brimming with tears. She thought. *I can't believe what's happening to me. Why am I crying so much? I'm never like this. Doesn't he know saying sweet things like that will make me cry. It's a good thing that I don't have mascara on, because the Qrie energies and my tears would have it running all the way down to my shoes!*

She just sat there. She couldn't talk. She couldn't say a word; her emotions were all over the place. She glanced at Tom and moved her hand over to his leg and squeezed. Tom put his left arm around her shoulder and laid his right hand down on his leg, palm up. She put her hand in his and interlaced her fingers with his. She squeezed, and he squeezed back. He pulled her close and kissed her gently on her forehead. She was trembling.

The warm, tingling sensation passed between them and was as strong as ever. She thought. *Is this what it feels like to fall in love? If it is, how does anyone survive it? My heart, my feelings, my emotions are going crazy. I can't even think. I've got to go to work in the morning, and I'm a wreck!*

Tom's heart was also racing. *I think I'm falling in love with this woman, and there doesn't seem to be anything I can do about it; not that I want to. I'm attracted to everything about her. When she put her hand in mine and squeezed, I felt electric chills up and down my back; I've got goosebumps. And when I kissed her on the forehead, it was electric. I can't think clearly. My mind is running a hundred miles a second. I can't function, and I've got a job to do tomorrow.*

They sat huddled together until Tom saw the waiter approaching. "Our order is coming." He gave her a good squeeze on the shoulder and squeezed her hand. She squeezed his hand in return and sat up, and he took his arm from around her shoulder.

The emotions between them were thick. Tom tried to break the tension. "Ah, here come the eats. Time for chow, and it looks great."

They ate slowly without talking. There were a lot of meaningful glances and smiles back and forth between them. They didn't say a word.

The moment Breath finished eating, she felt a massive wave of *Qrie Embrace* wash over her. The familiar voice came inside her head. *Talk to Crystal and Connie; they can help you.* Breath couldn't say a word.

Tom felt an immense wave of *Qrie Embrace* wash over him. A voice inside his head said. *Talk to Taylor and John; they can help you.*

Breath and Tom simply looked at each other and didn't say anything.

Both just sat there huddled close to one another and looking at their empty plates, thinking. *What just happened?* Both of their cell phones rang in unison.

Breath answered her phone first; it was Connie Bernard. She took the phone away from her ear and just looked at it for a moment. Then she put the phone back to her ear. "Hello, Connie. How do you do?"

"We'll be at the Talmages' compound when you get here. Bye now." And she hung up.

At about the same time, Tom answered his phone; it was Taylor Talmage. He was a bit stunned. "Hello, Taylor. How's it going?"

"The coffeepot is on, and we'll see you when you get here!" Then he hung up.

Breath looked at Tom. "Who was that on the phone? Was that one of our Mer family?"

"Yes. I guess we're going to the Talmages'!"

Breath and Tom stood up and started walking to the register. The waiter looked at Tom. "Is there anything wrong? Was the food okay?"

"No, nothing wrong or out of the ordinary — for this weekend, anyway. The food was great, and thanks for the cocoa. It was great as always." He paid the bill and left a generous tip.

No words were spoken in the car on the trip to the Talmages' compound. They both felt the energies flowing between them, now more powerful than ever.

When they pulled up, Taylor, Crystal, John, and Connie were all standing in the doorway.

Tom looked at Taylor, and Breath looked at Crystal. Breath said. "What's happening? We were sitting at Rebecca's. This tremendous feeling of *Qrie Embrace* washed over us. You called us, and here we are!"

Crystal and Connie took Breath in hand, and Connie looked over her shoulder at the men. "Sorry, boys; this calls for some serious girl talk."

Breath looked back at Tom with an expression of, "Help me; I'm being abducted," and all the women disappeared into another room.

Tom blankly gazed at Taylor and John. "What the..."

And then all three men went out to the backyard.

***

Breath walked into the living room and just plopped into a comfortable hagfish silk cloth overstuffed chair. Crystal walked towards the kitchen. "The coffee is ready. I'll bring some out for us. And I've some cinnamon rolls in the oven; they should be done in a little bit."

Connie started. "Breath, I know you've been through a lot this weekend. More than a normal person would ever go through. Oh, yes, I suppose you could go to a psychologist and discuss your feelings for a year. You probably won't gain anything because this doesn't have anything to do with your mental stability. A psychologist could analyze you — even Taylor could do it — but that isn't what you need. You're not human. You're also not Mer. We don't know what you are. We suspect you might be Qrie, since you emit Qrie energy, but you're physical, and the Qrie are all pure energy. What's going on in your psyche is out of the purview of that type of doctor and therefore couldn't help you. What you must do is reorder your thought processes and control the Qrie energies and forces that are emanating from you and amplifying your emotions. So, we're going to help you the Mer way, since you and Tom are now part of our family.

"Let me guess: You and Tom met during the crisis on your ship. You felt major sparks between you. No words were spoken other than those required to handle the situation. Later, you hooked up and found out the sparks were still there. You felt compelled to call us. I can imagine you found out more than you ever thought you'd ever know about something you didn't even know existed. Your feelings and emotions are out of control, and you don't know what to do. Does that just about cover it?"

Breath didn't say a word. She was dumbfounded and just nodded. About this time, Crystal walked back into the room with a tray of coffee and cups.

Connie continued. "When you and Tom saw each other, there were indeed sparks. If you were human, you might've called him or he might've called you, and you'd have gone out on a few dates and maybe even gotten to know each other better.

"As it was, you were inundated with Qrie energy. It was flowing from the Qrie Stewards and *Galactic Prime* into everyone, and it was everywhere. You couldn't avoid it. You and Tom already had an empathic connection without the Qrie energy, but with the Qrie energy, it was amplified immensely.

"We saw that empathic connection the moment you walked through that door Saturday afternoon. It was so strong and the Qrie energies were so powerful, we didn't know whether to say something at that time or not. We decided to wait. If you and Tom weren't strongly attracted to each other and weren't compatible, this symbiotic connection would dissipate over time.

"It's obvious now that there's a strong attraction between you two, and the empathic connection is powerful. All this Qrie energy flowing around makes the connection orders of magnitude stronger. In short, you've been swept up by an emotional cyclone, and you don't know what to do about it.

"The other part is that you've been inundated with the *Qrie Embrace* from the Mer and the Qrie, as well as *Galactic Prime*. Our feeble attempts at giving others this *Qrie Embrace* is nothing compared to what the Qrie can do. From what I understand from Neil, Kandy, and Sophianna the energies that occurred during the incident, with Morning and Beauty, are minuscule compared to those from *Galactic Prime*.

"You and Tom have been hit with a triple whammy. Before you answer this next question, think about it for a while. The answer will determine your destiny for the rest of your life. Now, do you want this to continue with Tom, or do you want it to stop?"

Before Breath could say a word, Crystal said. "Now, Love, it's not nearly what you might think. It's marvelous; trust me. Once you get a handle on your feelings, this *Qrie Embrace* is always with you, and it's an unconditional love directed towards you and — well, in your case, Tom."

Breath sat quietly for a few moments. "I know Tom is going through the same conversation with Taylor and John that we're having here. Why didn't we just do this together, Connie?"

"You know how guys are, Breath. They're always going on about boats, cars, fishing gear, and other stuff. Anyway, that's probably what they're talking about. At the end of their conversation, they'll come in and think they've got the solution to the whole problem."

Breath laughed halfheartedly, knowing that Connie was just trying to lighten the mood. She knew that she wanted to get control of these wild emotions. "I don't want to lose Tom, and I hope Tom feels the same way. What can you gals and I do to help me get a hold of these emotions so that they don't overwhelm me?"

"We've several exercises that we can use, along with flows of certain types of Qrie energy that'll help control your emotions."

Crystal continued. "We know from the large amount of Qrie energies flowing in and about you and Tom that both of you are quite compatible and that you do, indeed, like each other."

Breath was stunned for a moment. "You can sense that I have Qrie energies flowing in and around me?"

"Yes, Love, you've been touched by both the Qrie and *Galactic Prime* with rather large quantities of Qrie energies, and if I'm not mistaken, this heightened level of energy will be with you for a while.

"We don't understand why you're not floating, like our young Mer. You were floated out over the water at the incident by *Galactic Prime,* just like the dead RAN crewman and young Mer. Why do you think you're having such strong emotions now — when you haven't had these emotions any other time in your life?"

"I don't know," Breath muttered. "That'd make sense. I guess I'm just so... so..."

Crystal and Connie sensed that Breath needed a change of pace. They began to ask questions about what she did on her ship and what she liked about her job. Other things were brought up that they thought might be mundane, anything to help get Breath's mind off her emotions.

Breath liked the change of subject and asked. "Crystal, how is Neil doing with his energy problem? Is he still golden? Can he walk around on the ground? Will he discharge?"

"The field is almost down to normal. By the time he goes to school in the morning, it should be normal. No one will know the difference, I hope!"

Connie said. "Kandy and Sophianna are almost normal too. All three have clothes on, testing for school tomorrow. If they make it through the night, we'll know they can make it at school."

"That's great! I'm glad to hear it. When I first saw them on the access deck of the ship, I was afraid and concerned, I didn't know what to do. I was so glad that there was a doctor as well as an advanced paramedic to take care of the situation. When Doc informed us that they were dead, I almost passed out. I had to grab hold of the railing. I've seen some bad accidents, and those were some serious injuries.

"I'm glad that you didn't have to see that. I can't imagine what a mum would think — or a dad, for that matter! Seeing their child in that kind of condition! It was devastating for me. I can't imagine how you would have reacted! How's John doing?"

Breath noticed a tear moving down Crystal's cheek. "John is holding up pretty well under the circumstances."

"That's good. I was afraid for him. Neil and Cheyenne had the worst injuries, and both were dead. The damage to Neil's body was horrible. Except for Cheyenne's terrible head injury, from that piece of metal, she didn't look that bad; not much worse than Kandy. I'm so glad that he's going to be all right. I wish we could've done more for Cheyenne."

Connie lowered her head and nodded. "That makes sense. Kandy told us that Neil was the first one to the explosive container and Cheyenne was right behind him when it went off, so it makes sense that he'd catch the brunt of the explosion.

"We sensed when the situation occurred, although we didn't know what had happened. We were preparing to leave when Morning and Beauty told us to remain. That still didn't relieve our anxiety until Morning and Beauty informed us about *Galactic Prime* and the results."

Crystal said. "It's still difficult for us to believe that Cheyenne is gone."

Breath looked at Connie, concerned. "Why do you suppose *Galactic Prime* couldn't heal Cheyenne when it healed Neil?"

"According to Morning and Beauty, it was the head injury. Her brain was too damaged for even *Galactic Prime* to repair."

***

All heads turned as Tom, Taylor, and John entered the room. They were saying something about a ride along as they were walking through the door.

John was laughing and joking trying to put on a strong face. "I suppose you gals have been talking about us, or else our ears wouldn't be ringing like they are."

Crystal replied in the same laughing and joking manner. "Connie was telling us about what you guys really talk about — boats, fishing, and stuff."

Taylor's hands rose up in the air. "We've been found out boys. Can't keep anything from the gals. As a matter of fact, we were talking about boats. Tom has invited us on a ride along on his patrol boat. He says he can get it cleared. We can all go on an excursion. Maybe something even more exciting soon."

Connie, with an assured, knowing expression on her face, raised her index finger with an air of authority. "See, girls! Do I ever know my guys, or what!"

Crystal laughed and asked. "Well, guys, did you come to any conclusions?"

Taylor became serious. "Yes. Tom doesn't want to lose Breath, and he'll do whatever it takes to keep her."

Connie put her arm around Breath. "Breath expressed the same thing. I suppose we should get on with the exercises."

At that moment, the doorbell rang. Taylor looked around the room. "I'm not expecting anybody. And how did they get through the gate without ringing the gate bell?"

Crystal was closest to the door and went to open it. "Hello. Can I help you?"

8. JIM

A deep, soft, resonant voice filled the room. "No Crystal, but I think I can help y'all."

Breath erupted out of her chair, and floated in the air. There was no doubt in her mind who belonged to 'that' Southern drawl. Breath was beside Tom in less than a heartbeat, and they were both looking in the direction of the voice. She had an excited vise grip on Tom's arm that cut off the circulation to his fingers.

Tom's eyes widened as he watched Breath's reaction, and he felt a strange effect from her, what he thought could be a modified *Qrie Embrace.*

The Norse brawny, light blonde man, a hundred and eighty-five centimeters tall (over six feet), and perhaps thirty-five years old, walked into the room. He emanated immense power. He walked up to each person in the room, called them by name, and asked them how they were doing.

He then went over to Breath and Tom. "I've come to help y'all. Don't y'all agree that this is a much better venue than the café?"

Breath's eyes twinkled and her grin was almost ear to ear. She looked from Tom to the man standing in the middle of the room.

The man held out his hand to Tom. "My name is James Madison MacAvies, but please call me Jim, or Mad Mac if y'all want. All my friends do. Some people call me other names not mentionable in mixed company. The only thing I ask is, don't call me late for lunch." He chuckled.

Tom took his hand and felt a massive *Qrie Embrace* that made him weak in the knees. He had to use Breath for support.

He then extended his hand to Breath, who grabbed it with eager excitement. A great flash of multicolored light passed between them. She then dropped his hand and put both of her arms around him in a big hug. He hugged her back, and then she floated down, with a huge elated smile.

This took everybody in the room by surprise. Everyone just stood and looked at them, not quite knowing what to think.

John tentatively asked. "Uh — are you the Qrie Beauty or the Qrie Morning?"

"Nah, those guys are just a little bit stoic for me. I like things a little bit more relaxed, if y'all don't mind. Ya know what I mean?" He chuckled.

John asked. "We know you're not Mer, and if you're not Morning or Beauty, who are you?"

"I told all y'all my name is Jim; my nickname is Mad Mac. All y'all can call me that if ya want." He pulled Breath closer to him, then leaned close to her, and whispered in her ear. "Have y'all owned your name yet?"

Jim put his arm around Breath, pulled her still closer giving her a massive *Qrie Embrace*, and grinned like a cat with a mouse. "I must apologize to all y'all. I should've sensed your symbiotic connection and Tom's genetic differences at the unfortunate incident. I could've modulated my energy so it wouldn't have impacted y'all so much."

Tom and everyone except Breath were still stunned silent. Their mouths were agape at his knowledge of them.

Breath, on the other hand, gave him a mixed look of sheer exasperation and joy, having no doubt who he was.

Then Jim put a big smile on his face and a laugh in his voice. "Ah, come on, guys. I'm trying to be the guy next door. I guess I'm just not pulling it off. Man, this is a tough room. Must be my Southern U.S. upbringin'! Don't you blokes like Yanks?"

Taylor and John laughed at this.

Taylor was beginning to figure out what Jim was trying to do. "Come on, mates. Lighten up."

A buzzer went off in the kitchen. Startled, Crystal jumped up. "Oh, that's the cinnamon rolls. I'll be right back." She hurried off into the kitchen, with Connie close behind her.

Jim sniffed the air, and licked his lips. "Cinnamon rolls. Wow! I haven't had a cinnamon roll in a long time. They do smell good. I can't wait." He rubbed his hands together, laughing. "But then, I guess I'm gonna have to."

John smiled but wrinkled his brow and raised one eyebrow. "Well, you're not Mer. You're not the Qrie Morning or the Qrie Beauty, so you've gotta be..."

Breath interrupted with emphatic excitement. "You're GP, the voice that's been in my head all my life. And now I find out you're *Galactic Prime*! I guess that makes sense. GP — *Galactic Prime*, whatever that means. You've been my constant companion for eighteen years. I didn't know who you were until you showed up at the explosion site — And just why is that?"

Jim smiled at Breath and then turned to the rest of the group. "Ah, come on, guys. That's not even twenty questions. I guess my disguise isn't as good as I thought. I'm just gonna have to come up with something better. Do y'all think I could make a passable Easter Bunny? I don't want anything like a vampire or Frankenstein; that'd scare everybody off. I'll bet I could make a pretty good Santa Claus. I know; how about the Cookie Monster? I suppose I could become a Sorvolian crystal creature. They're quite beautiful, ya know."

Everyone laughed, except Breath. She just stared at him.

Breath projected with excited irritation, *Well, at least I know now.*

GP — or now Jim — bowed to Breath. *Yes, Breath, now y'all know.*

About that time, a ruckus came from upstairs. It sounded like a herd of cattle. Three teenagers, all talking at the same time, were running down the stairs. They ran into the living room, took one look at Jim, and stopped dead in their tracks. Both Neil and Kandy blurted. "Oh, My God, it's *Galactic Prime!*"

Jim threw his hands into the air. "Well, there y'all have it. I can't even fool Mer teenagers some of the time. What's a fellow to do?"

Jim put on a huge smile, walked over to the teenagers, glanced over at Taylor, winked, and asked with a thick Southern accent, "How're all y'all doin'? Is everthang workin' like it should? Y'all ain't got moles, have ya? Hope y'all don't get scales 'cause them things are really hard to get rid of. Does your back itch?"

Upon hearing him, the teenagers started looking at one another. All of them started checking for moles or scales.

Taylor elbowed John, and they started laughing. The teenagers realized they were the butt of a joke and went running into the kitchen, where the smell of food enticed.

Jim laughed out loud. "It's good to see teenage radar for cinnamon rolls still works perfect. It's good to know where one stands in the perspective of real galactic importance. Teenagers can give that to ya!"

***

Crystal and Connie came back into the room bearing cinnamon rolls, coffee, tea, and cups. They set the trays down, and Connie went back to get the milk, if the kids hadn't drunk it all. She came back a few moments later with a two-liter jug of milk and several glasses.

For a little while, everyone sat eating their cinnamon rolls and engaged in nervous conversation, awkward glances, and uncomfortable smiles. Everyone, that is, except Breath. After everyone had finished eating, they nervously wiped their hands.

Breath looked at her lifelong friend, GP — or, Jim, or *Galactic Prime* as she now knew him. She mused about their history together. She leaned her head back, closed her eyes, and smiled.

Neil and Sophianna came charging back into the living room to get a ball and started heading for the backyard.

Kandy jumped up and started to run out with them.

The tension was broken. Connie Bernard pronounced in a loud voice. "Kandy Bernard, you better not energize or flare with those clothes on. You take them off right now! I won't have you shredding another outfit just because you want something new."

Clothes went flying in every direction. Connie, Crystal, and Hilga all cleared their throats rather loudly. Kandy, now in the nuddy, picked up her clothes and placed them on a chair and went to join the game. Neil and Sophianna got the hint and placed their clothes on the nearby table as well. Then all three teenagers sprinted towards the backyard.

Tom said, "Now, that's something I never thought I'd hear in my life: mums telling their teenage son and daughters to strip naked before they go play a game — and with strangers in their midst."

No sooner had he finished that statement than both girls and Neil flared. Huge wings of multicolored, branching streamers of plasma light energy, each maybe eight meters across, came from their backs.

Connie called after the kids, as they left, "Play your game in the middle of the compound, and keep low to the ground. We don't want anyone seeing the lights of your flares from outside the compound."

Breath and Tom were startled by this, and Tom said. "That was fast."

John looked puzzled and asked. "What was fast?"

"Those wings... or whatever. They just sprouted! Where'd they come from?"

John understanding Tom's confusion smiled and replied. "That's what's called a flare. All Mer have it. It's how we Mer gather the Qrie energy when we want to heal or energize our bodies — or, in their case, float off the ground, fly, or go for a fast swim. The flare is also used to radiate energy away from the body if we happen to be overcharged, as the teenagers are now. You'll notice that all three young Mer have turned completely gold. And if you look closely, you can see the Qrie field around them."

Connie added. "The Mer flare appears as a multicolored, three-dimensional, wing like appendage carrying the *Qrie Embrace* and Qrie energy. Sometimes when we need a large amount of energy, the flare becomes like a huge ball, up to eighteen meters in diameter, with our physical body at its center. It comes from our back and is detailed in its fractal structure, and we can control its size, shape, and color. At night the flare can be well — resplendent."

Breath exclaimed. "We saw this before. I just didn't know it happened so fast!" She paused for a moment. "But Connie, how can you swim with the flare?"

"The flare is made of special Qrie energy and doesn't interact with physical matter. To the water, it's not there."

"Oh — I see! Then how can the other Qrie fields be discharged?"

Jim replied. "Because that type of Qrie field can interact with physical matter."

***

After the cinnamon rolls and some time spent in more nervous conversation, Crystal just had to ask. "How are you going to help Breath and Tom?"

Jim smiled a wicked little grin and said. "Don't quite know, 'cause I've never done anything like this before. Guess I'm just gonna have to wing it. Although I've read a bit about it, if that's any help."

Breath said dripping with sarcasm and a cheeky grin. "Well, GP, that just fills me with all kinds of warm, fuzzy confidence."

"Well, I'm glad somebody's got confidence. I'm a little shaky here myself."

Everyone in the room but Tom laughed.

Breath went over to Tom and pressed up against him. "Ah, come on Tommy. What's the worst that can happen? If he turns us into frogs, I'm sure he can turn us back!"

Tom, seeing and sensing that Breath was feeling better, relaxed a great deal himself.

Jim, seeing that both of them had relaxed enough and were comfortable, held out his hands. "If you'll take my hands, we can get started."

The teenagers came back into the living room to watch what Jim was about to do.

Breath reached out with her hand like a timid little girl. She'd never been in the physical presence of her friend GP before today. Tom wasn't much better, but they both put their hands out and grasped his. At that moment, both of them gasped for air and floated a few inches off the floor. A powerful strange light from the Qrie energies filled the room and surrounded her and Tom.

Breath felt and recognized the Qrie energy and the wonderful feelings that this energy brings with it. GP's soft inner mind voice filled them and began to teach them how to control their thoughts and feelings.

GP informed them that they were linked for eternity. The Qrie energy would always touch them. With these new exercises and his help, they'd gain better control of the energies than they ever had. He also told Breath she'd have to help Tom since Tom was brand new to all this. They began to communicate at a speed far faster than she'd ever experienced.

He told Breath that Tom's telepathic linkages were now activated, and he could use these linkages, with the energy, to communicate with her and the other Mer. However, he'd have to spend a fair amount of time with John, Crystal, and Connie to learn how to use these links and to control the Qrie energies. She could feel the excitement rise in her. She knew that she and Tom would soon be able to communicate the way she did with GP.

After what seemed to be a considerable period of time, GP left her mind. She looked around. Everyone in the room was looking at her and Tom. They glanced at one another and knew that the wild feelings were now under their control. They'd learned control and the self-discipline to maintain that control. All they needed now was a lot of practice to make it effortless.

***

Breath was a bit peckish and dizzy after her intense training session with Jim, and she had a wonderful floating feeling. She knew that the floating feeling would go away in a short time, perhaps if she had another cinnamon roll. She turned and started to walk over to get one. It turned out not to be quite so simple. As she put her foot out to make the first step, she felt herself falling. She caught herself and relaxed. She was floating in the air, something she and GP had practiced many times.

"Careful, Love." Crystal reached out to support Breath. "You can't go running off until your feet actually touch the ground."

Breath chuckled while enjoying the sensation. "I did learn to walk before I learned to fly. And I've been flying for a long time." And then thought to herself, *I should've realized I was actually floating off the ground, not just having a floating feeling. That training session was heavy duty.*

Jim looked at Tom with concern. "Y'all don't really want to do that right now. Why don't y'all let the field dissipate a bit? Then y'all can run your marathon."

Breath looked around and saw Tom also being held by John and Connie. She wondered if he'd tried to get a cinnamon roll too. "How long is he going to be floating here Jim?"

Jim beamed with a huge grin. "Did y'all hear that everyone? She called me Jim. She's the first person in this room to call me by my name — wow! It'll take just a few minutes, Tom, and then you'll be free to walk around."

"Oh great. He gets to hang here like a Christmas ornament until his field dissipates."

"Well, y'all can try to float around the room, if ya want. Y'all do have the energy right now. All you've got to do is think about balance and where ya want to go and then desire to go there," Jim explained.

Tom had already started moving. He was making little circles in the middle of the living room. He then tried his hand at floating around a chair, and that worked pretty well. He then tried a zigzag path across the room.

Breath saw this and with grace followed Tom. She tried the little circles; she was tracking Tom move for move. Of course, it wasn't long before the teenagers joined in on the fun.

Breath asked, "How long will this last, Jim?"

"Until it doesn't work anymore of course!"

Tom exclaimed. "This is wonderful!"

Jim laughed, with a sly grin, "Be careful what you wish for; it just might come true."

Tom asked. "Jim, why aren't we turning gold and our clothes ripping off? I thought that was what happened when the field was strong enough to lift someone off the ground."

"Well, that's because you're Qrie, not Mer. If y'all were Mer, your clothes would've been ripped off a long time ago. Y'all don't have the binder proteins with the gold particles. They're primarily to help the Mer protect themselves and breathe while in the water. This is also why Taylor, Jefferson, and Hilga can float off the ground without their clothes being ripped off. Y'all don't need protection right now — unless somebody throws a cinnamon roll at ya, and that's not going to hurt much.

"However, if y'all or someone else pours a considerable amount of Qrie energy through or around your body, your clothes will be damaged or disintegrate. Even if you can float in the air, it doesn't mean you can swim fast in the water. However, Breath, in your case, you can swim quite fast with your mermaid Aqume, *and in other ways.*"

Sophianna asked. "How can you three be Qrie? I've seen what the Qrie Morning and Beauty are like, and they're pure energy. I know you're not pure energy because I've touched you, and you're solid. How can you be Qrie?"

Connie looked at Breath and asked. "Are you human with special abilities like the Qrie?"

Breath frowned at Jim. *You always told me never to tell anyone that I was Qrie, and now you're telling everyone here.*

Calm down Breath. These people are our friends, and they know about the Qrie. They already control the Qrie energies well, and you're going to learn a lot from them.

Jim looked around the room. "Yes, everyone, Breath, Tom, and I are Qrie, but we're also human, and Breath is also a small part Mer. That'd make them similar to me, which is Qrie-human." He looked at Breath and then at Tom. "Tom the difference is, y'all need to learn how to control your Qrie part. That's why we're here, to help y'all."

Tom stopped flying in circles. "I can't be Qrie. I can't do anything like Breath or the Mer can."

Jim laughed. "Just what do you think you've been doing for the last twenty minutes, ice-skating? Yes, it's true. You're Qrie. Once you learn how to control your Qrie part, you'll be able to do similar things like Breath and the Mer. You'll even be able to feed the Mer Qrie energies, just like any other Qrie. Unlike the Qrie Morning and Beauty, you do have a physical body and will be able to do things they can't do."

Crystal sensed the tension in the room. "More cinnamon rolls, anyone?"

Jim said, "Without a doubt. I'm always ready for cinnamon rolls. By the way, Taylor, I analyzed you, Jefferson, and Hilga. I see you've got the communication link capability like the other Mer, Breath, and Tom. It has just never been activated. With your permission, I'd like to activate it at this time."

"Sure, I'm ready for it and I know Jefferson and Hilga want this too."

"Well then, I'll activate that capability, but you must know this: you three will have to work with Tom, John, Crystal, and Connie to learn how to use it. Practice makes perfect!"

***

When Tom came back down to Earth, Breath asked. "GP — err... Jim — just who and what are you?"

"Well, I suppose all y'all do deserve an explanation.

"Around a hundred and ten years ago, as a baby, I started hearing voices and getting images in my head like y'all Breath. And over the years they taught me, somewhat like I taught y'all. About four decades ago, I was approached in a more formal manner by the entities you know as Morning and Beauty, as well as the Stewards for the Galactic Memory.

"At first, I had no idea what was going on. Like you, I thought I was going crazy. They spoke to my mind with Qrie telepathy. I had a difficult time trying to figure out what they were attempting to tell me. They don't use language — only complex images, feelings, smells, sensations, orientations, complex mind expansions, and more. All these things are not translatable into human language. You know what I mean, Breath; you've experienced their methods of communication. Even after seventy years, I had difficulties, but I was able to understand the Qrie well after some period of time. At that time only one Qrie Memory Steward had learned to communicate in English, and it was bad English at best. I've been teaching them how to use proper human English — well proper for me that is. They haven't achieved full understanding and use yet, but they're getting close.

"Even though in the last forty years, they have somewhat learned to use human language, my training of you took much less time because we speak the same language.

"And if this weren't enough, they wanted me to become the primary Memory Steward and take over the Local Galactic Supercluster Memory, or just Galactic Memory for short, and become something called a *Galactic Prime*. I didn't know what was going on, but the more they communicated, the more I understood. I was persuaded, after some time, to become this *Galactic Prime*. When I did, I also got an assistant whose job it is to take care of my physical body. I call it Z because it hasn't chosen a human name. Z is quite young, for a Qrie, only a few million years young a recent split off from an older pair of Qrie. Knowing Qrie timelines like I do, it might be a few millennia before Z decides what it wants to be called.

"At that time, I was already over seventy. I had reached what they called Full Maturity. I laugh now, but at the time, I exclaimed, 'Full Maturity? I walk with a cane, and I'm almost dead!'

"It's apparent, the Qrie don't have a sense of humor, because they went on to tell me that I had at best twenty years left in my life. I asked them how long this selection process had been going on and when I had been selected for the position. They told me the process had been going on for over four thousand years, since the last *Galactic Prime* expired. And that my selection was made at the moment of my conception.

"They told me a rather scary story. The previous *Galactic Prime* was a being of artificial physical construction. It had on its body what the Qrie call a Genetic Stability Device. That device holds its physical artificial constructed DNA in place. It lost that device and died without producing an heir. They haven't seen fit to tell me what happened to the *Galactic Prime* prior to my predecessor, but I'm finding out by a thorough search of the Memory. It expired before the beginning of this universal cycle; it didn't have an heir, either. I use the term 'heir' because I've no idea how the selection process is exercised. I do know that this Genetic Stability Device had something to do with my being selected. Another of my impressions is that *Galactic Primes* pass on their genetic material after ten billion to one hundred billion years or so.

"About two million years ago, the previous *Galactic Prime* helped the Qrie Stewards place the aggression suppression rings around Earth, and the Mer were created. Homo erectus and then Homo sapiens evolved. Everything was going along fine until about four thousand years after the Toba volcano exploded, which occurred about seventy-four thousand years ago. This reduced the population of Homo sapiens to no more than fifty-five hundred breeding couples. The local Qrie Stewards called

Galactic Prime when there were only two thousand breeding couples of Homo sapiens left. At that time, *Galactic Prime* modified the genome of those two thousand couples, which changed their physical and mental capabilities so they could better survive their environment.

"It's unfortunate, that about four thousand years ago that *Galactic Prime* lost its Genetic Stability Device, here on Earth, that'd been keeping it alive these last many billion years. I now have all the memories of the past *Galactic Primes*. However, sorting through them is a bit problematic. That Genetic Stability Device is still somewhere on this planet." He glanced at Breath for a moment.

"Anyway, I guess I'm a slow learner, because it took me an entire lifetime to mature. After some persuasion on the Qrie Stewards' part, I opted to take them up on their accord. They did tell me I could get out of the agreement if I needed or wanted to. So, I thought, what the heck? I'm about dead anyway; I'll fall on that grenade for them. As it turned out, it was a great decision, and I love my job. It's challenging, exciting, and all the superlatives you can name. It's a unique job for which I'm the only being, in this Galactic Supercluster, that is qualified.

"There's one caveat; even though I get to experience things and speak with entities that no human being could even imagine, I still desire to be around my own kind. I know that I'm far more Qrie than I am human, but it's the physical human part that makes everything work.

"Breath, I've been teaching you all your life. The time has now come for you to take on the advanced lessons. The time of parlor games has come to an end. It's now time for you to learn how to be a 'true' Qrie. You can still play mermaid if you wish, but you're not a mermaid. You never were. You're so much more powerful and wonderful.

"The Qrie Stewards did the same with me. When I reached Full Maturity, I had to take on the advanced lessons myself. These lessons won't be easy, but I know you'll succeed, just as

I did. You'll also learn much faster than I did because the Qrie Stewards now know human language.

"Tom, you're also Qrie, although not as much as Breath. You'll also be taught in the ways of the Qrie. I'm confident that in time you'll be as conversant with the Qrie powers as Breath is at this time."

Everyone was silent for a few moments. Then Tom brought up this question. "I thought the Qrie were pure-energy beings, but you look like you have a physical body. How's that?"

Jim laughed and poked himself in the chest with his finger. "I do have a physical human body, but what you see here is a solid illusion. It's indeed pure Qrie energy, and a consciousness is here as well. In truth, there's only one consciousness here. At present, I've got well over seventy thousand of these illusion bodies, each in a different galaxy in the supercluster. Each body has its own consciousness; and all of them are connected to my personal section of the Galactic Memory. I can make as many of these bodies as I need. I'll teach you two how to do this someday. They come in quite handy.

"My physical body is sequestered. My assistant, Qrie entity Z, makes sure that my physical body is in perfect condition at all times.

"A physical body is required to control and maintain the Galactic Memory. The Memory is made of and requires a tremendous amount of Qrie energy. However, the Qrie are also made of Qrie energy; the Memory tends to consume the Qrie entities trying to control it. The Qrie continuum, the Memory, or anything associated with the Qrie energies cannot consume physical matter. They needed someone who was made of physical matter, and that entity also needs to be capable of handling the tremendous amounts of Qrie energies required to control and protect the Galactic Memory. They discovered my genetics and what they call personality structure before my birth.

"As part Qrie and part human, we've two bodies — one noncorporeal Qrie energy body and one physical body. If one of our bodies dies, which will occur, the other will continue until it dies. The chances are very high that the physical body will die prior to the demise of the Qrie body. If that occurs, a new physical body can be obtained."

Breath asked, "We don't become like the body snatchers or something, do we?"

"No, Breath. A Qrie can't do that. A normal human body can't survive our energies. We must find a suitable host parent on Earth, a Qrie mother. Or a human female who's in association with a Qrie Genetic Stability Device. That'd work for your grandmother and grandfather and for Tom. It wouldn't work for you or me. All our grandparents, mother, and father, would have to be Qrie. Your brother and sister, on the other hand, require that one side of their lineage be Qrie back to the grandparents and that their mother have the Qrie Genetic Stability Device. We would then combine our Qrie part to the physical part at the moment of conception. We'd then have to go through the normal gestation, birth process, and childhood.

"In all our present cases, we had the Qrie capability in our physical bodies prior to combining with any Qrie. In short, we were physical a fraction of a second or so before we were Qrie, at conception. That didn't make us any less Qrie. We've got the capability of taking on a Qrie memory and its powers. I did this when I became *Galactic Prime*."

Breath asked, "Are you kind of 'it' for the entire universe, or are there others like you?"

"There are many *Galactic Primes*. Right now, I'm the *Galactic Prime* for this Local Galactic Supercluster."

Tom muttered, "Wow!"

Breath glanced at him and rolled her eyes.

"I know it's a lot of information to take in, Tom, and I'd take notes because there's going to be a test. Maybe even a pop quiz!"

Tom just looked at Jim with a blank stare for a second. "You've gotta be kidding!"

"No test like in school. Your test will be life itself."

Breath was a little weary after all the excitement, but she had to know. "You mentioned earlier that they extended your life. For how long did they do that?"

"At first, I thought they'd extend it maybe a thousand or maybe five thousand years. They told me this was unacceptable. Their idea of life extension is more than ten billion years at the minimum.

"When I accepted their agreement. I merged my consciousness with the Qrie memory of the entity that founded the Galactic Memory in the first place. That memory is over ten thousand eight hundred times the age of the physical universe, or about a hundred and fifty trillion years.

"I assure you, I'm not the automaton of that founding Qrie entity. I'm the one and only James Madison MacAvies, but my history now is as if I were that Qrie entity. When any intelligent entity ceases its conscious existence, its memory can be used by another living being. That original Qrie entity is not conscious, and has no ability to control the new physical being in any way. Advanced humans can also link to these memories, human, Qrie, and even the Galactic Memory itself. They just won't have the Qrie powers to go with them."

Again, Tom muttered, "Wow!"

After the evening's events, Breath and Tom were quite exhausted.

"I think you two need to get some rest. You've been through quite a bit today, and that intense training session took a lot out of y'all. Besides, I find myself needed elsewhere. If you'll please excuse me, I'll go. It's been a great pleasure being here with y'all today. We'll do this again soon, say the next time both of you're in port."

And with that, Jim vanished. He left in his wake the usual powerful *Qrie Embrace.*

Breath and Tom excused themselves with a thank-you to everyone for the unique experience.

Before they left, Breath became silent and projected a personal thank-you to all her new Mer family. Each Mer responded in its own way. *Now you know Neil. See? I said you would find out. I just didn't think it would happen this quick.* She gave Neil a powerful *Qrie Embrace*, as she turned to leave.

Breath felt good about this revelation, and also because she would need to work with Tom to bring him up to his full capability.

"What an unbelievable day Breath. That flying part was a lot of fun. I knew that you could already fly. When did you first learn how?"

Breath looked down at her knees. "I've been able to fly since I was nine, GP taught me. I've been working with Morning and Beauty, and GP, or Jim all my life as far back as I can remember. He's been teaching me how to do all manner of things since that time. Up until the incident a couple of days ago, I thought the members of my family were the only people on Earth who could do these things. Now I know we're not alone. It's a great feeling."

***

Tom opened Breath's apartment door. He handed Breath her keys, came in and locked the door.

They paused and gazed at each other for a long moment. They both felt the Qrie energy between them, but now there was something different, something far more intimate.

Breath took Tom's hand and led him into the bedroom. She started removing his shirt, with slow deliberation. Tom started to help her, and she slapped his hand away at his impertinent intrusion.

"This is my job. I'm... exploring, just relax and enjoy."

Tom just stood there with an impatient look on his face. The more impatient he looked, the slower she did her job. After some time, it was his turn.

A couple of hours later, Breath was exhausted. *Making love with total control of your emotions, thoughts, and the* Qrie Embrace *is so fantastic. I wonder if it was as good for Tom.*

"Wow, that was unbelievable!"

Yep — he thought it was good too!

***

Breath looked at Tom. "Jim showed you how to make these energy fields around our bodies. When he did, I could see your field where it went through your clothes. And now that we're in the nuddy, I can now see a small field around your body; you should be able to see one around me as well. Let's make our fields stronger, at least strong enough to float off the floor, and see what happens."

With Breath's help, Tom was able to float off the floor. He said. "Yes, I see where you're going with this. You now look like one of our Mer friends, except not gold but with normal skin color. This field suppresses everything, making you look like a Barbie doll."

Breath said. "And you look just like Taylor did: a skin-colored mannequin — well maybe a Ken doll not anatomical at all. You can now understand why we don't like to wear clothes. This field is so much more intimate and comfortable. Tom, you know if you think about this energy as a rainbow, you can change its colors to anything you want. Watch this." Breath's Qrie energy field began to look like a rainbow. She started making the field into solid colors. She started with red and moved to other colors of the spectrum then pure gold.

"Wow! You look just like one of the Mer. Your hair color is not quite the same but it's close enough. You've got to teach me how to do that!

"John was telling me that the field will also protect us from cold and hot temperatures. This is so cool! I've gotta think about this."

Tom became introspective. Understanding his need, Breath left him alone in his reverie.

She did a mental review of the day and came to a realization. *Is it just my imagination, or is Jim's Southern drawl becoming lighter? I'm going to have to listen harder because only a couple times, did I notice that he used the thick Southern drawl.*

The rest of the time, he sounded well — almost normal. Or is it just me?

Later, they took a shower together. Tom told her he had to get back to the Station. He had some things to take care of to get ready for work tomorrow. Breath agreed that she needed to get back to *Morning Discovery* and prepare for work as well.

Breath gathered up some items and put them in an old, faded, pink duffel bag. Tom was gathering up his things as well.

Breath asked him, "Where'd you get the T-shirt and blue jeans yesterday?"

"Oh, I always carry several changes of clothes in the back of my Land Cruiser, just in case."

"Oh? Just what kind of case?"

"Just in case I meet a pretty girl. You can never tell who you might meet on the high seas."

"Yeah, you might meet a mermaid or something. You can't ever tell."

Tom stopped and with slow quiet introspection muttered under his breath. "Yeah — a mermaid — or something!"

They walked out and were standing beside Tom's car. "Some weekend."

"Yeah."

Tom put his arms around her and pulled her close. They shared a hungry kiss. When they parted, he said. "I'll call you ship to ship tomorrow. I hope we can get together later when we're in port, if that's okay with you."

"You better." She made a fist, bumped him on the chest, and then gave him a big hug. "Try to keep me away."

He hugged her back and gave her a tender kiss on the forehead. Both felt the energy link between them.

***

She parked her car at her assigned spot, took her bag, locked the car, and went aboard *Morning Discovery*. She saw Skipper and waved as she bounced down below to stow her bag.

She went back up on deck and found him looking at her with a shrewd appraisal.

"You look — different! What happened? You're glowing and have a bounce in your step."

Skipper turned his head and looked down at Breath out of the corner of his eye. "Am I going to have to find this Sub Lieutenant Haynes and discuss his future intentions, huh? Or did you just have a good weekend?"

Breath looked down and giggled. "Yes, definitely! Yes, I had a great weekend. It was exciting and scary and fun and everything in between. Wow!" More giggles.

Skipper turned back towards Breath with his usual twinkle in his eyes. "Well, I've got plenty of time. Tell me all about it."

Breath told him everything for about two and a half hours, starting with Tom and the evening at Rebecca's, Tom and the barbecue, Tom fixing her car, Tom and the meeting at Rebecca's, Tom and the meeting at the Talmage place, and Tom. She left out the Qrie, the Mer, and some of the juicier parts.

"Tom this and Tom that, I take it you don't like this Tom guy much, do you?" Skipper looked at Breath with a broad grin.

Breath blushed and looked down at her bare feet. "Well... yes. He's intelligent, a gentleman, a nice guy, and he's sweet. Did I tell you he fixed the battery in my car?"

Skipper laughed. "Yeah, several times. Tom this and Tom that did almost everything this weekend, as you tell it."

"He is nice and sweet and wonderful. I guess you can tell I like him a lot!"

Skipper raised his arms in the air with sarcasm. "I never could have guessed." Then he put his arm around Breath and hugged her close. "I'm so glad you've found someone at last. Let's just hope he sticks around." She folded herself deeper into his embrace.

They were looking down on the deck below when Ben Kavanaugh walked by. Skipper chuckled. "Breath, whatever you do, don't ask him about the shiner. It'll take longer than your explanation of your weekend with Tom this and Tom that."

"Well, I've gotta go down and see how he's doing on the acoustic array, and if he got it fixed."

Skipper grinned and winked at her. "Well, you're in for it now."

"He's okay, isn't he?"

"Yeah, he's fine, real fine! That's the problem. He's really fine!"

"Well, I guess I'd better bite the bullet. I'll go down and see how he's doing."

Breath went down two decks below and found Ben in the lab. Ben heard her come in, jumped up, and turned around. "Dr. Spring, you'll never guess what happened to me this weekend!"

"Wow! Ben, I can already see part of what happened. Did you get in some kind of fight?"

"No — oh you mean the shiner. No, that's only part of it. I got engaged! Me, Ben Kavanaugh — I got engaged! Can you believe it? I'm going to get married."

And for the next hour, he told the story over and over until Breath could repeat it word for word. Ben had been dating this young lady named Silvia for about two years. Silvia was a gourmet chef at one of the restaurants in town. This weekend he asked her to marry him. He had had the ring for six months and had just been waiting for the perfect time to ask her. Silvia got a little excited and ran to kiss him and say yes. However, when she got close, he bent down, and they collided with her forehead in his eye.

Breath thought. *That didn't take all that long to summarize. Why'd it take him an hour to tell the story? I guess you just had to be there. Anyway, I guess that's why Ben and I didn't get together when all the Qrie energy was flying around. He already had someone. Good for him. I'm so glad. I guess everything worked out as it should.*

***

After the intense exercises with Jim to control her thoughts and emotions, she mused that just because she could now control them with an iron will, it didn't mean they would disappear.

She could do all her work and wasn't bothered by the emotions and thoughts of the weekend, but they were still there. She knew she didn't want them to leave or disappear, and she thanked Jim for teaching her how to control them. She wondered how Tom was doing with his control.

That Sunday night in her bunk, she locked down her emotions with the control technique that Jim had taught her and went to sleep. Her sleep was filled with dreams of Tom and the energy link between them, of the Mer, of the Qrie, and of *Galactic Prime*. She was getting sleep, but the dreams were so intense that they were waking her up. She got up, got her phone, and called Tom several times. Each time his telephone was busy, so she texted him to ask how he was doing with his dreams and controls. Tom texted back. *Don't call me. I'll call you.* A few moments later, her phone rang. They talked for about an hour. She felt drowsy and decided to try going to sleep again. She didn't wake up any more that night.

9. MONDAY

Breath came awake with the alarm. She was confused. *Where am I? How? I'm in my bunk on the ship. I'm not in my bunk?* Sure enough, she was in her apartment — in her bed. She looked around for the alarm and saw Tom doing the same thing next to her.

She almost jumped out of her skin. She threw her arms around him and kissed him several times. Both felt the energy link again.

"Will you kill that stupid alarm?" She looked down at herself and saw that she was still in her birthday suit, and he was in his boxer shorts.

"How did we get here?" Tom asked. "I don't remember driving!"

"I don't either. Where're my clothes? Where's my phone?" She jumped up, ran out of the bedroom over to the window by her front door, and exclaimed, "Where's my car?"

"How did we get here?" Tom was right behind her. "No clothes. No phones. No cars."

Breath and Tom looked at each other and uttered one loud word: "Jim!"

No sooner had they finished saying his name than he appeared. "Okay, okay, I just thought you guys needed a little more togetherness time. The emotions and thoughts will never disappear; they'll always be with you. You just have to control them. You should spend a good deal more time together sorting all this out. It wouldn't be a good thing for you to be apart right now. You'll get it sorted out in time."

"We can't spend all our time together sorting," Breath blurted. "We've got jobs to do. We'll be at sea. We'll get fired. And how'd we get here?"

"I know that very well, and I teleported you here."

Tom was surprised, but Breath asked. "That must've taken a lot of energy. So why does Tom still have his shorts on?"

"If you teleport someone right, you teleport them as well as their clothes."

Breath's eyebrows went up. "Oh, I didn't realize that!"

"Well you should! You've been practicing teleportation now for a while. You just don't know everything about it yet.

"This is what we're gonna do. You two will spend your nights here in this apartment, which I'll handle, and your off-duty time together. Don't forget, you need to study with Crystal and Connie so you can learn to absorb the Qrie energy to help your control. You've no idea how unique you two are on this Earth. And never fear; I'm always here."

"Yeah — That's what we're afraid of." Was Tom's snide reply.

"If you two were Mer, the commitment you made to each other yesterday would've been imprinting and binding. However, you're not Mer. But you did make a commitment to each other, and with the increasing Qrie energies flowing around and through you, the symbiotic connection and the commitment will be powerful. It'll be with you for the rest of your lives."

Breath inhaled deeply and said. "That sounds an awful lot like a marriage contract for humans."

"It sure does." Tom said.

"It is!" Jim said.

"How do we know that we'll always be compatible?" Breath asked.

Tom said, with a confused expression and a little shyness. "Uh... Yeah!"

"You two are one of the most compatible couples I've ever encountered. But more on that later."

Breath put her left fist on her hip raised her right eyebrow and pointed at Jim. "I knew there was something more to that teaching exercise yesterday than everybody was saying. It was a ceremony, wasn't it? Was that a marriage ceremony? Did you marry us yesterday?"

Jim paused, to let Breath calm down a bit. Then he smiled. "You're — not married in human terms. You need a religious representative or a magistrate for that. When you showed up Saturday afternoon, the Mer knew that you two would always be together. In their eyes, you've imprinted. I know you've only known each other for a short time, but that doesn't change the situation or your commitment. The teaching exercise, as you call it, was necessary. Your Qrie part is fine. However, your physical brains would've been damaged and gone crazy. Too much too fast, you might say. The Mer, the Qrie, and I all knew this. We had to do something."

Breath and Tom looked at each other. "God bless us, we're married!"

"That's not at all how I dreamed of being married! Ever since I was a little girl, I was going to have a wedding dress and flowers and all that wedding stuff. I never even told him I loved him. Tom, I do love you, and I know I always will. I just... I just..." She hiccupped as her eyes grew moist. Then tears flooded down.

"I love you, too, Breath!" Tom said as he gathered her into his arms. "And for some reason I know I always will."

Breath looked up at Tom and blubbered, "But I wanted a 'real' wedding."

Jim laughed. "A real wedding? You mean a human-style wedding? I suppose being *Galactic Prime,* the most powerful being in the Local Galactic Supercluster and the Primary Steward of the Galactic Supercluster Memory just isn't good enough! Okay, what about this. Let's make a deal. You're gonna get with John, Crystal, and Connie and study hard until you master the energies that you need to control in order to keep you sane. Breath, you don't need much more training. But Tom, you have a long way to go to become proficient. When you complete that study and can prove your abilities, we'll have one whale of a human wedding complete with dress, flowers, and all your wedding... uh... stuff. Okay? Is that a deal?"

Tom looked down at Breath's tear-filled radiant face, and smiled. "It's a deal!"

Jim gave Breath a loving gaze. Tears were still streaming down her face. She smiled at him and nodded. She reached out and squeezed Jim's hand as she cuddled deeper into Tom.

"It's a deal, then. Breath, Tom, you know ship Captains have the power to marry people. Why don't you approach Skipper and ask him if he'll do the honors when the time comes?"

Jim looked at Breath and noticed that his last statement didn't help the tearing problem at all. If anything, it made them worse, but she gave Jim a huge smile, and again, she just nodded.

"There's some more important information you need. This may come as a shock to you. As you both are part human and part Qrie, this'll never change. Life as you knew it is over. You now have a new life, one that involves the Qrie within each of you. The incident on the ship with the Qrie Stewards and I have energized and activated your rather... ah... unique genetic structures. You two are much like me, part Qrie and part human.

"I knew Breath existed. Tom, I recently found out that you did also. I just didn't know I'd meet you this soon and together! Stranger things have happened. I'm going to have a long talk with Morning and Beauty.

"When your training is done, I'll ask you to link with two ancient Qrie entities, one for each of you. These entities are not capable of conscious activity or self-direction; that'll be your jobs. Yet their histories and their knowledge will be yours. The decision to do this is yours and yours alone. No one else can make it for you.

"You two were born this way. You've always had these abilities. You just needed to be taught how to use them. You each have the capability of handling large amounts of Qrie energy, and I'll teach you about this as time progresses. Tom, this might help to explain some of those strange things that happened to you growing up. If I'd known about you earlier, I would've worked with you as well. Having access to a gargantuan living Memory is challenging and can be distracting.

"Don't say anything about what I've just told you to anyone. Crystal and Connie and the adults of your Mer family already know about you. But don't let anyone else find out until you're ready."

Breath noticed Jim's thick Southern drawl had disappeared or at least was mild.

Tom asked Jim, "You know, I think I knew this for a long time because now that you've expressed it, everything makes perfect sense. Did my dad and mum know?"

"No, Tom, they didn't. Your mother and dad acted as channels for the Qrie energies that now flow through you. You're part Qrie, about the same as Breath's grandmother and granddad."

Breath asked, "I know my parents knew, so why didn't they tell me early on?"

"They told you some, but they didn't tell you everything, Breath, because Morning and Beauty wouldn't let them," Jim explained. "After you were born and were still quite young, I was still going through training. I could observe but not interact. They had me start training you when you were eighteen months old, as you know. Morning and Beauty were the voices in your head before I came along. I didn't know then why they kept the information from you. I didn't think it was my place at that time to interfere, since I was somewhat new at this too and had not completed my training. I do know that your mother and father were told what they were and what you are. Your brother and sister also know what they are; I'm training them as well."

"Thank you for telling me, Jim. I suppose I'm going to have to fuss at Mum and Dad now that I know — on general principles, of course. At least with Mum, a little fussing will be expected." Breath thought. *It's about time somebody told me what was going on.*

"Breath, I'm glad that you're taking this so well. Somehow, I thought you might have an explosion, if you know what I mean!" Jim looked at Tom. "I'm also pleased that you're taking this well, even if you're a bit stoic."

"Thank you, Jim. I'm not really sure how well I'm taking it, but yeah, I've got to agree with Breath. It does make sense."

Tom was a bit uncomfortable and decided to change the subject. "Where'd that crew and the contraband ship go after you, Morning, and Beauty left?"

"Well, Morning and Beauty didn't take the ship anywhere. They turned it and all its contents into energy and radiated it into space. Everyone on that ship is now at a special sequestered location. Morning and Beauty have taken them there to learn the error of their ways. Their bodies are in stasis, but their minds are fully active. They are reviewing the memories of their crimes, as well as their good deeds.

"Qrie non-sentient entities are instructed to add terror and horror to the negative memories each time the sequestered individual reviews its crimes and bad deeds. And they're to give love, peace, and understanding each time the individual reviews its good deeds.

"This'll continue until they all conclude with a full and firm understanding that crime and killing the Mer or anyone isn't a good thing; the idea of a negative thought will be terrifying and horrific to that individual. After they reach this firm understanding and have learned to love their fellow man, they'll be returned to help pass this understanding to others." Jim seemed to take some delight in this revelation.

Breath put her hand to her mouth and her eyes grew large, and Tom looked equally astonished.

"Was that the strange noise and shimmering light I saw when Morning and Beauty left?" Breath asked. She paused for a moment and then asked. "You mean they destroyed the ship, just like that?"

"Yes, to both questions. That crew was responsible for the death and injuries of Mer. The Qrie don't take kindly to anyone killing or injuring the Mer. It'd serve you well to remember that."

Breath, still astonished, said. "But they weren't all guilty of killing or injuring the Mer. Maybe the Captain and a couple others, but not everyone!"

"That may be true, but the Qrie don't see it that way. They were all members of the crew of that ship, so to the Qrie, they were all guilty."

"You mean, if someone in a village killed a Mer, then everyone in the village would be held responsible?"

"Not necessarily everyone. But those closely associated with the villager certainly would. The others would be given an opportunity for redemption. Actually, as it turns out, the Captain and his crew were not there by choice. The ship and crew were hijacked by the terrorists. That doesn't mean that they were innocent of everything they have ever done. And they have done some bad things in the past, not terrible just bad."

Breath was still puzzled but now a bit surprised. "That's a bit harsh, isn't it? Forcing someone to relive their crimes over and over would drive a person insane."

"No, the punishment fits the crime, and it's worked for the Qrie for many billions of years. You must also remember these people get to review their good deeds as well, and the other villagers get the message: don't kill Mer — or anyone else, for that matter. You must also remember that the Qrie are there guiding them every step of the way."

Jim turned to Tom. "Tom, you might be interested in one other thing. After going through the memories of the crew, we found there are some other containers dropped off by other contraband ships. From what we understand, these containers are in deep water, about four hundred to six hundred meters. I just thought you might like to know."

"Uh... thank you, I think. I'll figure out a way to tell Commander Tibbett."

"Now, let's get you kids back where you belong."

With that, a bright light formed around them. Breath found herself standing in her cabin. Tom found himself standing beside his bed in the BOQ on the Station.

10. SCHOOL

Crystal checked Neil for any errant Qrie energies that might cause a skin and clothing problem, on Monday morning, the first day of school after the incident. She was relieved when she found that the energy levels had dropped over the weekend to just above normal. She reminded him not to use any Qrie energy that day.

She also checked to see that he'd put on the eyebrow and eyelash darkener to help hide his golden eyebrows and eyelashes. For Neil, this was a normal daily inspection. He liked that ritual each morning, but he also knew he didn't need it. That was what mums did. He could almost imagine Connie checking Kandy and Hilga checking Sophianna for gold skin, darkened eyebrows, eyelashes, and energy levels.

As Neil got out of the car after being dropped off by Crystal. He saw Kandy and Sophianna stepping off their bus and called out. "Hey guys, wait up."

The two girls stopped and turned around as he jogged up to meet them. They walked onto the school grounds together.

Sophianna exclaimed. "Wow! What a weekend!"

Kandy nodded. "You can say that again. I don't want a repeat of 'that' anytime soon. If it hadn't been for those two ships out there to rescue us, Neil would still be dead, and I probably would be too."

Sophianna replied with some indignation. "It wasn't those two ships or their crews that saved Neil and the rest of us. It was the Qrie and *Galactic Prime* — Jim, Mad Mac, or whatever he likes to be called."

Kandy's face brightened. "Can you believe that we met and had in our house three physical Qrie! I knew something was strange about Doctor Spring and Sub-Lieutenant Haynes, and I never knew about or expected to see *Galactic Prime*!"

Neil also brightened and with excitement exclaimed. "Doctor Spring touched me on *Morning Discovery*. She gave me the most powerful *Qrie Embrace* I've ever felt. I knew at that instant that she had to be Qrie. She and Lieutenant Haynes were leaving after the barbecue. At that time, she gave me another even more powerful *Qrie Embrace* and projected into my mind that I would find out about her soon. I think she's probably more powerful than Morning or Beauty!"

Kandy smiled and glanced out the corner of her eye at Sophianna. "I wonder if those two lovebirds know now that they were imprinted by none other than *Galactic Prime*. OMG!"

Sophianna replied, still indignant. "Humans don't imprint; they get married. In my opinion, it's not as good as Mer imprinting. I know they're part Qrie, and I've got no concept what a Qrie ceremony would be like. It's still unbelievable being imprinted by *Galactic Prime*, the most powerful and ancient entity in the universe. As the humans say, 'that's really getting hitched.'"

Then Kandy and Sophianna began talking at once.

Neil looked towards the lockers and thought. *I'll just let the girls talk. I won't have a clue what they're saying, anyway.*
***

That afternoon after school, Kandy and Sophianna saw Neil walking ahead and Kandy called out with her telepathy. *Hey, Neil, wait up.*

Kandy queried aloud. "How was school today? Could you even concentrate with Cheyenne gone?"

Neil saw the tears in the eyes of both Kandy and Sophianna. He turned and wiped his own eyes with a quick motion. "Ah, well — I guess I was okay. Kinda rough, though. Not bad for having died Friday afternoon only three days ago. It's gonna take me a while to get everything sorted out."

Both girls made a simultaneous solemn reply. "Yeah — us too!"

They heard another human classmate yell to them. "Hey, wait up. I'm so sorry to hear that Cheyenne drowned. I know you guys must be absolutely devastated. We had our third period together, and I liked her. I just wanted you guys to know. Would you like to get a juice or something and talk about it?"

All three Mer turned in unison. "Grounded — forever!"

11. BARBECUE TWO

"**I** know, Tom, but I think we owe it to them because they've taught us so much over these last months. Don't you think being able to manipulate water and open locks with your mind is a good thing? I think it's exciting."

"Don't get me wrong, Breath, but — OMG another fabulous barbecue!" Tom said waving his arms in the air. "There's one every other Saturday, and sometimes Sunday, or at least once a month. Yes, I love them. I like being with everyone there. And I've even become used to being in the nuddy like you and they are. But we spend more time at the Talmage compound than we do here in our cozy little apartment. I don't think we've missed a single free night during the last three months studying with Crystal, Connie, John, and sometimes Jim. Yes, I've got a real handle on understanding the Qrie energy..."

Breath thought while Tom continued his rant. *I love his thinking! 'Our' cozy little apartment, is it!*

"Tom you've got to admit, that exercise we were teaching you this last week of jumping from high places and landing unharmed, will be valuable."

"Oh yeah! Jumping from a second-story balcony onto the grass has got be the greatest feat in the entire world! Let's alert the media. I've seen stuntmen in movies do that with ease. Now, if you taught me how to jump out of an airplane from three thousand meters with no parachute and land unharmed, that'd be a real feat! Besides, what are you worried about? You know how to fly."

"Well, you'll get there soon. Besides, you've got to jump before you can fly.

"On a different subject, you were also telling me you wanted to talk to John about using his salvage boat to retrieve something that a contraband ship dropped in the ocean. Or is that now ancient history?"

"That thing is still out there. We don't know where it is, just its general location. Jim mentioned it's in about four to six hundred meters of water. Human salvage divers can't get down to it, at least not without it being outrageously expensive."

"Haven't the Mer been helping *Queen's Shield* with some of your work? I know they've been helping *Morning Discovery* with fish counts and taking underwater photos along the reef. They've also been working with Ben to see if they can figure out a way to prevent them from being seen by his acoustic array. You know, you can't get human divers to do as good a job as the Mer can!"

"Well, that settles it. We have 'got' to go now. We have to talk the Mer into doing jobs humans can't possibly do." Tom had a dripping sarcastic grin on his face.

"You rascal." She giggled as she threw a pillow at him.

He exaggerated the giggle teasing her, and threw the pillow back.

"There's one little problem. I've got something to do on *Queen's Shield*. It should take about an hour or so. I'll meet you at the barbecue as soon as I get done. Okay?"

She nodded okay.

***

Early Saturday afternoon found the Mer family gathered at the Talmages' compound. Breath practiced her teleportation as she arrived in the backyard.

Breath laughed, waved, and called a greeting to everyone there. They were all working there Mer style, with a Qrie field around them, for protection. Each of them gave her a welcoming smile while cooking, laughing, talking, and having the best time visiting.

Taylor was cooking the meat on the barbie as Breath walked over to say hello. At the same time, Crystal came out of the kitchen carrying a large bowl of boiled prawn salad. "Breath, would you check the front door, Love? I think I just heard the bell ring."

Breath wound her way through the huge house to the front door, where Jim gave her one of his huge smiles. "Hello, Breath. You didn't think you were gonna get all the way through this fabulous barbecue without me, did you?" He gave her a big hug, and she escorted him towards the backyard.

"Why didn't you just port into the backyard instead of ringing the doorbell?"

"Well I guess I could have, but then you needed something to do."

Breath laughed and gave Jim a light punch on his shoulder. "I love you too."

"Jim, can I ask you a question?"

"Sure Breath." Jim chuckled while looking at Breath in the nuddy. "What you got on — your mind?"

Breath chuckled at Jim's lame joke. Then with a private projection to Jim. *Will my physical life be extended like yours, and will Tom's?*

Jim replied in the same manner. *Tom's life extension may not be as long as yours or mine, but the answer is yes.*

This is going to take some time getting used to!

Jim replied, with a sly smile. *Well, now you've got all the time in the world — literally.*

John waved at Jim. Taylor nodded and waved a pair of meat tongs at him and turned back to the barbie. "Boy, do I ever know when to show up! Just in time to eat. Who says I don't have impeccable timing?" He shook hands with John.

***

Later, Jim, Breath, and the Mer adults lounged in the large hot tub and watched the young Mer kicking their football around while trying to keep it from touching the ground. The adults were pumping Jim for more information about the Qrie.

Breath asked Jim. "I've noticed that things that made me angry when I was a kid now give me a mild irritation. Also, I tend to lose track of time. Why's that, and how's that work? I know we trained a lot when I was younger to control my anger, but that didn't include losing track of time."

"I'd have thought you'd have figured it out. It has to do with the Compulsions and flow existence. Anyone under the Compulsions, like you, me, and Tom have volunteered to inhibit our behavior from becoming angry. If you'll remember, the last time you got angry, at those Earth Only people and that building in California, you learned that little exercise I taught you about ramping up the Compulsion. It helps to prevent us from doing something rash. Ramping up the Compulsion allows us to remove the stress caused by strong negative destructive emotions. You know, the seven deadly sins. Allowing us to think in a rational manner so we won't cause mass destruction. It won't stop the minor irritations; it just prevents the strong negative emotions from taking over the rational mind.

"As for losing track of time, you're becoming more Qrie. Time doesn't work for us the same way it does for humans. We think in terms of flow existence instead of time.

"The truth is, you're learning to use your power and abilities the way the Qrie, not humans, understand the universe. You're beginning to embrace your inner Qrie. Another truth is that the physical universe resides within the Qrie continuum. Everything is endowed with the Qrie and is part of it. All humans have the

Qrie or the I AM within them and they can learn to use this Qrie power to a limited extent. It's not easy mind you, but it is possible. Physical telepathy is one example of this ability. As you know humans and other animals can communicate using telepathy when you are touching them."

John asked. "Can humans develop the same powers as the Mer or the Qrie?"

"Not at this stage of their evolution. It is possible that humans can soon learn to use and develop abilities by using the Qrie consciousness to achieve some of those abilities in the physical realm."

"Wow Jim, that's amazing.

"You keep talking about flow existence, like we all know what that means. What does it mean?"

Jim took a deep breath and chuckled at John. "I knew someone was going to ask me that question. I just didn't know when. There's no human term that can explain flow existence; the closest analog is time. The Qrie don't consider any such thing as time.

"I can sense that everyone wants to know as much as they can about the Qrie and the Qrie continuum. This is a long, boring, and complicated subject, so I'll tell you what. Let's get the kids in the water so I'll have a low energy connection to each person here, and I can teach you the Qrie way."

John asked. "What's the Qrie way?"

"Well, as you know the Qrie can communicate to the mind of anyone or anything with a brain. And the easy way is if we're in physical contact, such as touching or in the water. We can also use air as a connection, but it takes more Qrie energy, as the Mer also know."

Taylor called the kids over to join the adults in the pool.

When everyone was comfortable. Jim began the Qrie communication to each of them — on how flow existence, time, civilization cycles, gravity, and the expansion of the universe worked. This Qrie communication method took much less time than normal talking. He didn't go into detail because he didn't want to overload their minds.

Jim laughed and continued speaking aloud after the mind link was completed. "I heard a comment one time that when God created the universes, it also had to create time so that everything wouldn't happen all at once."

John and Taylor started laughing. John said. "Well, that's going to take some thinking. I'm not quite sure what you just taught us. I guess there's no dark matter either, for that matter."

Taylor groaned at the pun. "And I guess gravity blows instead of sucks, and everything is an illusion."

Jim chuckled. "Something like that. You guys aren't too far off the mark. Flow existence is the tracking and remembering the flow of events and structures. Yes, John, you're correct. There's no dark matter. When physicists have a better understanding of the universe, they'll see that there's no need for dark matter. Some physicists today already have inroads into that understanding. And, Taylor, this is due to the way gravity works, which is it pushes rather than pulls. There's more to gravity than Newton, Einstein, Feynman, Hawking, and most physicists today understand. Everything is just energy, and gravity is the propensity to allow this energy and energetic particles to follow the path of least resistance."

Jim laughed and made a motion like removing a hat. "Okay, guys, the class is over. If you want to know more about this, I'll tell you later, and we can go into it in more detail. This is supposed to be a 'relaxing' get-together, not a physics forum. We're here to have fun, relax, and eat some great barbecue. So, let's get on with it. This is just the beginning. We'll talk more about this at another... um... 'time.' All I can say is just 'Go with the flow.'"

Both John and Taylor groaned.

Breath in a private projection. *Jim, you came to me as GP at the Coral Sea explosion incident and told me that times were going to get exciting. Why'd you wait so long before you showed up?*

Jim opened the telepathic conversation to all the Mer and Mer/humans. *Neither Morning, Beauty, nor I were anywhere near the explosion when it went off. Morning and Beauty informed me soon after the explosion that Neil and Cheyenne had been killed. I came as soon as I solved a problem on a planet with emerging life, and Morning and Beauty were in another local star system. The sentinel that Morning and Beauty left to monitor the Mer can only relay messages from the Mer. Sophianna here, was the one that sent the message. Morning and Beauty informed me after they received the message, and then they went as quick as possible to the scene of the incident. I knew a few minutes wouldn't have made any difference with Cheyenne — or Neil. Morning and Beauty could take care of Kandy and Sophianna. The only way we could've saved Cheyenne was to have stopped the explosion in the first place. We don't predict the future. We're not gods.*

Why was Sophianna floating in a circle then?

She was trying to gather enough energy to heal her friends and herself. Unbeknown to you, you were her only available source of Qrie energy until Morning and Beauty showed up. Neither you nor she knew how much energy you were feeding her. You both did a pretty good job keeping Kandy alive.

Breath was silent for a moment. She looked down and smiled. *I did feel energy flowing from me but I didn't know where it was going. I now understand. Thanks for telling me.*

Sophianna and Breath glanced at one another, and Sophianna nodded.

***

The Mer teenagers were lounging in the hot tub when Kandy asked. "Dr. Spring, will you please tell us what it's like to swim with dolphins and whales as a mermaid?"

"It's great, Kandy, but don't you swim with them as well?"

"We have, but they seem somewhat shy around us. Maybe it's because we swim so fast, and they can't keep up with us, or we don't come up for air."

"Oh! I didn't realize that. I kind of — assumed... As you know, both dolphins and whales are smart. They do all the things that smart animals and people do. And one thing they do well is play. They..." Breath continued her dissertation on swimming with the dolphins until Taylor came out with a tray loaded with fresh drinks.

***

Tom arrived late to the barbecue and pulled Breath aside. Breath asked. "What's up?"

"The executive officer's hitch was up and he left the Navy. I have been made interim executive officer on *Queen's Shield*."

"That's great, Tom. I'm so glad for you." She gave him more than just her normal greeting hug and kiss.

***

Tom was talking to John Weber, away from the group. "Commander Steven Winslow, HMAS Cairns, Naval Station CO, has assigned *Queen's Shield* a salvage operation that CO Tibbett and I thought you and *Sea Gatherer* could help the RAN with.

"I don't know exactly where or what it is, but our informants have told us they thought that it might have toxic chemicals in a shipping container and it's approximate location.

"The RAN has been looking for the object using side-scan sonar, but they haven't found anything. Jim was no help, either, since he retrieved the memories of the contraband crew but not the location. I was wondering if we could use some of the Mer to help us find it."

"Well, okay. School is almost out for summer break. We could use the kids to find what you're looking for. They should be able to scan quite fast if you know the general area."

"John, the last time the kids got around something like this, Cheyenne was killed, and the others were killed and injured. I saw what happened, and I don't want anyone getting hurt or contaminated if it involves toxic chemicals or something worse."

John looked away for several seconds while he gathered his composure. He swiped his eyes then faced Tom again. "I — understand your concern. And I understand what we're up against. Odds are nothing bad should happen since the container is at such a great depth. It's obvious that they packed it right. We just have to make sure that the Mer are prepared."

"Well, still — John, I don't feel comfortable about using the Mer kids to do this. I'm sure that there's some law that says that we can't use them to do this kind of dangerous work."

"Well, Tom, there's always some kind of law. But if it makes you feel better, we can have the older Mer also help out with the search. That way, it won't be just the kids. And besides, the kids need the experience.

"Perhaps we should take this technical conversation to a more professional venue. I don't want to talk shop today, if you don't mind. We could do it on my ship, *Sea Gatherer*, or *Queen's Shield*."

Tom shrugged and felt a bit relieved. "Yeah — John. Why don't we get together Monday?"

***

After everyone was sufficiently stuffed from another fabulous barbecue, Breath was cuddled up as close as she could get to Tom. Tom had his arm around her. As they watched the kids kick the football around, she mused. *What a contrast from the first time we attended a barbecue here. The kids were gold, in the nuddy, and playing with a hard croquet ball instead of a football. They tossed it around at speeds inconceivable to an ordinary human. I sure don't want this to end, but I know everything changes.*

12. DEEP WATER

John Weber, Captain/owner of the salvage ship *Sea Gatherer,* and Tom Haynes were on the aft deck of *Morning Discovery.* John was summing up what Tom had said. "CO Tibbett told you this thing they dropped in the ocean is a shipping container? By the way Tom why isn't CO Tibbett here, talking to us himself?"

"I don't know John. All I know is CO Tibbett asked me to have the meeting here and not on *Queens Shield.* I don't know why he asked me that. I think this whole explosion incident shook him up a lot more than he would care to admit. He stays in his cabin almost all the time now. He looks and acts just fine when he's out of his cabin and about his duties. He's trying very hard to pull himself together. I have been running the ship for now.

"I understand Tom. It's affected all of us." He took a moment of silence.

"Well Tom, I wish him luck. But back to business. If it is a container, it should be easy to hook onto and lift, with the Mer and the right equipment."

Tom paused, thinking then said. "That'd be convenient and nice if it were, but I don't know. You know, Breath has a remote submersible with fifteen hundred meters of cable on *Morning*

Discovery. Once we find this container, if that's what it is, we might be able to use the remote to hook up to it." He looked around and found Breath exiting the galley with a tray of food. He waved to her to come join him and John.

Breath walked over to the two men. She handed them each a plate of shrimp and a lemonade from the ship's galley and sat down with her own plate. Tom asked her about the remote submersible and what its capabilities were.

"You know, Tom. It has a small arm and gripper. I don't think it'd be strong enough to hook up a large lifting cable. We also don't want to get it tangled up in the heavy cable."

"I don't think we should worry about that. All we need to do is get the cable down there in the general vicinity, and the Mer can do the actual hooking up. Do you think Dr. Kavanaugh can come up with some kind of scenario where we can fake hooking it up to bring up this box, or whatever it is? All that is required is to have something that's somewhat feasible for the salvage operation."

Breath frowned. "Why're you doing it this way? Why not just have the Mer hook it up in the first place? Or I could just lift it myself."

John paused, laughed, and then said. "You see, I have this young Tristan Dillon on *Sea Gatherer*. He's Troy Koch's wife's, nephew's, cousin's, uncle or something. Troy, my first mate and chief engineer, says Tristan is a good kid. He just doesn't have much of a family. No mom, his dad is a workaholic, and his dad's girlfriend hates him and won't have anything to do with him. He just got his deckhand license, so I hired him to replace a couple of deckhands who quit for better jobs. He'll be working weekends and all through the summer break. He's a high school kid, but he's really sharp and curious. I plan to put him with Troy on the winch to keep him busy during this operation."

Breath replied. "Oh! I see! The submersible operation is just something to keep him occupied. Won't he realize something's amiss with this remote submersible that won't be able to hook up a heavy line? If this young man is as smart as you say, he's going be pretty hard to fool."

John said, with a sly grin. "Well — what we do is we make Dr. Kavanaugh look like an absolute genius by allowing him to manipulate the submersible. We must convince the people on shore that we can do this. Showing up with a container dredged from the bottom of the sea six hundred meters down and no way to hook onto it might take some creative explanations."

"I see your point," Breath agreed. "Devious, but it just might work."

John raised his index finger and asked. "By the way, Tom, did the RAN ever get back with you on what was in the container that fell off that contraband ship and blew up?"

"It's all under investigation right now. They won't give an official answer as to what was in it until the investigation is over. However, the unofficial rumor is that we know the container was loaded with the bulk explosive ammonium nitrate fuel oil (ANFO). There were also some plastic explosives and detonator caps. The whole thing was timed to explode, to enable the contraband ship to get well away from the area. However, most of the ANFO didn't go off because it got wet. We still have no idea what their plans were. We also didn't find any identifier tags in any of the ANFO. These tags are sometimes put in explosive-grade ammonium nitrate to show where it came from and who bought it. The RAN and the Australian Federal Police think that it was something nefarious like smuggling or terrorism. They estimated that between sixty and seventy metric tons of illegal ANFO was in that container. That much ANFO can do a tremendous amount of damage. You were lucky that container sank. If it had floated, with that much ANFO, it could've sunk *Morning Discovery*."

***

"This Dillon kid's really good and strong as an ox," Troy Koch was telling John Weber. "He knows more electronics than I do. He's got a lot of book knowledge with the hydraulics and pneumatics. I'm glad you hired him. Is he going to be on deck when we raise that container?"

"Yeah. You're going to need some help with the winches. So, I'm going to put him with you. We just have to be careful. Anyway, it's a good way to keep him occupied."

"Yeah, we better keep an eye on him. I noticed that Sophianna is also keeping an eye on him." Troy nodded towards Sophianna at the bow.

John laughed. "Yeah, I think Sophianna has a class or two in school with him. And yes, I think she's got her eye on him. You think we should warn him about her? He's awful shy."

Troy grinned his evil grin. "Sink or swim, I always say."

John said with a chuckle. "Yeah, well, you 'are' kind of evil that way."

Both men laughed.

***

John stepped out of the bridge of *Sea Gatherer* and yelled. "Ahoy, *Queen's Shield!* Have you heard from *Morning Discovery*?"

Tom yelled back. "Yes, she's about twenty minutes behind us. She'll be here in a little bit. Are we ready to do this? By the way, where are the rest of the kids?"

John yelled back to Tom. "They're with Breath on *Morning Discovery*. They'll help her and her crew today. She's got them working... uh... below deck. We won't be seeing much of them."

Tom nodded understanding, waved at John, and ducked back into the bridge. He walked over and leaned against the bulkhead and did the Qrie energy-linking exercise. *Breath, let's hope everything goes as planned today, with no incidents. We've been working on this for some time now; let's not screw it up.*

Breath held on to the ship's railing, anticipating the joy of the warm and loving *Qrie Embrace* from Tom. When it came through, it was wonderful, as if she were in his arms. *Well,*

Tom, we'll see if all our planning was worth it. Good luck to everybody.

John sent a Qrie energy message of his own. *Hey, Tom, how's it goin'? Congratulations, I just heard your conversation. Welcome to the Mer club. Good on ya, Mate!*

Both Breath and John could feel the pride when Tom projected back. *Thanks, John, and good luck to us all.*

CO Tibbett on *Queen's Shield* turned to his new X. "Tom, we'll just keep out of the way until they need us. They know what they're doing. We've been planning this for a while, and if it works, we may have a new way to recover dumped contraband. We'll go in when we're needed."

Breath ordered the underwater remote deployed and then started moving *Morning Discovery* to where they thought the container might be.

Several groups of Mer had been scanning the ocean floor in this general area for a few days now. They had found and marked what they thought might be the container in question with a sonic buoy. They also informed Breath that they had found more than one container but didn't have sonic buoys for them.

About twenty minutes later, the remote reached the proper depth and began homing in on the sonic buoy. About thirty minutes later, they found it.

She turned helm control over to Dr. Kavanaugh to guide *Morning Discovery* and *Sea Gatherer* into position and to get the hooks down to the proper depth. Troy and Tristan were running the winches. This took another half hour. Then Dr. Kavanaugh began instructing John to maneuver *Sea Gatherer* into the proper position to grapple onto the container. John had earlier informed Dr. Kavanaugh that he wanted to be directly above the container when they started lifting. No one knew how much it weighed. John didn't want to take any chances. This whole process took about three hours.

When Dr. Kavanaugh thought everything was lined up, he told John over the radio that it was time to hook up. Dr. Kavanaugh tried to use the remote arm to maneuver one of the hooks into place. He almost got it. However, he decided he didn't want to damage the remote. He backed the remote off and let the Mer handle the hookup.

Another hour later, after some careful winching, the suspect container broke the surface. Troy and Tristan lifted it free of the water. John began to maneuver the *Sea Gatherer* into position to set the container on the salvage barge.

Once the container was safe on the barge, he called Tom to inspect it. He and three crewmen went over to the barge and checked the container. He closed it, locked it, and came back to *Queen's Shield.*

Tom projected. *John, Breath, it looks like we got what we came for. There are several suspicious-looking plastic drums in that container. So, John, if you'd take it back to port, the RAN will take it off your hands. CO Tibbett and I want to thank everybody involved for a job well done. You guys need to confirm this with CO Tibbett on the ship-to-ship communications.*

John replied. *Thanks, everyone. It went a whole lot smoother than I thought it ever would. Tom, Breath, I was inspecting that container when we were setting it on deck, and there are some strange things about it. It looks like there's an acoustic repeater mounted on it that'd allow some kind of automatic attachment crab to hook on to the container. Could you have Dr. Kavanaugh inspect it? It's possible the other containers will have the same systems. If so, we may be able to build some kind of crab that can use the acoustic system to bring these things up easier.*

Breath beamed and projected. *Congratulations, everyone, on a job well done. Tom, do you think we'll ever know what's in those drums?*

Tom considered her request. *If it's just toxic industrial waste, yes, the RAN will tell us. If it's something else, the RAN may not want to say. I can't promise anything.*

John asked. *Breath, ask Skipper, please, if* Morning Discovery *has a large repair weld on the starboard outboard hull up towards the bow. If it does, it could be a ship we salvaged when I was the first mate here on* Sea Gatherer.

Skipper confirms that there is a large weld starboard side. The ship was donated to Geoscience Australia several years before I came aboard. I guess it could be the one you salvaged. You'll have to tell me about it sometime.

13. DISCOVERED

Jim projected to Breath and Tom. *I'm going to need you two more than ever. Things are about to get, well — interesting. Tom, I've watched you over the past several months, and you've learned more than I'd hoped. You're now much farther along than I anticipated. You've passed all your challenges with flying colors.*

The time has come for you to make your decisions about the Qrie memories. These memories are the memories of no longer conscious Qrie entities. They are not self-aware or capable of conscious activity or self-direction. That direction falls to your discretion. As you become integrated, your history and their history become merged. You'll become an ancient Qrie-human, with your young Qrie-human part controlling everything.

Consider these memories as you would a well-stocked box of tools. As you learn to use these tools, they become part of you. I know you two have given this a considerable amount of thought. I don't want to influence you, but I must say that you lose nothing and gain a lot. Their knowledge, power, and abilities are immense; you'll have access to it all. I've chosen these specific memories because their personality structures are almost a perfect match to each of yours.

***

Captain Kathleen Harbits of Australian Naval Security was of medium build with mousey brown hair usually worn in a bun. She presented the same mousey demeanor but had a sharp and capable mind. She had arrived at HMAS Cairns Naval Station and was in the process of reviewing a strange briefing. She was trying to figure out what to make of the reports of high-speed underwater targets. Six had been received over the last eighteen months. There were four incident reports from three separate ships and two from guided-missile submarines.

Perhaps, she thought, *they could be artifacts of the new passive acoustic array systems that are on these vessels. At first, the analysts thought they might be dolphins. But they moved way too fast, and they seemed to move in an intelligent manner.*

She noted with interest that most of the incidents around Reeftown involved either the patrol vessel HMAS *Queen's Shield* or the Geoscience Australia survey ship *Morning Discovery*. She knew that *Queen's Shield* didn't have sonar that could detect these high-speed objects. She didn't know what type of scanning sonar *Morning Discovery* had. She did know *Morning Discovery* had bathymetric capability, but that wouldn't detect anything high speed.

She knew the HMAS *Newcastle* out of Cairns, with its passive acoustic array, was at present looking for a net-and-cable loss that could interfere with navigation off Reeftown. *Newcastle* could on occasion scan *Queen's Shield* and *Morning Discovery* without interfering with their search-and-recovery missions.

Captain Harbits knew from salvage reports that these two ships were working in close proximity with *Sea Gatherer* and would be in the area. She knew from other reports that the three ships were seeking to recover contraband and possible terrorist materials in several containers which had been dropped in that general area.

Over the next three weeks, *Newcastle* reported to Captain Harbits. Every time the crew scanned *Queen's Shield*, *Morning*

Discovery, or *Sea Gatherer;* they saw the same high-speed objects. The objects didn't seem to interfere with the recovery of the containers. They even seemed to be helping the recovery operation, which was going well and made her think that the objects probably were intelligent.

Captain Harbits thought. *I think we need to speak to the CO of* Queen's Shield *and whoever is in charge of* Morning Discovery. *If there's some kind of new technology out there, I'd very much like to know about it.* She typed a communiqué and orders to make it so.

***

Breath stood reading the communiqué from Geoscience Australia telling her to take *Morning Discovery* to the RAN Station at Cairns. She sent a Qrie message to Tom on *Queen's Shield.*

What are we going to do about this? Tom, they've seen high-speed objects under and around our ships.

Then John Weber joined the Qrie conversation with Breath and Tom. Tom projected to the group, *Yeah,* Queen's Shield *received orders to report to Cairns Naval Station as well. We can't tell them anything unless the Compulsions are removed, and I don't think the Qrie are going to do that.*

John projected. *The Qrie Beauty told me that both the Americans and Australians were getting quite close to discovering the Mer. It looks like the Australians now have. The Qrie haven't given me any indication of what they might do. I suspect that they'll confer with* Galactic Prime *and come up with something. They're not subtle. And I know they won't do anything to hurt anyone, but it might not go well for the Australian Navy.*

Tom projected. *Whatever they do, we still have to report to Captain Harbits at Cairns. Breath, I guess it's going to be you and me. Of course, CO Tibbett will have to speak for* Queen's Shield. *I think the best way we can handle this is just to evade — claim we don't know anything and say we're as surprised as they are. With the Compulsions, I don't know what else we can say or do. This isn't going to be comfortable. Maybe CO Tibbett won't call on us.*

***

Captain Harbits picked up the radio phone and answered. "Captain Harbits, this is CO Bristleton of HMAS *Newcastle*. I think you're going to like what I've got to tell you. Two of those high-speed targets got tangled up in that net-and-cable mess that we were looking for. If it hadn't been for them, we never would've found it. We called a fishing boat over and asked them to help us bring the net up. They got the net up on their deck, and the two targets were tangled up in it.

"Captain Harbits, you're not going to believe this. They look human, a male and a female from the looks of it, and they're upset. They seem to have some kind of telekinetic ability because they've been throwing things around the fishing trawler. Chief Johnson shot them with tranquilizer darts. They took two each, but they're nice and calm now."

"Thank you, CO Bristleton. I'll have CO Tibbett on *Queen's Shield* rendezvous with you as soon as possible. His patrol boat is quite a bit faster than yours. I'll have him coordinate with you about the hookup."

Breath projected to Tom and John. *Now that the RAN have captured these two Mer; you don't think the Qrie will do anything violent, do you? The RAN is a quite valuable service.*

***

John Kingman almost ran towards the OAI communications and code lab. He looked around until he found Tatelin Westworth.

"Tate, grab your ready bag. We're going to Australia. I just got an urgent telephone call from Admiral Lynch. All he relayed was. 'Get to HMAS Cairns Naval Station. 'Now!' It's going down. 'Now!' Two fast-moving targets have been captured.'

"I've got the new supersonic plane fueling up. We've gotta get there fast!

"I think he's trying to tell us they've captured two of the Kawreak and are preparing to transfer them to Cairns Naval Station. If we hustle butt, we might be able to see these Kawreak. I've also found out they're supposed to have a meeting tomorrow sometime. If everything goes right, we just might make that meeting."

Tate looked at John and frowned. "And if everything doesn't go right, we could have our butts handed to us."

Less than thirty minutes later, John and Tate were in the air.

***

Tom projected with apprehension. *Breath, Queen's Shield has new orders. We are to turn around and meet the* Newcastle *and pick up two Mer that were trapped in some netting that they pulled up. They've tranquilized a merman and a mermaid and want us to pick them up and take them to Cairns. Don't turn around; go straight to Cairns.*

Breath replied. *Tom, that can be dangerous. We don't know what the Qrie will do. You'll have two unconscious Mer on board. They're very protective. That's interference with the Qrie. Do you think you're going to be okay?*

Tom projected. *I don't have a choice, Breath. No matter what we do, somebody's going to be upset. I believe the Qrie will understand my predicament and help me out. I'm not gonna let them turn the Mer over to the RAN, even if it means getting kicked out.*

Well, just be careful Love.

***

Queen's Shield's new interim Executive Officer, or X for short, Tom Haynes, watched the transfer of the two Mer onto his ship and pondered. *Something doesn't seem right. Maybe because they're unconscious.* He didn't recognize the two Mer. They weren't from Reeftown or the Reeftown anchor point. The

CO had the Mer placed in the austere compartment of the patrol boat and instructed the doctor to stay with them.

As soon as *Queen's Shield* was again headed to Cairns, Tom went down to the compartment. "Doctor, are the two Mer okay?"

"Yes, Tom, they're fine, just unconscious, and will be that way for at least eight more hours. They've got good heartbeats; breathing seems to be okay. No marks on the body that I could find, so yeah, they're okay. Eight hours should give us more than enough time to reach Cairns."

Queen's Shield caught up with *Morning Discovery* about three hours later. Breath was standing by the railing when Tom came out of the bridge. They waved at each other, and Tom projected to Breath. *Has Jim or the Qrie contacted you? They haven't contacted me yet.*

Breath, Tom, I knew this was going to happen. So, I decided to make it happen now, on our terms. Your RAN people are good Tom, better than I'd hoped. It's hard to beat dedicated and quality people.

I'm glad you decided to show up, Jim. What do you want us to do?

Nothing for the moment, Breath. Once the ship gets docked, a contingent of naval security will come on board to remove the Mer. They'll take them to a holding facility. They'll be held there until the meeting tomorrow.

You're — uh — just going to let them — take them? I thought the whole idea was, they couldn't find out about us — or at least the Mer.

And they won't Tom. At least, not anything that counts. This is our discovery.

So, there's a scheme, Jim. A plot is afoot. Are we part of it?

Oh, yeah, Breath. You guys are going to be my star witnesses and emissaries.

Breath asked. *Then you're going to lift the Compulsions? So, what can we tell them?*

Jim said, with a chuckle. *Tell them whatever you need, but tell the truth. Just don't tell them how long you've known about the Mer. Be like politicians; say a lot, but reveal little for the moment. They will learn the whole truth in time. I'll be with you to coach you since you're not used to — evading.*

Tom asked. *What if they decide to do something you don't expect? Like not let the Mer go? You do want them to let the Mer go, right?*

I don't think there'll be any problem with that. As you know, there are a couple of Qrie here in the solar system. They're quite protective. They might have something to say about the RAN trying to keep the Mer. Hope to see you guys tomorrow. By the way, I need your Qrie entity memory decisions now.

They both projected. *What? You need the decisions now?*

Breath thought. *Hope? What's he mean by hope?*

Yes, to both of you. Events tomorrow will require you two being buffered. There'll be a lot of Qrie energy flowing. I've picked out appropriate entity memories for each of you. If you don't approve of these memories, they can be removed. This decision 'is' reversible.

Breath projected. *Well, I'm going to go for it!*

Tom projected. *Me too!*

In that case, I suggest that you two get to your bunks. This won't take long, but it's quite unsettling.

Both Breath and Tom excused themselves and went to their cabins. Breath's Qrie entity memory was a fraction of the age of Jim's Qrie memory, or about one and a half trillion years old. Tom's entity memory was just a bit younger than the age of the universe. Both entities had been loving, intelligent, warm, kind, and forgiving. Both Breath and Tom were staggered by the astounding age and power of these entities. And they both understood why Jim had told them to be in their bunks when it occurred. Unsettling was an understatement.

Both Breath and Tom understood now what Jim meant by the entities' memories being theirs. Breath could separate her human memories from the Qrie memories because they were her latest and strongest. On an intellectual level, she could perceive her human age. However, when she thought about herself, she knew her true age was now about a hundred and ten times the age of the physical universe, or about one point five trillion years. Tom felt and understood the same thing about his age. He knew his age was a little less than the present age of the physical universe. For both of them, there was no doubt. It was a perfect fit.

14. CAIRNS

The two ships pulled into Cairns Naval Station just a little after dark. Sure enough, no sooner had *Queen's Shield* tied up before a dozen naval security people came on board. They took the unconscious Mer off the ship to the holding facility.

Early the next morning, Jim woke both Breath and Tom. *We're going to have a rather exciting day today, you two. Take your showers, but don't get dressed. Leave all your clothes in your closets, including your underwear, rings, watches, earrings, and any other object that isn't you. I'll provide you with your attire for the day. I'm going to be pouring energy through you that'd cause problems with your clothing. No one except another Qrie can tell that your clothing is a Qrie illusion. Clothing illusions are something that you two are definitely going to have to learn. Before you leave your cabins, make sure you look at yourselves in the mirror. Make sure your clothing and everything is okay and properly placed.*

As Breath and Tom walked into the station's headquarters, they were told they had to wait. The station was under a high-security lockdown. Guards were everywhere and fully armed with automatic weapons. About fifteen minutes later, they understood why. The Governor General of Australia, the Prime

Minister, the Deputy Prime Minister, the Minister of State, the Minister of Defense, and at least a half a dozen Admirals and Generals, several RAN Captains, Commanders, Lieutenant Commanders, Lieutenants, and civilians, as well as the Director of Geoscience Australia, filed past as they watched in awe.

Jim, do I really have to do this? You know how I dislike crowds. This is a very high-powered crowd, and I've got butterflies already!

Breath, you'll do just fine. Do some of those calming exercises that Connie taught you, lock down your emotions, and everything will be okay.

Breath, Tom, I hesitate to bring this up right now, but you must know. These negotiations are critical to the future of the Qrie and the Mer on this planet. If things go well, we're home free, and we've controlled our discovery. If we can't convince these people of our good intentions, we could be in for a battle.

Tom projected. *I understand, Jim. I'll do everything I can to make this a positive outcome.*

Breath projected. *Jim, as I mentioned many times before, you just fill me with warm, fuzzy confidence.*

That's great, because it's sink-or-swim time!

***

Breath noticed two rather disheveled late arrivals. They ran up to the guards, who perused their paperwork with serious attention. They weren't allowed in. The older smaller man, who had a broken nose, showed something to the senior guard, and a few moments later, a Vice Admiral came out and spoke with the guards. They were then admitted into the conference room.

Sometime after the last of the brass had filed in, Breath and Tom were told they could enter. They went into a large conference room capable of holding twice as many as were in attendance.

Everyone in the room stopped what they were doing and watched the unusually regal, graceful elegance exuded by Breath and Tom as they glided in and took their seats next to CO Tibbett.

Breath noticed that the Vice Admiral and the two disheveled latecomers were paying particularly close attention to them.

Captain Harbits was surprised to see so many government officials. She knew she hadn't contacted most of them. She got up and welcomed everyone and began the briefing. She started by telling those assembled about the high-speed objects the various RAN vessels had been detecting over the last number of months.

"I now call on *Queen's Shield* Commanding Officer Lawrence Tibbett to discuss his impressions of the humanlike beings that he transported here."

CO Tibbett slowly rose and walked briskly to the podium. "Your Excellency Governor General, Prime Minister, Deputy Prime Minister, Minister of State, Minister of Defense, Admirals, Generals, — Um— and everyone else assembled. I'm Lieutenant Commander Lawrence Tibbett." He laid the briefing sheet that Captain Harbits handed him prior to the meeting, on the podium.

He related the events leading up to the capture of the two high-speed targets now being held at the detention center on station. He began to sweat and fidget and only briefly mentioned the contraband ship. He continued. "I — wasn't on board *Morning Discovery* except for a short time. However, interim Executive Officer Sub Lieutenant Tom Haynes was present there the whole time. I'd — like to turn the floor over to him — at this time."

"I hate speaking to crowds. They make me nervous." Tibbett whispered as he sat down beside Breath.

She gently placed her hand on his as he seated himself. "I fully understand."

Tom was nervous but slowly got up and smoothly moved to the front of the conference room and began speaking. He acknowledged those assembled in the room as his CO had, and then he continued. "I'm Sub Lieutenant Tom Haynes of *Queen's Shield*." He pointed to Breath. "This is Dr. Breath Of Spring of the Geoscience Australia ship *Morning Discovery*. The two individuals you have in holding are called Mer. Dr. Spring and I have known about the Mer for some time."

Everyone in the room sat rigidly upright with attention riveted on Tom.

He continued. *"Morning Discovery* was doing some bathymetric soundings. *Queen's Shield* was endeavoring to catch some contraband smugglers. The smugglers..."

For more than an hour, Tom told them about how the Mer had helped them on numerous occasions and as much about the Mer as he could without revealing too much, under Jim's coaching. His throat was raw, and his voice was becoming hoarse. He turned the floor over to Breath.

The people in the room were dead silent. Then a collective sigh could be heard. Two people raised their hands to ask questions. Even though Breath was nervous, she moved to the front of the room with her usual graceful elegance. She'd done the exercise that Connie had taught her, and she now felt calmer and much better. She pondered. *Why would these dignitaries with this much power raise their hands to ask a question?*

Because Breath, they are nervous and ill at ease. You are filling the room with the Qrie energies and some of the people in this room can't really take the energy.

Thanks Jim, is there anything to put their minds at ease?

Yes Breath, I'm already on it. I am giving them a mild form of the Qrie Embrace, *which will, as you say put their minds at ease.*

Thanks Jim.

She pointed to a General, who asked. "What do they want?"

Breath felt Jim's presence. Her tension eased as well. "Primarily, the Qrie are just watching. They feed the Earth their energy, hoping that mankind, through their guidance and protection, will move towards and achieve True Intelligence. Don't ask me what True Intelligence means." She paused a moment. "But that 'is' what they're doing. And as Sub Lieutenant Haynes has told you, they've been doing it for a really, really long time."

No sooner had Breath finished her statement than PM Amanda Everett asked. "What are these Mer like? What are their abilities? Do we have anything to fear from them?"

"As Sub Lieutenant Haynes mentioned earlier, the Mer were created by the Qrie. The Mer cannot kill other Mer or human beings. The Qrie are not so restricted. The Qrie are also quite protective of the Mer. Think of it this way. The Mer are like lion cubs. And the Qrie are the mother lions. If you mess with the cubs, mum lion will eat you!

"I've personally seen the Qrie exercise their justice. When they get done, you're completely removed from the face of this Earth. So, I'd think about what you're going to do with the Mer you have in holding.

"The Mer have considerable abilities. You've seen some of them, such as swimming fast, not having to come up for air, the ability to control gravity. They have the ability to pull light around themselves, and they have the ability to generate force fields. They can lift loads inconceivable by a normal human. Three of them retrieved and moved the contraband ship a considerable number of miles at high speed during the Coral Sea incident.

"Most Qrie are pure-energy beings. The Qrie exist and live in the Qrie continuum. This continuum is what the universe exists in and expands into. Needless to say, it's incomprehensibly enormous. The two Qrie Stewards for this solar system are known as Morning and Beauty. They're about as old as the universe itself. These beings are the ones that *created* — that's my term; they prefer the term *assembled* — this solar system, and they're responsible for it."

The Minister of Defense immediately asked. "Exactly how powerful are these Qrie? What can they do?"

Breath practiced the breathing exercise Connie had given her. "They assembled and can control the Sun. They can make it cool down or heat up. They can cause it to go nova or make it into a super red giant, or they can turn the entire solar system into gas. None of these things would be good for life on Earth. If they can do that, they can certainly do anything they want with Earth or any other planet in the solar system."

A Minister asked. "You two have told us one whale of a sea story. I don't know how much of it is true. Can you prove any of this? I know there are two of what you call Mer in holding. How do we know that these Mer are not just some human actors? As far as I can see, there's absolutely no way you can prove any of this bullshit. What else haven't you told us?"

Breath looked around the room and saw quite a number of frowns, scowls, and nodding heads. "I was just getting to that. There's one other entity that you should know about. This entity, as far as I know, is by far the most ancient and powerful being in this universe. From what I understand from the Qrie, this entity is many thousands of times older than this universe. This entity is known as *Galactic Prime*. It's responsible for creating or 'assembling' the hundred thousand or so Galaxies in this Local Galactic Supercluster."

At that moment, the universe opened, and everyone in the room was severely startled and experienced an expansion of mind that was incomprehensible without the Qrie. With this expansion came unconditional love, peace, understanding, and the *Qrie Embrace*.

I am the Qrie Beauty. You have been briefed by Dr. Breath Of Spring and Sub Lieutenant Tom Haynes. I have authorized my Mer to leave your facility. Do not detain any more Mer. They and the Qrie are not your enemies unless you make us so.

At this time, a loud ripping sound was heard outside, followed by gunfire. People in the conference room turned to look out the window. They saw the entire roof of the retaining facility ripped completely free of its walls. The Mer floated up, caught the roof, and gently placed it back where it had been, making absolutely certain that no one was injured.

The Qrie Beauty projected. *Galactic Prime comes.*

Everybody in the room was acutely aware that the opening of the universe a few moments earlier was minuscule compared to the presence of *Galactic Prime* and its immensity of age. Everyone could see and experience all of the Galactic Supercluster. The black hole at the center of the Milky Way Galaxy was intimately experienced on all sensory levels. All the colors of the Galaxy were seen. Colors of light that have never been encountered or comprehended by humans before were brought into sharp focus, from long-wave radio waves to gamma rays.

An immensely powerful but gentle projection emanated into the room. *I AM* Galactic Prime *of the Qrie. Dr. Breath Of Spring has mentioned before the Compulsions placed upon them. I have placed Compulsions on every person on this station who now knows of us. You cannot speak of this to anyone. You cannot disclose to anyone about us or even of our existence. If you have any individual who absolutely must know of us, you must contact Dr. Breath Of Spring.*

With that. *Galactic Prime* was gone, leaving in its wake the *Qrie Embrace.*

Breath, Tom, when anyone asks you about your abilities, just tell them you're unique but still human, at least for the time being.

Everyone in the room was stunned. No one spoke. A few had tears in their eyes. There was no doubt in anyone's mind that Breath and Tom had stated the absolute truth. The room was silent for a full five minutes. Most of the people in the room were still dazed and unmoving, trying to comprehend what they'd just experienced.

The reverie was broken by a knock on the door. Tom went over to the door and opened it. A young Acting Sub Lieutenant was standing there. "Sir, the detainees are gone. They lit up like a huge bolt of lightning. They lifted the roof off the building, flew out, caught the roof, and put it back where it was. Then they just simply flew away and vanished." The young Acting Sub Lieutenant was obviously shaken.

PM Amanda Everett stood up, shaking while holding firmly to the table in front of her, and contritely asked, "Dr. Spring, are you or Sub Lieutenant Haynes Mer or Qrie?"

"We were born human just like you." Breath stated bluntly, without further comment or deliberation.

The Prime Minister asked again. "Do you have powers like the Mer or the Qrie?"

"That's best left for later. Please, I know there are many more questions, but I think it'd be good for us to take a lunch break at this time. We can continue this after the break. I think we could all use one, thank you. I know this has been a considerable shock to all of you. It will take some time for you to process." Breath turned, walked to the door, and walked out. She almost ran to the loo.

Breath came out of the loo and saw Tom exiting the men's room, and went over to him. *What do you think? Is this going to work?*

Guys, it's working great. I'm going to flow considerable energy through you two. Breath, I want you to shake hands with everyone in that room.

Jim what are you up to?

You'll find out, Breath. Tom, just go along and follow Breath's lead.

***

Breath and Tom were walking back towards the conference room. Everyone was slowly filing out. Several Acting Sub Lieutenants and petty officers were directing the dazed and disoriented dignitaries to a special dining room that had been set up to accommodate the assembled officials.

As they were walking, Breath heard someone call her name. PM Amanda Everett was trying to catch up to her. She reached out and touched Breath on the right shoulder, trying to get her attention. When the Prime Minister touched Breath, she made a huge gasp, dropped and almost hit the floor.

Breath spun around and held out her hand, caught her, and righted her without touching her. She placed Amanda's left hand in her left hand, then put her right hand and arm under Amanda's elbow. Breath held her close for several seconds, waiting for the Prime Minister to become stable. While still supporting her this way, Breath started walking and talking to Everett and the rest of the group as if nothing had happened. Everett was still dazed from the experience. Several other people in the group saw this.

Breath thought. *I must be more careful; I can't flood people with energy like that. They're not used to it. It's one thing skin to skin, but through clothing. Oh! That's right, I'm not wearing any clothing; all I've got on is an illusion. I've gotta be careful. And to do that to the Prime Minister, of all people! OMG!*

The Prime Minister stopped in her tracks and just looked at Breath. "I sensed every word you thought in my mind. You didn't open your mouth or move your lips — I was looking. It was just as clear is if you had spoken. I also noticed that you can pass on this inconceivable love, peace, and the unbelievable expansion of mind that we experienced earlier just by touching me."

Well, this didn't go as planned! Then Breath said aloud. "Prime Minister, the atmosphere is highly charged due to what we're teaching you. That sensation you just felt is called the *Qrie Embrace*. The inrush of the Qrie energy can be quite — startling."

Breath and the Prime Minister continued small talk arm in arm until someone caught Breath's attention. The moment she looked away, Everett looked at her and thought. *What else can you do? Can you swim fast like the Mer?*

Not as fas... Breath stopped. She looked back at the Prime Minister, gave her a little smile. *Okay, you caught me. Your mental voice is almost like your physical one. You had me fooled there for a second. From now on, let's try to use our physical voices. Is it a deal?*

Everett just looked at her and nodded. *Oh my God! This is actual telepathy, and I'm doing it. It's hard to believe, but it's real.* She then realized that Breath was looking at her. She focused on Breath. She said, with a big grin. "It's a deal."

Everett reached out with her free hand and grasped Breath's hand and thought. *What did she mean by her clothing being an illusion?* as they walked into the special dining room.

Breath smiled at Amanda and projected in private. *Tom and I are highly energized. That much energy passing through our bodies would disintegrate normal clothing. The clothes that you see are illusions of pure Qrie energy. Please, Amanda, let's just keep that little tidbit between us. Okay?*

Amanda smiled, nodded, and had an unsettling thought. *My goodness, I just touched a naked God.*

***

Everett brought Breath over to her table, where the Governor General, the Minister of Defense, the Minister of State, a Vice Admiral, and a Rear Admiral were seated.

Everett and the Governor General looked at a Commander who was also seated at the table. It was obvious they wanted the Commander to move.

The Commander looked over at Breath and stood. When she saw him, she walked over to him and gave him a big hug. "George, it's so good to see you again. I was wondering what happened to you since we last saw each other in Melbourne. Where've you been? We must get together later and talk about old times. By the way, you told me you'd keep my secret. Yet for some reason, the U.S. Navy knows all about what we did in Port Phillip Bay. What do you have to say for yourself?" She lightly bumped him on the shoulder with her fist, a grin and a twinkle in her eye, and then gave him another hug.

Everett and the group were all puzzled at this and had expressions to match.

Both Breath and George turned towards the group. "Everyone, I'd like for you to meet Commander George Marsdurban. Years ago, we worked together on a whale problem for the RAN. He was a Lieutenant Commander at that time, while I was attending University of Melbourne."

She reached her hand out to the Governor General and greeted him. He almost collapsed to the floor. Then she greeted each of the dignitaries in turn, and, last, the Rear Admiral, with the same results. She took her seat. All of them, after recovering, seemed relieved and surprised to lower themselves into their seats.

From the expressions of the people around the table, it was obvious they understood that Breath Of Spring was a force to be reckoned with and that they'd better tread lightly. They also looked over at the table with Tom and understood the same thing about him. They looked at Commander Marsdurban seated next to Breath and had no idea what to make of him. Breath smiled to herself.

The Vice Admiral looked at the Rear Admiral. The Rear Admiral looked at Marsdurban, then back to the Vice Admiral, and nodded. The Vice Admiral nodded back.

Everett noticed this and asked, "Admiral, is there something you'd like to share?"

"Yes, Ma'am. The Admiral Staff in the United States has known about Dr. Breath Of Spring for some period of time now. They've known about her since she was at University of Miami. We here in Australia knew her through Commander Marsdurban, who's known her longer.

"We also know about her father and her siblings in Canada and now Texas, and her mother in Fremantle. We were given this information as a courtesy by the U.S. Navy and another U.S. agency that holds Dr. Breath Of Spring in high esteem. We've known from that time that she's quite special."

He turned his attention to Breath. "Dr. Spring, I'm honored to make your acquaintance at long last. I'm Vice Admiral Winston Lynch, Chief of the Royal Australian Navy."

"It's also my pleasure and honor to meet all of you as well. I know all of you have many questions."

At Jim's request, she had to be vague with some of her answers. It was obvious that these government officials wanted to know more about what was going on with her, the Mer, the Qrie, and *Galactic Prime*.

Towards the end of the meal, she stopped and looked at Tom. Their eyes met and held for several moments. The energies and the *Qrie Embrace* passed between them. Everyone in the room noticed this.

Breath, Tom, these people have way too many questions to be answered. So, here's what we're gonna do. We're going back to the conference room, and we're going to do a little mind-to-mind teaching. Tom, if it's okay with you, I'm going to use Breath for this. She's got a better rapport.

Breath, I know this is your first major Memory link, but you've been practicing, and I know you can do it. Look at what you've just accomplished!

***

After the meal and dessert, Breath stood up. "Ladies and gentlemen, may I have your attention, please. You have many more questions than can be answered in this short time. When you file out of this room going back to the conference room, I'd like to shake hands with each of you. I must warn you; this can be startling, but I know that you're all strong government and military people and can handle it."

She shook the hands of every person in the room, as they filed out after the meal. She gave everyone time to become comfortable.

When everyone was back in the conference room, she had them sit down, take a few deep breaths and relax. She started projecting to them using her mental voice to teach them, from the Memory, what they needed to know. What would've taken a day only took an hour.

Everyone was astounded and apprehensive by what she'd done.

Breath said. "I want everyone to think about what's occurred here, where you want to go, and what you want to do with this information.

"I want to thank you all for coming to this conference. I think an important amount of information has been transferred to you today. What you do with it is up to you.

"I didn't call this conference. Captain Harbits did. I also know that it didn't follow any agenda that she'd set out. I'd like to thank Captain Harbits for her foresight and this opportunity. If you need to contact me, please go through Geoscience Australia or Sub Lieutenant Haynes. I think you all know how to contact Lieutenant Haynes. I now turn the meeting back over to Captain Harbits."

Captain Harbits was slow to stand and walk to the podium. "There's nothing I can say that'll add anything to what's gone on here today. We have a lot to think about, so let's get to it. If there are no more questions..." She surveyed the senior staff. "This meeting is adjourned. Thank you all for coming."

***

Breath was walking out of the conference room and took a glance over at the detention facility.

Breath, would you and Tom please proceed to the detention facility. We should repair it for these good people. Breath, you're going to do this; I'll coach, but you're still going to do it. Now, this is what I want...

Tom, you can wave your hands around in the air to make it look like you're doing something if you want. Better still, just follow Breath's lead.

Jim, you're giving everyone here the wrong impression of us. It makes me somewhat uncomfortable.

Yeah, Jim, me too. These people are my military family.

Well, if it's only 'somewhat' uncomfortable, I think we can live with that. Breath, you've been training for this for a long time, and I know you can do it. Besides, it's going to be fun. Just remember what I taught you.

Breath and Tom both projected. *If we must!*

Wow, I'm not sure I can stand the extreme wild anticipation of it all.

Breath projected. *I love you too, GP.*

Tom just chuckled.

CO Winslow of HMAS Cairns Naval Station was walking just ahead of them. Breath tried to get his attention. "CO Winslow!"

Steven stopped and turned around, a little flummoxed that she knew his name. He saw Breath standing directly behind him. For a moment, he looked like a kangaroo in headlights. "What? Err... oh, yes, it's Winslow. What can I do for you... um... Sir?"

"It has come to my attention that you've had some recent difficulties with your detention facility. If you'll please guide Tom and me to that facility. We might be able to do something about it."

CO Winslow stammered, "Yes... ah, Sir, Dr. Spring. Tom... Sir, this way, if you please."

Breath projected to Tom. *This is getting a bit out of hand. Here's the Station Commander calling you and me 'Sir.' I didn't think he was supposed to do that.*

Jim projected. *Don't either of you correct him for now.*

Tom projected back. *I think he's in about the same condition I was when we first encountered the Mer. I do know that he has no idea what to do with me now. I don't know where that puts me in the scheme of things.*

Everyone in the conference room followed CO Winslow, Breath, and Tom to an area outside the detention center. The building had seen better days. And those better days were only a few hours ago. The building was sturdy, reinforced concrete, including the roof. The roof was sitting on top of broken concrete and bent rebar.

Breath asked. "Is the building clear?"

The CO looked over at a guard standing in front of the building. The guard indicated that no one was in it. CO Winslow turned to Breath, started to say something, then just nodded.

Breath looked at Tom and projected. *Here goes. I'm not going to make any big motions. I'm just going to be subtle.*

Breath crossed her hands at her waist and stood silent. Tom was following suit. For a moment, nothing happened. Then

Breath put a powerful light around them. They floated about a foot off the ground. Tremendous tendrils of lightning-like multicolored-plasma moved from them and wrapped around the detention building. The roof was lifted three meters. The walls seemed to repair themselves.

The roof started descending. What looked like molten rock formed on the top of the wall and on the bottom of the roof where the roof and wall would attach. The roof settled itself onto the top of the wall. The molten rock hardened in a matter of seconds.

A fresh coat of what looked like military gray paint spread itself over the building. The light then dissipated. Breath and Tom floated over to the door of the building and went inside. A short time later, they emerged.

Breath was fascinated. *I did it, Jim! I did it! With your coaching, of course, but I did it!*

Well, you trained long enough! Congratulations!

She then floated over to CO Winslow. "I think that should do it. Is the restoration to your satisfaction? If you don't mind, you should let the paint cure for a few hours before occupation."

CO Winslow, like everyone else watching, stood there agape.

Breath spoke in a more commanding voice. "CO Winslow, please inspect the building and see if it's to your satisfaction!"

He stammered. "Err, oh — uh, sorry. Yes, Sir, Dr. Spring. Right away, Sir." He hurried over to the building and went inside. A few moments later, he came out and walked around, looking at the building.

He came back over to Breath and Tom. "Everything is satisfactory, Sir. Thank you, Sir."

"Very well. Lieutenant Haynes and I have a few things to discuss on *Morning Discovery*. So please excuse us." Everyone seemed to have been able to get their mouths shut by the time Breath and Tom floated towards her ship, over the water, and onto the aft deck.

Jim, don't you think that was way over the top? These people have no concept of how to deal with us now. And it's going to make Tom's job way more difficult, if not impossible!

It's for sure that they'll put surveillance on us. And I mean serious surveillance! We won't even be able to chew bubble gum without them knowing all about it. We're gonna be in a fishbowl.

Yes, I know — 'Sirs.' Both Breath and Tom could feel Jim's laughter. *There's one thing for sure. Without a doubt, they'll not take you for granted. If you want or need something from them, they'll know you are serious. I want you to put an energy field around yourselves so they won't be able to take your picture. Every time they try, it'll be overexposed and out of focus. They also shouldn't be able to record your voices unless, of course, it's authorized by you. Don't forget the Compulsion that's been placed upon everyone. Unless the surveillance people are on the station, no one can order surveillance on you or us without violating the Compulsion.*

Jim, I didn't think the Mer were powerful enough to rip the roof off a building like that.

They're not Breath. Those two detainees weren't Mer; they were me, as illusion images of the Mer. Any readings, tissue samples, blood work, ad infinitum that they took is now gone. However, it did give me an idea.

Oh no! Here we go again. Another idea!

Yes Breath, about the explosion incident with the contraband container. I've also been thinking about the lifting of the containers that you two and John have been doing. And the pushing of that contraband ship makes me think that the Mer need more power. We're going to have to come up with some way to protect the Mer from tranquilizers, explosions, and small-arms fire as well. Up to now, the Mer haven't needed it. But with the capabilities of the various militaries, I think it's now necessary. I'm going to get with the Qrie Stewards and figure out just how to do that.

15. MEETING

The entire conference group was standing and watching the glowing forms of Breath and Tom on *Morning Discovery*.

PM Everett turned to no one in particular and commanded. "Get the Minister of Security here as soon as possible. She's got to know what's going on. Captain Harbits, would you make arrangements for that conference room after the evening meal, and would you also contact Dr. Spring and have her make arrangements so we may speak with the Minister of Security? I want everybody who was in attendance today in that conference room after dinner. It's going to be a long night, people."

Captain Harbits put her phone to her ear, left the group, and started walking over to *Morning Discovery*.

Tom, Breath — Captain Harbits is coming to ask you if you can put a Compulsion on the Minister of Security, that I can do. But here's what we're going to do... Tom, you need to get over to your ship. I think you're going to be called on the carpet.

Breath and Tom stepped back into the confines of the covered aft deck. They kissed, and Tom turned and began floating across the water towards *Queen's Shield*. Breath floated to the end of the deck and waved as he left.

Jim, I don't feel comfortable with this. You've always transported us, and now you want me to do it. What if I make a mistake and turn someone inside out? Then what?

Breath, you'll do just fine. Besides, you've done it before, and you need to learn the finer points. I'll be with you every step of the way. I won't let you do anything that's gonna hurt anyone. Besides, consider it a good training exercise.

If I must.

There's that positive spirit that I always like to hear.

Still smiling, she turned and floated down the gangway to the dock and met Captain Harbits, whose eyes widened in apprehension.

Breath extended her hand, and Captain Harbits started to say something. "Sir, or... Ma'am, I..." At that moment, their hands touched. Breath let the Qrie energies flow into Captain Harbits; she felt the great power from the *Qrie Embrace.*

Come with me, and we'll get the Minister of Security.

A strong light formed around the two of them. When the light dimmed, they found themselves in a small office at the Perth security building, where Minister of Security Helen McElroy was speaking with her first Deputy Minister.

Breath looked at McElroy for a few seconds when Jim projected to her. *This one is different, but she's also a handful. I suggest you keep a close watch on her.*

Breath projected back to Jim. *Will do.* Captain Harbits had moved her hand to Breath's shoulder for support. Then Breath reached out and touched both women and projected, *Minister of Security, Deputy Minister, you need to come with us.*

Both women looked at Breath and the Captain. The Deputy Minister exclaimed as light formed around all of them, "Oooh shii..." She finished, as they formed on the aft deck of *Morning Discovery,* "...it."

McElroy asked. "Wha... what's going on here?"

Ministers, you're needed here in a conference. You know Captain Harbits of Australian Naval Security. She'll take you to the Governor General, the Prime Minister, and others. You have a lot to discuss and decisions to make. You also have a Compulsion placed upon both of you. I'll let Captain Harbits explain that to you. My name is Dr. Breath Of Spring. I'm pleased to meet you. Captain, please, if you will. She made a grand gesture towards the gangway leading to the dock.

When Captain Harbits got the two Ministers to the bottom of the gangway and onto the dock, both Ministers turned and looked back at Breath with mouths agape and astonishment in their eyes. The Captain started talking to them to explain the situation.

Jim, this is way over the top. They're going to think that we're some kind of gods or something. We've gotta stop. It makes me uneasy! Besides, that took a lot of energy.

I want them to think of you in that manner. Breath, you were excellent! You only need to work on a couple of very minor points, and we'll get to those later. As far as the energy usage goes, you never get something for nothing. So far, everything is working as it should. It's going according to plan. These are high-powered politicians and military people with overinflated egos; they need to eat a little humble pie. Trust me, it'll all work out.

Trust you? I do trust you, but every time in my past when someone said, "Trust me," the situation turned all pear shaped!

Oh, how you do wound me! I thought I was doing you a favor.

A favor? A favor is when you give someone an ice-cream sundae with whipped cream, not something like this!

At that moment, a chocolate ice-cream sundae with whipped cream and a spoon formed just before her. She reached out and took it and started eating.

Jim, this is extraordinary. But I can't make out all the flavors! I've never tasted anything quite like it! You do know how to make a sundae!

Favors and flavors for favors.

Breath chuckled, smiled, and projected. *Okay, I love you too.*

***

Tom floated into the old Romanesque station headquarters building, that had once been a bank in the early part of the twentieth century, and into CO Winslow's outer office. He had walked those familiar granite floors many times. He came to the desk of a nice-looking yeoman with a pencil in her mouth, working on her computer with intensity.

He told her if she didn't mind, he'd wait in the CO's office. "He wants to see me. He'll be here in a few moments."

She looked up at him floating in front of her desk, and the pencil dropped.

She stammered. "You're the... you're..."

Tom floated past the stammering yeoman into the CO's office and closed the door.

"You're... okay!" she finished with a large gulp.

CO Steven Winslow came in and closed the door behind him. He looked at his longtime student, friend, and drinking buddy with confusion while still trying to hide his concern. "Tom, what the hell have you gotten into? And what've you 'turned' into?"

"Now, Steven, don't get all upset. It's okay. Everything's going to be fine."

"I doubt that. There she is, talking to me! I sounded like a blithering idiot! I called her 'Sir' several times. She's gotta think I'm the dumbest, most idiotic CO in the Navy. And you didn't help matters at all, just standing there with her, repairing that stupid building. She asked me once and then had to order me to get me to move, and all the while, you two were blowing happy sunshine up our collective butts! What's all that about? And what am I going to do with you?"

"Well, Steven, you pretty well confirmed the blithering and Sir part several times, but I don't think she thinks you're dumb or an idiot. Absolutely not the dumbest, most idiotic CO in the Navy. I'm not a CO, but the dumbest, most idiotic position is firmly held by me. Of course, the look on your face was priceless. I'd love to have a picture of that."

Steven gave his longtime friend a lopsided grin and said, "Oh, shut up. I'm sure you didn't have any better expression on your face when you first encountered these entities. I'd like a picture of 'that!'"

"It's ancient history now. We've got to figure out what our next steps are. I don't know what *Galactic Prime* has in store for Breath and me. Right now, it seems to be pulling our strings. As far as I know, there's nothing anyone can do about it. And, if I'm being honest, I like it this way!"

"Sure, you like it. You're the all-powerful pooh-bah. What about all us other blokes having to put up with you? What's Larry Tibbett have to say about this?"

"Until today Tibbett didn't know anything about me except, I'm the interim Executive Officer Sub Lieutenant on his patrol boat. Steven, I'm not going to lie to you; it's an awful lot to take in. I've been working with these beings for quite a while now. I haven't seen a single time where they've been anything other than what they purport to be — and I've looked. As soon as all this... well, settles down, I want to bring you down to Reeftown and introduce you to some of the Mer. They're really great people who can do some amazing things. I think you'd like them. When they're in their human form, you can't tell them from anyone else. When they're in their Mer form, they're nude. That should excite an old letch like you!"

Steven said. "Yeah, I saw the ones we had in the detention facility. They were pure gold and nude. I can't say much for the male, not being wired that way, you know. But that woman, even unconscious, was an absolute breathtaking beauty."

"You get used to it."

"Tell me the truth Tom. I've seen you do some strange things in college that I couldn't and you wouldn't explain. How long have you had these abilities? Dr. Spring told everyone you weren't Mer. She didn't say anything about you not being Qrie. Are you Qrie? And if so, how old are you in actuality?"

Tom hesitated and just looked at Steven for a moment.

Jim projected to Tom. *This not telling a lie is gonna bite us in the ass. Tell him the truth, Tom. But make him swear not to tell anyone.*

"Steven, you've put me in a difficult situation here. You must swear to me and to the Qrie never to tell anyone what I tell you here unless I say it's okay. Do you so swear?"

Steven looked at Tom for a moment. "Yes, I swear."

"I was born this way, with these abilities. I had to learn how to use them, but I've always had them. I'm part Qrie. I'm a little younger than this universe, over thirteen point five billion years."

Steven plopped into his office chair. "What about Dr. Spring? How old is she?"

"The same restriction goes for her as well." Tom looked at his friend, and Steven nodded. "She's older than I am. She's about one hundred and ten times the age of this present physical universe. You realize that these ages are just estimates. Time doesn't work for us the same way it does for you." Tom gave Steven a strong *Qrie Embrace*.

It took Steven several minutes to compose himself and wrap his brain around what he'd just heard and felt. "My God, Tom, what was that? Is this what you feel all the time?"

"Yes, and it's called a *Qrie Embrace*. It's how we Qrie greet one another."

The yeoman came into his office. "They want you back in the conference room, Sir. Just you, Sir, not... uh."

"Call me when you get out of the meeting, Steven. We'll go have a beer, okay?"

"You got it, Tom. See you then."

***

The Minister of Defense, seated at the conference table, bumped the arm of the Prime Minister, seated next to him, and pointed towards the door as three women were walking through it. Captain Harbits was leading Helen McElroy and her first Deputy Minister. All three women looked shaken. However, Captain Harbits was trying hard to put a good face on. They all walked over to Everett.

McElroy was still shaken up. "What's going on here? One moment we were in an office in Perth. This one" — she gave a dismissive gesture towards Captain Harbits — "and another woman calling herself Dr. Breath Of Spring appeared out of nowhere. She spoke without words, into our minds. She told us we had to come with them, and bang! Here we are. She moved us more than thirty-four hundred kilometers in — well — less than a second! How's that possible?"

Everett looked concerned. "No one in this room can answer that question. We'd all like to know more of what's going on. I sent Captain Harbits to give you a message to come here. I didn't think she was going to go herself and pick you up. Could you please explain that to us, Captain?"

The Captain looked at all of those standing in front of her and stammered, "I... I did like you instructed. I went down to *Morning Discovery*, and she met me on the dock. The next thing I know, we're in Perth with the Minister of Security and the first Deputy Minister. She informed them that they had to come with us. The next thing I... I know, we're back on *Morning Discovery*. That's all I know. She knew precisely what I was there for and just did it."

Everett looked at the three women as if she were sensing something. "Would you three like a bite to eat before getting this meeting underway? It could be quite a while before we take a break. I'd recommend the spare ribs."

"Yes," McElroy replied. "I haven't had anything to eat since last evening, and I'm famished. Perhaps with some food in me, I can make more sense of what's going on here. Captain Harbits, brief me as best you can before we get to the conference room."

16. DECISIONS

CO Winslow told the door guards that no one was to disturb them after the meeting began.

The Prime Minister stood up at the end of the conference table. "Today we discovered we're not alone. We're not the only intelligent beings on this planet. We're also not the most intelligent, and for sure not the most powerful. The entities that we've encountered here today are, very much, out of our league.

"We've met our creators today. We know that they've been here for billions of years. Their created beings, the Mer, have been here for over two million years. The *Galactic Prime* entity is incomprehensible!

"I don't know what to make of Dr. Breath Of Spring or Sub Lieutenant Tom Haynes. These two people, if they are human beings, which they say they are, wield immense power and don't mind using it. The primary question we must answer here tonight is: What do we do about them, our Country, and our Security?"

Helen McElroy stood up. "I'm not going to roll over and play dead until I know what's going on. I know that I wasn't in this conference here today, and I didn't see anything, so I'm coming at it from outside, playing catch-up. As head of security for this country, I want to know everything I can about them, and is there someone here who can brief me?

"First, I need to get some security people on them and track their every move. I want to get someone close to Dr. Breath Of Spring on her ship, to watch her. And I want to get someone on *Queen's Shield* to watch Sub Lieutenant Haynes.

"I hate putting spies on our own people, if they are our people, but I don't know how else we can do it. I also want to put people on as many Mer as we can find in this country, if we can find them. They may be what they claim to be, then again, they may not. I for one want to make certain. I won't rest until I know for sure.

"Does anyone know what they've been doing since they went back to their respective ships?"

"Yes, Minister." A young lieutenant stood up. "Lieutenant Jackson here; I'm head of station security. I've had people on both Dr. Spring and Sub Lieutenant Haynes since the meeting. If you'll allow me, we have a video of both Sub Lieutenant Haynes and Dr. Spring."

McElroy made a proceed motion with her hand. "Go ahead, please."

Lieutenant Jackson placed a flash drive into the overhead projector. Nothing unusual could be seen happening until Breath and Tom repaired the detention facility. After that, they floated back to *Morning Discovery*. A few minutes later, what could have been Tom was now a huge, fuzzy, out-of-focus ball of light floating over to *Queen's Shield*. It disappeared into the ship and came out a few moments later. The ball of light then floated over to the headquarters building and went inside.

Captain Harbits could be seen walking down the dock towards *Morning Discovery*. A ball of out-of-focus light floated down the gangway and met her. There was a huge blaze of light, and they disappeared. A few moments later, they reappeared on *Morning Discovery*. Captain Harbits, Minister McElroy, and the Deputy Minister could be seen stumbling down the gangway, stopping for a moment, and walking away.

The fuzzy ball of light remained on the ship for a few moments, and what looked like an ice-cream confection formed in front of it. Something that looked like a hand reached out and took it, and then everything went into the ship. A moment later, the video reversed and then started again and zoomed in on the confection, which appeared to be a chocolate ice-cream sundae.

McElroy blurted with mild anger, "Okay, so she likes chocolate ice-cream sundaes, and we can't get a decent picture of her. We've gotta find out a lot more."

She reached over, picked up her cell phone, hit a couple of buttons, put the phone to her ear, and waited. "Yes, it's me. I want you to get several top people and..."

Her face was turning red. Veins and arteries were sticking out of her forehead and her neck. She was straining hard to say something into the phone, but she couldn't. Nothing happened. The harder she tried, the redder she got, and the more the veins stuck out. She punched the phone off. Her face began to return to normal. "What the bloody hell was that?"

Captain Harbits said. "That may have been the result of the Compulsion that's been placed on us all. We didn't know what would happen if we tried to violate it. Apparently, now we do."

McElroy spat with unleashed fury, "I don't like this one damn bit. This bloody Compulsion crap is preventing me from doing my job."

The Governor General quite calmly replied to Helen McElroy's fury. "I do not think expletives like that will gain you influence with the entities that we have encountered here today. I think it would be a good idea to control those outbursts in the future."

McElroy shot him a look that could rip the paint off a battleship but she averted her eyes. "Yes, Sir, I think you're correct."

Everett continued. "We know we must keep a close eye on these people. One thing that we do have to consider is how we're going to do it. They know what we're thinking, just like Captain Harbits said earlier; Dr. Breath Of Spring knew what she was there for. How can we do anything without their knowing? The point is, we can't!"

CO Winslow spoke up. "I was speaking with Sub Lieutenant Haynes in my office. He told me he's been working with them for — a considerable time now and has been looking for anything that could point to them not being what they say they are. I trust Tom. We've known each other since he was in his first year at college and I was about to graduate. We've stayed close friends since that time, and I know him to be honest and honorable. I, for one, am ready to take him at his word. I'll keep in close touch with him, seeing if he finds anything that could be a chink in their armor."

A Rear Admiral spoke up. "How do we know that Sub Lieutenant Haynes hasn't been compromised? How do we know that he and Dr. Spring haven't been with them for a long time? We know that they're Mer or Qrie themselves, especially after what we've just seen."

McElroy asked. "How was it that everyone got a message to meet here today? I got one from the PM. I just couldn't be in two places at once."

As it turned out, everyone in the room had gotten emails or communiqués from other people in the room saying that there was an urgent meeting at Cairns Naval Station. The original email communiqué had come from Captain Harbits.

McElroy said. "Well, how about that? They got into our communication systems. What other systems have been compromised? What else can they do?"

The Prime Minister commanded. "People, check with all your departments. Check every system. Make sure of their proper function and that nothing has been compromised. If they got into our communication systems, they can get into other systems. Let's make sure that everything is up and running as it should."

Captain Harbits thought. *This is an exercise in total futility. From what I've seen of these entities, if they wanted to disrupt our systems, they could've done it a long time before now.*

This fruitless activity continued into the next hour, creating more questions than answers.

***

Meanwhile, McElroy and Everett asked the RAN Admirals and Commander George Marsdurban to join them in a private room.

Everett began. "Admiral Lynch, why is it that you knew about these beings for years and didn't inform your government?"

Lynch replied. "Primarily there were the Compulsions. The U.S. Navy and another top-secret U.S. agency, the OAI, made this information an eyes-only briefing. The President of the United States doesn't even know.

"When we first found out about Breath Of Spring, we knew her only as a capable swimmer who could communicate, in some manner, with sea mammals such as whales and dolphins. We later learned much more about her. We were told to be extremely cautious around her and her family due to their unusual abilities. This particular U.S. agency has been in communications with a large alien consortium known as the Anasso, and they informed..."

At the end of this portion of the discussion, Vice Admiral Lynch nodded to PM Amanda Everett. She spoke up. "There's another problem, or perhaps an opportunity, that we must discuss. Sub Lieutenant Tom Haynes is scheduled to be promoted to full Lieutenant. Lieutenant Commander Tibbett, the present CO of *Queen's Shield,* is being promoted to Commander and assigned to another ship. This leaves no one in command of *Queen's Shield* except for the possibility of Tom Haynes, if we allow him to stay in the RAN and promote him to Lieutenant. The question remaining is, do we allow a Qrie to be in command of an Australian Navy ship?"

This portion of the discussion continued for quite some time with no resolution.

17. RESTAURANT

Breath heard a knock on her cabin door. She walked over and opened it.

It was Tom. "Hey, you want to hit the town? Wow! You look — uh — amazing. I can't wait to entice you to take that off — very slowly — just for me. You just can't surprise a guy like me with a dress like that. I'm going to have to carry a really big stick."

Breath replied, striking a sultry pose and a come-hither side-glance look. "Well, before we do all that, you're going to have to buy me dinner."

Tom said with a huge leering smile. "Absolutely! Fast food, really fast."

Breath replied with the same look. "No way. Steak and lobster for this Sheila."

"Well, if we must, but maybe a little dancing later. I'd like to show you off."

"I'm not up for dancing tonight. I wouldn't mind getting a bite to eat. Is there any place within walking distance that's pretty good? I'm glad you like my 'little red dress.' Hilga made it for me a couple of weeks ago and haven't had a chance to try it out. I was trying for the sophisticated, sexy look, but not too prim and proper."

"Yeah, well, I think you achieved your goal, especially on the prim-and-proper part. You look fantastic. I'm still going to have to carry a big stick. Okay, back to food. Let's see... uh there's a little place about four or five blocks south of the main gate. They've got anything you want if you like seafood."

"That's great. I'm up for a walk. Besides, Skipper talked me into leaving in the morning instead of this evening. Let me grab my bag, and we're outta here."

"Ok, what are you up for? I'm kinda leaning towards lobster."

Breath looked up and to the right in thought. "I think I've got a yen for some fried shrimp instead of steak and lobster. I haven't had any in a while."

They strolled towards the seafood place, talking about anything except the day's events.

Tom glanced behind as they strolled along. "You know, if we go any slower, our security details back there'll pass us bye."

"Yes, I know. Maybe when we get in the restaurant, we can invite them over for dinner. Do you think that'll bother them? I know they're not 'her' people, but I think Helen McElroy is going to have to teach these new people how to follow someone a little bit better." Breath chuckled.

They continued this line of scheming until they got to the restaurant. The place was popular. There was a line. The maître d' greeted them and gave them a number. He showed them to the waiting area. Even the pub area was filled with people standing around talking.

While they were waiting there, Tom heard his name called. It was Jim. He waved them over to his table. They walked over, and Jim shook hands with them. They seated themselves on the high bar stools. The waitress came over and took their drink order. Tom got a Carlton Draught, and Breath ordered a Shiraz, after they both showed their ID's to the waitress.

Tom asked. "What happened to your not liking wine?"

"Well, it's gotten better the older I get. It's not near as bad as when I was young."

Both Jim and Tom laughed. Then Tom asked. "What've you done with my Breath? A sexy red dress, and now wine. Jim, I think the world is coming to an end."

Jim continued laughing. "I hope not. We've spent a lot of effort on this one. We don't need to start over. Anyway, what'd you think about the meeting?"

Breath became serious. "Look, guys, I don't want to talk business such as the Mer, the Qrie, the Navy, or government of any kind."

Jim laughed. "Okay, so how about the price of tea in China?"

All three laughed, puns started flying, and the quality of the conversation went downhill from there.

A few minutes later, the maître d' walked up to their table. "Madam, sirs, we've a table in the restaurant for three that's just opened up. If you don't mind sitting together, I can seat you now."

They all agreed that sitting together would be a good thing.

The table turned out to be a rather strange booth. It was a small booth with a pie shaped table that fit in the corner.

They were all looking at their menus. Breath saw the day's house specialties, American Gulf Coast–style, peeled, butterflied, deep-fried shrimp, with tartar sauce. She mentioned this to Tom and Jim. "I've had them several times. I fell in love with them when I was studying in the Southern United States, where they fry everything. If they fix them the same way, I'll be happy."

The waitress came and took their order. Tom ordered the lobster, Breath ordered the shrimp, and Jim ordered a small appetizer plate.

They continued with small talk until their order came.

Breath asked Jim. "How's the plan coming? Is it still on track?"

"I thought you didn't want to talk about what was going on today."

"Well Jim, I don't think I have a choice. I know what's going on in that room, and I know I'm going to have to go back in there to get our accord. So, what's your assessment?"

"Well, it's kind of got a snag. Our good Minister of Security, Helen McElroy, has got everyone asking questions about everything in the world. I think security people are paranoid of their own shadows. They have to be because they're afraid of everything else.

"On the other hand, I was telling you about giving the Mer more power to handle emergencies. Well, I got with the Qrie, got into the Memory, and we figured out a way to do it without having the Mer be gold all the time. We did have to modify the Mer a bit, but it didn't change them much. It just allows them to handle much more power and prevent them from being injured by explosions and small-arms fire.

"It's unfortunate that it won't stop high-powered or armor-piercing-type bullets or high explosives. It's far superior to what they had. The Qrie can now channel continuous power to all the Mer, no matter where they are. It did take us a while to get the logistics worked out.

"The situation isn't unique in the universe. This need has occurred many times; we just adapted it for our Mer, and it's a beautiful solution. Morning and Beauty have been instructing the Mer worldwide in the use and safe application of this new added energy. When you guys return to Reeftown, I'm sure the youngsters there are going to be showing off their new Mer muscles."

"That's super, Jim; I can't wait to see it and them again!"

Tom asked. "I agree, but what are we going to do about Helen?"

"Well, you know, it just so happens that I've got this Memory thing. It has a complete history of the solar system and all the life on this planet from the get-go. I'm kinda thinking that they need a history lesson."

"Jim, I can see another fiasco coming."

"Hey, what are emissaries for if they're not for emissarying?"

Tom almost choked, but he held it together.

Breath laughed. "Jim, that's not even a word."

"Sure it is, because I just said it!"

Breath laughed. "Okay, okay. What must we do?"

"That's the spirit." He leaned over and said, with conspiracy and a twinkle in his eye. "Here's what we're gonna do..." For the next few minutes Jim laid out his plan.

"Why me? Why not Tom? Why do I always have to be the bad guy here?"

"Oh, so now 'you're' the bad guy, huh. Gosh, what's that make me? Well, let's see. You've built a considerable rapport with these people. The majority in that room are men. You're a lot more appealing to them than Tom, although Helen might not agree. They already know that you can do all these things. Should I go on, or do you want some more wine?"

"Why can't Tom and I do this together?"

"Breath, we know what this is all about and where we're trying to go with it. Besides, I don't mind playing second fiddle to you, with you in that 'little red dress.'"

Breath looked at Tom and blushed. "This feels like a conspiracy."

Jim leaned close to her and then winked at Tom. "Well, guess what, Breath? It is!"

The three of them sat and talked for several more hours. The place had cleared out. They were the only ones still there, with the exception of their tails.

"Well, Breath, I guess we're going to have to do this. It's well after midnight, the staff look anxious to go home, and that bunch in the conference room hasn't made any definitive decisions at all. They're just like a bunch of politicians."

Breath laughed out loud. "Jim, they 'are' a bunch of politicians." The three of them started laughing, got up and headed towards the cashier. "Just a moment, guys. I'm going to get our tails, if you don't mind."

She walked back to the table where the two military-looking security people were seated. "Come on, guys, give me your check. We're leaving; come join us."

She walked back, their tails in tow, to where Jim and Tom were standing by the cashier. She handed Tom the other check. "Add this to our bill."

"You guys got the meal. I'll get the tip." Jim walked back towards their booth, pulled out a wad of cash, and left it on the table.

As they were all leaving the restaurant, Jim turned. "Nice bumping into you guys here tonight. We'll have to do this again sometime. Have a good evening — or well morning now I guess."

Breath and Tom and their two security details were walking back to the station, when Breath turned to the two guys. "What are your names? I'm Breath. This is Tom. Of course, you already know that."

"Yes, Ma'am we do. My name is Don."

"It's nice to meet you, Don." Breath then looked at the other man. "And your name is?"

"Zachariah. Most people just call me Zach, Ma'am."

"Zach and Don, it's nice to have two such strong young men to protect us from harm on our walk back to the station. I want to thank you for such a nice service."

Tom chuckled. "Yeah — nice service."

All four laughed. They knew the jig was up, and there was no reason to extend the charade any further. The men begin telling one another about how they'd come to the service and how long they'd served in the RAN. The small talk continued until they got back to the dock and *Morning Discovery*.

The two men didn't remain with Breath and Tom but followed a discreet distance behind them as they walked towards *Morning Discovery*. Breath and Tom went on board, walked back onto the aft access deck, put their arms around each other, and kissed several times.

Breath looked up at him. "I wish you were coming along with me on this escapade. I need some moral support because I'm not comfortable intimidating people."

"Do you think Zach can follow me across the water to *Queen's Shield?*"

"Oh, Tom, that's almost mean. They're just doing their jobs."

Tom took a long slow look at the 'little red dress.' Then with severe disappointment, he floated back to the aft end of the access deck, over the railing, and across the water towards *Queen's Shield.*

Breath smiled and watched him leave. "Hey big boy, why don't you come back and see me sometime."

Tom stopped in mid float. He hung his head turned, and continued on without turning around.

She went into her cabin, changed back into illusion clothes, came back out, and walked down the gangway towards Don.

"Walk with me, Don. I'm going to the conference."

"Yes, Ma'am. May I ask a question?"

"Yes, please do."

"The other fellow, Tom, flew over to his ship. I know you can fly. Why aren't you doing it now?"

"Tom is just having a little bit of fun with Zach. He's yanking his chain. I'm not doing it now because I've got a real gentleman with whom to walk."

This put a big smile on Don's face. He extended his elbow to her, and she took it.

Breath and her gentlemen escort walked arm in arm into the administration building. They went down the hallway to the conference-room door. The two guards at the door became agitated. They glanced back and forth at each other, wondering what to do. They strolled up to them and she turned to Don. "Thank you, Don, for being such a fine escort."

18. ACCORD

Breath approached the two guards. "Please, open the door." One of the nervous guards said. "I can't do that, Ma'am. We've — got our orders."

"You know who I am. I won't ask a second time."

The guards turned in unison and opened both doors.

"Thank you, Gentlemen." She floated through. The doors closed behind her.

Every eye was on her. Everyone was seated around the large and now-cluttered conference-room table. The men's jackets were hung on the backs of their chairs, their ties loosened, and the women had removed their uncomfortable shoes. The strain on the faces of those gathered around that table was obvious. She started floating with grace around the table and the group.

She began speaking in a calm manner. "You've been in this room for well over seven hours now. You've made no progress whatsoever towards your decisions. I've come to speed things up. We were hoping that you'd come to the conclusion that we, the Qrie, wished to make an accord with the government of Australia. You haven't come to this conclusion. You've only worried about whether we're here to usurp your security, your sovereignty, and your freedoms."

She stopped floating behind Minister Helen McElroy and PM Amanda Everett, who were seated next to one another. When everyone turned towards her; she continued speaking.

"If we wanted to do that, we would have done it before civilization began. We are not here to take anything away from you. We are here to help you and all the people of Earth.

"We 'will' have an accord. We only want your promise of silence, that you'll not expose our existence to the public, and leave us alone to do what we're here to do. For this, we'll give you information to help you guard your borders and to protect the people of this country. We'll not do it for you, but we'll help you.

"The only question is. Do you want to do it the easy way, or the hard way? I would recommend the easy way. You wouldn't like the hard way. The easy way will be most enjoyable. You'll learn a lot about us and what we do. This'll entail my taking you on a little trip through time. I'll take you to the nebula from which this solar system was condensed and let you see the evolution of the Solar System from its birth to today. That is the easy way. If anyone is concerned, I'll tell you about the hard way." Breath stopped talking, and the room was deadly silent. She continued floating around the table.

McElroy took a deep breath and asked. "What's the hard way?"

"All your military infrastructure and — 'toys' will be moved to a convenient location on the moon in full view of Earth or space-based telescopes. Your 'toys' will be preserved until such time as you come to the conclusion that having an accord with us is a good thing."

Everett asked. "You can do that?"

"We can take Earth in its entirety and put it into the atmosphere of Jupiter or the Sun. However, neither of these actions would bring about True Intelligence on this planet."

Everett placed her hand on her chest and leaned back. "Oh, my goodness! If we do agree to your accord, what are the details?"

Breath paused a moment to make sure everyone was listening. "They're quite simple. You'll agree to do as I've just asked. We'll help you as I told you. The strong Compulsions that are on you at this time will be somewhat relieved. There'll still be a Compulsion, but it just won't be as strong. You'll maintain your free will.

"If you make a mistake and start telling someone about us, you'll be reminded of our accord. If you continue, you'll have to make a powerful concentrated mental effort to break the accord. Either way, we'll be alerted." She made a deliberate glance at Helen McElroy.

"You'll be able to tell anyone with a strong need to know about us. Anyone you tell, we'll put under the Compulsion. Anyone they need to tell will also be put under it. Anyone you tell must be told about the Compulsion. We, the Qrie, will decide whom you can tell.

"You cannot communicate in any manner information about us to any member of the media; a foreign agency of any kind, including corporations; and foreign governments, unless authorized by us. In short, to the outside world, we don't exist. We'll not advance your technology. We'll not save you from your intellectual or political inadequacies. We will not heal your sick or resurrect your dead unless the circumstances affect the Mer or the Qrie. This is for you to learn. We'll not enter your wars or disagreements; your battles are yours, not ours unless that war affects the Mer and the Qrie. If you're attacked, we'll render aid. We do not predict the future. However, we'll give you information to help protect your nation and your people. This accord will be honored in its spirit." Breath paused for a moment and then commanded with emphasis, "No exceptions will be allowed.

"There'll be no paperwork with this accord. It'll be pressed into your being and become part of your life."

McElroy asked. "What if someone's determined and violates the accord?"

"That individual will find itself in different conditions. Its life will be no longer as it knew it."

"So, you'll take that individual and stick it in a cold, dark place. Is that it?"

Breath turned to McElroy and looked into her inner being. *The universe is overwhelmingly a cold, dark place.*

Helen McElroy had always used personal and physical intimidation to get whatever she wanted. She considered herself ruthless and driven. She knew there was no one on this Earth she couldn't intimidate. However, when she looked into Breath's eyes and Breath looked into her inner being, she knew there was no way on Earth this woman could ever be intimidated — by her or by anything else.

"This accord isn't onerous or difficult. It means keep your mouth shut, leave us alone, and everything will be all right."

Everett asked. "This easy way — uh — you say it's enjoyable, and we can learn a lot?"

"Yes, it's quite enjoyable, and you'll learn. This isn't a requisite for you to agree to the accord. It's just something we thought you might like."

PM Everett passed her gaze to everyone around the table. "Is there anyone here who doesn't want to experience this? Raise your hands if you don't."

All hands remained on the table.

"Wonderful! I must warn you; this trip will take a while. I'd recommend you go to the loo before we embark. Let's meet back in this conference room in, say, twenty minutes."

Breath and everyone else filed out to the loo. She saw her escort, Don, standing over with the door guards. She walked over to him. "Hi, Don. Would you like to take a little trip with us? If you would, I'd suggest you avail yourself of the loo and meet us back in the conference room in about twenty minutes."

After everyone had returned to the conference room, Breath went to the door and told the two guards, "Gentlemen, we'll be gone for a couple hours. Don't let anyone into the room until we return. If someone comes in, there could be a rather nasty accident. Someone could get hurt, and we don't want that. Thank you." She closed the door.

Breath turned to everyone in the room. "At first, you'll be somewhat disoriented. You'll feel yourself standing with no floor and no walls around you. Be assured gravity will exist, and you'll be on a solid surface. It'll just be invisible. If you feel the need to sit down, do so, and an invisible seat will anticipate your need and catch you."

Breath paused a moment and then asked, "Is everybody ready? If so, I'd suggest you take the hand of the person standing next to you. This'll help with your disorientation."

She thought. *I feel like a tour guide on a theme-park ride.*

Jim chuckled.

Breath lit up with a beautiful, powerful multicolored light. Tendrils of this light reached out to everyone in the room and encompassed them. At that moment, they disappeared from the room. Their perception was that they'd been transported in time to a nebula in deep space. Breath began to play into each of their minds the history of the Solar System from its beginning point in time forward. The scope and immensity were staggering. They saw and understood what was going on as time unfolded, even though there was no narration. They experienced unearthly sounds that were the actual sounds of the universe. No group of human beings had ever experienced this before.

Breath projected to Jim. *You know, other than the weird sounds, this reminds me a lot of that piece in Walt Disney's* Fantasia.

Jim replied. *Those guys were good, but they had to guess. Where do you think I got the idea? But I'm better. I've got the real thing.* He laughed. *I hope you like it.*

Oh Jim, this just gets better each time I experience it. I do have a question; do you think any of these people will realize that they're actually in the Talmage's Qrie protected compound?

Not if you don't tell them.

***

Breath ported all the conference members back into the conference room. "Why doesn't everyone take a quick break and continue your discussion as soon as you return? I'll return in a short time. I have other urgent business to attend to at the moment. Please continue without me." She vanished, thinking she'd give the conference members some time to mull over what they'd just experienced.

After an appropriate amount of time, Breath flashed back into the conference room. Everyone was discussing the grand tour.

"You now know some of who and what we are, and some of what we're trying to do. I trust you found it enjoyable. We must now address the matter of the accord. Are you ready to enter into this accord with us?"

She remained still and waited.

The Prime Minister stood up after a few moments. "Ladies and Gentlemen, I don't think we've got anything to fear from these beings. They've been here for millions and billions of years. If they were going to do something, they'd have done it long before now. This may be an agreement with god, or it could be a deal with the devil. The way it's been laid out for us, we don't have a choice. Either way, we'll have to agree to the accord. I know we've got most of the top government and military officials here, but we don't represent a quorum of Parliament. I don't see any other way to do this. Let us vote now with a show of hands. Those in favor of the accord, raise your hands."

She raised her hand. "Those opposed to the accord."

No hands raised.

"The accord has passed." Breath gave everyone a huge comforting smile. "The conditions of the accord are now in effect. Congratulations, and thank you." She spread a shield of light to each person in the room and gave them each a strong *Qrie Embrace*.

***

The concussions were powerful and towards the back of the room. Breath's first thought was *Earth Only*.

"Tom did you sense that? I put a shield up over everyone just prior to the explosion. I'm not certain why I did that, but I am glad I did.

"Admiral Lynch thinks it was a rocket propelled grenade that burst through one of the large windows."

"Yes Breath, I did sense it, and heard it as well. The Admiral is correct they were rocket propelled grenades. They were fired from a hard-bottom inflatable boat on Chinaman Creek with three men in it. Queens Shield *is returning fire at this moment. We're launching our own boat to go get these guys. Just in case you were concerned, those guys' hard bottom inflatable boat is not so inflated anymore and is about to sink."*

"Thanks Tom, good work. I'm a little busy right now several people are injured."

The shield that Breath put up was powerful but not impenetrable. She floated up and began clearing the room. There was debris, dust, smoke, fire, and the stench of burning plastic. She hurried to reach the people closest to the explosion. Armed guards burst into the conference room. They could not penetrate the shield. All they could do was watch. Three unconscious victims were lifted up and placed on the long conference table. She returned to the explosion site and dug three more injured out of the debris. She brought those three to the long table. One of the victims had died before Breath could get to him. He was Deputy Minister Wilson.

Breath you're going to need a little help with that one. She realized Jim had sent an invisible consciousness to help her. No one in the conference room except her knew he was there.

I know Jim. What do I need to do?

You already know how to project the healing Qrie energies so I would say start there. You also need to separate the one who died from the others on the table and everyone needs to stand back from that one. We will be sending a considerable amount of energy into that one to bring him back to health.

What can we do Jim? He's dead.

Well yes Breath, but there's merely dead and then really dead. This one is only merely dead and you and I can do something about that.

Are you saying we can bring him back from the dead?

Yes! Just like Neil.

"Everyone please stand back. Do not touch anyone that has the glow of light about them. The light can discharge and cause you and the victim pain."

She did as Jim said.

She could sense the fear, apprehension, and horror of everyone there including the guards and began to project the healing Qrie energies into everyone. The intensity of the healing Qrie energies was such that everyone in the room was healed of all their injuries including those maladies not caused by the explosion. She continued her projections until all the injuries, fear, and anxiety were healed and gone.

Tom, can we expect any more problems?

No Breath not from that boat. We're looking to see if there are any more. So far, we haven't found any.

Breath went over and helped the people she had healed off the table. Then she turned to everyone in the room. "If you will all please step back, I must attend to Deputy Minister Wilson."

Someone in the group said. "There's nothing we can do for him. He has a large splinter of wood going through his body and heart. I was a paramedic before I got into politics and I know death when I see it."

Breath chuckled to herself and Jim. She thought she would use Jim's little quip. "Well Sir you see this man is only merely dead not really dead, and something can be done about merely dead!

"I have communicated with Sub Lieutenant Tom Haynes, and he says there is no more danger. I will drop the protective shield when Deputy Minister Wilson is healthy, up, and about."

She floated over to him and placed healing light around him.

Okay Jim, what do we do now?

Well Breath, I think we ought to get that great big piece of wood — out.

I think that would be a wonderful idea Jim. What do you suggest — just pulling it straight out?

Yep. Then we have to heal the wound and make sure everything is back in its right place.

This procedure took about fifteen minutes, and everyone else in the room was trying to get a better look.

Okay Breath, here comes the tricky part. I have only done this two times before.

As Breath stood over the Deputy Minister, Jim placed a powerful bright light around both her and the Minister. Then he took great care placing the Minister's memory back into his brain.

The bright Qrie energy light had destroyed the Minister's clothes. But Breath had enclosed him in a field of light that hid his embarrassment. Jim was making certain that the Minister was in perfect condition before he started removing the light that had caused the destruction of his clothes. The Minister was floating above the table and Breath moved him off the table and into a vertical position.

Breath you're going to have to take this gentleman to the station hospital here, while the Qrie energy around him dissipates. You might want to have a couple of the young Mer come and watch him. What do you think?

Well Jim, I think that would be a good idea because they've been through it once. And everyone here knows about the Mer.

Jim teleported Neil and Kandy, in their Mer form with full flares, into the destroyed meeting room. They arrived just about the same time that several doctors and nurses came streaming into the room.

Neil and Kandy floated to the suspended Deputy Minister. Breath asked one of the nurses to show them where to take him.

"Well that was — interesting." Helen McElroy came over and touched Breath's arm to get her attention and received a *Qrie Embrace.* "Wow," then caught her breath. "I don't think

I want to go through that first part again. The last part where you gave us all the feeling of well-being, I would 'like' to do that again."

Breath looked at Helen with intensity. Then she placed her hand on Helen's shoulder. "I think I can do that." She then gave Helen a very strong *Qrie Embrace*. It was strong enough to make Helen go weak in the knees. "Something like that?"

Helen's eyes and mouth flew open. "My God, and Saints preserve us — yes something like that!"

"Is everyone okay there?"

"Yes Tom, everyone here is okay now. We had a few anxious moments and several people were injured in the blast but everyone is okay now."

"That's great. We got the three guys that were doing the shooting. They came armed to the teeth. They had three rocket propelled grenades and a fifty caliber semi-automatic rifle. They didn't stand a chance against one of our fifty caliber machine guns. They fired two of the rocket propelled grenades. They didn't have a chance to fire the third. I suppose the guy that was getting ready to fire that third grenade was a little distracted by our fifty-caliber machine gun shooting holes in his boat. He never got the shot off. Those three guys are headed to the detention facility that we repaired. We're just lucky no one got killed — as in really dead. Would you like to meet Steven and me there?

Yes Tom, and I'll bring Admiral Lynch.

***

Breath could sense the fear in the guards as she and Admiral Lynch walked into the detention facility. She gave the guards a mild *Qrie Embrace* just enough to relieve the fear but not the intensity.

"Well Admiral, we have three bad guys here. Have they said anything?"

The Admiral glanced at the guard in charge and raised his right eyebrow.

"Not a peep Sir. They won't tell us anything not even their names."

Breath stepped forward. She could smell the fear on the three men. "Did TDog or Dixon send you?" Their fear intensified by several times. Breath, knew at that instant, who these men were.

She turned to the Admiral with a sly smile. "These men work for an agency called Earth Only, run by a man named Melvin Blanchard, codenamed TDog. This group has made several attempts on my life and have injured friends of mine."

"What should we do about them?" The Admiral queried. "Is this a Qrie problem or should we handle it?"

"It's a Qrie problem. Their target was me." The smell of fear from the men was again intensified and almost made Breath nauseous. *Jim, did you get anything from these guys like the whereabouts of TDog and Dixon?*

No Breath. We went to the place where these men got their marching orders but the big dogs weren't there, and we don't have any idea of where they went. Their movement patterns our quite random. Sorry Breath we didn't catch them this time, but they can't evade us forever.

Thanks Jim, please take these guys and put them with the others.

No Breath, it's now your job, and here's where you need to send them...

Gladly!

A bright light formed in the prisoners' cell. One of the men screamed as they disappeared.

Helen McElroy, who had just come into the detention facility, looked concerned and upset when she saw Breath begin to glow and the three men disappear. "What are you going to do with those men. They could've killed the Prime Minister and several senior members of our government. All of this happened in our jurisdiction."

Both Breath and Tom turned to Helen. Breath placed a gentle hand on Helen's arm, and could feel the confusion and consternation in the Minister of Security. "Don't worry about these men. They have gone to a place where they will learn how not to kill anyone or interfere with the Qrie for as long as required."

Helen looked uncertain at Breath. "Will they be punished or killed?"

"We Qrie don't kill if we can avoid it."

Breath could feel Helen's uncertainty and gave her another mild *Qrie Embrace* to calm her consternation.

Everyone in Breath's small group strolled back into the lunch room, to where the attendees had evacuated from the conference room. Breath again gave everyone a mild *Qrie Embrace.* "Please let me assure you that everything has been taken care of. The men who are responsible for the destruction of the conference room are now in custody and will no longer cause anyone harm. I want to thank you all for agreeing to the accord. It is now in force. Sub Lieutenant Haynes and I must now leave your presence."

They walked from the room. It was early morning, and the Sun was just rising above the horizon.

As soon as Breath left, McElroy picked up her phone and called her office. She didn't know what was going to happen or if she could even finish the telephone call. But she had to know everything she could find out about this Breath Of Spring and Tom Haynes. One of her assistants answered the phone.

"Yes, this is Helen McElroy. I want all public information, everything you've got, on a Dr. Breath Of Spring and Sub Lieutenant Tom Haynes. That's right, Haynes — H-A-Y-N-E-S. I want to know their ancestry all the way back to Adam." Helen was surprised and pleased that she could complete the call without being strangled.

Breath decided to walk out of the building, and as she did, she sensed Helen making her telephone call. *Little does Helen know; I placed her entire office under Compulsion.* She smiled and made a mental note. *I'll have to keep an eye on this one.*

***

CO Winslow looked at his phone and noticed he had a text message from Tom, which said.

"Have to run. The Mer gave me and CO Tibbett some information on some suspected smugglers. The Mer are tracking them now. Must investigate. Have to save the world. I L B C N U later. Tom."

CO Winslow picked up his phone and called Tom's number.

"Hello Steve, what's up?"

"You were on duty earlier this morning when the explosion occurred, right?"

"Yes, I took over the watch at 0400 hours. CO Tibbett was in his cabin when everything started. We were watching the boat for a while thinking it was just going down Chinaman Creek to do some early morning fishing until we saw the rocket propelled grenades fired. We knew at that moment what was happening and returned fire. They got off two shots and tried to get a third shot off but it failed."

"I know all that Tom, but what I want to know is what were these guys thinking by attacking a military station on high alert. They had to know that they would never get away with it. It was suicide. It's amazing that none of the three got hurt with all those bullets flying around. How do you explain that?"

"Let's just say that the Qrie try never to kill or even injure if we can help it."

"So, what you're telling me is that you put some kind of field thingy around those three men to protect them."

"There is that — possibility."

"That's what I thought. It still doesn't explain their extreme insanity and stupidity for attacking a fully armed Naval Station."

"Well, there 'is' a possibility of curing insanity, but there is 'no' cure for stupidity. Sorry Steven, got to run, duty calls. Talk to you later."

CO Steven Winslow mumbled as he punched the button to terminate the phone call. "This could get complicated. I wonder who actually runs this operation now — me, or Tom and the Mer?"

***

Breath, you've exceeded all expectations and tests that I've put before you. You're now ready for your next step, and I believe that the other Qrie Stewards will agree. I'm so proud of you.

What are you telling me Jim? You've been dangling this carrot for a long time now. It'd be nice to know what this great 'thing' is.

I'd love to tell you right now Breath, but I've got to wait until the other Qrie Stewards agree. Until then, we'll both just have to wait and see.

Yeah, yeah, I've heard that before.

19. OAI 2

The two pilots on the supersonic jet were laughing. They were flying back to OAI headquarters in Roanoke, Virginia. They had no idea why John Kingman and Tatelin Westworth were so excited, since they had not been in the meeting.

John and Tate were talking like excited teenage girls on their first date. They were going over every minuscule aspect of the meeting in exuberant detail.

Tate was saying "I've never experienced anything like what that *Galactic Prime* entity did. It was out of this world, literally."

"I know! And when the Qrie entity Breath Of Spring touched me, I felt it all over again. She also told us our entire team, including the pilots and the National Security Adviser are under Compulsion. Just like that, she can control stuff halfway around the world. What else can she do?"

The pilots continued to laugh as Tatelin said. "That history lesson we got was out of this world. Can you believe that..."

The conversation continued like this on the flight all the way back to the United States.

Towards the end of the flight to Virginia, Tate, still eager and excited, said. "I can't wait to see the comments the Anasso are going to make about this Breath Of Spring entity."

John, just as excited, said. "I can't wait to see what they'll say about this *Galactic Prime* entity as well. This'll be a hard-ten-month wait."

20. A SCIENTIFIC LOOK

One evening the Mer family adults were lounging in the hot tub. The three young Mer were honing their telekinesis skills by tossing around an old bowling ball at the Talmage compound. The adults began to badger Jim about how the universe works.

John Weber asked, "Jim, you always talk about flow existence as if we know what that means. So, since there are no kids around to interrupt us, tell us about that."

Jim laughed. "You guys are real gluttons for punishment."

John chuckled. "I suppose so, but we still want to know."

"Well, okay — If anyone jumps up and runs screaming into the night, because your head is spinning, don't blame me. Because you asked for it, so here goes.

"Flow existence is the dynamic interaction of events and structures in the universe. It's the marking of events that happen in the physical universe with respect to themselves and the Qrie continuum, regardless of their physical speed, distance, or gravitational influence. Flow existence within the Qrie continuum takes place without time. Time in the physical universe is distorted by Einstein's general theory of relativity. Since the Qrie have near-instantaneous links to the entire universe, this relativistic time distortion is a severe inconvenience. Qrie don't think in terms of time. Not having time in the Qrie continuum, we Qrie carry that lack of time into the physical universe.

"Some physicists are bringing forth the argument that time is not a true dimension. Time is an understandable mathematical construct created by man and is the nondimensional numerical order of material change. Clocks can be used to measure the numerical order of this material change — that is, physical motion in space. Physical material change can move in space only, and time is the nondimensional numerical order of this motion.

"Time is a simplifying mechanism for human use to keep track of, understand, and interact with dynamic events. It allows a physicist to mathematically break into incremental segments a dynamic event. This allows one to understand the event. In simpler terms, time is used to break up and have placement for the events you experience. However, to a relative extent, a universal object and even universal space itself cannot exist without a duration of universal time. This restriction does not exist in the Qrie continuum.

"Let's take the example of the Earth orbiting the Sun. A year is a term man has given to the measurement of the movement of one complete orbit of Earth around the Sun. However, that measurement is just one aspect of that event. In order to measure that movement, you have to have an object, the Earth, in relation to another object, the Sun; a trajectory; the distance and shape of that trajectory; and arbitrary starting and stopping points of that movement; and so forth, as well as the actual movement that you're measuring, all of which comprise and define a dynamic event. That particular dynamic event is just one example of a particular flow existence. In addition, each aspect comprising that particular flow existence is a flow existence itself. The Earth, the Sun, the trajectory, the movement, the distance, events on the Earth, the planets, and the Sun, etc., are themselves individual flow existences. Each is then clustered together to make the flow existence; that's called a year. In a sense, we could say that to describe a particular flow existence is to tell its complete story. Human language cannot express this complete story. Human language becomes a small part of the flow existence story itself.

"Consider another example — an object held with respect to another object, such as a ball above the ground. If the ball is released, gravity causes the two objects to accelerate together, you understand it as exhibiting movement. In other words, the ball falls to the ground. The ball simply follows the standard laws of interaction physics of least resistance. This entire interaction happens regardless of time. Only the movement of the ball could be measured by units of time, if so desired. But then there's the distance it fell, the ball itself, the ground, the device or person holding it, gravity, the interaction of air movements, et cetera. These are a cluster of flow existences. They come together to make a larger flow existence, that of the ball dropping. This, in turn, makes an even larger flow existence. Until you end up with the great flow existence, which is the totality of the universe.

"It's like bartering for items. Two people each have an item the other needs. They trade items; now each person has something he or she needed. This is also an example of a flow existence. To interact with humans, the Qrie have agreed to use the term *time* and its concept. As long as there's no relativistic distortion, there is no such thing as time. As a point of interest. Some of your physicists now argue that there's no time and can write equations for dynamic interactions that don't use time. Without the time construct these equations are complicated, convoluted, and difficult to understand.

"Don't get me wrong; there are cycles such as the day-night cycles, lunar cycle, and orbits around the Sun. There are also other types of cycles, such as the circadian rhythm, your heartbeat, the swinging of pendulums, the oscillations of molecules and atoms. All of these cycles are somewhat regular and predictable.

"There are also cycles of societies, whether they're human or some other entities. All these cycles follow a similar structure. Civilization on Earth had its foundations: along the mouth of the Indus River, the grassy plains west of the Nile, the grassy areas in eastern Turkey, and the Tigris-Euphrates Valley approximately twenty to thirty thousand years ago. Each of these groups began to cultivate cattle, goats, and sheep. They'd move these animals from pasture to pasture just as the animal herders do today. Horses were herded on the steps of Russia, and were tamed to ride. Those people were able to use the horses to herd cattle, sheep, and goats.

"Of course, the various groups had conflicts as well as gathering places. These gathering places became settlements where they could trade. As the settlements grew, societies began to form, and agricultural farming started.

"This would be the beginning of a new cycle of that civilization. When all the people who'd been alive at the beginning of the cycle died, the cycle would end and a new cycle would begin. These cycles have been known to man since ancient times, and there are books written in the latter part of the last century detailing these cycles.

"These human societal cycles are what's known as a *saeculum*. The term comes from the ancient Etruscan civilization, who put a name to the cycles; it has two meanings. One meaning is a century; the other meaning is a very long life. All human societies from the beginning of recorded history have followed a saeculum. Two to two and a half saeculum cycles is the average life span of a democracy or a representative republic. This is also an example of a flow existence.

"A saeculum is composed of several parts. There are two main parts: the crisis and the awakening. The crisis changes the society, usually an economic situation followed by a war, which is followed by several small crises, usually inconsequential wars that don't cause a societal change. That doesn't mean that these inconsequential wars aren't bloody, and, in some cases, they can cause more death and destruction than the society-changing crisis. An example of this type of society-changing crisis is the Revolutionary War between the American colonies and England, and the Civil War in the United States. Another was World War II. The War of 1812, the Spanish-American War, and World War I are examples of inconsequential wars or non-society-changing wars for the New World, North and South America, Australia, and the Pacific. However, World War I 'was consequential' in Eastern Europe and the Middle East. This shows that more than one saeculum can be running at a time. Many can be running simultaneously in different societies.

"The awakening phase is a crisis of spirit or intellect where society questions perhaps religion, the governmental structure, or social norms. Examples of this type of awakening would be the beginning of the Christian Reformation brought on by Martin Luther. Another one was the anti–Vietnam War riots in the 1960s and early '70s. These crises and awakenings all changed societies and the psyche of mankind, usually for the better.

"The Qrie have a long memory and have understood that each of these saeculum cycles can improve human civilization and bring all civilization towards True Intelligence. However, True Intelligence forms when the saeculum is no longer needed, since that species obtains telepathy or some form of it. The brains of all sentient beings emit radiation and can be detected by a telepath. The brain of a telepath develops into a very sensitive receiver, not unlike a radio receiver, that can pick up the electrical emanations of another brain, and interpret those emanations as thoughts and emotions. The telepath looks at the individual's personality structure and can detect lies, deceit, omissions, subversion, and the truth. The telepath can also detect the megalomaniac, the narcissist, the psychopath, the sociopath, the egomaniac, the greedy, the power-hungry, the manipulator, the thief, and the other mentally deficient individuals and groups and their machinations and not allow them any influence. Then that species can fully remember and understand its actual history and make positive changes in order to move out of its insanity. Each entity then becomes a responsible individual unto itself and society.

"A problem always arises as telepathy evolves. The above-mentioned mental deficient groups always endeavor to destroy and eliminate those who can discover them. As a result, the telepaths must live in secret until they outnumber and can defeat their destroyers.

"You, as Mer, know yourselves that no human can lie to you even though you may not know what that person's thinking. This is what the Qrie are waiting for on this planet; it'll take a while, what you might call a long flow existence.

"I must say, a society going through the saeculum can be devastating. Sometimes that society is destroyed. Such as, the end of the Etruscan civilization, the fall of Rome, and the destruction of the Aztec empire.

"The end result is there's no true time, but there are cycles that man can consider as keepers of it."

Connie asked. "When a civilization comes towards its end, couldn't you or the Qrie remove the power-hungry megalomaniacs and keep the free civilization moving forward?"

"We've tried that several times here on Earth and other planets. The only thing that happens is that the civilization starts over and functions for another two hundred years or so, until the same attitudes and the types of people arise again. Removing the destroyers of the civilization doesn't work. We now know that for a civilization to remain stable without the destroyers, that civilization must evolve into True Intelligence, where these destroyers are removed from the society and not allowed to gain power."

Crystal asked, "How long does that take?"

"It takes anywhere from a thousand to sometimes one hundred thousand generations. That's two hundred and fifty to twenty-five thousand saeculum cycles, assuming the destroyers don't wipe out all intelligent life on the planet. It's unfortunate but it happens all too often. Human beings on this planet might be able to achieve True Intelligence sooner through genetic manipulation, and developing telepathy or true mind-to-mind communication. Did that answer your question, Crystal?"

"Well, somewhat. How do all the humans get to be telepathic?"

"Good question Crystal. Like everything else in evolution, it takes a few to get the ball rolling, so to speak. What happens is a genetic variation will occur, through natural, or genetic editing and manipulation. This process has already started on this planet.

"When this occurs, those with the telepathic capability tend to stick together. They become somewhat like a network or a secret society banding together for their mutual benefit. They'll be able to detect both the truth and the negative aspects of the people around them. This can also occur in those with negative aspects to their personality structures. You might ask, doesn't this poison apple spoil the rest? It's not necessary that this occurs. Because the rest of the telepaths can sense the deviant personality among them with ease. Association with that person tends not to occur within the group network. When the positive group learns how to block their interactivity from the deviant personalities, those negative personalities become isolated from the positive group network. The positive group develops a win-win structure with the members of their group network. Each member then contributes its special capabilities to the group and the network contributes the combined group capabilities to the individual. Everyone wins, and everyone benefits. The larger the network becomes, the more resistant to intrusion it becomes. The narcissist, psychopath, sociopath, egomaniac, megalomaniac, and other negative personality types can't become part of the positive telepathic network and are isolated.

Connie asked. "Why can't the negative people form a negative telepathic group?"

"The answer to that question is, they can. But have you ever seen two narcissists work effectively together? Have you ever seen two or more sociopaths, or, for that matter, two or more psychopaths work together and be effective? Megalomaniacs can work together, but not for long. So, you see, negative personalities can't be effective and work together. Positive telepathic personalities can always read the negative personalities. This occurs in physical beings as well as in Qrie beings."

Crystal looked a bit confused. "Are there any none telepath groups of humans that can work together like positive telepathic groups?"

"Yes, Crystal, there are groups that can do things somewhat like the positive telepathic entities. A prime example is the military, among the enlisted personnel. These people, by necessity, must form a positive supporting group utilizing the talents of each individual. They must be a cohesive group, and each individual supports the group. The no-man-left-behind attitude.

"The narcissist, the psychopath, et cetera, cannot function within this type of group and still allow the group to maintain its integrity. These negative personality types are moved to the outside of the group or transferred to some other part of the military, or expelled from the military. There are other examples of this, such as doctors, nurses, orderlies, etc. forming a cohesive unit.

"The United States militaries are now screening and verifying all of their inductees, to make sure that none of these people with these negative traits remain in the military."

Taylor asked, "Why can't you make humans telepathic like the Qrie and Mer?"

"Good question, Taylor. The problem with that is, we'd have to make all humans Qrie capable. That's not possible. This has been tried. It turns out that even with the telepathic capability, the Qrie power causes more problems to the physical civilization than if they didn't have that Qrie power to start with. A negative person with Qrie power can be destructive, to the extreme. The Qrie have ways to handle their negative individuals. It's unfortunate, that physical entities don't have those same capabilities.

"Naturally evolved telepathy using universal energies such as electromagnetic, acoustic, optical, or other physical means is far safer for a physical society than giving everyone Qrie power. What you must understand is, telepathy isn't the only thing that's required. People must also evolve true rational intelligent sympathy and compassion to prevent their destruction. The best way is to allow people to evolve in a natural way. The Qrie have developed the aggression suppression ring system around intelligence-bearing planets to allow and encourage this evolution."

There was silence among the group for a few moments. Then John asked, "I'd like to learn more about universal creation and gravity. What can you tell us about that?"

"Are you sure about that, John?"

John looked around the group. No one was saying anything. "Well, I for one would like to know about creation and gravity. Especially since the Mer can manipulate gravity."

"Well, okay. The Qrie are not the creators of the universe, we are the assemblers. Creation is produced by what we call *Prime Cause*. *Prime Cause* creates what you humans call quirks, leptons, gluons, forces, energies, etc., and then space from the cosmic quantum vacuum, at the beginning of a Big Bang for a universe. We Qrie take those gluons, quarks, leptons, and energy and make them into protons, neutrons, electrons, etc. We then turn those into hydrogen, helium, and lithium atoms. Gravity is a weak evolution of space itself. Space is a field that pushes on everything not unlike the repulsion of the like poles of magnets or like electric charges.

"The Qrie and the Mer can fly, move, and lift objects. We do this by using the Qrie energies to manipulate the physical electromagnetic forces as well as manipulating space itself. Physical space permeates everything in the physical universe and is what gravity emerges from. We can manipulate the electromagnetic forces as well as the strong and weak force associated with matter. Lifting and moving objects requires that we change space, or the space force surrounding matter. It's much easier for us to manipulate space and let space itself move the physical matter than for us to use electromagnetic forces to move that matter. We can do either, but for us manipulating space is like lifting a feather, where using electromagnetic forces would be like lifting a truck.

"The Qrie make disturbances in the matter of the subatomic nebula to begin the formation of atoms such as hydrogen, helium, and lithium and ultimately stars. After that it's just a matter of pushing stuff around to make planets, clusters of stars, galaxies, and clusters of galaxies.

"The space field pushes on everything, such as quarks, leptons, gluons, photons, atoms, etc. including the force fields between all these particles. The space field or force is about ten to the fortieth times smaller than the electromagnetic force. The subatomic particles makeup all other matter and as the space field interacts with matter, the space field is — scattered or reflected. The more mass the more — scattering or reflection. Not unlike light pushing on a solar sail. Except that space is not absorbed by the mass. A shadow will form between two masses due to the scattering. The masses will then be pushed together by space itself in an effort to remove the shadow.

"Stars in a galaxy don't move like planets around a star. Nor do they move as Newton and Einstein say they should, which is like water flowing down a drain. Where the stars closest to the center of a galaxy move much faster than the stars out at the edge.

Stars in a galaxy move somewhat like paint spots on a merry-go-round or items on a lazy Susan, except at the very center of the galaxy. This characteristic is caused by what the Qrie call 'The Shadow Web.' This web is formed by the space shadows between the stars and tend to tie the stars together like a spider web.

"Several physics theories today including Modified Newtonian Dynamics, Modified Gravity, Emergent Gravity, and others show that gravity doesn't work the way most people, including Newton, Einstein, and most other physicists today think. The universal constants that physicists count on as always being constant, such as the fine structure constant alpha designated (a) the speed of light designated (c) and Newton's universal gravitational constant designated (G) in physics and mathematical equations, haven't always been quite so constant.

"The speed of light changes with the temperature or energy of the universe. In the early universe when the temperature was extremely hot, i.e. very high energy, the speed of light was much faster something like ten to the fortieth power times the speed of light today. As the temperature dropped and the universe expanded the speed of light also dropped. The inflation of the universe is different than what physicists imagine today. The age of the universe is a little greater than suspected.

"The universal gravitational constant G changes with respect to the distance from very large masses. G close in around a star, for example, tracks close with Einstein. Throughout all of this, matter still manipulates space, and space tells matter how and where to move. Physics, as we know it today, needs a little rethink.

"An old idea of gravity known as the Le Sage theories say that gravity pushes. This is true but also problematic because of the way Le Sage was thinking. He theorized that particles like light or gravitons will push or collide with particles of matter. The principle of least action causes the universe to expand, with the so-called dark energy. There is no true dark energy just space. Space itself pushes and causes the universe to expand and accelerate from its birth i.e. the Big Bang which is set into action by *Prime Cause*. It pushes on space as long as there is power to expand space, and that power comes from the universal background temperature of space itself. When the universal background temperature drops to absolute zero the universe is out of energy and stops expanding, and gravity diminishes to zero.

"This is the maximum expansion of a universal cycle. The expanding universal matter and energy approaches its Qrie domain limit or maximum expansion limit. This limit is many, many times larger than the present universe. The universe reaches its pressure balance volume limit with respect to the Qrie continuum. As I said before, this is the point where the universe runs out of energy and can no longer expand. Then, at that point, the physical matter and energy are again broken down and absorbed back into the universal quantum vacuum.

"This vacuum exists in the same volume as the observable universe and is coincident with it. It doesn't interact with the universe except through virtual particle generation and annihilation. Hawking radiation is an example of this. The cosmic quantum vacuum and the universe are both part of the physical and are not — Qrie. Neither physical matter nor universal energy can ever escape its physical universal Qrie domain limit.

"At the outer universal boundary or edge, the universe can't expand into the Qrie continuum any longer. It then begins to shrink as its mass and energy are converted back into the cosmic or universal quantum vacuum. The Qrie outer domain limit always remains the same with respect to that particular universe. The size of the Qrie outer domain limit for all universes are about the same. When all the universal matter and energy have been converted, it is returned to the cosmic quantum vacuum. Since there's no gravity in this vacuum, the pressure from the Qrie continuum — shrinks this volume. The Qrie continuum is contiguous throughout the continuum. Each universal bubble is separated and contained within the Qrie continuum.

"The energy in this vacuum becomes unstable when a pressure balance is achieved between the cosmic quantum vacuum and the Qrie continuum. At this point, a new universal cycle is initiated by *Prime Cause*. A new observable universe begins, space and gravity again forms. A new universal flow existence begins, and its ultimate conversion back into quantum vacuum ends that universal flow existence. The cycle is continuous. All energy and matter are conserved, retained, and recycled within the Qrie/universal domain bubble.

"The Qrie continuum is filled with these Qrie/universal domain limit bubbles. Each of these bubbles contain all of the universal energy and/or matter required to build a universe. Universes expand and contract within these bubbles. These Qrie domain limit bubbles are like marbles in a jar of infinite size, with each marble surrounded and separated by the Qrie continuum.

"The bending of space-time was a construct by Einstein. I might add he did an excellent job, considering the limited cosmic universal information he had. You're right, John; there's no dark matter, for that matter.

"As I say, there are a few physicists who now have a better mathematical understanding of how gravity works without dark matter. However, they have some way to go yet. They'll have a much better understanding when they realize Newton's constant G changes around massive objects such as galaxies and star clusters, and that the speed of light changes with the temperature of the universe. Once they do, they'll have better insights into things such as galaxies, galactic clusters, black holes, the early universe, and the bending of light."

John looked puzzled and asked, "You told us earlier everything was energy, but I'm matter, and the ground is matter. What about that?"

"Well John, there are two main types and subtypes of energy. One is Qrie energy; the other is universal energy. Qrie energy can affect universal energy, but not the other way around unless controlled by a Qrie intelligence. All objects such as you and I are made of energy. I happen to be made of Qrie energy. I look and feel solid, but I'm still pure energy. You and the Earth and all things on it are universal energy. You and the Mer can also manipulate Qrie energy as well which allows you to manipulate gravity to a limited extent, as well as other universal forces.

"When a universe is first born, it's only energy; there is no matter. As the universe ages or flow exists, the energy begins to condense and matter forms, but all the matter is still made of energy.

"What the Qrie do is learn from the universal entities of each past universal cycle to build the next better universe."

Taylor said. "I'm a medical doctor. I don't understand all this gravity and universe-building stuff. What I'd like to know are two things: One, what about all the other consciousnesses and bodies you say you have? How do you keep track of all of them? It seems to me the human brain can't handle more than one consciousness at a time. Two, you mentioned, the bad guys who had interfered with and attacked Breath were placed in stasis with their minds active. I would think this would drive someone insane."

"Taylor, you're exactly right." Jim chuckled. "To your first question. The human brain can handle only one consciousness at a time. All Qrie entities that live within the confines of a physical universe have access to a Galactic Supercluster Memory. Each living Qrie, whether noncorporeal or physical/Qrie, has a section of that Memory devoted to that individual Qrie. Each consciousness for that Qrie is located in the Supercluster Memory and has an intimate link to that living Qrie such that that living Qrie can know what the other consciousnesses are doing. Each of the consciousnesses are exact copies of the consciousness within that living Qrie. Once linked with the various consciousnesses, it becomes like a group think of one mind for that particular Qrie.

"And now for your second question. The physical bodies are placed in stasis so they do not age. The minds however, are left active. Their brains are still in stasis, and they are conscious They have a place in the Supercluster Memory for that consciousness. They are not in total isolation. They are guided by the non-sentient entities in the Memory towards love and rational compassion for their fellow man. They are not isolated from their companions. The non-sentient entities introduce into these consciousnesses strong negative emotions; when the consciousnesses are reviewing their negative emotions and events with their companions. The entities also introduce strong positive, loving, and compassionate thoughts and emotions, when these people are reviewing positive emotions and events. They're not in some dark gloomy place. They're shown scenes and given strong positive emotions of places of great beauty. From their own memories, they are shown strong positive events in their lives. The Memory entities amplify the strong positive feelings of these events. The entities also show these people their negative events and evil deeds. At the same time, they amplify the negative feelings with disgust, fear, and terror. This allows these people to make up their own mind as to how they feel about others and themselves. The entities will recycle the good feelings, the bad feelings, the good scenes, and the bad scenes until these people learn to be loving and have rational compassion. In the end they learn how not to harm or kill other people and how not to interfere with the Qrie."

Jim could see the glaze in everyone's eyes and stopped talking.

Taylor caught Jim's attention. "The other day Sophianna asked me if I knew how fast Qrie could fly as Qrie. You told us one time that you could move from one side of the Laniakea Supercluster to the other in about an hour Earth time, how fast is that?"

Jim kinda rolled his eyes. "Well Taylor, let's figure it out. The far edge of the Laniakea supercluster is about 500 million light years distant from this solar system to that point. If we do the math then it comes out to be approximately the speed of light or C times 5 times 10 to the twelfth power. It's pretty fast." He chuckled.

Taylor barked. "No kidding, Jim!" As he laid his head back laughing.

"Oh! And it's also the speed of quantum entanglement; since, under certain circumstances, physical matter and other things can link via the Qrie energies. So, when you have entangled things at one point, the Qrie energies transfer that information to the entangled things at the other point. It would be nice if the Anasso could get their stressor communication systems to work with quantum entanglement. But they've never been able to make it work reliably."

"Is that also the speed of the Qrie and Mer telepathy?" Taylor continued.

"No Taylor, Qrie telepathy is instantaneous throughout the Qrie continuum, which includes universal space. Over great distances the Qrie energies must be focused in a tight beam, somewhat like a laser beam. Otherwise, the Qrie energies required for long distance communication becomes quite high."

Connie raised her hand.

"Yes Connie, what is it? And you don't have to raise your hand to ask a question."

"How do the Qrie reproduce? You know — have babies."

"It's much like reproduction in the physical world. We don't call it birth. We call it merge-emergence. It's the English term for an extraordinarily complex Qrie to Qrie entity linking flow existence event. When two Qrie obtain sufficient maturity, they can merge. During this merge everything that the two individual Qrie are, combines and becomes one being, and a third part is formed. This part contains the minimum and essential elements to form a new Qrie entity. Then the emergence occurs, where the original two Qrie entities separate leaving the third new Qrie entity. Then after a million years or so this new Qrie entity can function on its own. The Qrie Z, who is responsible for maintaining the health of my physical body is a good example of a young Qrie entity."

Jim leaned forward towards the rest of the group and put his hand up beside his mouth, as if no one outside the group could hear. "Don't tell anybody I told you this, but I think Morning and Beauty were the ones that merged and Z is the result."

Taylor looked puzzled and asked. "How do Qrie-humans, come about because they don't have a million years or so?"

"Well Taylor, when a Qrie-human female or a human female with the Genetic Stability Device conceives, the combination of the Qrie and human energies forms a kernel like seed. It then combines as part of the human fetus and grows as part of that fetus. It learns to become independent as the human child learns and progresses. This is far faster than a pure Qrie can accomplish on its own."

Then John popped in with a question. "Then why does it take an hour to move your illusion bodies and consciousnesses across the Galactic supercluster?"

"The consciousness and telepathy are pure Qrie and can move instantaneously. The illusion body can't because it has weak links to the physical universe, to produce the physical light for the illusion, and the illusion of solidity. Illusion bodies are formed using our physical body. Forming an illusion body using the separated consciousness requires a considerable amount of time and energy. It requires much more, than the simple transporting of the illusion body in the first place."

Crystal floated up out of the pool and headed for the kitchen. "I've got a few cookies and some ice cream. I'll get them. I need something besides physics right now because my head is spinning."

Connie floated up as well. "I'll help you. My head's spinning too!"

Jim laughed. "Okay, I agree Crystal, enough with the physics. What this group needs are some cookies and ice cream. But you know what I'd really like is some Cinnamon rolls or even Apple fritters. I'd be glad to zip out and get some if that's okay with everybody."

Crystal stopped in mid float and replied. "That would be great Jim, since I don't think I have enough for everyone — especially not the kids."

"Great I'll be back in a second."

No more than a second later Jim returned with several boxes and bags full of Cinnamon rolls, Apple fritters, and several flavors of ice cream.

"I also need to take a little time, with you guys to tweak the added powers that I gave you. I see our energetic young Mer over there are having a little problem controlling these added powers."

Two bright indistinct lights formed in the back compound and Jim became quiet for a few moments. Tendrils of plasma reached out from Jim and the indistinct lights, who everyone there knew were Morning and Beauty, and touched each Mer assembled there. A few moments later the tendrils ceased and Morning and Beauty vanished.

John said. "Wow! That was one whale of a rush!"

All the other Mer, said in unison. "Yeah!"

Later, Jim indicated towards the young Mer. "I think we can all see now that their abilities with the bowling ball is much smoother. I think they're ready for some more advanced adventures. Don't you think so, Tom, Breath?"

FIN

THE CURSE OF THE WAND
THE QRIE, MAD MAC AND THE MER BOOK 2

The continuing saga of the Qrie, the Mer, and the Spring family

Three Golden Mer teenagers came flying out of the water, and landed on *Queens Shield's* foredeck. Kandy Bernard and Sophianna Heilsvien the mermaids, and Neil Talmage the merman, surprised the recently promoted, and new CO Lieutenant Tom Haynes. All three were gold and were in full view of the crew and guards. Their flares, that emerged from their backs, looked like huge three-dimensional wings of light.

Several Cairns Naval Station harbor guards watched the Mer from outside their guard shack. Tom waved to them, knowing that everyone on the station was under the Qrie Compulsion and couldn't communicate in any way to anyone not under compulsion about the Mer or the Qrie.

Then he thought as he watched the guards. *I just wonder what those guards are thinking right about now.* He chuckled, paused, looked at the Ken and Barbie dolls, anatomically incorrect golden young angelic Mer. Their translucent Qrie protective shields tightly covered every square millimeter of their skin, only the golden hair on their head, their eyebrows, and eyelashes protruded through the Qrie field. Tom watched the Mer teenagers in their translucent Qrie energy — leotards for a moment and chuckled. *Nope, I can't 'possibly' imagine!*

The Qrie-human Lieutenant Tom Haynes, Commanding Officer (CO) of Her Majesty's Australian Ship HMAS *Queens Shield* had his crew up and moving. CO Commander Stephen Winslow of Her Majesty's Australian Cairns Naval Station, Queensland of the Royal Australia Navy (RAN) had just sent orders to *Queens Shield* to investigate a yacht of suspected human slave traffickers. Tom, now standing on the walkway just outside of the bridge with the three Mer teenagers watched as his new but experienced female Executive Officer (X) Sub Lieutenant Alieka Zander competently maneuvered the refitted and modified Armidale Class Patrol Boat out of the harbor.

All of the Mer teenagers started talking at once. They were trying to tell Tom about their new abilities; that the Qrie entity *Galactic Prime,* who is James Madison MacAvies also known as Mad Mac, or Jim as he prefers to be called and Morning and Beauty, the solar system's Stewards, had given them. It was all a bit confusing for Tom. He raised his hands and told them he could only understand one person at a time.

Neil excitedly told him. "I lifted John Weber's salvage ship *Sea Gatherer* all by myself."

The two girls bounced up. "Watch this" and they started flying circles around *Queens Shield*. They were going so fast it looked like two solid gold rings of light.

After the girls landed back on deck Kandy exuberantly exclaimed, "We've learned how to evade the passive sonar array that Doctor Kavanaugh built on Doctor Breath Of Spring's ship *Morning Discovery* and we've been practicing on a RAN submarine off Brisbane."

Sophianna, while dancing in the air, told him, "The Qrie Morning and Beauty, told us the submarine couldn't see us. But being invisible underwater is a jillion times harder than being invisible in air. We all love these new abilities, they're just super."

Neil telepathically projected to Tom Haynes. *The boat's heading out of the harbor. Are you going anywhere special or just a patrol?*

Tom laughed and thought. *These kids are so excited they can't contain themselves.* He replied to Neil by projection. *Queens Shield is headed out to catch some sex slave traders that've been preying on young girls, along the east coast of Australia.*

Jim thought so Lieutenant. That's why he sent us out here to help you catch these slaver people. We're more than ready to catch these guys and show you what we can do.

Well Neil, we've got to catch them first. We just learned about them. We know where they are and where they're going. We've gotta get this boat moving fast to catch them before they get to international waters.

Jim-*Galactic Prime* projected via telepathy. *Tom, let the kids strut their stuff they've been practicing. I think they're ready to take on a good challenge. All you've got to do is tell them what to do and how to stay safe.* Tom felt the pride Jim had for his young protégés.

Tom slowly said as if he were being coerced, and chuckled at the excited teenagers. "Well, okay come with me." They landed on deck collapsed their flares, and filed into the ship towards the aft of the bridge. Tom told the helmsman to head at maximum speed to the coordinates they had marked on the chart earlier and told his X Zander to join them.

After everyone was gathered and the Mer were introduced to Zander, Tom said. "The Mer here're going to do some exercises with *Queens Shield* to catch the slavers boat. Don't be surprised at what happens. Just be ready to hang on to something in case it gets a little rough." He cast a raised eyebrow towards Neil. "It's not going to get rough, is it?"

"No Sir CO Haynes I'll make it smooth as glass."

CO Haynes is it. I guess the young Mer haven't yet earned the right to use our first names, Tom and Breath. He then projected to the young Mer. *You guys need to be more careful; someone could have seen you.*

Tom started laying out a plan to get *Queens Shield* moving fast enough to catch the high-speed yacht now headed for international waters. Neil would lift the RAN patrol boat. The girls would fly to the suspect yacht turn it around and push it onto a small sand island they found on the chart. He then went into detail about how to keep the Mer safe during the operation by keeping to the plan, staying invisible, and out of sight.

Neil was able to lift *Queens Shield* but he could only do about seventy kilometers an hour.

Neil this's quite a bit faster than the boat could do under her own power but smooth as glass it isn't. Do you need some help? I can fly out and help stabilize.

No thank you, Lieutenant, I think I've got it; just a few more minutes and I'll have it smooth as glass I promise.

Tom stepped out on the catwalk surrounding the bridge, and looked up at Neil suspending *Queens Shield* with his Qrie field. *It's okay Neil do your best we've been through a lot worse. It's going to be close if we're going to catch that yacht.*

When *Queens Shield* arrived at the island, Tom noticed the girls had done their job. Not only had the yacht run aground on the sand island; it sat in the dead center of the island.

He couldn't contain his laughter. *Well, leave it to teenage enthusiasm to get the job done right.*

Neil, put us back in the water so the yacht's crew won't see anything unusual, other than a normal RAN ship approaching. And get back on board. Because, what I've heard about these people, I suspect we'll meet with armed resistance.